Mostyn has worked as a bookseller, copywriter,
list and fictional agony aunt. She lives in her hometown
nchester with her partner. *The Love Delusion*, a
nion novel to *The Gods of Love*, is her second novel.
Nicola on Twitter @nicolamostyn and on Facebook
olamostynauthor, or visit www.nicolamostyn.com to
ver Nicola's musings on relationships, phallus museums
e inevitable apes-versus-robots apocalypse.

Plea
on th

To r
or co

Your

Also by Nicola Mostyn

The Gods of Love

THE
LOVE DELUSION

NICOLA MOSTYN

piatkus

PIATKUS

First published in Great Britain in 2019 by Piatkus

13 5 7 9 10 8 6 4 2

A CIP catalogue record for this book
is available from the British Library.

ISBN 978-0-349-41571-0

Typeset in Sabon by M Rules
Printed and bound in Great Britain by
Clays Ltd, Elcograf S.p.A.

Papers used by Piatkus are from well-managed forests
and other responsible sources.

MIX
Paper from
responsible sources
FSC® C104740

Piatkus
An imprint of
Little, Brown Book Group
Carmelite House
50 Victoria Embankment
London EC4Y 0DZ

An Hachette UK Company
www.hachette.co.uk

www.littlebrown.co.uk

For my mum and dad

Prologue

We've been on the road for ten minutes when I get a bad feeling, an uneasy prickling on the back of my neck. It could just be a reaction to my new pineapple-scented suntan lotion or maybe even a simple case of abject paranoia, but a) I've never been the sensitive type and b) if these last few months have taught me anything, it's that things aren't ever as awful as they seem – they're always so much fucking worse.

I keep my gaze fixed on the wing mirror, watching the vehicles weave in and out of the motorway lanes. One car, big and black, is positioned a suspiciously subtle distance behind us and there's that prickle again. Definitely not the lotion. I turn to see Dan's eyes flick to the rear-view, then he indicates and overtakes and the black car disappears into the receding traffic.

'Probably nothing,' he says, his eyes meeting mine for an instant.

'Probably,' I pretend to agree, though probably isn't nearly good enough and both of us know it. I want to tell him to turn around, then. We could be back at my flat in fifteen minutes, drinking wine and eating noodles and making fun of a Liam Neeson action movie. You know, all that mundane, wonderful stuff that, if we were a normal couple, we'd get to indulge in for the rest of our lives (or until they stop dyeing Liam's hair burgundy and making him run everywhere, whichever comes sooner). I go to speak, ready to call this whole thing off, but then stop. There's no point. I know what Dan will say, because I'd say it too. We can't hide from this. We have to do it now. The longer we wait, the more dangerous it gets.

I think about Dan's family. How they've had their minds wiped clean of any threat, thousands of years of inherited knowledge undone in an instant, as easily as taking a wet cloth to a whiteboard. And unless we can stop this, Dan and I are next in line for the damp flannel effect.

The Damp Flannel Effect. Didn't I see Liam Neeson in that once?

I'm dragged away from my whimsical ponderings on ageing action heroes as Dan swings the car into the left-hand lane and takes the junction. This is it. We're close. For a moment I think I see the suspicious car behind us again, but no, I blink, and it's just a big black family saloon, a googly-eyed pug on the parcel shelf nodding a gentle benediction as their car speeds on to some happier destination.

Lucky bastards.

I check my phone. 'It's the next right,' I say and Dan takes it. There are no other cars on this thin, rutted country lane and Dan puts his foot down, his old silver hatchback juddering over every bump. The track threads between sun-bleached fields piled with bales of hay, a pretty, bucolic scene. But the further we get from the motorway, from life, from people, the more that dark dread blooming inside me becomes something closer to terror.

We're too isolated out here. It's not safe.

'Anyone behind us?'

I look. 'No.' Somehow that still doesn't soothe me.

'How much further?'

I consult my phone again. 'About a mile along this road.'

Dan looks into the mirror then flashes me a glance. 'We're nearly there, Freed. We can do this.'

'I know,' I say, trying to force a smile that ends up more like a grimace. We travel the last mile in grim, concentrated silence, as though we can reach our destination safely by sheer force of will. Then I see the turn-off for the car park up ahead. The forest stretches out, lush and green, and a sense of relief sweeps over me, so powerful it's like a rush. I turn to Dan and this time my smile is genuine.

'We made it!'

He smiles back and turns into the car park just as a vehicle emerges, blocking our entrance. I dart an anxious glance as Dan slams on the brakes, turning the wheel so we skid back on to the road and slide into the dry-stone wall. I'm thrown forwards, the seat belt snapping me back, as the engine stalls, spluttering into silence. Dan turns the key. The engine gives a sickening cough but refuses to fire. I twist in my seat and see, with horror, that the car is red.

Black is bad.

Red is also bad, just in a different way.

The car stands at the entrance to the forest, the sun shining on its windows, obscuring any view of who is inside. Or what.

I turn back to Dan. 'A speedy escape anytime now-ish would be marvellous.'

'I agree,' he says. 'Mind telling the car?' He waits for another second, two, and then turns the ignition key again, but still the engine refuses to cooperate. Behind us, the doors to the red car open. What emerges are Anterist guards, their heavyset bodies clad in red suits, their blank, bovine faces the only clue that they are not quite human.

'Dan . . .'

'I know! Come on,' Dan mutters to the car, 'come on!'

We wait, breath held, every nanosecond spooling out like an hour, then Dan twists the key again and – miracle! – the engine springs into life. He grinds the gears into reverse, straightens up and speeds down the narrow, stony path, away from our destination. But it's okay. We can find another forest, another time, another way. The main thing is we're safe. As Dan drives on, the road narrows even more, allowing enough space for only one car. On either side, walls of closely packed stone rear up claustrophobically. That prickling feeling comes again and my heart starts beating too fast. I have just enough time to understand that this is a mistake, that we should have gone back, when a large black SUV rounds the corner and slows gently to a stop, blocking the road ahead. Dan slams on the brakes and we screech to a halt, rebounding painfully against our seat belts again. Behind us the red-suited Anterists advance.

4

We're trapped.

I feel a flickering in my heart, a golden thread travelling to my hands, a faint trace of power sparking at the presence of our pursuers. But it's not enough to stop this. Nowhere near. And, besides, I don't want the occupant of that black car to know what I have inside me, however slight. It will be worse for us if he does.

I meet Dan's eyes. I can see his fear now and it breaks my heart.

'We could run,' he says, but I shake my head. We're out-numbered. Outplayed. This stage of the game is over. And maybe we always knew that this was how it would go. We've left insurances in place for just this eventuality; the smartest thing we can do now is salvage what we can while there's still time. I reach into my bag and my hand closes around something small and smooth. I hold it out.

'Hide it,' I tell Dan. 'Somewhere he'll never find it.' Then I open the car door.

'Frida!' Dan shouts, but I'm already gone, out on the road and staring towards the black car, swallowing down my rising panic as the passenger door slowly opens.

Because it's him. It's really him.

Anteros.

He's calling himself by a different name these days but he can't hide who he is, not from us. He's flanked by two more red-suited, blank-faced guards and as he makes his way towards me, leisurely, enjoying this, smiling that terrible smile, all I can do is watch. He's a thing of beauty: dark hair tumbling to his shoulders, black-brown eyes, cheekbones of a movie star. Black jeans, black boots, black shirt. His followers wear red to honour him, but he only ever wears black. Don't they wonder about that?

He only has a few hundred mortal devotees right now, but we know there will be more. Dan has seen it: in time, there will be thousands upon thousands of mortals following this man who is not a man, lapping up his message, their hearts slowly turning to stone, their worship giving rise to a kind of darkness that we haven't even begun to understand. I glance over to the expanse of green that spreads, temptingly, just a few metres away. Whatever answers there are lie in those woods. Too late now.

Dan's door opens and then he's standing beside me, our backs against the wall as Anteros and his guards advance. I look up at Dan, thread my fingers through his, and see my own feelings reflected in his clear green eyes. We didn't ask for any of this. It's our burden, our fate. *But at least it brought me you, Dan*, I think. The last seven months have been the most messed-up time of my life, but also the happiest. And because of that, I wouldn't change a single thing.

I want to tell him that, or say *something* at least, a poignant last phrase, a witty aside. But I can't seem to speak. Some things, it seems, are too big and too terrible for words.

'Hey,' Dan says.

I look into the face that has come to feel so much like home. Dan leans down, his lips brushing mine. 'Mmm,' he murmurs, 'you smell like a pina colada.'

My eyes swim with tears and a sob escapes me.

'What?' he says. 'I happen to like pina coladas.'

6

'Dan,' I say, pulling him closer, 'I can't lose you.'

'Freed, listen to me. We'll find each other.' He strokes a curl away from my face. 'And we'll stop him. I promise you.'

'I know,' I say. 'I know we will.'

He gazes at me with so much tenderness, this man who knows me like no one has ever known me.

'I love you,' he says.

'I love you,' I return, my voice breaking. And I wrap those words around us, a three-word talisman. Surely it is enough to protect us from what's to come?

But Anteros and his guards are almost upon us. I lean my head on Dan's chest and cling to him, trying to imprint him on to my cells, and I make a vow that, whatever happens, whatever Anteros takes from me, I won't go back to the Frida I was before: cynical, superficial, blind to the dark magic of this world. The time I've spent with Dan – the incredible things I've seen, the love I've known – it has changed me irrevocably.

I won't forget who I am.

I'll never, ever forget.

Chapter 1

Two years later

'The problem with love,' I tell him, 'is it doesn't actually exist.'

Lee Hatton sits across from me, pale and dishevelled, his brow furrowed in confusion.

'Well, of course it does,' he says reproachfully. Lee turns to his wife, a miserable gleam in his bloodshot eyes. 'That's what I'm trying to tell you. I love you, baby. I love you so much it hurts.' He shakes his head. 'All this divorce stuff, it's just … a mistake, a misunderstanding. It'll blow over,' he mutters. 'You'll see.'

Karen shoots me a look. She told me her husband would be a tricky prospect, that her attempts to divorce him were going nowhere. I told *her* that I could handle it and I will. But Lee's going to take a little convincing. Most people do. They've been in the delusion for too long. They can't grasp the truth. It's like trying to explain water to a fish.

But then, I have always been very persuasive.

'Lee,' I say soothingly, 'Listen to me. Your. Marriage. Is. Over.'

'Over?' He stares at me dully.

'Yes,' I say. 'This divorce is happening.' I look down at my papers. 'You must understand that your wife's terms are incredibly generous. Take another look at what Karen is offering, please.' I push the documents over to Lee. He hunches over the desk, his pale blond hair falling into his blotchy face. After a cursory glance at the settlement offer he shakes his head, a mulish, sneaky expression arriving on his face.

'I want at least three times that.'

'Three times ...?' Karen explodes before I can interject. 'And how exactly am I supposed to give you that? Sell the company?'

'Yes. YES!' her husband says, sitting up straight and actually rubbing his hands together. I suppress a sigh. Why not just twiddle an imaginary moustache for good measure? Lee turns his pale face to me, a manic look in his eyes. 'Can I make her do that?'

'Oh, so you can drink away more of my money?' Karen shoots back.

Lee pooches out his lip. 'I've quit the booze now,' he whines, emitting a whiff of whiskey breath that strongly suggests the contrary.

Karen glares at her husband and I can sense how dearly she would like to wrap her hands around his throat and squeeze. Fair enough. I only met him ten minutes ago and I'm experiencing a similar compulsion myself.

10

As the couple eyeball each other, I mentally track back through my notes. Karen Hatton née Waters built up her consultancy company years before she met her husband, then a successful estate agent. I picture them as they must have been back then, a golden couple with a life that photographed beautifully. Until five years ago, that is, when Lee was suddenly made redundant and took to sitting around that big house all day in his lucky pants, drinking and gambling and neglecting his personal hygiene.

There's no filter on earth powerful enough to airbrush *that* reality.

Poor Karen has been carrying Lee ever since. She's tried all the usual ways of dealing with the problem: rehab, screaming, ignoring it and hoping it will go away. Then, as the desperate often do, Karen found herself at a Love Delusion meeting, her car crash of a marriage being explained to her in simple terms: You haven't failed. You've been trapped in an unwinnable game. But The Love Delusion can set you free.

I glance over at Lee, who is currently engrossed in picking his teeth with the corner of his wife's settlement proposal. Perhaps unsurprisingly, Karen was quick to get on board with the idea that her affection for this man was merely part of a society-wide delusion. (People are at their most open to seeing the truth while in the midst of a marriage breakdown and I have the conversion rate to prove it.) And, naturally, my name is well known in the meetings. When an Anterist finds themselves in the unfortunate position of being married to a person who still believes in love, I'm the lawyer they come to. I've a knack for easing the transition. For making the other party see sense.

I stare at Karen's husband, who is now attempting to hold his estranged wife's hand. Sense and this dude parted ways a long time ago. Still, Karen has done the hard part: persuading Lee to my office. Now all I have to do is convince him to accept her offer. And he really should. Because, unlike most lawyers he'll meet in his lifetime, I'm actually telling Lee the truth. Karen's terms are way too generous. If Lee had any sense, he'd snap her hand off. But then, Lee isn't holding out on signing the papers because he doesn't think they're fair. He's holding out because some poor, broken part of him wants to retain contact with Karen. Even this kind of painful, humiliating contact, it seems, is better than nothing.

Lee is a typical addict and pining for Karen is his fix (along with online slot machines, Southern Comfort and, by the whiff of him, a complete avoidance of underarm deodorant). Yes, on the face of it, Lee is a tricky case. He doesn't want to let Karen go. He'll be determined to cling to his obsession. Unless, that is, I can find something powerful enough to replace it.

Luckily, I know just the thing.

Taking a copy of *The Love Delusion* from the pile in my drawer I slide it across the table, Karen looking at me in surprise and with more than a little scepticism. I know she thinks her lovesick husband is an unlikely candidate for The Love Delusion. But about that, she's dead wrong.

'Lee, I want you to read this before our next meeting.' I touch his arm encouragingly, and in response Lee picks up the book. He wrinkles his nose at the cover photo, an image

12

of a real human heart seeping with blood, an arrow stuck through it. It *is* pretty disgusting, but not as disgusting as, say, oh, pretty much all the crimes that have ever been committed in the name of love, so I think we can let it slide. 'Has Karen told you about The Love Delusion movement? About the message R. A. Stone is trying to spread?'

'It's nonsense,' Lee says miserably, but he turns the book over to read the blurb.

'It might seem like that at first,' I agree, 'but ... let me ask you, do you believe in a deity?'

'A deity?' His brow furrows, he gazes at me with cloudy eyes. 'What do you mean?'

'Do you pray to a god of some kind?'

Lee shakes his head.

'In that case it might help you to think of romantic love as just another deity. Something millions of people have believed in and worshipped and shaped their lives around for a very long time and yet something that other, more rational, people have concluded is just a myth, a sort of virus of belief wedded to a biological imperative that has been passed down, unchallenged, through the generations. Until now.'

I've got his attention. It's a line of argument I use often and it's almost always effective. 'And just like religion,' I continue, 'belief in love can make people do terrible things.'

I watch as Lee flicks through the pages, chewing his lip.

'If you care about Karen,' I venture, 'then why not read the book? If only so you can try to understand where she's coming from.' I smile and shrug, like it's no big deal. 'If it makes no sense to you, that's fine. What do you have to lose?'

13

Lee nods balefully. 'Okay,' he says, 'I'll give it a try.'

'Great!' I rise from my chair. 'Let's meet again in two weeks and see how you both feel then. Speak to Serena on the way out and she'll make an appointment for you.' I watch the pair leave with a feeling of real satisfaction. There's a shift in Lee's body language as he walks out of the door, clutching the book to his chest. He'll probably be half-converted before he's left the building. In a few weeks, he'll be a more devoted Anterist than Karen could ever be.

The addicts always are.

After the couple have gone I make my notes on the session and then grab my bag.

'I'm heading off,' I tell Serena on my way out of the office. 'Anything I should know about before I go?'

My PA checks her list and smiles. 'No, that's you done. Enjoy the meeting. You're speaking, aren't you?'

I nod, appreciating her enthusiasm. I had another PA before Serena but sadly we had to part ways. She just couldn't get on board with my conversion to Anterism and it caused some friction between us. Then I met Serena at a Love Delusion meeting and when I discovered she was looking for work as an assistant, I hired her on the spot. It's nice to be surrounded by people who get it, you know?

I check the clock. It's time I was on my way.

$\longrightarrow$

The church is a five-minute walk from my office and since it's a beautifully sunny day I decide to get some sun on my skin. I love my work but I spend so much time indoors these days, I'm beginning to turn decidedly mole-like.

As I approach the grand building I get that familiar tingling excitement. This huge, beautiful church was derelict before R. A. bought it, as he has bought similarly abandoned churches the world over. Well, God has been dead for a while now, so his house-clearance was a tad overdue.

I'm walking up to the foot of the church steps when someone gets in my way. A protester. I haven't seen this one before, but half a dozen or so of them usually hang about outside every meeting and we let them stay. People are free to believe whatever they want. Still, I draw the line at physical confrontation with the delusional. When the man declines to move, I push up my shades and meet his eyes.

'Help you with something?'

The guy's gaze sweeps my red sundress and Love Delusion badge and then he nods towards the church. 'You're going in there?'

'Congratulations, you have working eyeballs.' I smile pleasantly.

'I'd like to give you some literature.' The man pushes a flyer into my hand. 'An alternative view.'

I glance down at the flyer and catch sight of some of the text: *Dangerous Anti-love propaganda. Isolating individuals from their support networks.* The usual nonsense.

I take a good look at the protester. He's in his early thirties, maybe a little older. Longish dark brown hair, stubble, white T-shirt and sleeve tattoos adorning strong, tanned arms. Good-looking, with kind green eyes. We could use someone like him.

15

Shame he's an idiot.

'Sorry to break it to you, Che,' I say, 'but you're on the wrong side of the revolution. The Love Delusion *is* the alternative view.' I smile at him brightly. 'Hey,' I continue, 'why not come inside and have a listen? I'm giving a speech. You never know, you might learn something.'

The man just laughs, those lovely eyes crinkling, and I think again what a shame it is that he's one of the deluded.

'No way,' he says. 'I go in there, I'll come out a pod person. That's what happened to my friend's husband.' He nods towards a red-haired woman in combat-pattern dungarees who is currently engrossed in haranguing another unfortunate Anterist. 'That's what has happened to you.'

'You watch too many films.' I roll my eyes.

'And that guy running things in there, the lanky weirdo? You're seriously telling me there's not something very disturbing about him?'

'A typical lookist attitude.' I sniff. 'So small minded.'

The guy laughs again. 'Is it lookist to say he resembles an evil pencil?'

My lips thin as I glare at the protester. Then, shaking my head, I continue up the steps. But the guy just follows me, like an annoying fly buzzing in my ear. 'It's a cult,' he says. 'Plain as day.' He pauses. 'You seem like an intelligent woman. How is it you can't see that?'

I stop and face him. 'Do you know what the markers of a cult are?' I say, ticking them off on my fingers. 'An ideology that discourages scepticism about its validity; a group that shames non-members; ritualistic symbols and practices; a

16

façade of happiness when, actually, everyone inside the cult feels miserable and trapped.' I look around at this guy's fellow protesters, glum faced in the sun, carrying placards decorated with childishly drawn hearts and slogans reading: 'Love will save the day' and 'Love conquers all'.

'Remind you of anything?' I raise an eyebrow. 'Now, if you'll excuse me, there's a pod in there with my name on it.' I flash him a wink to show him he hasn't bothered me. He squints up at me in the sunshine and there's something in his face that makes me falter.

'You really don't see it, do you?' he says softly, wonderingly, and I notice his voice has a gentle Mediterranean burr. 'How weird it is that this movement is spreading so quickly? How slavishly you all follow it?'

The sun beats down. I'm starting to perspire uncomfortably. I fold my arms. 'And you really don't see how much happier Anterists are? How much more focused? Successful?'

'What about all these reported instances of discrimination against couples?'

'Well, hey, now they know how it feels!' Beads of sweat have broken out on my forehead. I blow my hair out of my eyes. Why am I standing on this step in the heat, arguing with this guy, when I should be inside the lovely air-conditioned church preparing my reading? *Come on, Frida*, I chide myself, *you can't convert them all*. But still, I just can't seem to walk away. For some reason, I want this man to see things my way. Maybe even to join us. Some of our finest Anterists were once hardened sceptics, after all.

'Listen,' I say, 'Anterism offers enlightened people a different way to live. It's a psychological evolution.' I shrug. 'Those who fail to adapt get left behind, that's the way evolution works. Besides,' I add, 'single people have been denigrated for too long.'

'Oh bullshit!' the man snorts. 'I'm single and I don't feel *denigrated*.'

'So just because you haven't felt it, it doesn't exist?' I widen my eyes. Typical ignorant white male privilege. 'Well, good for you, but you're in the minority. Society has a template for what's acceptable, what's considered normal, and that's pair bonding followed by offspring. Except, why is it this supposedly ideal template doesn't work? Huh?'

'Do you want me to answer that or—'

'The divorce rate is at an all-time high of eighty-five per cent,' I thunder on, 'and the other fifteen per cent are just sticking it out for the kids, who'll grow up totally dysfunctional and helplessly following the same insane model. Don't you see, we keep asking the impossible of our species, instructing them to find their soul mate, telling them from birth that they're only half a person and making them spend their lives searching for something that doesn't exist, so either they pretend they have found it, and feel like a fraud, or they stay single and are shamed for being alone? How can you say that is not totally fucked up?'

'All fair points,' the man says, meeting my gaze evenly. 'I'm not denying that there are things about society that are totally messed up. And I'm not saying that some of what The Love Delusion is trying to change *shouldn't* be changed.' He shakes his head, serious now. 'But the way this movement has spread, it's disturbing. It's like brainwashing.'

'You know what, maybe you should actually read the book. Perhaps then you'll get it.'

'I have read the book.'

I blink at him. I wasn't expecting that.

'And it just confirmed my fears. It's manipulative rhetoric. A conniving intellectual takedown of something the author has clearly never experienced and, I believe, actively despises. It's also insanely extreme—'

'Well, maybe we need extreme!' I say. 'Perhaps you've not been paying attention but this world is absolutely fucked. Our outdated beliefs about how we're supposed to live are contributing to a downward spiral of self-destruction. We need a radical change,' I glance around, eyebrow raised, 'and that's going to take a damn sight more than some good intentions and crappy placards.'

The protester's eyes rest on me, his head cocked to one side. 'I feel sorry for you, if you think a loveless world is a better world.'

'You feel sorry for me?' I splutter, incensed. 'What is it to you, what I believe? You don't even know me!'

'I know but ...' He shrugs. Smiles. 'I just seem to like arguing with you. Weird, isn't it?'

I seem to like arguing with you, too.

Okay. That's enough. I thrust the flyer back at the guy, ready to storm inside. As my fingers touch his I feel something, like a flicker of electricity. I step back, confused, and the protester stares at me, brow furrowed. Did he feel it too?

19

I shake my head to try to clear it. It's just the heat frazzling my synapses. I need to get away from this infuriating man; I need to get inside, where everything is cool and calm. Where everything makes sense. I turn on my heel and, without looking back, I walk away.

I try to rid my mind of this guy as I head into the church. He's so wedded to his false belief, he just can't see what The Love Delusion is doing for humanity. For people like me. I was lost when I first heard about this movement. Depressed and isolated. Empty inside. It seemed as though nothing could reach me. But after I saw mention of the movement online, and idly searched for the book (expecting just another self-help charlatan), I saw that title, that cover, with its bloodied, punctured heart, and . . . something awoke in me. When the book arrived the next day, I tore it from its envelope and started to read it right there in the hall. I devoured the whole thing that afternoon, eyes wide, heart racing. R. A.'s words reached that lost and empty part of me like a torch in the darkness. His clarity, his vision, his promise of freedom beyond suffering, it led me out of the hole I'd found myself in. Ceased the wretchedness. Gave me back to myself. No, more than that, it gave me a community, a sense of shared purpose.

And I'm not about to let some small-minded protester ruin that.

Inside the cool church, hundreds of Anterists are patiently seated awaiting this evening's sermon. I hurry over to the pulpit where Sehda, our centre leader, is waiting. And okay, yes, maybe Sehda does strike an unusual figure. I think he's Scandinavian or something, from one of those countries where it's 90 per cent darkness, and, at around seven feet tall, with long grey hair, a sharp pale face, narrow pale blue eyes and a penchant for cloaks, it's fair to say that he's unlikely to be a candidate for the cover of *Men's Health*. But that's another great thing about The Love Delusion: these days, life isn't just one long beauty contest. We Anterists are preoccupied with loftier pursuits.

I flash Sehda an apologetic smile as I approach.

'We have a special announcement, Frida,' he says in his soft voice. 'I thought you might like to do the honours?'

I stare at him, nonplussed. I had a reading from the book prepared, one of my favourites, about how the concept of love is just an existential crisis in reaction to the challenges of human consciousness and our separation from the natural world. But then Sehda hands me a piece of paper and when I see what's written there, I forget all about my reading. I forget all about the protester outside. I stare up at the centre leader and as he sees my expression, his thin red lips part in a knowing smile.

'Is this true?' I ask, and my voice is shaking. 'Is it really happening?'

Sehda nods, eyes gleaming. He gestures to the congregation. 'Go on. Tell them.'

I approach the mic and as the assembled crowd hushes, I give them a warm smile.

'My fellow Anterists,' I begin, 'I have some incredible news.' In the expectant silence, I gaze out at all those faces, all these heroes championing change. 'At this church, a week on Sunday, we're going to be graced with a special guest.'

A murmur of excitement goes through the congregation. There have been rumours about this but the Anterists aren't convinced that it can possibly be the thing they hope for.

'R. A. Stone will be coming here, to this church, to give a very special Love Delusion sermon.' I deliver the news, triumphant.

The place erupts. For two years we've followed R. A.'s message and now we're finally going to meet our guru in person. As I look out over the gathering of Anterists, butterflies gather in my stomach, a feeling of excitement so intense it almost feels like fear.

R. A. is coming. And it's going to be amazing.

Chapter 2

After the meeting we spill out on to the church steps, the air still warm, the buildings holding on to the heat of the day. I find myself unaccountably scanning the crowd for the protester, but the area seems to have emptied of placard-holders and, anyway, I'm quickly distracted by the throng of Anterists who gather around me like excitable puppies. There's always a strong buzz after a Love Delusion meeting, but the news of R. A.'s arrival in just over a week has cranked up the atmosphere to a fever pitch. Sehda, typically, has made a quick getaway (by his own admission he's not much of a people person) so that leaves me as the spokeswoman, standing at the top of the steps, surrounded by frothing Anterists and fielding a barrage of questions.

Yes, this is really happening. No, R. A. is unlikely to have time to sign books. Yes, he's going to deliver the sermon in person. No, he won't be able to speak to Anterists individually. Yes, we guarantee a place in the church for all our members. No, I don't think you should pitch your sleeping bag tonight just in case. Yes, as aforementioned, this is really happening. No, R. A. will not have time to autograph your Deluxe Love Delusion Wall Calendar. Yes, R. A. probably *will* be tired after his journey here. No, R. A. will not require a space in your bungalow/box room/bunk bed. No, R. A. cannot cure your mother's glaucoma. Yes, I would like you to let go of my arm now.

Yes, yes, yes, for the last time, yes – this is really happening. R. A. is coming.

It's after nine when I finally extricate myself from the giddy masses, my brain fizzing, clutching an extra piece of news to myself like a gift. Sehda has asked me to deliver the introduction to R. A.'s sermon. I'm actually going to meet my idol!

I wonder if he'll sign my first edition.

I can hardly believe that Sehda is trusting me with such an honour. Immediately I think this, anxiety gnaws at my stomach. How can I possibly come up with the words to express what R. A. has done for us? I ponder it as I walk home. Maybe what I'll say is that, before R. A. came along, single people had got used to being treated as less than. That it took R. A.'s audacious vision to upend that reality. That once the movement gathered momentum, the money began to follow, and that we Anterists have watched, amazed and delighted, as the focus previously directed at families, couples or singles in search of love has gradually been redirected on to this new and burgeoning demographic: the singles who

24

intend to stay that way. I mean, why not? We're the ones with all the disposable income.

I'll say that, thanks to R. A., the world is being remade with Anterists in mind, which means everything from reasonably priced single-serve products to cheap single-occupancy hotel rooms, and from government bursaries for solo house-buying and child-rearing to Anterist-only matchmaking sites providing opportunities for no-strings, guilt-free sex. Yes, that's it; I'll say that thanks to R. A., we finally feel complete just as we are. We finally feel like we belong.

I cut through the park, enjoying the evening air, breathing in the drifting aromas of BBQs and cut grass. One of the things I used to hate most about being single was how unsafe I felt walking alone at night. Not so now. After persistent lobbying by some influential Anterists, all city parks now have security teams patrolling twenty-four hours a day. For the first time in my life I can take a walk in nature without the threat of some pervert flashing their genitals at me. Just another thing we owe to R. A.!

Probably best to avoid any mention of flashing genitals in my speech, though.

Lost in further thoughts of my grand tribute to the Love Delusion leader, I emerge through the park gates and head over to my apartment building. I notice a figure standing outside. A woman of around twenty. She wears loose khaki harem pants and a black vest top, and she leans against the building, one espadrille-clad foot against the wall, languidly smoking a cigarette. As I get closer I notice that she's

25

ridiculously beautiful, with a creamy complexion, large grey-blue eyes, rosebud mouth, pale blonde hair pulled up into a messy bun.

I offer a friendly smile as I approach the front door, presuming that she's a visitor or someone's daughter or even a new arrival. I make a point not to socialise with my neighbours in case I get stuck in awkward hallway conversations, and these days I'm barely here enough to register the comings and goings of new owners. But when the woman stares right at me, my smile falters. There's something unsettling in that look.

'Hi,' she drawls and at the sound of her voice something strange happens. I have a sudden, bizarre and overwhelming urge to keep on walking. No, not to walk, to run. But that would be crazy, of course. Not to mention rude. I think about my equally odd reaction to the protester earlier and consider the very real possibility that I am suffering from heatstroke.

Collecting myself, I turn to the young woman and force myself to smile. 'Hi! Are you okay? Do you need help with something?'

She watches me silently for a moment and I decide, no, she's far older than twenty. It's in the eyes.

'You don't know me?' she asks, her voice low, sultry, matching her exotic appearance.

'No, sorry, are you new?' My keys dangle from my fingers, jangling. 'Must have missed you moving in.'

The woman's eyes rove over my crumpled red dress and linger on my Love Delusion badge. Something crosses her face, an expression I can't quite read, then she smiles

26

and it lights her up and she's not just beautiful then, she's magnificent.

'I wonder, could I come in with you for a moment?' She gives a husky laugh – she should probably stop smoking, doesn't she know those things kill you? 'I've locked myself out,' she continues. 'And I'm feeling a little faint in this heat.'

She actually looks dewy and fresh, which is more than can be said for me. Next to this lithe vision, I am suddenly hyper-aware of my diminutive status, my sundress sticking to my thighs, the nail polish on my toes that has chipped since this morning, my once-straightened hair sprung into erratic curls in the humidity. I blow a sticky lock off my forehead. There's nothing like meeting a tall, beautiful supermodel after a long day to bring out your inner Oompa Loompa. Do I really have to spend another minute in the company of this stunner, when all I really want to do is get in, take a cold shower and start planning my introduction? Again, that strange something deep inside me urges me to run to my apartment and dead-bolt the door.

'I could really do with a glass of water,' the woman says, and I blink and return to myself, appalled. She's a young woman stranded in the baking heat. I can't leave her out here. What was I thinking?

'Of course!' I say, flushing at my impoliteness.

'Thanks,' she says, '*so* kind.' She stubs her cigarette out on the wall, sending sparks flying as I open the main door to the apartments, fumbling my key under her gaze.

Once inside the flat, I grab the filter jug of water from the fridge and pour two glasses, adding a slice of lemon. I turn to offer one to my guest, only to see that she's wandered off into the adjoining lounge area and is currently engrossed in my bookshelves.

I walk over. She doesn't look up. 'Um ... here's your water.' The woman turns those cool grey eyes on me and takes the glass from my hand. Despite her alleged thirst, she doesn't take a sip but just stares at me, a strange look on her perfect face.

'You live here alone?'

'Yes,' I say. 'And you?'

'And me what?' She frowns.

I stare at this beauty. Is she a bit slow? 'Do you live here alone?'

'Oh, yes,' she says airily. 'I've been alone for years.'

'What number are you?' I ask. 'Is it Pat and Phil's place?' They're the only neighbours I know any more and I haven't even seen them for months. Maybe they finally decided to move to Spain like they've been promising each other. Or perhaps they've sublet to her?

'Yes,' the woman says faintly, 'that's the one.' She reaches into her pocket and takes out a packet of cigarettes. Then she sees my look and laughs. 'Second-hand smoke is the least of your worries right now, Frida, believe me.'

My skin prickles. 'How do you know my name?'

She flicks her lighter once, twice, and the cigarette ignites with a thin sizzle. She takes a lungful of smoke and smiles. 'Your neighbours told me. How else would I know?'

How else indeed? I stare at the woman. Despite her angelic face, looking at her gives me a bad feeling in my gut.

I consider telling her that the apartments are non-smoking and that, as a matter of fact, I don't care for the smell. That she can drink the water outside; hell, she can keep the glass. Reluctantly, I decide against it. I'm stuck with this woman as my neighbour and I don't need the hassle of a feud. I've seen these court cases and they never end well. One minute you're arguing over the exact positioning of a boundary hedge, the next you're clutching a pair of bloodstained secateurs and facing life without parole.

Instead, I walk around the lounge opening the windows – not just because of the smoke, it's hot in here anyway – all the while feeling the strange woman's eyes on me. When I turn back, yes, there she is, assessing me with that forensic gaze. She flicks her ash into my pot plant and stares at me as though willing me to challenge her. With a tight smile, I walk to the kitchen, collect an old saucer from the cupboard and, returning, place it pointedly on the coffee table. (I've got to hand it to myself, I'm accessing black-belt levels of passive aggression here.) Then I stand in front of her, countering our height differential by placing my hands on my hips, the trusty Wonder Woman pose. Oh, for a weaponised tiara.

'I didn't catch your name,' I say, in an attempt to claw back some authority in this situation.

She blows smoke from the corner of her mouth. 'Psyche.'

'Seriously?' I laugh. I can't help it. 'Were your parents big psychology fans, then?'

She tips her head to one side and surveys me, unsmiling. 'It's actually taken from an ancient myth of Eros and Psyche.'

She pauses. 'But I suppose you're going to tell me you've never heard of that?'

'It rings a bell,' I say vaguely, though actually I've no idea what she's talking about. But that settles it; she's definitely an actress or a model. They all have weird abstract names like Charisma and Fortitude, don't they? Makes them memorable. Also, a lot of models take drugs and I'm pretty sure she's off her head on something.

Psyche gives me another once-over, the cigarette dangling from her fingers, scattering ash on to my new rug. 'What do you do for work, Frida?'

I hesitate. I don't want to tell this woman anything about me, but equally, I can't find any good reason not to.

'I'm a solicitor,' I say, 'specialising in quick, mutually agreed divorces.'

'Oh dear.' She raises an eyebrow. 'Old habits die hard, I see.'

I stare at her, puzzling over this bizarrely rude utterance. Psyche plucks a copy of *The Love Delusion* from the shelf. 'And you're a Delusionist, I gather?'

I flinch. 'The correct term is Anterist,' I say stiffly. 'Atheists don't believe in the concept of a god and Anterists don't believe in the concept of romantic love. What's the difference?'

'No difference at all,' Psyche says, with another of those maddening smiles. 'Anterists,' she muses, almost to herself. 'How he must love that!'

I shake my head. Total nutjob. 'And what do you do, Psyche?' *Model. Actress. Asylum escapee?*

'Me? Oh, this and that,' she says vaguely and twiddles her finger dismissively. 'I travel.'

I knew it. A model with a side-hustle in being absolutely crackers. Why doesn't she just admit it? I decide to prod her a bit, just to show her that she can't intimidate me, even if she is twice my height and ten times as beautiful.

'It's funny,' I say, 'when I first saw you, I thought you were around twenty, but I think maybe you just look very good for your age. Had some work done, have you?'

'Oh, like you wouldn't believe.' Her rosebud mouth twists into a smirk. 'If you're very lucky, I might let you into my secret.'

'I don't hold with facelifts and the like. I'll just age gracefully, thanks all the same.'

'Well, darling,' she says darkly, 'some of us don't get the choice.'

There's a long awkward silence then as I try to work out what to say, which just stretches on to infinity as I fail to come up with anything suitable. It's hardly my fault if the modelling industry demands youth and beauty, is it? I head to the kitchen, pick up a cloth and start wiping down the kitchen surface, really just for something to do. Hopefully Psyche will drink the water she was so thirsty for but has hardly touched and then get the hell out of my flat. This, I remind myself, is why I don't get friendly with my neighbours. There's always a high chance you'll end up trapped in an unwelcome situation with a lunatic.

'So, where's Dan?'

I frown at this non sequitur. 'I don't know a Dan. Is he a new resident too?'

Psyche's face is inscrutable. Then she sighs. 'That's what I thought. It doesn't matter. You're no use to me, are you?'

31

'No use . . .?' I stare at her. What the fuck? Okay, that's it. The time for politeness is over. In truth, the time for politeness whooshed by a good five minutes ago. She might be some sort of gorgeous goddess-like creature, but no one speaks to me like this.

'I'd like you to leave now, Psyche,' I say, my voice firm but pleasant. No need to rile her. 'I have things to do.'

'Oh, I'm going,' she says, and stubbing her cigarette out into the soil of my plant she heads for the door. I watch her for a moment, filled with relief, but then I hurry after her, through the hall and over to the front door, just to make sure she's actually leaving and not, say, secreting herself under my bed so she can jump out with a knife at 3 a.m.

Psyche opens the door and then turns. Her eyes look storm-grey now, the antithesis of the clear blue sky outside. She steps towards me, close enough that I can feel her breath on my cheek. 'If this is a trick,' she says in a low, menacing voice, 'if you're faking, tell me now.'

'Faking?' I repeat wonderingly. What the hell is she talking about? As I look into her fierce gaze, I get a chill. Perhaps this woman is more than a little bonkers. Maybe she's actually dangerous. She's slender, yes, but – I eye her biceps – she also looks pretty strong.

'You really don't know me?' she says.

Then the penny drops. The absolute cheek of it! She's famous and she thinks I'm pretending I don't recognise her! Fury floods through me at the arrogance of this glorified giraffe. Does she think I have nothing better to do? Doesn't she know who *I* am? I step towards her, hands on hips, rooting my feet firmly on the laminate flooring. Admittedly I only come up to her boobs, but still, I like to think I can be pretty threatening when I want to be.

'Listen,' I say, keeping my voice calm and level, 'I've got no idea who you are and I couldn't care less. Now get out of my flat.'

The strange woman doesn't move for a moment as her eyes search mine. And then, seemingly satisfied, she nods. 'I'll be seeing you, Frida,' she says softly and then she's gone.

$$\longrightarrow$$

For a long time afterwards I have a weird feeling. Call it intuition. I wait by the window and when I see a familiar car come through the automatic gates, it just confirms what I already suspected. I grab my mail-box keys and pretend to be checking the slot so that I'm standing in the hall as they enter.

'Oh, hi there,' I say, in an attempt at breezy that I'm not sure I quite pull off. 'Been doing some late-night shopping?'

Pat peers at me over his box of groceries, just a pair of brown eyes and a tuft of auburn hair visible. 'Hey, Frida. Yeah, stocking up on all things cold. They say it's going to be another hot one this weekend!'

'You're still here, then?'

Pat looks at his partner, Phil, and they both offer me a bemused smile. 'Last time we checked. Why wouldn't we be?'

My heart sinks and my smile frays at the edges. 'Oh, nothing,' I say brightly. 'I must have got confused. I heard someone was selling up?'

The pair shake their heads.

'We do have a newcomer to the building, though?' I ask. The guys look at me blankly. 'Blonde woman?' I continue. 'Looks like a supermodel?'

Phil frowns. 'Not that I'm aware of.' He looks to his partner. 'You?' Pat shakes his head.

'Though,' Pat says animatedly, 'if we're attracting supermodels to the area, maybe the prices have gone up again! Let's hope so.' Then his gaze passes over my Love Delusion badge and his eyes cloud over. He flashes his husband a look. 'Anyway, we'd better get this stuff in the freezer before it melts.'

'Of course,' I say faintly.

Back in my flat, I feel even more uneasy. I knew it. The woman outright lied to me. She doesn't live here at all. Which is great news except, why on earth did she say she did? What did she want? Maybe she was casing the building? Except, come on, burglars don't look like her, at least not outside the movies. *No, stop catastrophising, Frida,* I scold myself. She just wanted to get out of the sun and thought the quickest way to do that was to con me into letting her into my flat. I'm sure that's all it was.

But as I remember the woman's brutal, assessing stare, a shiver passes over me despite the heat. And what she said as she left: *I'll be seeing you, Frida.* Words that sounded less like neighbourliness and more like a threat.

Chapter 3

The next morning I wake with a whole sunny Saturday stretching out ahead of me. But I feel itchy-eyed and unsettled. I had planned to sit in a pavement café and work on my introduction to R. A.'s sermon, but even after two cups of coffee my brain feels too frazzled to compose a coherent thought, let alone a tribute to the most revolutionary thought leader since Charles Darwin. So, instead, I decide to do something that always makes me feel better.

I go and see my mother.

An hour later I'm sitting in my mum's garden under a huge daisy-patterned parasol, a cup of Earl Grey tea in front of me, a biscuit assortment laid out neatly on a plate. My mother looks over at me, her small blue eyes bright with excitement.

'I can't believe it, Frida!' she says, reaching for a shortbread finger. 'R. A. is really coming – and you're introducing him?'

I nod over the rim of my teacup, quietly beaming. To see the look of pride on my mother's face is everything to me. That my mother is a devoted Anterist would be painfully obvious to anyone taking even a cursory glance at her décor. She has half a dozen glossy pictures of R. A. framed and hung on the walls, a set of Love Delusion coasters featuring a close-up of our great leader's handsome face, multiple copies of *The Love Delusion* proudly displayed on her bookshelves and, on her tinted-glass dining table, a half-completed 4,000-piece R. A. Stone commemorative jigsaw.

Mum doesn't go to the meetings because she's phobic of large crowds, but she's finally got to grips with computers so that she can chat on The Love Delusion forums. I know she likes to tell the other Anterists all about her important daughter, Frida McKenzie; yes, the Anterist divorce lawyer who practically runs the city's main Love Delusion chapter.

'It's an incredible honour,' I say. 'There will be thousands of Anterists there.' As I speak, the protester's words come back to me. *You really don't see it, do you? How weird it is that this movement is spreading so quickly? How slavishly you all follow it?* Those kind eyes judging me. Pitying me. Why does that bother me so much? I distract myself from the memory by reaching to the plate of biscuits and crunching down on a fig roll.

'What's wrong, Frida?' So perceptive, my mother. No detail of my life or my mood escapes her.

'Oh nothing!' I chew the biscuit, forcing a smile through the crumbs. 'It's just that there were some more of those doomy protesters outside the church.' I pause. 'It bugs me how they can't see the good R. A. is doing.'

My mother leans towards me and locks her shiny eyes on mine. 'Don't even engage with these people, Frida. You can't convince them. They can't see because they don't want to see.' She shakes her head and her greying curls give a little dance. 'But they can't stop this movement. And eventually everyone will understand.'

I nod, reassured, and tip my head back to feel the sun on my face. I'm so glad I popped round. I feel better already. It's hard to imagine it now, but for a long time my mum was a difficult person to be around, a difficult mother to have. Because of my dad. We don't talk about my father, never really have, and since I don't remember much of anything about him, it doesn't come up. Besides, I don't need to know the details to know the story. I've seen it over and over again in my office. Two people meet, mistake loneliness and need for love, have kids and then … the delusion fades. There follows arguments, blame, recrimination, hurt, betrayal on a loop – a veritable Wheel of Fortune of bad until eventually, the spinning stops, leaving just the relief that it's all over. Except, of course, anyone who isn't an Anterist just begins the whole sorry cycle all over again, deciding that they must have chosen the 'wrong' target for their love and that they'll do better next time.

Sure. Because that's been working *wonderfully*.

At least my mother was never so stupid. She was ahead of the curve where Anterism was concerned. There was no one after my dad and when, two years ago, I introduced her to

The Love Delusion, it gave her a peace she'd been sorely lacking. And it gave us something to share. I look at my mother now, at the animation in her face, the light in her eyes, and I am so grateful for what this movement has done for us both.

'You're right,' I say now, picking up a pink wafer. 'These things can't be hurried. Everyone will understand the truth in time.'

'Of course I'm right,' she says happily and reaching for the teapot, she tops up our cups. 'Now, let's hear what you're planning to say in this speech of yours.'

$\longrightarrow$

I'm leaving my mother's house when I see a familiar figure heading down the street. *Oh fuck*. What abominable timing. I duck my head and turn, walking in the other direction, but it's too late, I know she's seen me and, what's more, she'll know I've seen her. Still, I walk on, hoping she'll do us both a favour and feign obliviousness like I intend to.

'Frida!'

Damn. I stop and arrange my face into something resembling a smile.

'Bryony!' I say as I turn, faking surprise badly as my friend approaches. 'How lovely to see you!'

As Bryony reaches me she holds out her arms for a hug and then seems to change her mind and lets her hands drop to her sides. Great. This is not awkward at all. Bry darts a look at the house behind me.

'Visiting your mum?'

38

'Yes.' A pause. 'You?'

She nods. 'Just dropped the kids off there. Justin and I are having a date-day and—' She stops mid-sentence as she remembers what I think about things like that and we stand there in yet more uncomfortable silence.

I stare at her. She looks pretty for her 'date-day', like she's made a real effort, in a strappy sapphire top, jeans and sandals. Her pale milky skin has broken out in freckles and a slender bracelet flashes on her wrist, a thirtieth birthday present from her husband. She's curled her strawberry-blonde hair especially for the occasion. How long has it been since I last saw her? Months? No, longer than that. I turned thirty and she wasn't there, because of what I did, what I said at *her* thirtieth. That's where it all started, where our decades-old friendship reached breaking point.

The silence just stretches on. 'How *are* the boys?' I ask, grasping for safe conversational ground.

'They're great.' She pauses and when she meets my eyes, I can see her deciding something. 'They ask after you sometimes. Wondering what happened to Auntie Frida.' I stare at her, a sinking feeling in my guts. She's really doing this now?

'Well, you know how it is,' I say brightly. 'I'm busy with work.'

'And with The Love Delusion?' She eyes my red top, my Love Delusion badge. 'You're still with them, then?' And there it is, sparking in her eyes. Judgement. Blame.

I set my jaw firm. Bryony has been furious with me ever since my outburst at her birthday party, but what was I supposed to do? A meal out with all of those smug, repressed couples, and they couldn't see, couldn't understand, how deluded they were! And *they* pitied *me* for being single! One guy told me that if I acted more demure, swore less, *earned* less, then maybe I'd have more luck finding a man. Truly, I tried my best to keep a lid on it but after a few sambucas, some demon inside me arose and I let rip. My memories of the event are a little hazy (see the aforementioned sambucas) but I do know that one wife left the party in tears after I pointed out that, while she may believe in true love, she might not be so attached to the concept if she knew that her husband had been fucking his badminton partner while she, his wife, was six months pregnant. Oh yeah, and I may have outed Bryony's GP partner. In front of his fiancée. And the whole restaurant.

But fuck it, I was only telling the truth.

I'm sure Bryony was expecting a call afterwards, an apology for ruining her special night, but I couldn't pretend I was sorry when I wasn't. Those people deserved to know the reality behind the love pyramid scheme they'd signed up to.

And when my apology didn't arrive, something changed between us.

'Yes, I'm still a member of The Love Delusion,' I say now. 'Things are going really well, actually; they've asked me to deliver an important speech next week. The founder is coming and . . .' I trail off. The days when Bryony was interested in my accomplishments are long gone. Her expression says it all. 'Sorry, I'm boring you,' I say. I paste on a smile. 'I need to get going anyway . . .'

'What happened to you, Frida?'

I stare at her. 'What's that supposed to mean?'

'You know what it means,' Bryony says. 'All this Anterism stuff, it isn't you! I mean, sure, you've always been a little cynical, because of your dad and everything, but this is another level.' She shakes her head. 'I just don't understand what could make you join *them*.'

Her tone of voice when she says 'them' – so disparaging, so disgusted with the people I now call my friends. My comrades. Anger twists inside me, a thin blade.

'Of course you don't understand,' I say. 'You never did. You've been in your bubble with Justin for, what, twelve years? How could you have any idea what life is like for me or for anyone who doesn't live like you do?'

Her eyes darken. 'I know more than you think. I can always spot an Anterist in my surgery, even without the badge, and you know why?' Her face is pale but there are high spots on her cheeks. She pushes escaped wisps of hair back from her face, a familiar gesture that gives me pangs of homesickness for our friendship. 'They're angry. Really angry. Just like you. You say this movement is about bringing peace to the world, Frida, but you're wrong. There's nothing peaceful about this.'

'Well, sometimes peace comes at a price,' I retort. 'And, anyway, don't they have a right to be angry at how society has disregarded them, treated them as failures?'

'But it isn't—'

I hold up a hand. 'You know what, just forget it. It's like Mum says, there's no point trying to convince people who just don't want to see the truth. It's a total waste of breath.'

'That's another thing!' Bryony says, her eyes flashing to the house behind me, where I'm certain my mum will be twitching the curtains. 'How you are with your mum these days, it's not natural! You two never got along and now you're her number-one fan?'

I blink at her. 'Wow,' I say slowly. 'I'm so sorry I'm no longer playing the part of the dysfunctional fuck-up to your well-adjusted saint, Bryony. I guess you'll have to find someone else to look down on.'

She stares at me, hurt in her eyes. 'That's not it, and you know it. Freed, I'm just trying to understand,' she says in a low voice. 'I'm your best friend and you've gone full-on Stepford and I just want to know why! God, I even read the book to see if I could work out why it has such a hold over you, but . . .' She shakes her head. 'Frida, it's just dogma.' She pulls her hand through her curls. You'll flatten them, Bry, I want to tell her. You never could get used to anything fancy. 'I keep thinking,' she goes on miserably, 'was there something I could have done?'

I sigh. 'What do you mean?'

'I don't know.' Her pale brow furrows. 'Did something happen, back in February two years ago?' she says. 'Because that's when this all started.'

'What are you talking about, Bryony? I didn't even become an Anterist until August two years ago.'

'I know that,' she says. 'But still, February was when things changed between us. When you ended up in hospital, discharged yourself when I went to get you coffee, wouldn't answer my calls. You lost a week of your life. There were things you wouldn't tell me.' She frowns. 'Then you send me a weird text about NeoStar on Valentine's Day . . .' Her eyes are far away as she recalls these things. I stare at her blankly. I have no idea what she's talking about.

Bryony bites her lip. 'But then in the months after that you seemed,' her eyes brighten, 'different. Different but definitely happier. I was *sure* you'd met someone.' She gives a sad smile. 'I was just waiting for you to introduce me, to tell me you were in love. But then, the next time I saw you . . .' She spreads her arms towards me. 'You were like this.' Her eyes are shiny with tears now. 'If I could just understand, if you could just explain to me, Frida, what happened, what did this to you? You know you can tell me anything, don't you? Anything at all?'

'Bryony,' I say softly, 'nothing did this to me. Nothing happened to me. I chose Anterism because it is the right path for me. That period of time you are talking about, it's just . . . blank to me. I was working so hard, I hit rock bottom.'

'But the guy you met. Did he leave you? Is that why you joined up?'

'There *was* no guy! I was having a breakdown. You saw me in that hospital and how I was afterwards. I was in a bad place. Anterism saved me. I don't know where I'd be without it.' I reach out and touch my friend's hand. 'People change, Bryony. They make choices and they grow apart. And honestly, I'm so much better now. If you're really my friend, can't you just be happy that I'm happy?'

She stares at me for a long moment and then her slim shoulders slump. 'I have to go,' she says. 'Justin's waiting.' She walks away heavily and I watch as she unlocks her car and slides into the driver's seat. She pulls out, eyes on the road. She doesn't look back at me as she drives away.

$$\longrightarrow$$

When I get back to my flat, I'm unsettled and antsy. The visit to my mum was supposed to make me feel better but bumping into Bryony has rattled me all over again. I pour myself a glass of water and drink it straight down. Close my eyes. I can't very well write my introduction now, with my brain buzzing with frustration.

Instead, I decide to clean the flat. It's my weekly calming ritual, usually reserved for Sundays. It always clears my mind and makes me feel like I have turned a new page. Admittedly, it's hardly ideal cleaning weather but I'm determined not to waste this day brooding, so I open all the windows and place a fan on the kitchen counter. I change into a pair of old denim shorts and a baggy T-shirt tied in a knot at my navel, tune the radio to my favourite classical station and make a start.

And it does help. As I dust all the surfaces, spritz and wipe down the bathroom, hoover through the flat, scrub inside the microwave, I start to feel better. With every surface that sparkles, I feel replenished and virtuous and, also, very sweaty. Who needs hot yoga? Once I have finished, and with energy still to burn, I decide to do something I avoid every Sunday – I'm finally going to clear out the sideboard, the only messy area in my flat, where I keep all the papers, instruction booklets and magazines I can't decide what to do with.

As I feared, it hasn't been sorted for months – God, maybe

even years – and is stacked high with old bills, battered books and trinkets that don't have a home. With a determined exhale, I pull everything out on to the rug and set about sorting it into piles. As I reach for a tall heap of old *New Yorker*s I'll never read but can't bring myself to throw away, the top of my hand brushes something. Intrigued, I slide the magazines from the shelf and then stick my head into the cupboard, peering upwards. There's a piece of paper taped to the underside of the cupboard. I reach in and, easing it away, I bring it out to look at it. It's an unopened envelope with my name written on the front. It must be an old Christmas card that got stuck up there, or maybe a thirtieth birthday gift card from someone I've neglected to thank. Oops.

I tear open the envelope. Inside I find not a lost Christmas card, but a photograph. Weird. I look at the photo. The picture shows two people sitting on a rug in a field. One of the people is me – there I am, smiling up at the camera. But my breath stops in my throat when I see the figure sitting next to me, his lovely green eyes smiling up at the camera.

It's the protester.

Chapter 4

Have you ever had that feeling when you wake up in a strange hotel bed and you go utterly blank for a few seconds, unable to remember where you are or how you got there? Looking at this photograph makes me feel like that; my mind is just scrambling around, blindly, trying to make sense of it. But it can't.

Because this photograph doesn't make any kind of sense at all.

It's like one of those logic riddles. How the hell can a picture of me and a man I only spoke to for the first time yesterday come to be taped to the underside of my sideboard? I stare and I stare, as though the photograph might assemble itself into some sort of answer. But no matter which way I look at it, I cannot come up with a single reasonable explanation for this picture's existence. Then I turn the photo over and see with a tiny shock what's written there – the words: FIND DAN.

SHOW HIM, an address written underneath and then, in tiny, cramped handwriting in the corner: *Anteros*.

I frown at the names. Anteros sounds like Anterist. But what does it mean? And FIND DAN?

I flash back to my unwelcome guest of yesterday. *Where's Dan?* she asked, as though I should know who she meant. Darts of anxiety pierce my chest and for a moment I forget to breathe. What the hell is this? I place the photo down on the rug with shaking hands and then I notice something written on the back of the envelope in a different pen: *Cupboard under sink*. I stare from the photo to the envelope and it's only then that I see something truly horrible: all the notes are written in my handwriting.

I get up unsteadily, sending piles of magazines and papers scattering as I wobble over to the sink, my heart pounding. *Don't be stupid, Frida*, I tell myself. *There won't be anything there. This is just some sort of joke or misunderstanding.* But it doesn't matter. I know if I don't check I'll never stop thinking about it. I'm cursed with a vivid imagination. My mother always said so.

Opening the cupboard, I kneel and carefully remove all the items: box of miscellaneous light bulbs, pile of clean dusters, three-drawer toolbox, plastic bag stuffed with a million of its brethren. When everything is removed, I stare down at the cream shelf, the cupboard base. There's nothing here. Thank God! Just as I'm about to put everything back, I see it. A small triangular-shaped gap where the base meets the wall. I stare at it, gnawing on my thumbnail. *Just walk away, Frida. Nothing to see here.* Except what if there is?

With sudden decision, I open the toolkit and take out the thinnest screwdriver. Sliding it into the gap, I ease up the cupboard base. There are pipes under there and the scuffed, brown-grey granite of the floor, discoloured with rust from old water spills. But there's something else. Something that has no place being there at all. A purple plush-velvet drawstring bag. Gingerly I remove the bag and, still squatting there by the sink, shake out the contents.

There's a thin gold chain with a pendant heart shot through with an arrow, and a small clear bottle, almost like an old-fashioned perfume decanter, containing a viscous orange substance. There's another note wrapped around the neck of the bottle, secured with a small blue elastic band. I tip the necklace back into the bag and, picking up the bottle, I remove the note. I'm hardly even surprised to see that it looks like my writing.

For memory, it reads. *Only take if no other option. Don't tell Dan.*

I stare at the words. Dan again! What the hell does he have to do with any of this? Placing the note down, I turn the bottle in my hands. It's really quite beautiful. I remove the stopper and gingerly give the amber liquid a sniff. Immediately, a sultry scent assaults my nostrils, a heady aroma both intensely musky and impossibly sweet. It's all I can do not to take a swig, except that anyone who takes a swig from a bottle of something they found hidden under their sink almost certainly deserves to wind up in A&E with a tube down their throat.

I take one last sniff of the liquid and then reluctantly reinsert the stopper.

After checking the sideboard and the nooks of the kitchen cupboard, I establish that this is the extent of the mystery objects and notes. I gather them all on my dining-room table and look at them in turn, trying to put them together in a way that makes some sort of sense. What are these things? What do they mean? Who put them there? And why?

I stare at the photograph again, at these two people who look as though they're on some sort of picnic. Could someone have mocked up this image? The idea gives me a dark feeling of foreboding. It's one thing to be seen debating with this man outside the church, but it's quite another to be pictured cosied up on a picnic blanket tucking into a Scotch egg.

An idea comes then, and once it worms its way into my brain it is both ridiculously paranoid and horribly convincing. The supermodel freak planted this. Maybe she and the protester are working together. To ruin my reputation. To blackmail me. The timing is too neat: first I am chosen to introduce R. A. at the sermon, and then this incriminating photo turns up, along with – I glance at the bottle – this strange liquid, which, from its enchanting effect, is probably some sort of illegal substance.

And all this happening one week before R. A.'s visit?

But why are those notes in your handwriting? a voice inside me chimes in. *And how could that woman have hidden the bottle when she went nowhere near the kitchen?*

I shake my head. Maybe she was scoping the place; maybe she broke in after I went to my mother's and planted the bottle then? And how hard would it be to copy my handwriting? There are examples of it on contracts all over the city.

Where's Dan? the woman asked me. Taunting me.

I flip the photograph and read the address. I vaguely know that area. It's on the other side of town, by the train station. And that scrawled word, *Anteros*. What the hell is an Anteros? One thing is for certain, I have to get to the bottom of all this. I won't feel safe until I do. I get up and, stuffing the photo into my bag, I grab my keys.

FIND DAN.

I bloody well *will* find Dan. And then I'm going to demand some answers.

Chapter 5

I take a taxi to the address on the photo, muttering to myself on the back seat until the cab driver flicks me a nervous glance in the rear-view mirror and I settle for staring out of the window and silently seething.

Eventually the driver drops me off at the street given. This district is slowly becoming gentrified and building work is in evidence all around, with dozens of cranes towering overhead. Around me, shiny new-build apartments and artisan delis have popped up among the sex shops, Vape stores and second-hand book emporiums. The result is an area caught between two very different demographics, like a 'before' subject unexpectedly exposed midway through a makeover.

Taking the photo from my bag, I check the address one more time. Yes, this is the place, except the building in front of me appears to be an eatery, a tired-looking place with a grubby sign proclaiming it to be Tony's Café. Poor Tony, is all I can say. Then I spot a shabby-looking door to the right of the café entrance, realise that 'Dan' must live above this grotty establishment, and extend this sympathy to myself. I really don't want to have dealings with anyone who chooses to live somewhere like this.

Sighing, I walk to the flaking door and press my finger to the bell, my anger rising to simmer just below the surface as I think about how someone – maybe this man – must have broken into my flat to hide all those weird objects. I wait, straining my ears, but I don't hear anything. I ring again, keeping my finger on the bell for a full ten seconds. More silence. Okay, he's not here. Fine. I'll just take all of this straight to Sehda. That's probably what I should have done in the first place. Best to get everything out in the open. After all, I've done nothing wrong. I've got nothing to hide.

I'm already a few steps away when I hear the bang-bang-bang of footsteps on stairs and then the door flies open.

I turn and stare. It *is* him, the same guy from yesterday. He's wearing cargo shorts and a light grey T-shirt and, as I watch, he wipes his black-stained hands on a yellow cloth. There's a streak of something dark on his cheek and forehead. What's he been doing up there, fixing a car?

The guy looks at me, all innocence. 'Can I help you?' he says. I think he's actually pretending not to recognise me. Ha! Nice try.

'Are you Dan?' I demand as I walk back towards him.

He nods.

52

'Then yes, you can help me.' I narrow my eyes at him. 'You can tell me what your game is!'

He stares at me for a moment, his brow furrowed, and then a light goes on in his eyes. 'Oh, it's you! From the church! I didn't recognise you in your ... um ... casual-wear.' He grins. 'Well, until you started shouting at me, that is,' he adds, 'then, strangely, it all came flooding back.'

I glance down and see that I'm still in my sweaty cleaning outfit of shorts and T-shirt. I was in such a fury to get over here I completely forgot to change. Damnit. Not quite the authoritative presence I was aiming for. Still, it's more about the attitude than the outfit.

Dan is now smiling at me pleasantly. 'So, what's this? Have you come for another debate on the merits of love?' Then he frowns. 'Hang on, how did you find me?'

'No, I have not come for a debate,' I say stiffly. 'And as to how I found you, you kindly left your address on the back of this!' I brandish the picture. 'Now just what were you hoping to achieve?'

The man's brow crinkles further as he tries to catch a glimpse of the photo I'm furiously waving. 'Er ... I'm afraid I don't understand the question.'

God, this guy is insufferable. I thrust the photograph under his nose. 'I found this in my flat, as if you didn't know!'

With studied calm, the protester stuffs the yellow rag in his back pocket and takes the picture from me. As he inspects it, his eyes darken and when he looks back up, his face is a picture of confusion. 'I don't get it. What's this supposed to be?'

'You tell me!'

'How can I tell you?' he asks reasonably. 'You've just brought it to my door. I've never seen it before.'

'Well, *someone* planted it in my sideboard!' I snap, though I'm momentarily wrong-footed by his 'oblivious innocent' act. 'Maybe your supermodel friend?'

'What supermodel friend?'

'Your glam sidekick who conned her way into my flat yesterday!'

The protester looks at me, widens his eyes as though I might be a tad unhinged, and then looks at the photo again. 'You found this in your sideboard, you say?' He pauses. Then hands the picture back. 'I'm sorry, but I honestly have no idea where it came from.'

I pause. This wasn't the outcome I was expecting and it leaves me feeling oddly deflated. 'Well, there has to be some explanation,' I mutter, having lost some steam.

'There does, doesn't there?' Dan says. 'I wonder what it is.'

I meet his eyes and then we stare at each other for a long, intense moment, and though I try, I can't seem to break away from that gaze.

'Look,' he says eventually, 'do you want to come in? Maybe if we put our heads together, we can work out what's behind all this.'

'No,' I say, 'I will not be putting anything together with you, thank you very much!' But the protester has already turned and begun climbing the threadbare stairs and obeying a magnetic pull I don't understand, I follow.

$\longrightarrow$

Up in Dan's living room, he clears a space at the table for me while I scan the area, looking for evidence that he is, in fact, a psychopath who gets off on planting photos of himself with his victims before dismembering them with a saw. For instance.

The room is small and cosy, with a tan leather sofa, a black-and-white throw rug and a seventies-style gas fire. In the corner near the window there's an easel on which sits a half-completed charcoal sketch of a dragon. Not a mechanic, then, but an artist.

Elsewhere, a large TV attached to a game console displays a stocky green chap wielding a massive hammer; an electric guitar leans against an armchair; triple-stacked bookshelves are bursting with graphic novels, epics the size of house bricks, and DVD boxsets: *Buffy*, *Battlestar Galactica*, *Game of Thrones*.

One large shelf is devoted entirely to vinyl, their sleeves displaying the names of various rock bands. On a higher shelf is a row of plastic toys, all still in their boxes. I peer up at them and spot, amongst the dozen stacked there, a Spider-Man, a wizard and a little fellow in a school uniform clutching a guitar.

'You have kids?'

Dan looks over. 'What?'

'Your dolls.' I nod to the shelf.

'Those aren't dolls,' he says, indignant. 'They're collectible vinyl figures.'

'Right.' Pause. 'Why are you collecting little boys in school uniform?'

'That's Angus Young!' Dan splutters. 'The guitarist from AC/DC!'

I stare at him. 'Righto. Grown man in short shorts. Nothing disturbing about that.' Shaking my head, I walk over to join Dan at the table, only to find yet more toys: some sort of board-game map thing with tiny figures positioned on it. I pick one up. 'I suppose this isn't for kids, either?'

Dan's face takes on a worried aspect. 'Be careful with that, I painted it myself.'

I see now that I needn't have been concerned about him murdering me. All I'd need to do to overpower this guy is threaten to snap the head off one of his figurines. I bring the teeny creature closer to my eyes. 'What on earth is it supposed to be, anyway?'

'It's a half-dwarf Cleric of Moradin,' Dan says.

I raise my eyebrows. 'Okay, let me rephrase that. *Why* is it?'

'It's a role-playing game. A group of us go on fantasy quests and these figures represent our characters.' He sees my face. 'It's great! The adventures can last for years. They're really incredibly detailed and inventive.'

'Wow, you really are a gigantic geek, aren't you?' I place the little figure back where I found it. 'Meanwhile, back in the real world, we need to get to the bottom of this bizarre picture.'

'Okay, let's have another look.' The protester holds out his hand.

I pass it to him and watch his face carefully as he stares at it. Then he turns the photo over, reads what's written, raises his eyebrows and looks at me. 'This is very odd. We've never

56

met before, have we?' he asks. 'Like, we didn't have a date at some point before you converted to your cult?'

My gaze roves over his sleeve tattoos of skulls, symbols, jewel-coloured images of elves and dragons and other mythical creatures. 'Doubtful.' I smile. 'Don't take this the wrong way, but you're really not my type.' *Except*, a little voice chimes in, *for this really strange sensation I have when I'm around you. Like, I don't want to be anywhere else.* I shake the thought away. That's it. I definitely have sunstroke.

Dan just laughs. 'Right back at you.' He returns his gaze to the photo. 'And was this all you found? Just this picture?'

I think about the bottle in my bag. *Don't tell Dan.* 'Yes, just the picture.' I give voice to an argument that a tiny part of my brain is making, that this guy's confusion seems completely genuine. 'So are you seriously saying that you didn't mock up this photo and then plant it in my flat?'

'Well, of course I didn't! What kind of a weirdo do you think I am?'

'No comment.' I pause. 'Then it must have been the supermodel.'

Dan places the photo on the table. 'Okay, slow down. Who is this supermodel you keep talking about?'

'After the meeting last night, I got home to find her on my doorstep.' I gnaw at my lip. 'She talked her way into my flat, pretended she lives in my block but she doesn't. She was . . .' I search for the words. 'Strange. Aggressive. Said her name was Psyche.'

'Psyche, like in the myth?'

I blink. 'Apparently so. And she mentioned you.'

This gives him pause. 'In what context?'

'In the context that she said, "Where's Dan?"'

'Right.' He looks worried at this. 'Okay, so maybe I *do* know her. What did she look like?'

'Tall, blonde, beautiful. Like, head-turningly beautiful. But,' I squeeze my eyes shut, remembering, 'sort of tough-looking, too.' I see something cross his face. 'What?'

'I think I saw her.'

My heart starts to flutter. 'What? When?'

The protester rubs at his jaw, just spreading that charcoal around. 'This morning in the café. She was sitting at the next table. She asked me if I'd seen anything.'

'What do you mean, seen anything?'

He shrugs. 'I didn't understand. I just said, "Like what?", thinking maybe there'd been a mugging outside or something.' Dan's brow furrows and the charcoal smudge gathers to look like an inkblot test – I see a butterfly; no, an eagle. 'Anyway, then she just gave me a strange look and said, "Oh wonderful, you too." And then she left.'

'"You too"? She said that?'

He nods.

'Did she mention my name?'

He looks at me oddly for a moment. 'What is your name?'

'Frida.'

'Ah!' He smiles. 'After the Mexican painter?'

'After the singer in a Swedish pop group, but don't judge me.'

Dan grins. 'No, she didn't mention you.' He looks at the photograph again, turns it over. 'What about the writing on the note? Does it look familiar?'

I hesitate. 'Well ... it looks like mine.' I nibble at my thumbnail then realise what I'm doing and pull my hand away from my mouth. 'Someone must have copied it.'

'Why would they do that?' He gazes at me.

'I don't know!' I say helplessly. 'Maybe the same reason they've mocked up a photo of the two of us together – to mess with us!'

'That's one theory.' Dan turns the photograph around again and stares at the image of himself. 'Those are my clothes,' he says thoughtfully. 'I still own that T-shirt and ... Hey, what's that there?'

'Where?'

I scoot closer to get a better look at what Dan is pointing at and feel an overwhelming urge to lean in and touch the smudge on his cheek. I catch myself actually reaching out and pull my hand back as though I've been burned. What the fuck is wrong with me?

Oblivious, Dan taps the photo and points out something I'd overlooked in my panic and fury. There's a book on the rug.

'That looks like James Joyce. *Ulysses*.'

'And?'

'And ... I don't know,' he says. 'Wait a sec.' He moves away, heading to his cluttered bookshelves, and the room suddenly feels cold. I have to fight the compulsion to follow him over to the shelves. Oh God, why am I acting like this? I hope I don't have a brain tumour.

As Dan flips through the titles on his overstuffed bookshelves I watch him frowning in concentration, the hair curling at the nape of his neck, T-shirt stretched across his strong back.

ARGH! STOP IT!

'Do you own this place?' I ask, in a bid to distract myself from his lovely arms.

Dan looks up briefly. 'Rent it,' he says.

'How long have you lived here?'

'About four years.'

'Where are you from – originally, I mean?'

Greece. He's going to say Greece.

His gaze is back on the shelves. 'Greece,' he says absently.

My stomach jolts but I don't move, don't say anything. I just keep myself very still. What is going on here? Was he right? Is it possible that we have met before and somehow I have forgotten? I think back to those dark few months a couple of years ago, the time Bryony was referring to. Everything from back then is a bit hazy, it's true. But surely he'd remember us meeting, even if I didn't?

'Here!' Dan says, triumphant, and pulls out his copy of *Ulysses*, a thick tome with a battered cover, Post-it notes protruding from the pages.

'Great,' I say. 'And this proves . . . what?'

He ignores me and flicks through the book. Stops. 'Fucking hell.'

'What is it?' I walk over to take a look at what has got Dan so bug-eyed. 'Oh.'

A shallow hole has been dug out of the pages at the end of the novel. It's about the size of a matchbook. In the hole, taped down neatly, is a key. A key in a book. What fuckery is this? I look up at Dan. He stares back at me and I see very clearly then that he genuinely doesn't have any more idea about what's happening than I do. My head begins to pulse with the effort of trying to make sense of it all. I track back through everything that's happened in the last twenty-four hours. The R. A. Stone announcement, the psychotic blonde, the photo, the strange substance, this key. And then I ask the most crucial question I can think of.

'Do you have any coffee?'

$\longrightarrow$

'So you're absolutely sure you didn't put it there?' I ask once I have a steaming mug in front of me.

Dan looks at me askance. 'Well, I think I'd remember digging a hole in a book and hiding a key in it.'

'Unless, like you said, there are things we've forgotten.'

'Both of us?' he asks, seriously considering it. 'Like, collective amnesia?'

I pause, wondering how much is safe to share with this man. 'About two years ago I gave up my law practice for a while.' I see his questioning look. 'I'm a divorce lawyer.'

'Oh, well, that explains a lot.'

I ignore this. 'Anyway,' I say, 'I had a sort of ... well, I don't know what it was, maybe a sort of breakdown. Or, a life crisis. Everything from that time is a bit unclear, to be honest. So I'm thinking, maybe we met then?' I hate this idea a huge amount but I have to consider it as a possibility. 'What were you doing from February to August two years ago?'

Dan thinks about it. 'Not much. I lived here. I'd just come out of a relationship. Was finding my feet with my illustration business.' He shrugs. 'Just normal stuff.'

'So we might have met then?'

'It's possible, except why wouldn't we remember?'

'I don't know.' I think about that time I turned up in hospital after I was found unconscious in the street. 'Maybe you sold me drugs?'

'I don't even smoke!' He laughs. 'Maybe you sold *me* drugs; I know what you lawyers are like.'

I close my eyes. I feel like I'm drowning. Yesterday life made sense, today everything is unsteady. And there's something else about this whole situation: it feels odd but also incredibly familiar, a spooky, doubling déjà vu.

I pick up the key. It has a small silver disc with the number 19 printed on it in orange paint. I turn it around and the disc catches the light. 'That was definitely your copy of your book?'

'Yeah. It still has all my notes in there.'

'Okay, so how long has the key been hidden inside it? Any idea?'

Dan shrugs. 'Impossible to say, I probably haven't touched it in years.'

I stare at the thick, battered tome. 'It doesn't make sense. Why hide a key in a book where anyone could pick it up and find it?'

'Clearly you've never read *Ulysses*,' Dan says drily. 'If you wanted to hide something in a book that no one was going to touch, that's definitely the book you'd choose.'

I take out my phone and snap a picture of the key, then save it and navigate to a search engine. Dan watches me silently as I carry out a reverse image search and after scrolling down the page, I get a hit. I show him the result.

'Look familiar?'

Dan moves closer to me to look at the phone screen and my skin fizzes from the proximity. I shift incrementally away. The key on the screen is identical to the one on the coffee table, just a different number. I click through the link and land on the website of EZStore, a storage company branded in the same orange and purple. I pull the phone away and click on the locations one by one.

'The nearest store is twenty-five miles away.' I stare down again at the key. 'None of this makes any sense at all.'

'That we can definitely agree on.'

'But isn't it strange that all this is happening just a week before R. A. Stone visits the city?' I bite my lip. 'I think someone is trying to frame me.'

'Frame you?' Dan snorts. 'What for, crimes against picnicking?'

'Are you really that obtuse?' I glare at him. 'I'm pictured looking chummy with a vocal protester of Anterism. Maybe this lock-up has more incriminating evidence. I'm supposed to be introducing R. A.'s sermon in a week! The timing is just too neat.'

'Or it might have nothing to do with R. A. bloody Stone,' Dan says. 'Not everything revolves around your precious movement, you know. It's probably just a coincidence.'

'There's no such thing as coincidence,' I snap and then

stare at Dan in surprise. I don't know why I said that. I don't believe it. Our eyes meet for a moment and something deep inside me leaps, though whether in fright or something else I can't tell.

'Look,' I say hurriedly, 'either we've met before and forgotten, which is freaky, or we've never met and I'm being set up, which is equally bad just in a different way.' I drain my coffee cup. 'Whatever it is, you clearly don't know any more than I do, so it was pretty pointless coming here.'

'Hey,' Dan protests, 'I found the key, didn't I?'

'Forget about the key.'

'Well, that's not going to happen.'

'Forget about the key,' I repeat firmly. 'Look, I'm just going to destroy this photo and hope nothing else happens.' But my heart sinks. You know you're in bad shape when 'hope' turns up on your to-do list. 'And,' I say, more forcefully, 'if anything else weird occurs, I'll report it to Sehda. He'll know what to do.' I stand up. 'I need to get going.'

'That's it?' Dan stares at me. 'Aren't you even curious as to what's in the lock-up? You don't want to take a trip out there? I can drive us tomorrow.'

I shake my head. 'No, I do not. Bad idea. Terrible idea.'

'Why?'

'We've no idea what's out there. It might be a set-up!'

'Fine,' he says. 'I mean, you came all the way here to find out what this was about, but now you don't want to know?' He shrugs. 'No worries. Go home.'

I blow out a long breath. 'Well, what are *you* going to do?'

'I'm going to that lock-up tomorrow.'

I stare at him and find my thumbnail in my mouth again. I pull it away. 'Dan, listen to me. I think you should leave this alone. I've got a bad feeling. I think it might be better for both of us if we forget we ever met.'

'Seems like we've done that once already,' he says. 'This is a mystery, Frida,' his eyes flit to the table-top game, 'a bona fide adventure. I can hardly just ignore it, can I?' Dan gets up and walks over to his bookshelf. When he returns he hands over a business card.

'Here's my number, in case you change your mind.'

I meet his eyes and set my jaw firm. 'Thanks,' I say, 'but I won't.'

$\longrightarrow$

When I get back to my flat I tidy away all the magazines and papers, stuffing them back into the sideboard and slamming the door shut with considerable force. I wish I'd never started the big clean. If it wasn't for Bryony, if it wasn't for that blasted supermodel, I'd be contentedly writing my speech right now instead of gnawing at my nails (which were perfect just yesterday and are now being slowly massacred) and worrying about something I don't even understand.

Thoughts circle in my brain and I'm grateful when I can finally go to bed. I slide under my cool sheets and try to put the whole business out of my mind, thinking of happier things like R. A.'s arrival a week tomorrow, his sermon and how amazing it will be. But shards of worry slice through these pleasant musings: why was my handwriting on those notes?

Who has gone to this much trouble to plant all of these weird items? Someone is messing with me. Someone means me harm. It strikes me suddenly how stupid it is to let the protester, 'Dan', go to the storage facility alone. How do I know that he'll be honest about what he finds? How can I be sure that, if he does find something there, he won't use it against me? It could make a bad situation even worse. Knowledge is power, ignorance can be dangerous. Any lawyer worth their salt knows that. As I lie there, unable to sleep, I reluctantly conclude that, though I would like nothing better than to put this entire mess behind me, I have to know what's being kept in that storage facility. Sighing, I get up, find the business card and stab out a message to Dan, not even caring that it is impolitely late.

The reply comes back within thirty seconds. Almost as though he was waiting for me.

Chapter 6

And so it transpires that on a bright Sunday morning I find myself meeting a relative stranger on an anonymous ring road in order to head to a storage facility that is hiding God knows what. As Dan pulls up in a beat-up silver hatchback – oh, the glamour – I climb hastily into the passenger seat, enjoying the cool blast of the air con as I slam the door and belt myself in. The car is well worn, though it appears clean enough, a fragrant purple tree dangling from the rear-view mirror.

'I could have picked you up at your place, you know,' Dan says.

'No, thanks. I don't want anyone associating you with me.'

He studies me for a moment, and then, shaking his head in apparent wonderment, he pulls out into the traffic. Dan turns the radio on and in the second of silence before the music kicks in I think, *Classic Rock FM, he loves Classic Rock FM,* and the song plays and the Eagles sing 'Hotel California' and you can check out anytime you like but you can never leave, and oh dear God, how do I know these things?

Dan catches my look. 'Everything okay?'

I nod. It doesn't mean anything, I know he listens to classic rock, any fool could see that just by looking at him. I open my bag and check the contents even though I only checked them two minutes ago. The perfume bottle is zipped into the side compartment. I feel oddly conspicuous with it in there – *Don't tell Dan* – even though the man next to me doesn't know it exists and I have no idea what it even is. We drive to a backdrop of heavy guitar for a while, my mind ticking over the situation. Then Dan breaks the silence with his un-endearing bluntness.

'So, you've heavily bought into this Love Delusion crap?' He glances over to me. 'I mean, that's the only reason you're here, isn't it? To protect your precious reputation as a leading Anterist?'

'Everyone is entitled to believe what they want,' I say stiffly. 'I know what's true.'

'You seriously believe that love is just a myth?' He flashes me a glance. 'Haven't *you* ever been in love?'

I think about all of my doomed relationships. Boy, *have* I. 'I bought into it for a while.' I shrug. 'Before I realised that leaving this delusional belief system was an option.' I reach to the dashboard and turn the radio dial so the music becomes background noise. I frown at him. 'What is it with you, anyway? What does it matter what other people choose to do with their lives?'

Dan focuses on the road. He seems to be thinking something over. 'My friend at the church the other day, she was the one who printed those flyers.' He flicks a glance at me to see if I remember. I nod. 'Her husband works in a bookshop. Two months ago, he took a look through *The Love Delusion* when some rep came to try to persuade the shop to stock it.' Dan pauses. 'He packed a bag and left that same night. Told her their entire relationship had been,' his mouth twists, 'what was it he called it? "An unfortunate misunderstanding."' Dan shakes his head. 'I went to their wedding. I *know* what they had. And after reading this book,' he shrugs, 'it was all gone.'

'That's not how it works,' I protest. 'He must have been unhappy. Their marriage would have been in trouble before . . .'

'Marriages are complicated,' Dan says, shooting me an impatient look. 'Relationships aren't all bliss. That doesn't mean there isn't any love there. What happened to my friends is not normal.' He shakes his head. 'And there are rumours, too. About your R. A. Stone. That he's serving a bigger agenda, with all this behaviour modification, brainwashing . . .'

I've heard all this conspiracy nonsense before. And anyway, my interest has been piqued by his first statement and his tone as he said it. 'Have *you* been married?'

Dan nods.

'Did she leave you for The Love Delusion? Is that what this is all about?'

'No, no, nothing like that.' He frowns. 'Janie and I

69

divorced a couple of years ago. There was no major reason. It was amicable. We're still friends.'

I fall silent. So that was the relationship he referred to before. I marvel, now, how this man has not converted to our cause. He's a prime candidate: single, divorced, passionate and, judging by his collection of fantastical paraphernalia, desperately searching for some greater purpose in life.

'You know,' I say gently, 'you should open your mind to Anterism. It isn't all—'

'No chance!' Dan says, and the look he shoots me silences me. 'That's how you get them, isn't it? Find them when they're vulnerable, give them something to believe in?' His jaw flexes. 'Relationships can be difficult, painful, yes, but even when they fail, they can teach us about ourselves. Love isn't for everyone, I respect that. But anyone who promises such a simplistic, extreme, one-size-fits-all solution to something so nuanced is not doing it to benefit the human race, but because they're after something.'

I fall quiet as Dan's words needle into my brain. The magnitude of the movement. The speed with which people are converted. *Is* there something strange about that? I shake the thought away. No, it's just that we have been waiting for a solution for so long. We need it so badly. I can't let a guy I barely know make me doubt a movement that has given me so much these last two years. Given humanity so much.

'Well, if love is so great,' I say to him, 'then why are you still single?' And when he doesn't answer, I reach over and turn the radio back up, letting Pink Floyd's 'Comfortably Numb' drown my doubts away.

$$\longrightarrow$$

Twenty minutes later, Dan pulls the car into the entrance of EZStore. We follow the arrows and find ourselves on a narrow road blocked by an orange barrier. There's a small brick cabin to the right and as Dan winds down his window a man in an unfortunate purple and orange security uniform peers out at us. The guard has florid cheeks, yellowing eyes and the bulbous nose of a man who enjoys a drink or twenty. 'Receipt,' he says, in a bored drone.

Dan hesitates, because of course we do not have a receipt, what with having found the key hidden in a carved-out cranny in a work of classic literature. Something tells me that the guard would not be particularly sympathetic to our situation should we try to explain that. As Dan flashes me a look – *What now?* – the security guard's frown deepens, his face creasing inwards like a drawstring bag. 'Receipt,' he says again in a no-nonsense tone and nods to the rows of garages waiting tantalisingly on the other side.

Dan offers up a rueful expression. 'The thing is,' he says in a pleasant we're-all-sensible-here sort of voice, 'we've mis-placed our receipt. We have the key, though,' he adds. Then he dangles it out of the window, the garish purple and orange fob undulating gently.

'Could've found that anywhere.' The guard shakes his head, pursing his lips. 'No entry without receipt.'

71

Okay, that's quite enough. This idiot is clearly enjoying his little scrap of power. I lean over Dan, about to give ol' drawstring face a piece of my mind, but just as I lock eyes with him, ready to pierce him with my best withering gaze, the guard's curmudgeonly face breaks into a huge and rather alarming smile.

'Oh, it's you!' he says, in a light, breathy tone entirely unbefitting his bulk.

I blink at him. 'It is indeed me,' I say, for want of a better response.

The guard beams and, Jesus, is he blushing? 'You look lovely today, if I may say so.'

I look down at my plain black sundress and then glance at Dan. He just stares back at me, eyebrows raised. I turn back to the guard. 'You too, er . . .' I catch sight of his name badge, 'Maurice. Orange and purple are definitely your colours. Now, Maurice,' I say, doing that thing people do, using Christian names to create familiarity although, let's be honest, this guy seems altogether too familiar with me already, 'I am *so* sorry we forgot the slip. You know how these things go. Busy, busy, busy. So, we were wondering, is there any possibility that you could . . .?'

Maurice nods and blinks and then nods some more. 'Absolutely, absolutely!' he says. He leans over the counter, eyes for me only now, his finger lingering over the button. I will him to press it. He doesn't. Instead, he stares out at me with the wet eyes of a doting spaniel.

'I didn't think you would ever come back,' he says mournfully.

I actually feel Dan go on high alert next to me. Oh Christ. It *is* amnesia. That, or I have a very convincing double. Or a twin. Oh my God, am I a twin?

'Yes,' I say carefully, 'it *has* been a while. How long would you say it was since I was last here?'

Maurice casts his eyes skyward, looking ridiculously pleased to have been asked. He thinks about it for a moment, squeezing his eyes shut and then popping them open and smiling a touch madly. 'Two years, two days, one hour and forty-eight minutes.'

There's a long silence. 'Exactly,' I say, though I'm having trouble getting air into my lungs.

'Yes,' Dan pipes up, 'that's right. And this was when I was with Frida, or . . . she was alone?'

Maurice frowns at Dan. 'Yeah, yeah, you were here,' he assents begrudgingly. Then he turns back to me and his rheumy eyes are bright. 'I kept your names off the records like you asked,' he whispers, conspiratorial, and then he taps his big red nose. 'Mum's the word.'

My smile is rigid as I nod at him. 'Wonderful,' I say. 'That's just wonderful.'

Satisfied, Maurice presses a button and the barrier begins to ascend. Dan releases the handbrake and eases the car forwards. There's a very pointed silence.

'What the hell was that?' Dan asks once we've traversed the barrier.

I glance back at Maurice, who is leaning, chin on his hands, looking mooningly at our receding vehicle. A sick feeling is starting in the pit of my stomach.

'I have absolutely no idea.'

$\longrightarrow$

73

We follow the signs past row upon row of purple and orange garages that fair boggle the eye until, eventually, Dan pulls the car up outside number 19. There's no one else around – and little wonder, since any sane person would have far better things to do on this baking hot Sunday than hulk furniture around or go poking about in dusty old storage rooms.

As we get out of the car the swirling sensation that began in my stomach makes its way to my throat. My heart is beating too fast and I feel faint and woozy, though that could be due to the over-abundance of orange and purple. *It's not too late*, I tell myself, *you could just walk away from all this.* Whatever this is. I watch as Dan approaches the garage, key in hand. No. We're here now. We just need to do this. Anyway, it's burning inside me now, the need to know. How that photo came to be; why we hid that key; who Psyche is; what the hell I did to Maurice.

Dan glances back and his gaze turns to concern. 'Are you okay?' he says. 'You look a bit green.'

'I'm fine,' I say, pasting on a smile. 'Let's just get this over with.'

Dan fits the key into the lock and then, with a heave, swings the garage door upwards. I hold my breath. I have absolutely no idea what to expect but given the bizarre nature of events thus far, I'm putting money on a dead body.

Instead, what we see is a small square room with concrete walls, carpeted and painted the same migraine-inducing orange and purple combo, and empty except for a table holding a laptop. I sniff the air. It smells dank, like this place hasn't been opened in a very long time. Say, two years, two days, one hour and forty-eight minutes. Dan walks over to the table and I follow. The laptop is plugged into a power socket on the wall, the switch flicked off. I bend down and turn it on. On the table top, next to the computer, there's a memory stick. I open the lid of the laptop and it springs into life, revealing a backdrop of mountains in the mist. A few seconds later, a box appears. The laptop is password protected.

'Shit,' Dan says as we stare at the blinking cursor. 'Any guesses?'

'Try my name? F. R. I. D.A.'

He does. *Incorrect password.* 'Yours?'

He types D.A.N. and when that fails, DANIEL.

'It could be anything.' Dan thinks for a minute. 'Maybe we should just take it with us and one of us can try to crack it at home?'

'Maybe,' I say but I don't move. Instead, I open my bag and take out the photograph. Turn it over. Stare at that word on the reverse, scribbled in the corner. Driven purely by instinct and ignoring my rational brain, which is telling me that there is no way this is going to work, I say, 'Try "Anteros".'

Dan types it in. I can tell he's not expecting anything but this time when he presses return the screen flickers and the mountains disappear and we're staring at a plain blue screen empty of icons. Dan picks up the USB and slides it into the port. A box pop ups: the laptop has detected a new drive. Do we want to open it? Dan and I look at one another, suddenly reluctant. Can of worms, springs to mind. Pandora's laptop . . .

Do we want to open it?

We don't but we do.

Contained within the drive we find a single folder. Underneath that, a video file. The folder is called: 'Everything You Need to Know'. The video file is called: 'Watch This First'. Dan flicks me a glance and I nod, though my heart is hammering as Dan hovers the cursor over the video and clicks. When two figures appear on the screen, I let out a small choked sound. Because it's us, me and Dan, and seeing us on the screen like that fills me with a great and unnameable terror. As we stand there, staring at our doppelgängers, mouths open in silent shock, the on-screen Frida smiles.

'Hi, Frida and Dan,' she says. 'If you're watching this, then you've forgotten who you are.'

Chapter 7

The Frida in the video looks different to me, though I can't put my finger on exactly how. It must have been summer there, too, when she filmed this because she's wearing a bottle-green sundress that I still own. She hasn't straightened her hair, though, and that's how I know it can't really be me. I never wear mine curly, it looks far too unprofessional. She's sitting on a tan sofa, the same sofa I saw yesterday at Dan's flat or at least one very much like it, and unless he has a twin brother the man on the screen is the man standing next to me now. The only difference being that screen-Dan has one sleeve tattoo. The Dan next to me has two.

My mind fills with silver stars of panic. What is this? How did they do it? Who is *they* anyway? What does this all mean?

And an answer comes from somewhere deep inside me: *Nothing good.*

Dan is very still, watching himself on the screen, sizing up his counterpart and feeling perhaps the same emotions that I am. I realise now that we were wrong to come here. I thought that it would give me answers but instead we've stepped further into the fun-house, the ground continually shifting, the hall of mirrors refusing to reflect back anything I recognise as reality.

'I hope that you're both watching this,' screen-Frida is saying, 'that somehow we ... I mean you ... found each other again.' Her eyes are sad. 'Because you have work to do. Of course, none of this will make any sense right now because you've been dosed with water from the River Lethe and it has made you forget everything about the magical world.' She pauses. 'And that includes each other.'

I look at Dan. *River Lethe? Magical world?* What the actual fuck? But Dan is just staring at the screen, looking as shocked and bewildered as I feel.

'We don't know how long ago it happened,' screen-Frida continues. 'It could be weeks, months, maybe even longer.' She looks at screen-Dan. 'What date is it today?' When he answers, she nods and turns back to us. 'Well, however long it is from that date, that's approximately how long you've had this magical amnesia for.'

My stomach lurches. The date screen-Dan gave was over two years ago.

Screen-Dan speaks now and the Dan beside me jumps at the sound of his own voice.

'We have no stock of the antidote to the Lethe water,' screen-Dan says. 'Can't find any; we've tried everywhere and everyone we can think of. We reckon he's destroyed it all.' Screen-Frida looks as though she wants to add something, and the words on the note float into my mind – *For memory. Only take if no other option. Don't tell Dan* – then screen-Dan continues and Frida glances away and the moment passes. 'So, in the absence of any way to get your memories back, we've done the next best thing. We've written down everything you need to know about who you really are and what you're facing. Read it all and however fantastical and mad it sounds,' screen-Dan smiles ruefully, 'and trust me, it will at first – please, please, believe that this is real. It's dangerous for you if you don't.' His face darkens. 'Anteros is planning something. Something terrible. You have to find out what it is and you have to stop him.'

Screen-Frida says something then, but it is low and the mic doesn't catch it. Dan nods, his eyes flick away, and then he looks back at the camera and says, 'We have to go.'

Screen-Frida stares out at us now, her large dark eyes serious. Whoever she is, she's haunted by something I don't want to know about. 'Frida,' she says and I start. (It's really very disconcerting to be addressed by yourself.) 'I know you don't believe a single word of what you've just been told.'

I frown at the screen. She's got me there.

'I didn't believe it either, when Dan first told me,' screen-Frida continues. 'Right now you're probably thinking this whole thing is a trick, played by someone who is trying to ruin your reputation.' She shakes her head almost fondly. It makes my blood boil. 'It's not your fault,' she says. 'After all, you've not been fanciful Frida for a long time, have you? You stopped believing in magic when Dad left. You toughened up. Built walls around yourself. Became force-to-be-reckoned-with Frida.'

Dan is watching me curiously. I stare straight ahead at the screen.

'But despite how hard you'll try to rationalise all this, something inside you knows it's real.' Her gaze is intense now, her voice low. 'Trust that feeling, Frida. Believe it. It's the only way you'll find your way back to yourself.' She smiles then, and there's a fleeting wistfulness in that smile. 'You can do this, Frida. I have faith in you.' Then she leans in and stops the recording.

There's a very long, very shocked silence as Dan and I stare at the static screen. Then Dan turns to me, his face a picture of bafflement.

'Well, whatever I was expecting, I—'

'Shhh!' I hold up a hand and cock my head to the open garage door. 'Did you hear that?'

Dan stops stock still and listens. I hear again the faint sound of raised voices. Maurice? Flashing a warning look at Dan, I nod at the laptop and then I move quickly to the door. Far in the distance I can just glimpse Maurice reprimanding someone in a sleek black sports car. In the driver's seat, a flash of pale blonde hair.

My body reacts even while my mind scrambles to catch up. That prickling primal fear I experienced is back, and stronger than ever, telling me only one thing: we're in danger.

'What did you see?' Dan asks, laptop under his arm. 'Who's out there?'

'The psycho supermodel has followed us,' I say grimly. 'We need to go.'

Back in the car, Dan starts the engine and I stare numbly ahead, my mind scrambled by having seen a version of myself I don't remember talking to me from that screen. I shake my head. *Focus, Frida.* Right now, the priority is to get the hell away from Psyche. I don't know why, I just know that I can't let her catch up with us. I hold my breath and don't release it until Dan has eased the car down the lanes, following the arrow signs to the exit, which – thank the stars – is on the opposite side to the entrance. Maybe Psyche won't see us. Maybe she won't even know we were there.

'Where to?' Dan asks.

I think about this and realise I have no idea. We can't go to mine or Dan's, Psyche knows where we live. Right now it seems we're safest in motion. 'Just drive for a while,' I say, chewing at my thumbnail. 'I'll think of something.' Dan nods and accelerates, crossing two lanes and provoking rude hand gestures but at least putting a healthy distance between us and our pursuer. I open the laptop and mouse to the file our screen counterparts left for us. It's a huge text document.

I double click it but before I can read a word, the battery dies. 'Fuck!'

'Read anything?' Dan glances at me.

'Nothing.' I slip the memory stick in my bag and close the laptop. Stare straight ahead, thinking, thinking. We drive in silence for a while.

'Could that video have been faked?' I ask eventually. 'Could those people be . . . someone other than us?'

Dan thinks about it. 'No,' he says, reluctantly shaking his head. 'I don't think so.'

I take this in. 'Those words she ... I mean, *I* said.' I close my eyes, trying to remember. 'The River Lethe. And Anteros again. Do either of them mean anything to you?'

Dan looks straight ahead, eyes focused on the road, brow furrowed. 'Well, the River Lethe, that's the river of forgetfulness. In the Underworld.' He flicks me a glance, sees my blank expression. 'You know, from Greek mythology?'

'Is that from one of your role-playing games?'

'No.' He frowns. 'Well, actually, the River Styx in D&D is sort of a catch-all, inaccurately attributed with the powers of the Lethe, which some players are *really* not happy about but—' He sees my expression. 'Sorry, sorry, not the point.'

'And Anteros?' I press.

Dan shakes his head. 'I'm not familiar with the name. Don't you know? Isn't it connected to you Anterists?'

'I'd never heard the name before I saw it written on that envelope.'

'Anteros,' Dan ponders. 'Well, that sounds Greek too. Maybe it's something connected to the Greek god Eros? Hey, yeah,' he says, nodding, 'the supermodel's name was Psyche. Psyche was Cupid's wife in ancient myth. Eros is the Greek name.'

'And you just happen to be Greek,' I say darkly, my mind turning furiously over the facts, putting all these clues together to form the only possible conclusion. Dan shoots me a confused glance.

'What does that have to do with anything?'

'Isn't it obvious?' I glare at him. 'Clearly we *do* know each other; presumably we met during that hazy period of mine two years ago.' I rub at my aching head. 'You must have somehow got me involved in one of your stupid fantasy quests, one with a Greek legends theme, and we . . . I don't know, forgot about it somehow.'

Dan falls silent. 'I suppose it's possible,' he says eventually. 'But there's just one thing, Frida.' He meets my eyes, his gaze intense. 'If this is only a game, why are we running?'

Chapter 8

'We'll have to stop soon,' Dan says, casting an eye on his petrol gauge. 'I'm going to need to refuel.'

I glance at the wing mirror. No sign of the black sports car. 'Let's stop at the next services. I want to plug that laptop in anyway, find out what the hell is on that file we left for ourselves.'

Five minutes later, Dan is filling up the car at the petrol station. Then he pulls into the sprawling car park and finds a spot between two other silver vehicles. I glance at him. It's almost like he's done this kind of thing before. With no sign of Psyche, we head into the services, past the arcade games and burger joints and towards the chain coffee shop. We pass the usual mix of families on their way to their holidays, kids with sticky-ice-cream faces, babies asleep in their carriers, businessmen working the weekend. I inhale the aroma of coffee and sugary pastries with a sigh.

'You find somewhere to plug in,' I tell Dan, 'and I'll get us coffee. What do you want?'

'Double-shot mocha.' Dan glances to a quiet corner booth. 'I'll be over there.'

'Dan,' I call. He looks back and at the sight of his face I have a rush of feeling I don't understand, am gripped with a sudden urge to say, *Be careful! I don't want to lose you!* Instead, I give a tight smile and ask, 'Do you want a muffin?'

As I queue for the drinks, I work methodically through what I know. Dan and I were friends two years ago, evidently playing some sort of role-playing game together. That much is clear from that video we left ourselves. Maybe that's what Bryony meant about how I seemed different back then, how she thought I'd met someone? Perhaps this is what I was into when I went off radar?

But then what happened? How did we lose our memories of it all? Did we include memory loss as a plot point, and then get so deeply involved in the game that we somehow convinced ourselves to forget? Or – Jesus – maybe we arranged to have ourselves hypnotised so we'd forget? Is that even possible? A cold thought comes upon me. If Psyche is our pursuer in the game, what if she doesn't know it's just role-play? Maybe she genuinely believes she's after us.

If this is only a game then why are we running?

I feel very tired all of a sudden. I knew I'd hit rock bottom two years ago, but I never for one moment imagined that my nadir could have encompassed live-action role-play. The barista eyes me warily and I realise that I just laughed out loud in a semi-hysterical fashion. Oh dear. I'm losing it. Again.

I am suddenly very sure of something. Clearly, I was quite ill two years ago. If I indulge this charade, if I read the notes we left ourselves about this Anteros and his dastardly plot, then I'm in danger of getting sucked back in to the madness and – I think about screen-Frida's earnest face, her haunted eyes, how she didn't look like someone playing a game, but someone fighting for her life – I may even start believing this craziness is real.

I can't let that happen. My life is so much better now. I have so much to look forward to. I need to contain this.

But how?

Ahead of me, I spy an Anterist, wearing his badge proudly as he claims his customer discount, and I experience an ache of longing for my church. I should be at home, writing my speech, looking forward to next Sunday's event, not uncovering disturbing secrets from my hazy past in the company of an admittedly attractive but entirely unsuitable near-stranger. Then it comes to me. I know what I need to do next, what I should have done as soon as I found that photo. I have to contact Sehda and tell him everything. The Love Delusion's influence spreads around the city; he is sure to have a connection with an Anterist psychologist or a hypnotist or even a freaking professional Dungeon Master who can explain what the hell has happened to us and help us put it right. Pills, CBT, whatever it takes. As soon as I make this decision, I feel better. Yes, that's it. Anterists are my people. They care about me. Of course they'll help me!

Keeping one eye on the entrance for the arrival of the psycho supermodel, I send a text message. To my delight, I receive a reply within a minute, and as I read it, some of the tension leaves my body. In all of this weirdness in the company of Dan, I've almost forgotten who Frida McKenzie is. I'm important. I have influence. I don't have to handle this alone. I order the coffees and muffins, then I make my way over to Dan. He looks up from the laptop screen at my footsteps and I see a flicker of alarm in his eyes before he sees that it's me. God knows what he's read in that file, what insane depths we sank to back when we wrote it.

'Listen,' I say, sliding the tray on to the table and sitting down opposite him, 'it's going to be okay. Help is coming.'

'What help?' Dan asks sharply.

'Sehda.'

Dan's face turns the colour of putty. 'Frida, please tell me you didn't just call the evil pencil and tell him where we are.'

I glare at him. 'Put your prejudices aside for a minute, Dan, and think. This is some serious psychological shit. Sehda can help us sort it out.' And protect us from the crazy woman on our tail while he's at it. But Dan is already up, slamming the laptop closed.

'You've no idea what you've just done,' he says. 'Come on!' And then he's off, laptop lead trailing in his wake as he hares across the café and out towards the door. With a mournful look back at the coffees, I make after him.

'Dan, wait a second! What the hell is wrong with you?' I grab his T-shirt and yank him to a halt. He turns to me, his face grim with fear.

'You were right, Frida. This *is* all connected to The Love Delusion.'

'What are you talking about?'

'Two years ago it seems we were investigating R. A. Stone. Except, according to our previous selves, he's not called R. A. Stone, he's called Anteros. And he's not some charismatic guru, he's ...' Dan shakes his head. 'Doesn't matter. I'll tell you later. Anyway, we were digging into his plan and someone must have caught us.' He meets my eyes. 'Frida, they wiped our memories. Every trace of what we knew about them and each other, gone.' He shakes his head. 'If your friend catches us now, I'm guessing we'll forget this weekend ever happened, too.'

I stare at Dan sadly. I was right. He read the notes and it must have triggered something in him, he's been pulled back into the game, he actually thinks this is real. 'Dan,' I say gently, 'listen to me. None of this is true. It's all fantasy, don't you see? There is no evil Love Delusion plot. It was just a game we made up.'

'Then how do you explain our memory loss?'

'I don't know. A psychotic break? Hypnotism? Anything but water from a magical river that only exists in books!'

'Look,' he says, rubbing at his jaw, 'I know this sounds mad. I know it does. But what I read on that file doesn't seem like a game.' Dan meets my eyes. 'And it doesn't *feel* like a game. It feels real. Doesn't it to you?'

I think about screen-Frida's words: *Something inside you knows it's real*. About my terror when I saw Psyche at the lock-up – pure, primal, undeniable. 'It does feel real,' I admit. 'But maybe that's because of what happened to us two years ago. We got fantasy mixed up with reality and now the boundaries are blurred. We can't trust ourselves to know one from the other.'

Dan chews his lip.

'We need to sort this out,' I insist, 'before it gets any worse.'

Dan stares at me searchingly then his shoulders sag. 'Okay,' he says, 'maybe you're right . . .' Then his gaze travels over my shoulder and a flash of fear crosses his face. He clutches the laptop more tightly, knuckles white.

'What is it?'

'Your rescue party,' Dan says, 'and they don't look very happy. In fact, I'm probably just having another psychotic break but they don't look very human, either.'

'What are you talking abo—' I turn around and, sure enough, a group of Anterists are heading straight for us, seven of them, all wearing red suits. Wow! Sehda has sent a team. For a moment I experience a burst of pride that the centre leader values me so much. Then I look at the Anterists again and see that something is wrong. This group doesn't look like any Anterists I know. They're thickset, strong-looking, more like a mob and – a shiver goes through me as they draw closer and I see them more clearly – Dan's right. There's something disturbing about the way they look. They have blank faces and dead eyes.

I turn back to Dan. 'I don't understand,' I stammer. 'Why do they look like that?'

Dan doesn't answer; he's scanning the surrounding area. He nods over to the service station where several large tankers are fuelling up. 'Over there,' he says, 'behind the trucks.'

And then he's off again. I run after him, my mind reeling. What was wrong with the Anterists' faces? Were they wearing masks? Are they actors in this game too? Too many questions, zero answers. Right now all I can do is obey the same instinctive reaction that I had to seeing Psyche, and not walk, but run after a fleeing Dan.

Stumbling in my sandals, I follow Dan up to the service station and across the forecourt. He's making for the sprawling service station shop. Yes, I think, we need to be around other people. That will keep us safe.

I have no idea why I believe this.

As we approach the building, I see something. There's a black limo parked up on the garage forecourt. 'Dan,' I say, grabbing hold of his arm, 'wait.'

Too late. The window of the limo rolls down, revealing Sehda's long pale face. As we stand there, stock still, his small blue eyes lock on to mine.

'Frida!' The centre leader smiles. 'So glad I caught you.'

'Sehda!' I say. 'You're here!'

A small frown furrows his brow. 'Naturally. You requested my help, Frida, and here I am. And yet you do not seem altogether pleased to see me.' Sehda's gaze travels to Dan and then back to me. He smiles a thin-lipped smile. 'Get in the car. Your friend, too. And we'll ensure this nasty business is sorted out.'

I look over at Dan. He gives a tiny, almost imperceptible shake of his head.

'Frida,' Sehda says, in that beguiling voice of his. 'Come on. Let me take you home. I can help you.'

I don't move. This is my chance to sort things out, so why do I hesitate? I stare at Sehda and I notice something strange about him. His eyes seem like small chips of ice, his red slit of a mouth looks hungry, and once again a strange, deep instinct is screaming at me to get the hell away from him. But why? This is Sehda, my centre leader. Surely I can't believe that he means me any harm? I look about me and see that the area has entirely cleared of passers-by. The truck drivers at the petrol pumps are sitting in their cabs, staring straight ahead. Bewildered, I look to Dan again, his clear eyes shining a warning, and I am suddenly certain of one thing: whoever Dan is, whatever is happening here, I can trust him. Maybe only him.

And so, constructing what I hope is a rueful smile, I return my gaze to my centre leader.

'Sehda,' I say, 'I am *so* sorry but I'm afraid I've wasted your time. When I said I was in trouble and needed help, what I meant is I had ... um ... heatstroke! And because I was feeling muddled, I accidentally sent that message to you, when actually it was for my friend here.' I nod over to Dan. 'He's going to take me home. Again, I'm so sorry to have troubled you,' I babble on, 'and I won't keep you a second longer. I'm sure you've got lots of important things to do before next Sunday. So,' I say brightly, clapping my hands together, 'we'll be off now and you can get on with your business.'

Then I give Dan the eye and we start walking.

'Stop,' Sehda says and I do. I mean, I don't want to stop but for some reason I stop anyway. Dan, still walking, looks back at me, his eyes urging me to come the fuck on but then Sehda turns his gaze on Dan. 'You too, Dan,' Sehda says in that silky-smooth voice. 'Come back here.' *He knew his name; how did he know Dan's name?* I marvel, as Dan does a neat about-turn, efficient as a soldier, and walks stiff-legged back to my side.

I goggle at Sehda, utterly thrown. What on earth is happening here? Is Sehda some kind of magician-hypnotist? That would definitely explain his dodgy dress sense, as well as how Dan and I forgot all the things that we did. I saw a programme once in which a guy was mesmerised to think he was being attacked by zombies. Maybe none of this is real. Maybe I'm imagining it all, starting with meeting Dan on the steps of the church?

'What's on the laptop?' Sehda asks silkily. 'What stories have you been telling yourselves?' As his seductive voice trickles into my ears, I have an overwhelming urge to tell him everything – about my visitor, the photo, the lock-up, the memory loss, the quest – but another part of me is seething with fury. How dare Sehda violate me like this, using some mentalist's tricks to take control of my body, my mind? No way am I going to tell this fucker anything—'

'It's information about everything we've forgotten,' Dan blurts.

I stare at him. So much for the resistance.

'Really?' Sehda says. 'And what, pray, does it tell you?'

Dan's eyes bulge, his jaw clenches, but oh God, he can't stop himself from talking: 'R. A. Stone is an evil god,' he stutters, I can hear his throat click, click, clicking as he fights to stop the flow of words. 'I'm the Delphic Oracle, Frida is a descendent of Eros. And you're . . . you're—'

'Enough,' Sehda says with a wave of his hand and Dan's mouth snaps shut, helpless, desperate eyes meeting mine as my centre leader casually smooths the sleeves of his robe.

I stare at Dan. Delphic Oracle? Descendent of Eros? What the hell crazy fiction did we create? I also don't understand how Sehda fits into this. I mean, is he playing too? Did he also forget this was a game? This whole thing is lunacy.

'Come for a ride with me,' Sehda says in a sing-song voice. 'Come for a ride and I promise you that this recent unfortunate situation will all go away. That's what you want, isn't it, Frida?' He turns his chilly eyes on me. 'For things to go back to normal? For you to join our merry band again? You'll be important, admired, envied.' He smiles, showing his little sharp teeth. 'I can see it in you, how much you want that, Frida. Well then, what are you waiting for?'

The door to the limo swings open and my sense of panic is mirrored in Dan's eyes, because we're both moving towards the car, our limbs no longer our own. And maybe Sehda is right, maybe I do want whatever oblivion he's promising. Maybe if we go with him, I'll wake up tomorrow and every inexplicable thing that has happened since the supermodel turned up at my door will be gone. I'll be myself again, with no memory of any of this horrible, confusing, games-become-reality weirdness and that would be *so good*!

And even if I wanted to, I can't resist whatever mind control Sehda has over me. We are lambs gambolling to the slaughter. Powerless.

Not entirely powerless. Her voice in my mind. Screen-Frida's. My thoughts flit to the bottle in the zipped pocket of my bag, forgotten until now. Obviously it's just a prop from whatever game we were playing. But if Sehda believes the game is real, might it work to break his hold, even so?

I'm attempting to reach for the bottle, my hand only moves an inch, it's like gravity has increased a thousand-fold, when I hear something. Sehda hears it too, his focus wavers and I feel a momentary loosening of his hold over us, as a black sports car screeches onto the forecourt and comes skidding to a halt millimetres from the chief Anterist's immaculate limo.

I meet Dan's eyes and watch them turn from hope to despair. Psyche.

Now we have not one enemy, but two.

Chapter 9

Psyche steps from her car, looking ridiculously stunning in a navy playsuit and gladiator sandals, a regular magazine-cover star except for one small detail – she's holding a gun. Holy fucking hell, a gun. A guard emerges from the driver's seat of Sehda's limo, and with a jolt to the stomach I see that it's another of those red-suited Anterists with the disturbingly blank faces. Sehda himself seems unalarmed by the whole gun situation and simply regards the scene calmly from his window seat.

'Psyche,' he says with a thin smile. 'Well now, what an unexpected pleasure.'

So, these two know each other. Are we all playing the game? Just how many players does this blasted thing have?

'Let them go,' Psyche says. I exchange a surprised look with Dan. Okay, wasn't expecting that.

'Or?' Sehda arches one silver eyebrow, his gaze lingering on the weapon. 'Bullets won't stop me, dear, you know that.'

'Oh, these will,' she says. 'I had them made specially. Ophiotaurus bullets can really sting an immortal, even one as leathery as you.' She smiles broadly. 'How about a little demo?' Then she aims the gun at the Anterist guard and fires. There's a soft whizzing sound and then the guard's leg begins to smoke and he collapses to the forecourt emitting a keening bellow. I have a moment to think how very persuasive these special effects are and then Psyche swings the gun around to Sehda's head. 'I said let them go.' She smirks. 'You don't want to risk me messing up that lovely hair of yours, do you?'

Sehda stares at Psyche with pure, concentrated rage and my guts pool to liquid – I would not want to be on the receiving end of that look. But Psyche's eyes are shining and I get the feeling she's actually enjoying herself. He shrugs his thin shoulders. 'Oh fine.' He waves his hand and immediately Dan and I have control of our limbs again. As we half-collapse, Psyche jerks her head at us.

'Over here.'

We hastily obey, hurrying over, unsteady on our newly reclaimed limbs, as another guard appears from the limo and helps the wounded Anterist back into the car, casting a nervous look at Psyche.

Sehda surveys her. 'I heard you'd turned.' He purses his cruel lips. 'My, my, so many flip-flops, Psyche, it's a wonder even you know whose side you're on. It's the wrong move, of course. All we immortals must now choose who to align ourselves with, but you do not want to be opposing Anteros,

96

not this time.' There's a delighted glint in his eyes. 'Not with what's coming.'

Psyche waves the gun at him airily. 'What can I say? I like the long odds.'

'Er, excuse me?' I pipe up.

Psyche and Sehda glance over.

'We'd like to stop playing now.'

Psyche frowns.

'I mean,' I continue, 'I presume we all signed up to play this game a while ago and it all seems very professional and awfully ... um ... convincing but ... we'd like to throw in our cards or little figurines or whatever now.' I look at Dan. He nods enthusiastically. Meanwhile, Psyche and Sehda look at me with expressions by turns curious and pitying.

'Is there a password or something that tells you we want to quit?' I ask. 'Because if there is, unfortunately we seem to have forgotten it.'

'I see you Lethed them, then?' Psyche rolls her eyes at Sehda.

Sehda gives her an icy smile. 'Oh, not me. Anteros himself did the honours.'

'Really?' She frowns. 'Unusually hands-on of him.'

'Well, he wanted to ensure the job was done properly,' Sehda says. 'There's much at stake, Psyche, and even Anteros has greater forces he must answer to.'

She stares at him then. 'Greater forces? Meaning what? Who?'

Sehda just smiles. 'All in good time, my dear.'

I look at them both, incredulous. They're still playing. You can't fault their commitment. I shoot a glance at Dan and cut my eyes towards where his car is parked. *Shall we get out of here?* He nods. I clear my throat.

'Well!' I say brightly. 'If that's everything, we'll be off now . . .'

Sehda turns his gaze on me and instantly pins me to the spot. That is some Derren Brown level shit he's got going on.

'Frida, Frida, Frida,' Sehda says. 'What a disappointment you are.' He gives me the most terrible, empty grin. 'Still, this could be useful. While it has proven inconvenient that we are not able to kill you, there is no celestial law that says another mortal can't. And when the Anterists find out what you've done, how you lied to them, pretended to be one of them to gain their trust so that you could infiltrate the movement to destroy it from within, well,' he shrugs, 'I can hardly be held responsible for anything they do when they find you.' He bares his teeth. 'And they will find you, Frida. I'll make sure of it. In a few hours, every Anterist on the planet will know your face and want your blood.'

I seem to be having trouble breathing. 'Woah,' I say. 'Did you just say kill me? And infiltrate? Who infiltrated? I never infiltrated!' I look wildly from Sehda to Psyche. 'Look, I don't understand what's going on here. Is this still part of the game? Sehda, you're not really going to tell the Anterists I'm some sort of spy, are you?'

But the limo window is closing now, concealing Sehda's satisfied grin behind tinted glass. I run to the window and shout into the narrowing gap. 'Stop! Sehda! I wasn't pretending to be anything! I'm an Anterist, you know I am! Please tell me if this is just the game!' The car pulls away, almost catching me under its wheels, and I stare after it, bereft, as it rounds the corner of the service station and disappears.

When I turn back, Psyche is looking at me with an expression of utter disgust. 'You really have no idea who that was, do you?' she says.

'Of course I do! I've known the man for two years. He's my centre leader.'

Psyche rolls her eyes. 'That was *Hades*. God of the Underworld. R. A. Stone is Anteros.' She stares at my blank expression. 'They're anagrams! Fuck, I mean, I know they wiped your memories but did they carry out a lobotomy too?'

I give Psyche a pitying smile. 'Listen, Psyche or whatever your actual name is, I know this might be a bit hard to understand at first but,' I pause, 'it looks as though we were all involved in a role-playing game and somehow we lost our memories and now some of you think it's actually real.' I cast a worried glance after Sehda's receding limo. 'Apparently Dan was playing the Delphic Oracle, probably because you're Greek,' I say to him, 'terrible typecasting, really, and I'm some sort of descendent of Eros.' I smooth my dress. 'I suppose I do have a sort of goddess air about me.'

Psyche snorts.

'And evidently you're playing the wife of Eros,' I say. 'And it seems that poor Sehda thinks he's playing Hades, which is presumably why he's taught himself those hypnotist tricks.' I nod. 'But the main thing to remember here is that none of this is real.'

'Except that it is,' Psyche says.

'And,' I continue, ignoring her, 'the issue I have is that it

99

appears that Sehda may have gone a little rogue and could possibly cause a teensy bit of trouble for me with the Anterists by claiming that I am some sort of enemy of The Love Delusion.'

'Because you are.'

'So,' I press on, 'I think the best way to proceed is for us to contact whoever is in charge of the game overall and have them clear up this mess.' I look from Dan to Psyche. 'Agreed?'

Psyche stows her gun in her belt. 'You need to hide,' she says. 'Sehda's right, there's no law that stops you being killed by a mortal.'

I blink at her. 'Well, except, you know, the actual law.'

'Frida,' Dan says softly, 'what if this isn't a game?'

It takes me a moment to speak. 'Dan, we've been over this. Of course it's a game. Gods and Oracles and immortals and plots and mind-wiping Lethe water. What else could it be?'

'Reality,' says Psyche grimly. 'It's reality. And somewhere inside that thick head of yours, you know it, too.'

'No,' I say. I walk over to Dan. I can't lose him to this madness again. He's the only ally I've got in all of this mess. I take his hands and look into his eyes, and experience again that spark of something at his touch. What exactly were we to each other two years ago? Because, frankly, the feelings I have seem a little bedroomy for mere board-game buddies.

'Dan,' I say, 'please try to stay connected to sanity for a minute. This isn't real. It's probably some global, high-stakes, no-expense-spared, live-action performance, like ... what happened to Michael Douglas in *The Game*!' As I say this, I warm to the notion. That does sound rather glamorous and definitely more the kind of thing I would be involved in. 'Anyway,' I say, 'the important thing is, now we know it's just a role-play game, we need to find out how to contact the organisers and ask them to release us.'

'The thing is,' Dan says, 'I only got into role-playing games two years ago.'

I drop his hands. 'Your point being?'

'We left that video a month before that.'

'I don't follow.'

Dan rubs at his temple. 'Well, I'm just thinking, is it possible that it's the other way around. What if the reason I got into the fantasy role-play stuff was because of the life I had as this Oracle person, which Anteros made me forget?'

'Give that boy a gold star,' Psyche says and casts a scathing glance at me. 'You always were the more obtuse of the two.'

'You stay out of this,' I tell her. I meet Dan's eyes. 'Please, Dan, you can't seriously believe all this is real.'

He shrugs helplessly. 'I know it sounds mad. But the faces of those Anterists? What Sehda just did to us? And what about the way that security guard behaved towards you? How do you explain all that?'

'I told you, this is a complex, clever, very expensive game! You said it yourself, there are role-playing games that are inventive and layered and can last for years.'

He shakes his head. 'Not like this, though. Not something that seems so much like reality. You and me, together, like this, it feels familiar, doesn't it?'

I touch his arm. 'Because we knew each other. But that doesn't mean that magic and gods and monsters are real. It just means that we played a game together and we got confused.

Dan, please don't lose the plot on me now. We have to find out who organised this game and tell them it has got out of control.'

Psyche is looking at us with impatience. 'Okay,' she says, 'time's a wasting and I've got an evil love god to foil, and I'm down an Oracle and a God-descendent so, here.' She reaches into her pocket and draws out a bundle of money. I stare at it. Guns, bundles of money, sports car, the ability to face down Sehda without breaking a sweat: whatever game we are playing, Psyche definitely landed the best part.

'My advice is move fast,' she says. 'Catch a plane out of here. Never come back.'

I look at the money. It's a lot of money. 'But you can't go,' I say weakly. 'We need your help to get out of the game.'

Psyche flicks me a scornful glance. 'Trust me, darling, you're well and truly out of the game. Now take the money. I can't be responsible for you, not with you in this,' she waves vaguely in our direction, 'condition. You're a liability. The best thing you can do now is run.'

'I've lived in this city my whole life,' I say resolutely. 'I'm not running anywhere.'

She shrugs. 'Then the Anterists will find you and they will kill you.'

'Stop it!' I shout. 'Stop acting like this is real! I told you, Dan and I are not playing this ridiculous game any more. Just drop the stupid role-play, okay?'

She regards me for a moment. 'Fine. Whatever.' She throws the money on to the forecourt and reaches for her car door. I look down at the cash. It's bundled with a little yellow rubber band and the sight of it reminds me of the bottle of golden liquid. I have to hand it in. I don't want anyone coming looking for it, and starting this whole mess all over again.

'Wait!' I say. 'I've got a prop I want to return.'

I reach into my bag and pull out the small clear bottle. Psyche is fixed to the spot for a moment and then in one smooth movement she's over to me.

'Let me see that!' She reaches out and grabs the bottle. Stares at it, eyes widening. 'Where the hell did you get this?'

'It was hidden in the cupboard under my sink.'

'It was *what*?' Dan says, turning to me. 'I asked you if there was anything else and you said no! Why didn't you tell me about it?'

'There was a note telling me not to tell you.' I shrug.

'Why?'

'Well, I don't know, do I? I wasn't there!' I turn to Psyche, who is still marvelling at the bottle. She must be a method actor, she never drops her character.

'Just give it to whoever is in charge,' I say. 'Tell them we're out. Or use it yourself, I don't care.'

'What else did the note say?' Psyche asks.

I blow out a breath. 'Something like, "for memory only if no other option".'

Her grey eyes meet mine. 'This is ambrosia.'

'Yep. Okey, dokey. Ambrosia. Whatever you say.'

'No,' she says, and there's a thrum of excitement under her cool tone. 'You don't understand. This can bring your memories back. That's why you left it for yourself.'

I wave a hand. 'It's fine. I'm happier without them, to be honest.'

She appraises me for a moment, as though thinking something over. 'You really want out of the game, don't you?'

At her words, I experience a powerful wave of relief. Finally! Finally, she admits it is a game. Jesus, I think I was even starting to question reality myself for a moment there. I give Dan a beaming smile: *See, I told you!* I turn back to Psyche. 'I do. We do.' I turn to Dan. 'Right?'

He nods uncertainly. 'I guess so.'

Psyche smiles. 'Okay, well, this is how it works. You take a single drop of this and it . . . completes a phase. After you drink it, you can leave the game if you want to. Both of you.'

I eye her suspiciously. 'And you'll keep to your word on this?'

'I promise.'

I look at the bottle. 'All I have to do is drink one drop?'

'Exactly. But no more than one drop,' she warns.

'Why?'

She gives me a tight smile. 'It's the rules.'

'Mortals can't take ambrosia,' Dan pipes up.

I look at him. 'This isn't real, Dan, remember?'

'I know, but I'm just saying.' He flushes. 'If we *were* playing some sort of role-play game, you wouldn't be able to take ambrosia without dire consequences.'

'No, *you* wouldn't be able to take it,' Psyche says, 'because you're human. Frida, though . . .' She surveys me, smiling. 'Frida is something else. In the *game*, I mean.' She does air quotes round the word. Stares at me, a challenge in her eyes. It strikes me that I really do not trust this woman at all.

'How do I know it's safe to drink?'

In answer, Psyche uncorks the bottle, tips it to her mouth for a second and drinks. Then she smiles. 'See, it's fine.' I stare at her. Is it my imagination or does she look a little brighter in the eyes, a fraction more gorgeous than before? I shake my head. *Come on, Frida, don't get caught up in this insanity. There's no such thing as ambrosia!*

Psyche holds out the bottle. 'So, are we agreed? Are you ready to complete this phase?'

After a hesitation, I take it. Dan's face is drawn with concern.

'There was nothing in the notes about ambrosia,' he says. 'If this is some sort of role-play, there would still have been a mention of ambrosia, surely?'

'I don't know,' I say. 'Maybe keeping it secret was part of the game, too?' I shrug. I can't make sense of any of this. All I know is I want out. And if drinking some pretend-magical potion is the price, then, as childish as it is, I'll pay it. One drop, and all of this is over.

'I'll do it,' I tell Psyche. 'But as soon as I have, then you make the call and get us out, right? That's the deal.'

Psyche nods. 'As soon as you drink that,' she says, 'you go back to your real life. You have my word.'

'Good,' I say. 'Fine.' Certainly, there's a very high chance that Psyche is lying through her teeth, that this is just another twist in this infuriating game, but frankly at this point I'm willing to try anything.

Under the watchful eyes of Dan and Psyche, I tip the bottle to my lips.

Here goes nothing.

$\longrightarrow$

And indeed, at first, nothing is what happens. As the sweet liquid lands on my tongue and coats the back of my throat, I have enough time to recork the bottle and slip it back into my bag and I'm about to tell Psyche that okay, I did it, now make the call and remove us from the game, and then I feel it.

It starts as warmth radiating through my body, an amber wave pulsing through me, electrifying my insides. For a few seconds I know nothing but the most intense and buzzed-up bliss and all I can think is that I want this moment to last, I have to stay here, bathed in this amber glow for ever, and then, in one powerful pulse, my memories are back, not slowly in gentle waves but suddenly and violently, like a punch to the face. One moment I am the Anterist Frida who believes that all this magical stuff is a game. And the next, I'm myself.

Or no, not quite myself.

More.

I am golden.

Dan and Psyche are talking to me, their mouths moving, but I can't hear their words because of their feelings, their feelings are so loud, demanding my attention, overwhelming my senses. Dan's are greeny-blue, a swirl of confusion and fear and amazement and concern for me, and oh, my poor, darling Dan, how I have missed you, except, this is a different Dan, a Dan two years on, without his memories, who only knows a Frida he met two days ago . . . Before I can follow this disturbing train of thought too far, I'm pulled from Dan's emotions into Psyche's. Hers are a deep purplish red, complex, contradictory; she betrayed us once and now she wants to help us; she's reluctant to engage with us, but she needs to stop Anteros, she fears what is coming ... The power pulses and pulses within me, growing stronger, expanding, and now more emotions elbow their way in, more colours, not just Dan's and Psyche's, but the feelings of every mortal within a mile radius around me: the maroon repressed fury of the guy sitting in his truck; the butter-yellow patience of the woman feeding her child in the passenger seat of the Fiat; the burnt-orange happiness of the child in the coffee shop holding a purple balloon; the pale, almost colourless indecision of the man who wants to leave his soulless job but knows he never will. I feel them all, the emotions of dozens, and then hundreds in a circle around me, wave after wave, and as my power extends effortlessly across the city, I become aware of something else, something different.

Blackness over the hearts of so many.

I reach out towards them, wanting to understand, to help, to heal. These are the Anterists, and their hearts have grown dark with anger, sorrow and fear, these feelings not eradicated by The Love Delusion, despite the great R. A.'s promises, just sublimated deep inside where they can do secret damage. My golden power itches to return these mortal hearts to their former state, to break through that blackness and allow their colours to shine, but I don't have that power, I only took a drop, and already the magic bestowed on me is fading. I pull away from the shadowed hearts, then, back towards the colours, back towards the golden light but the glow inside me is fading now, growing dimmer and dimmer until, eventually, all the lights go out.

Chapter 10

When I open my eyes I find myself on a sofa in a large, open room. I suck in a breath, and let it out, blink up at the ceiling as my new-old reality settles awkwardly into place like a badly shuffled deck of cards. I'm back. After two years, I'm really back.

'Hey.'

I turn to the voice and see a figure in the adjacent armchair, watching me intently.

'Dan!'

In an instant I'm up off the sofa, and into his lap, my arms around him, breathing in his familiar scent and laughing with pure joy. 'We did it! We found each other!' It's only when Dan stiffens in my arms and gives an awkward cough that I remember one crucial detail. I may have my memories back, but Dan doesn't. Right now, as far as he's concerned, he's getting an affectionate mauling by a woman he only met two days ago.

'Oops . . . sorry!' I extricate myself from his lap and scoot back to the sofa. Smooth down my sundress. I meet his eyes ruefully. 'I forgot. You don't know me. I mean, the old me. Of course, you know me but that me is . . . er . . . a different me than the me I am now.' I stare at Dan's increasingly bewildered expression. 'It's complicated,' I say, putting in a bid for understatement of the century.

Dan blinks at me. 'Are you feeling okay? Would you like some water?' I nod, grateful for the activity to focus on. He hands me a glass, I take a sip, and then another, then place the glass carefully on the coffee table. Then I stare at him. Two years since I have seen him. He looks different. He looks good. His hair is longer, he has new tattoos, he's thinner, but oh his lovely green eyes, his precious face, the way he rubs at his jaw when he's worried about something, like he's doing right now. It's still him!

Except, he's not him, is he? This Dan doesn't know that he loves me. And . . . does he still love me, if he doesn't remember it? Is this still the Dan I love? My head starts to ache with the cognitive dissonance of it all. With a great effort I shelve this train of thought and, dragging my gaze away from my beloved, I look about me. I appear to be in a very stylish open-plan apartment.

'Where are we? What happened?'

'We're at Psyche's,' Dan says.

Fuck. Psyche. Of course.

'You agreed to drink that stuff to get us out of the game,'

Dan reminds me, 'and then . . . well, there's no other way to say this, Frida, you started glowing.'

'Glowing,' I repeat.

'Yes, definitely glowing.' He nods, as though trying to convince himself. 'And then you blacked out.' He pauses. 'You'd stopped glowing by then. Actually, I'm really worried that the stuff you drank was radioactive, but Psyche just laughed at me and said to bring you back here, that we can stay with her, and that when you woke up you'd explain everything.'

'That was nice of her.' I look past him to the window. The summer light is already fading. 'How long have I been out?'

'About five hours.'

'And where's Psyche now?'

Dan nods to the other side of the room. 'Out on the balcony. Frida . . .' I meet Dan's eyes. I can feel his confusion and his fear rising to the surface.

'Don't worry,' I say, trying to give him a calming smile, as if that's going to soften what's to come. 'That stuff wasn't radioactive.' I meet his eyes. How exactly to do this? 'Dan,' I say gently, 'Psyche was telling the truth. The contents of that bottle was ambrosia. It brought back my memories. It's not a game. It's all real.'

He stares at me, rocked by my words. And God, I've never seen Dan look like that. By the time I met him, he seemed all but unshockable. He's silent for a very long time, so long that I think I might have broken him.

'Dan,' I venture after a while, 'did you hear what I said?'

His mouth works for a bit, but nothing comes out. Then, his voice slightly choked, he says, 'Gods, real?'

'Yes.'

'Monsters, real?'

'Yes.'

'Oracles, real?'

'Yes.'

'Minotaurs, real?'

I hold up a hand before he can take me through the entire *Dictionary of Greek Mythology*. 'All of it, Dan,' I say. 'All of it is real.'

'And you're absolutely sure that you're not just having another psychotic break?'

I give a small, sad laugh. 'Right now, a psychotic break would be something of a holiday.'

Dan goes very silent again. I watch him carefully. I knew the old Dan so well, but I don't know how this version of Dan is going to handle this. He's known about this stuff his whole life but now all those memories are gone. I'm not sure where that leaves him. Or, indeed, us.

Eventually, to my relief, Dan lifts his eyes to mine and nods. 'Okay,' he says.

'Okay?' I raise my eyebrows. 'Wow, I really thought it was going to be more difficult than that.'

He smiles wanly. 'I think I knew all along that it was real,' he says. 'I mean, it's so insane, it can't be real but somehow I just knew that it was.'

'There's something else,' I say carefully. 'You can't take ambrosia. And as we said back on that video, all the Lethe antidote is gone. There's no way to get your memories back. I'm so sorry, Dan.'

He meets my eyes. 'Yeah, I figured as much from what Psyche said.' He shrugs. 'It's okay. At least I have the notes.'

'The notes,' I repeat. Right. The laptop. The clues we left for ourselves. The backstory of everything that happened to us two years ago.

'So, it's true that my family are the Oracle line? They know all about this magical stuff too?'

'Knew. They don't remember any of it now, though. Anteros made sure no one was left to remind us.'

He stares at me. 'That's horrible.'

I nod.

'So, I was right about The Love Delusion?' Dan says. 'It's ... some fantastical, evil plot by this Anteros, who is actually a god?'

I pick up the glass of water and stare at its clear depths. 'That's about the size of it, yeah.'

And I've been helping him, I think. For years, I've been lauding Anteros's false prophet, spreading his message, converting mortals to his cause. When Anteros captured us, I swore I wouldn't forget who I was, who *he* was. In my naïvety, the worst thing I could imagine was that I would stand by and do nothing. I get a foul taste of bile in the back of my throat at the horror and humiliation of what I've done. Then I swallow it down. There will be time enough for self-hatred when all of this is over.

'But we've stopped him once before?' Dan says now.

I force myself to focus. Nod briskly. 'Two years ago, on Valentine's Day. Anteros had a plot to send mortals mad with violent passion using a golden arrow. We prevented that from happening. Destroyed the arrow. Brought down his empire.'

'We were heroes,' Dan says wonderingly.

'Yes,' I say faintly, 'heroes.' For all the good it did us.

'And Anteros shot you in the heart with the golden arrow, right? And it left you with magical abilities?'

'Only very faint powers associated with love. The ability to read people's emotions and, in some cases, influence them.'

He looks at me, eyes bright. 'So *that's* what you did to poor lovesick Maurice!'

'Yeah,' I say. 'I wanted to make sure he'd keep our secret.'

Dan nods, taking this in. 'And I have a power too, right? I read in the notes that I have visions of the future.'

I nod.

'So, how do they work? I mean, how do I go about having one? Is there something special I have to do? An incantation or a sacred ritual?'

I stare at Dan sadly. 'You haven't had a vision these last two years?'

'I don't think so.' He frowns. 'But maybe I did and I didn't know it?'

'You'd know it,' I say grimly. 'They really hurt.'

'Oh.' Dan pauses. 'So, why haven't I had one? Isn't that the whole point of the Oracle, that they have visions?'

I study his lovely face. 'The visions weren't coming through the way they should have been, even before you were Lethed. We never worked out why.'

'Oh,' he says again and then falls into silence. I can practically hear his mind turning all of this over. 'So, if we were supposed to be fighting Anteros, how did you come to be an Anterist?' His sits up suddenly, wide eyed. 'Wait, was the evil pencil controlling you that whole time?'

I let out a long sigh. 'I wish I could tell you yes,' I say with a grimace that tells him I don't want to talk about that right now.

Dan shakes his head. 'It's amazing. Just amazing. All the books and films and games I love and I'm actually living in one. Jonesy will never believe this!'

I smile. 'It's a headfuck all right.' Then add hastily, 'And you can't tell Jonesy, whoever he is. You can't tell anyone, okay? I mean, they wouldn't believe it, even if you did.'

'Got it.' Dan nods. 'I won't tell anyone.'

I watch him and try to square this tangled situation I find myself in. Dan can read the story of what happened to us two years ago in the notes we left, but he won't see the truth between the lines. How Dan had feelings for me before he even met me. How we fell deeply in love. How we promised to be there for each other, for ever. And I can't tell him. I couldn't bear to see in his face the guilt, the pity, of him knowing I love him when he doesn't love me, can't love me, because he barely even knows me. To lay that past-life on him would just add one more burden, an extra twist of weirdness making what we have to do even harder. Anything Dan feels for me should come naturally, not from some edict from his previous self.

Easier if he believes we were just good friends.

Easier for who? a little voice asks.

I ignore it.

114

'So, everything in the notes is true, too?' Dan asks.

'Yes.'

'Shit. In that case, we can't trust Psyche, can we?' He darts a nervous glance to the balcony. 'I read that . . .'

'She betrayed us?' I finish. 'That, twenty years before that, she led my father into the Underworld and his certain death?'

Dan nods. Looks down at the rug and then looks up to meet my eyes. 'I'm sorry,' he says. 'About your dad.'

'Thank you,' I say softly. I glance out at the balcony and see Psyche looking out on to the city, cigarette in hand. 'Yes, she fucked us over. And ordinarily I wouldn't trust her as far as she could throw me.' I think about what I saw in Psyche before I blacked out, the emotions I felt. 'But I believe that she wants to stop Anteros. She's strong, she knows this world and we need her protection.' I shrug. 'So we let her help. For now, anyway.'

Dan nods.

'But, listen, the only people we can really trust is each other, okay? We were . . .' I swallow the lump in my throat. 'We were a good team, you and me. We only knew each other for a few months but we became firm friends.'

'I thought that we must have been. I feel that.' He smiles. 'You remind me a little bit of my sister, Kara, back in Greece.'

'Do I?' I smile through gritted teeth. *Kill me now.* 'You know what?' I say brightly, desperate to change the subject. 'I know we have lots to talk about but I'm feeling pretty tired. Does Psyche have any coffee?'

'Yeah, sure, I'll go and make you one.' Dan smiles suddenly. 'White, extra strong, no sugar?'

'You remembered?' My heart lifts.

'Oh. No.' Dan's smile falters. 'It was in the notes. In big type, bold and underlined. Seems like coffee is pretty important to you.' He sees my face. 'But I'm sure I'll start to remember stuff, you know, as we go along.'

'Yeah,' I say. 'Yeah, of course you will.'

$\longrightarrow$

As Dan busies about in the kitchen, I have a moment alone. I stare around the room, with its white walls, pale grey curtains, teal throw rug, geometric paintings. This is Psyche's place? It's not what I would have imagined. Then again, I would never have imagined that I would be teaming up with the woman who left me for dead with my head down a manhole.

Terrible times call for strange bedfellows.

I take out my phone and see many, many missed calls and messages. I open a few and the blood drains right out of me. Then I listen to my phone messages. Big mistake. There are seven horrified guilt trips from my mother, a handful of threatening expletive-filled rants from Anterists who have managed to get hold of my mobile number and one very terse message from Serena telling me that she's handing in her resignation, effective immediately. Hades has been as good as his word. The Anterists want my blood.

I block all the numbers, my mother excluded, and then put down the phone with a shaky hand, a sick unease in my stomach. The balcony door clicks softly and Psyche enters. As I lock eyes with her, she raises her eyebrows.

'It worked, then.'

'Well, I remember that you're a lying, manipulative psychopath,' I say, 'so I'm going with yes.'

'Tough talk.' She tips her head to one side and surveys me. 'Tough couple of years.'

Psyche takes a packet of cigarettes from her pocket and lights one then flops into the armchair. 'Ambrosia is dangerous stuff to be playing with, Frida. You do know that if you'd taken more than a drop it would have changed you irrevocably? Turned you into something other than human?'

I meet her gaze evenly, trying to hide the jolt of fear spiking my insides. How close I came to the edge of an abyss. I force a smile. 'Then it's a good job I didn't take more than a drop, isn't it?'

She narrows her eyes. 'You must have been desperate to leave that for yourself. Though,' she adds, 'I'm awfully glad you did. The Lethed you was even more of an idiot than the *you* you.' She sucks in a lungful of smoke. 'If you can believe that.'

'Why are you back, Psyche?'

She smiles admiringly. 'Straight to the point. I like it.' She blows smoke from the corner of her mouth. 'I came to help. And before you say it, this isn't another con.'

'Oh, I know that,' I say. 'I saw it in you.'

I enjoy her look of surprise. 'You can read people?' Then understanding dawns in her eyes. 'Ah, so it's true? I heard Anteros had shot you with a golden arrow and you'd transformed into some sort of love goddess. It left you with residual power, is that it?'

117

I pick up the glass and take a cool sip of water. 'Yes. The ambrosia must have boosted it temporarily.'

'Well, good,' Psyche says, hitching one sandalled foot over her knee. 'So, you'll know that I really do want to stop him.'

'I also know that you're scared. The question is, why? What is it to you if the mortals stop believing in love? You never had a great opinion of us anyway, as I recall.'

Psyche shrugs. 'You're right, I didn't care at first. I figured Anteros was just up to his old tricks, tormenting the mortals.' Her eyes grow dark. 'But I was wrong. There's something bigger afoot.'

I get a cold feeling at this. Like it's something I knew but have been pushing away for a long time. 'What do you mean, bigger?'

'There have been augurs, portents.' Psyche meets my eyes. 'Whatever he's planning, Frida, a loveless world might be a part of it, but that's not Anteros's endgame.'

That chill goes through me again and seems to settle in my bones. 'Then what *is* his endgame?'

She takes a long drag on her cigarette. 'I don't know. But whatever it is, it's bad. Worse than anything I've ever seen and trust me when I say that's a pretty high benchmark.'

'Trust you?' I say. 'What, like my father trusted you?'

Psyche looks at me. 'Okay,' she says, 'let's just get this over with. Yes, I helped your father enter the Underworld to face the terrors that, by the way, he was fully aware would be down there. He knew you'd be burdened with destroying the last golden arrow and he wanted to find it himself, to save you from your fate. He was determined.' She flicks a tower

118

of ash into a hexagonal ashtray. 'I thought, hell, maybe he'll even do it!' She shrugs. 'Who was I to refuse him his suicide mission?' She raises an eyebrow. 'And if we are talking old offences, need I remind you that, not so long back, you left me to be mauled for eternity by a Minotaur?' she points out. 'And I still came to help you.'

I shake my head wonderingly. Strange bedfellows indeed. Still, whatever her role in my father's horrible death, we're going to need Psyche if we are to stop Anteros. And so I mentally shelve my grudge, along with all the other awful things I'm boxing off to deal with later. Any more, and I'll need an EZStorage facility to contain them all.

'Okay,' I say. 'So what *do* you know?'

She takes a long drag on her cigarette. 'Not much. No one does. And there's something very wrong with that.'

'What does that mean?'

'It means that if what Anteros is planning is half as big as the augurs suggest, it should have been prophesied thousands of years ago. But there's nothing. I came to see you two, assuming Dan would have seen something but . . .' She tails off. Then she looks at me. 'Did he receive any information about what's to come in the time before he got wiped?'

I think about the first vision Dan had about The Love Delusion, back in July two years ago. The one that left him shaken and silent for hours afterwards, unable to find the words to explain what he'd seen. 'Thousands and thousands of people in red,' he told me, when he could eventually speak, his voice faltering, his face pale. 'And then . . .' Dan shook his head and went to his sketch pad. When I saw what he had

119

drawn, icy fingers crawled across my skin. It was darkness, only darkness.

'He did,' I say, 'though we couldn't make much sense of it. It was just . . . black.'

'Well, that does *not* sound encouraging.'

'No.' My mind returns to the service station forecourt, all of those feelings crowding in on me, and then to the blackness, the emptiness of the Anterists. Is that what Dan saw in his vision? No. It wasn't the shadowed hearts of the Anterists he drew in that picture. It was something worse.

Psyche studies the glowing end of her cigarette. 'Has he had any visions since he's been Lethed? Anything that might help?'

I sigh. 'No. He only had two after that Valentine's Day – both in July, weeks after we'd already found out about The Love Delusion.' My whole body feels heavy as I remember that time. 'That's why we were so slow to act. We didn't think Anteros could be behind it. We figured no visions, no problem.' I shake my head. 'We never did work out why Eros and Zeus stopped helping us.'

Psyche taps her cigarette into the ashtray, thoughtful now. 'Maybe they didn't.'

'What other explanation is there?'

'Hades said something about immortals aligning themselves with Anteros, or against him. Maybe the gods are taking sides. In which case,' she raises her eyes to the ceiling, 'whatever messages Eros and Zeus are trying to send to you via Apollo, you can bet others – Aphrodite and Ares, for example – have been blocking them.'

I stare at Psyche. This horrific possibility had never occurred to me. 'But why?'

'Perhaps they don't want you to stop Anteros. Perhaps they want him to succeed in his endeavour, presumably because it benefits them in some way.' She ponders this. 'Or because they're scared of going against him.'

'Why would they be scared?'

'I don't know,' she says. 'But do you remember what else Hades said?'

'About what?' I say, managing for the moment to repress the fact that I've spent two years treating the lord of the dead as my line manager.

'He said that Anteros Lethed you himself because he had to answer to greater forces.'

The words come back to me. It didn't mean much when Hades said it, since I assumed he was just performing a role. But now, as I replay the memory, a dark feeling grows in me. 'But who? Who could he be answering to?'

'I don't know.' She shakes her head slowly. 'But whoever or whatever it is, it's big enough to draw Hades up from the Underworld to lend his power and to spook a bunch of immortals into pledging allegiance.' Psyche looks evenly at me. 'So, the question is: what now? Do we have anything at all? What did the second vision you mentioned contain? Did you two have a lead before they caught up with you?'

'I . . .' I stop, frowning. 'I can't remember.' I close my eyes, try to focus on the memories. But they keep slipping away when I look at them, hazing out like old instamatic pictures in reverse. 'We did go and see someone . . . and then, we were in the car . . . heading into the countryside . . . we thought we were being followed.' Where were we going? Why? I shake my head, frustrated. 'It's not there.' I open my eyes and stare at Psyche, alarmed. 'Why isn't it there?'

'Give it a few more hours,' she says. 'After Lethe, memories come back in fragments and the most painful ones will come last.'

Painful. Because that was the day they tore Dan away from me. Right.

I look at Psyche. 'Listen, can you promise me you'll protect Dan until this is over? You owe me that much.'

She nods.

'And Psyche . . .' I shift uncomfortably on the sofa. 'Look, Dan doesn't know that he and I were together and I don't want him to. It'll only confuse things.'

Psyche lifts an eyebrow. 'If that's really how you want to play it.'

'It is.'

'Okay, well, that could be interesting.'

'Why?'

She smirks. 'Because you two former lovebirds are going to be sharing a room.'

Chapter 11

When Dan returns with the coffees and hears that Psyche intends us both to sleep in her spare room, he gallantly volunteers to bed down on the couch, an offer that fills me with equal amounts of relief and sorrow, and one which, anyway, Psyche outright refuses.

'I don't want you hanging around the place,' she says. 'Bad enough that I've got to have you stay here at all.'

All hail our gracious host.

And so, as the city grows dark and we can put it off no longer, Dan and I get to making up the beds, moving awkwardly around each other in the confined space. I had somehow managed to blank out the whole Dan-doesn't-remember-that-he-loves-me situation, but there's no escaping it now I'm stuck in a box room with it.

As Dan lays a sheet on the carpet and smooths it out, it's all

I can do not to reach out, take his hand and pull him to me. I want to go to that nook in his neck where I fit so neatly, for him to wrap his arms around me, to pull me close, for him to brush his lips against mine and tell me I smell like pina colada, to pull me on to this single bed and—

'You want the big one?'

I blink. 'Excuse me?'

'Pillow,' Dan says, offering the cushion to me. 'There's an extra one.'

'Oh,' I say, stammering. 'Yes. Thank you.'

I carry on making up the bed, sneaking more glances at Dan's strong arms as he shakes a pillow into a case, my eyes drinking him in, the way his T-shirt hangs on his broad shoulders, his hair curling at the nape of his neck, the tattoos I made up stories about in bed in the morning, tracing their colourful lines with a teasing finger. But he has new tattoos now. He's had a life without me for two years. He ... oh God ... he might have slept with other women. Loved other women. I want to know and yet I can't stand to know, even if I could find a casual way to ask. *Hey, Dan, how many women did you have sex with in the last twenty-four months? Just a ballpark figure, plus names, ages, descriptions, positions ...*

He said he was single, I remember now and I cling to this. Oh, thank God he's single.

Dan catches me watching him and I quickly look away and start to stuff a duvet into a cover with excessive violence. On a rational level I understand that, to Dan, I'm a person he's only known for two days. And yet, here he is in the flesh, and it's impossible to believe that I can't just flip a switch and have my

124

Dan back. How far away can those feelings for me be, when they were once so strong? When his love for me, his search for me, was the thing that brought us together? Is his love for me still there inside him somewhere? Or did the Lethe destroy it along with his memories of me?

My head begins to hurt again. I take the spare clothes Psyche has lent me and go to the bathroom to change. They're all far too big, of course, but they'll have to do for now. It's not like I can exactly pop home for supplies. I stare into the mirror. My hair, straightened yesterday morning, has sprung into hectic curls from the humidity. My mascara has smudged under my eyes so that I look like I've been punched, which coincidentally is just how I feel. I rub my finger on my bottom lashes to wipe away the black rings of make-up. It only makes it worse.

'Hello, you,' I say to myself. 'Joined any evil cults while I've been gone?'

My mirror-self stares back blankly.

When I return to the bedroom, Dan is on the floor on top of his makeshift bed, in boxers and T-shirt, laptop balanced on his thighs. I look at his long, bony feet. I love those feet. Dan gives me a strange look and for one horrible moment I think I have said this out loud and I blush crimson, but then I see he's just laughing at my nightwear. I look down. On Psyche, they're a T-shirt and shorts. On me? More like a boilersuit. This is how to win back the love of your life. Seduce him with plumber-chic.

'I borrowed them from Psyche,' I say, pulling at the hem of the shorts awkwardly.

'Very nice,' he says diplomatically.

I look at Dan's simple and not very comfortable-looking bed on the floor. 'We can swap,' I say. 'Take the bed on alternate nights.'

'Nah, I'll be fine,' Dan says, stretching his arms above his head and rolling his neck. 'Don't worry about it.' He looks at me. 'So, what happens next?'

'Next, I get some sleep so I can find out what to do next.' At his quizzical look I explain. 'There was somewhere important we were on our way to, but I can't remember where. Psyche says it might take a few hours for all my memories to return. I'm hoping that by the morning I'll know where we were going.'

'And then we resume the mission?' Dan asks, his face a mixture of excitement and apprehension.

'Hopefully. That's if Psyche is right and the memory comes back.'

'And if it doesn't?'

I shrug. 'We'll cross that bridge when it starts to burn from under us.'

I wait until Dan goes to use the bathroom and then I pick up my bag and find the bottle of ambrosia zipped into the compartment. I locate the small purple pouch, tip it up and the necklace falls into my hand, glinting golden. A heart shot through with an arrow. A gift from my father on my eighth birthday. My chest aches with all my unshed tears. How many times will I have to forget my dad and then discover, anew, that he's not absent but dead? That he's never coming back.

I fasten the chain around my neck and then slip the ambrosia under my pillow as there's a gentle knock-knock on the door and Dan comes back into the room.

He looks at me. 'You okay? You look a bit . . . sad.'

I smile. 'Just tired.'

'Yeah,' he says, 'me too. Big day.'

'The biggest.'

'Want to sleep?'

'I think so. To try, at least.'

As Dan gets back on to his floor bed, I snuggle down under the thin duvet and click off the bedside lamp.

'Goodnight, Dan,' I say.

'Goodnight, Frida,' he returns.

I lie there, hyper aware of the sounds of sirens, the odd hoot of a Sunday-evening merrymaker and Dan's steady breathing. It's only now I'm alone with my thoughts that it really hits me, what has happened, what I've lost. My eyes fill with tears.

You knew this was the cost when you left yourself the ambrosia. You knew Dan wouldn't be able to take it.

Yeah, but knowing and experiencing are two very different things. Salty tears soak my big pillow as I say all the things in my head that I can't say out loud: *Oh God, Dan, I've missed you. I love you so much. Dan, I'm scared of what's coming; it's so much bigger than we knew. Dan, I need you.* As I lie there, I'm bone-weary but my brain is busy. I know I won't sleep. There's too much I need to do, too much I don't know. Why is Anteros doing this? When mortals renounce love, what happens next? The news that Anteros may be in the service of someone else fills me with horror – going up against the love god last time was hard enough. Who on earth is a greater threat than him? These worries could keep me awake for the rest of my life but the ambrosia has taken its toll and soon enough weariness overtakes me. Comforted by the familiar sound of Dan's breathing just metres away, I'm soon drifting off and dreaming, dreaming.

In my dream, I'm watching a scene: there's a dark-haired handsome figure in a black robe on an altar, and approaching him, a woman who looks just like me. She has a dagger concealed in the sleeve of her red robe. She has to end this. She knows she can do it this time. Sacrifices have to be made. I watch as my doppelgänger withdraws a golden knife, but as she plunges it into Anteros's chest, the golden blade transforms into a rose, and as the flower falls at the love god's feet, my other self understands with horror that she hasn't come here to finish Anteros.

She's come to worship him.

Chapter 12

I wake the next morning, fresh and revived. The moment I open my eyes, I look immediately for Dan but the makeshift bed is empty. I stare at the shape in the pillow his head has left, a bitter-sweet ache in my chest.

I'm so glad to have him back.

I'm so heartbroken he's not mine.

Then I catch myself staring at his pillow indentation like some sort of lovesick stalker and I give myself a shake. *Come on, Frida, there's no time for self-pity. You have a mission to finish.*

I head to the bathroom and take a quick shower. Then, wrapping myself in a large fluffy grey towel, I squeeze toothpaste on to my finger and scrub my teeth and gums, staring unseeing into the fogged-up mirror, rinse and spit. When I turn off the tap I can hear voices – Dan and Psyche are already up – so I head back to the bedroom and quickly dress, pulling on a grey mini of Psyche's, which translates to a midi on me, securing it with a thin tie belt. I fasten my sandals.

When I finally look at myself in the mirror, I'm taken aback. Yesterday I looked shattered. Today my eyes are bright and clear, my lashes and brows dark, my cheeks have a rosy glow. My skin is smooth and even, despite the lack of concealer or foundation. I look like those women who spend three hours in the mirror to achieve a make-up-free look, except I'm genuinely not wearing any make-up. And where last night I felt achingly weary, today I feel light and filled with energy. I locate a bobble in my handbag and smooth my hair back into a low chignon, and for a change, my hair actually does what I ask.

Damn, that ambrosia is good stuff.

I follow the sound of voices down the hall and over to the kitchen table, where Dan and Psyche sit, a pot of coffee in front of them.

They fall suddenly silent when I walk in.

'Morning!' Dan says, effortlessly cheerful. 'How did you sleep? Wow, you look much better than yesterday, you were—' He sees my face. 'You looked fine both times.'

'Thanks,' I say, stifling a grin. I take a seat at the table, grab an empty mug and pour myself some coffee, add milk and take a long swig. I look up to find their eyes on me.

'So, what's up?'

'Nothing,' Dan says shiftily.

My eyes flit to the tablet on the table in front of them. I smile. 'Dan, you're a terrible liar, do you know that about yourself?'

Dan rubs his jaw and exchanges a look with Psyche. She shrugs and turns the tablet around. 'You're in the news.'

She presses play and a video image of Hades fills the screen. 'Hello, dear Anterists,' he says, giving it his best grave-face. 'I'm afraid I have something terrible to tell you. We have discovered that our trusted member Frida McKenzie is a spy, a mole, who has been posing as an Anterist in order to infiltrate our movement and corrupt it from within.' His red lips thin. 'We consider this woman to be very dangerous, both to individual Anterists and to our cause. We are especially concerned about the sermon on Sunday. We fear that she may mean harm to R. A. Stone.'

Hades leaves a silence. I picture the Anterists reacting to this news, imagining how I would have responded. Would I have fallen for it? Would I really believe that someone was planning to assassinate our prophet? Oh God, yes. In a heartbeat.

Hades' image is replaced by a photograph of me and Sehda taken outside the church on Friday night, right after I'd delivered the news of R. A.'s upcoming sermon. With my wide, open-mouthed grin and my manic eyes, even I'd have to admit I look a trifle unhinged.

'If you see this woman,' Hades says, 'you must act immediately. She must be stopped, at all costs—'

Psyche clicks the video and Hades is paused, mid rant. 'You get the gist.'

I stare at Hades' frozen face, his tiny horrible eyes, his slit of a mouth. *Well, Frida, you've really done it now. Your face is known to every Anterist in the world and you're on their hit-list*. I refill my mug. This is going to require a lot more coffee.

'Are you okay?' Dan eyes me uncertainly.

'Yeah, I'm fine.' I shrug. 'It's what we knew he would do.'

'But I mean are you okay after yesterday—'

'He means did you get all your memories back,' Psyche interrupts.

Dan flushes. 'No, well, I . . .'

'It's okay,' I say. I smile. 'I remembered.' After a night of troubled dreams, the ambrosia working its way through my system, I awoke this morning with all of my memories intact. More than that, it's like they're playing in HD on a loop through my brain. The smile on Anteros's face as he approached us in that lane. The blank expression of the red-suited guards. Dan's agonised face as they dragged him away from me. And yet here Dan is, eating toast, with no memory at all of that event. It's freaky, having been through that trauma with him and not being able to share it. Does it affect Dan, even though he can't remember it? Does he dream of it?

'What were we doing?' Dan asks eagerly.

I clasp the mug with both hands and try hard not to take his enthusiasm personally.

'You had a vision about a nymph called Daphne who is keeping a secret prophecy about how to stop Anteros.' I swallow more coffee. 'We were on our way to see her when Anteros and his guards ambushed us.'

'A secret prophecy?' Psyche sparks up a cigarette. 'Well, that's more like it.'

Dan listens to this, his brow furrowed. 'But there's nothing

132

about Daphne in our notes. Or anything about a secret prophecy.'

'Because we didn't have time to update them. It all happened so fast. The day after you had the vision, we went to find Daphne and . . .' I flashback to Anteros approaching us, that terrible smile on his lips. 'They caught us.'

'Okay,' Dan says. 'So who is this Daphne? Where does she live?'

'She was a naiad, a water spirit, who was turned into a Laurel tree.'

Dan blinks at me. 'Oh.'

'She lives in the woods.'

'Which woods?'

'Doesn't matter. Any woods will do. But we don't have much time. Whatever Anteros was building up to, I think it's going to happen soon.'

'The sermon?' Psyche flashes me a look.

'I think so. Why else would he come back here?'

Dan stares from me to Psyche and back again. 'Hang on. You're not saying you think this something bad that's coming is going to happen at R. A. Stone's sermon . . . As in the sermon on Sunday?'

I nod.

It takes Dan a moment to form words. 'We . . . we have less than a week to stop him? That can't be right.'

'That's the way it is,' I say.

'But they had six months in *The Lord of the Rings*!'

I look at him.

He flushes. 'I'm just saying, it seems an awfully quick

turnaround for something that we have barely any information about!'

Draining the coffee mug, I put it down and grab a chocolate croissant. 'Yeah, well, we had two years and you spent it playing Dungeons and Dragons and perfecting your guitar solo and I spent it helping to destroy the concept of love. So now we have a week.' I look at him. 'So, are you ready, Frodo? I'm going to need you for this next bit.'

He recovers himself admirably, his eyes shining with anticipation.

'Where are we going?'

'To a shadowy barren wasteland filled with poisonous fumes in pursuit of a small gold object,' I say and take a bite of the croissant. 'Don't forget your car keys.'

$$\longrightarrow$$

The underground car park of Psyche's apartment building is hot and muggy and stinks of petrol. I peer into Dan's car, dishevelled and despondent. We've been searching for an hour and found precisely nothing. I sigh. Why didn't I ask him where he hid the blasted thing? Come to that, why didn't I stay in the car while he did it?

'*There* you are!'

I jerk up excitedly at Dan's voice and smack my head on the car door. 'Oof!'

Dan looks over at me. 'Sorry, didn't mean to startle you.'

'That's okay.' I rub at my temple and stare at him, expectant. 'You found it?'

'Oh. No, sorry,' he says, holding up a compact disc. 'It's just a Lynyrd Skynyrd album I lost a couple of months ago.'

I look at him with raised eyebrows and then resume poking around under the driver's seat.

'So,' Dan says, as he sifts through the contents of the dashboard for the third time. 'A golden acorn.'

'Yep.'

'A magical golden acorn.'

'Uh-huh.'

'That will lead us to some enchanted woods.'

'Exactly,' I say, and then I stand up, easing my aching back. I stare at the vehicle in exasperation. We've checked everywhere – emptied the dashboard, the door pockets, under the seats, in the cracks, we've even prised away the door fittings. We've searched every inch of the car that Dan could have reached from his position in the driving seat and several that he couldn't. Nothing.

'It's no good,' I say with a sigh. 'It's not here.'

'Maybe I ate it?' Dan offers. 'I saw this film once where someone hid a coin by swallowing it and then, um, finding it and re-swallowing it, over and over again.'

I stare at him. 'Firstly, ewww. Secondly, that wouldn't have helped because by the time you'd have found it, as you so delicately put it, you wouldn't have known what it was for. And thirdly, ewwwwww.' I survey the car. 'When was the last time you had the car valeted?'

'Never. I clean it myself.'

'And you never found an acorn and just … threw it out?'

'I don't think so. No, I'm sure I'd remember, because an

135

acorn is not exactly a normal thing to find in a car, is it? Unless you happen to be Squirrel Nutkin.'

He smiles at his own joke. I arm the sweat off my forehead and let out a long frustrated breath. 'This isn't a film or a book, Dan. It's real. We need that acorn.'

'I'm sorry,' Dan says. 'I know. I'm trying. I just wish I could tell you where I hid it.' He scrubs at his stubble. 'It's pretty awful, knowing I've got years of memories that just aren't there any more.'

I look at him and soften. All things considered, he's dealing with this whole situation valiantly. It's only that it's hard to adjust to me being the sensible, knowledgeable one and Dan being the naïve one who asks all the questions. I much preferred it the other way around.

'Well,' I say, 'we've looked everywhere. It's not here. They must have searched the car after they Lethed us.'

'So what now?'

'Now, I try to get us another one.' I brush down my dusty borrowed dress and pick up my bag.

'Great,' Dan says. 'Where do we get it from?'

As I look at his handsome, eager face, a swell of feeling comes over me. This isn't the old Dan. This one is giddier, more vulnerable, but he's still Dan and I can't risk anything happening to him. If he got hurt because of me, I couldn't bear it. And where I'm going, well, foolhardy men are this creature's speciality. Not to mention that being around him while we are in this altered relationship is too confusing. I keep forgetting and going to touch him, grab his hand, and then have to remind myself I don't have the right to do that any more.

Just some more emotional baggage for the storage unit.

'I think it might be quicker if we split up on this one,' I say now. 'You go back to the flat and do some research on Anteros's arrival. I'll see you back here in a couple of hours, okay?'

I start heading for the lifts. Dan follows me. 'You're not supposed to do this alone,' he says. 'We're a team. You said so yourself.'

I press the lift button. 'I know, Dan. But it's dangerous out there and you've only just found out about all this magical stuff. Where I'm going ... it might be too much, too soon. Plus,' I reason, 'there're the Anterists and Hades to think about. I'd feel better if you stayed here where Psyche can protect you.'

'What about you? That video? Hades has practically put a price on your head!'

'I can handle myself.'

'Frida—'

'Dan,' I say, 'I'm doing this for your own good, and I really don't have time to argue. Please.'

The lift arrives. I step into it.

'Is this because I said that thing about eating the acorn?'

'I'll see you in a couple of hours,' I say firmly.

I know I'm doing the right thing. I know I am. Still, when the lift door closes, concealing Dan's disappointed face, I'm grateful.

Chapter 13

I leave the building by the rear entrance.

With my hair tied back, my shades on, wearing Psyche's grey dress and my sandals, I look like a thousand other women in the city. Generic. Anonymous. I pace through the streets. In my pockets, two protection spells borrowed from Psyche. They should help keep me hidden from view.

Although I just told Dan he's not ready for what's out here, the truth is, I'm little more prepared for how it will feel to walk around with my memories returned, knowing what I do about The Love Delusion.

I'm hit by that same double-vision, seeing the streets as they were two years ago and also as they are now. It's eerie and unsettling, like waking from a coma to find myself on an alien planet. When I left it was my city, my home, the place I have always loved. Now everything feels different. Now, everywhere I look, I see *his* influence. Anterists everywhere, Love Delusion propaganda abounding, shop windows blazoned with Summer Sale adverts dedicated to single life:

LOVE THE ONE YOU'RE WITH
treat yourself to our singles' beach breaks

ALL YOU NEED IS YOU!
Gourmet meals for one

ANTERIST DISCOUNT
on all purchases!

SOLO IS THE WAY TO GO

You have to hand it to Anteros, he's a master manipulator. After centuries of fucking up mortal love, he switches tack and gives us the thing our poor beleaguered souls are crying out for: a way to give love up. Create a problem, sell the solution. It's Marketing 101. I walk past the library, with its grand stone lions standing guard, and it comes back, with heartbreaking clarity – that blissful time that Dan and I had together, after we defeated Anteros but before he made his return. The day Dan told me he loved me.

It was May. We'd picked up a couple of coffees and were strolling around the city in the weak spring sunshine, talking, laughing, happy just to be. Outside the library, Dan had stopped and looked at me and he said, 'You know I love you.' Not a question, more like he was stating something that already was. And it was so easy then, so natural, I just looked at him and smiled and said, 'You know I love you, too.' And there it was. *Us*. We were so happy. We'd fulfilled the prophecy. We'd done our part. We told ourselves it was over.

Really, wouldn't you think I'd know better?

The first thing we saw was the name, The Love Delusion. Just a whisper on social media around the end of June that same year. We didn't think anything of it or, if we did, we assumed it was some sort of fad, a harmless craze – a reaction to the dysfunctional love obsession that had so long dominated the western world. We didn't imagine Anteros was behind it. Eros and Zeus would have warned us if Anteros was still a threat and Dan hadn't received a vision. Not one. So, no, it couldn't be Anteros back so soon.

No way.

But in July, the book began circulating and we saw the name of this anti-love guru: R. A. Stone. And unlike our Lethed counterparts, both Dan and I were highly attuned to evil anagrams. Then 'R. A.' made his first appearance and we saw him and we knew our honeymoon was over. In a matter of days, articles started popping up online and in newspapers, their tone moving from amused scepticism to analytical curiosity to outright admiration. The world wanted to hear more about this gorgeous, charismatic messiah and his ideas for a brave new world.

140

Then Dan had his dark vision.

And all the while, Love Delusion churches were springing up all over the world. We waited and waited for another vision, a sign, something or someone to tell us what to do, how to stop whatever was coming. For a while, nothing else came. And then, finally, Dan had the vision about the secret prophecy.

I glance at a trio of red-clothed Anterists standing on the corner, deep in conversation. One of them looks up as I approach and stops talking, frowns slightly, as though trying to remember something she can't quite place. I lower my head, slipping away down a side street, and when I glance back, the group have returned to their debate. Watching them, I feel a strange pang of homesickness.

I head to my destination, keeping an eye out for groups of Anterists who may be actively searching for me. As I walk, I think about what happened after I was Lethed. I woke up at home, with no memories of Dan, our mission or what Anteros was up to. All I knew was that months before I had shut down my law practice and I had nothing in my life to replace it except a deep, abiding depression and a need for something I couldn't explain. I was broken-hearted with loss, with no idea why. When I finally learned about The Love Delusion, it seemed like just what I had been waiting for.

Because I had lost Dan, I chose R. A. Stone. And the sickening irony of this slays me.

I try to stick to the back streets, but there's no escaping the Anterists, they are everywhere. I can *feel* them. Even were they not wearing red or sporting their Love Delusion badges,

I could pick them out in a crowd. Maybe it's a hangover from the abilities the ambrosia gave me, but there's a feeling emanating from them. What I saw back there on that garage forecourt. A darkness over their hearts.

Bryony's words come back to me and with them another stab of grief. When I think about how I've treated her, my behaviour towards her friends, my stomach contracts with anxiety and shame. She's my oldest friend. My best friend. How could I have been so cold? So much damage has been done these last two years, to my friendships, my relationship, my life has been torn apart. But that's nothing to what I've helped Anteros do to this city, and to the world.

As I walk, I try to ascertain the extent of the damage. One thing my two years immersed in the Love Delusion fold has given me is an in-depth understanding of how far this movement has spread. It's disquieting knowledge. I know, for instance, that one third of people who live in cities are Anterists now. That we – I mean they – are converting people at a rate of thousands every day, *The Love Delusion* book is in the homes of millions across the world. When Dan and I first learned of the movement, it was a small, cult thing, attracting only those who were wide open to its message: the heartbroken, the mistreated, the bereft. But in the last two years the book's power has grown. And its reach is extending.

I shake my head in frustration. Despite all my time served as an Anterist, I still don't know the one thing that would help me: why is Anteros turning the mortals against love? What does he have to gain?

In less than a week Anteros will be here and we still don't

even know what it is that he wants. As I weave through the crowds, I sneak glances at the Anterists, my mind turning it over and over, trying to find the answer to this terrible puzzle. Ancient history recounts that Anteros likes a spectacle – he and his mother kicked off the bloody Trojan War, after all – which is why, whatever the love god is planning, I know he's going to do it at the sermon with all his devotees watching.

Dan is right, we have so little time to stop Anteros, and it frightens me how close I came to never waking up at all. If Psyche hadn't turned up; if I hadn't seen Bryony; if I'd never found that photograph; if Psyche hadn't tricked me into drinking the ambrosia . . .

If, if, if . . .

With an effort, I shake these thoughts from my mind. Don't think about that, Frida. Don't think about the life you wanted and can never have. Don't think about how your mother must have known you were Lethed and said nothing. Don't think about how you've been working side by side with Hades for two years. Don't think about how you have preached the gospel of Anteros, converting hundreds of mortals, aiding his cause. Don't think about how there is no more antidote, how the Dan who you loved and who loves you is never coming back.

All of this, everything Anteros has done, has been to push you off course. And what does that mean? It means he believes we can stop him.

So, don't think about any of that, Frida. Think only of one thing: making Anteros pay.

Chapter 14

The place I'm looking for is underneath a railway arch on the west side of town. There are no other shops, bars or restaurants in the area and the building doesn't even have a sign. You'd never find it unless you were looking for it, unless you'd been told it was here. Luckily Dan and I had contacts. When we realised that finding Daphne was our first priority, we were told that a certain person could help us locate her. What we didn't know, on that first desperate visit, was whose side this contact was on and whether we could trust them.

But by that time, we had little choice. We knew this was our only chance.

As I walk under the arch, the sunlight shadowing to gloom, I stiffen at a noise behind me in the tunnel. Footsteps, a shuffling. Have I been followed? I stand very still and listen. Try to feel for them. Anterists? A last vestige of golden arrow power tingles in my fingertips. I don't have much, but it might be enough to convince a couple of Anterists that they never saw me. Deciding, I turn and head towards the noise.

'Who's there?' The archway is dim, but I can see a shape, a shadow looming, elongated on the mossy brick roof. My heart races and I pull my shoulders back, prepared to fight. 'Show yourself!'

The figure steps out.

Oh, for fuck's sake. My heart rate slows down fractionally then rises again in a confusing mix of annoyance and joy.

'Dan, what on earth are you doing here?'

'I followed you,' he says, a tad redundantly.

I meet his eager gaze. 'It's too dangerous, Dan. I told you!'

Dan shoves his hands in the pockets of his cargo shorts and a stubborn expression crosses his face. 'I'm not scared.'

'You don't even know where I'm going!'

'No, and the only way to find out is to come, see?'

I sigh. 'Dan—'

'No,' he says, holding up a hand. 'Listen. I know I don't have any memories, but I've already been fighting The Love Delusion in my own way.' *While you joined them*, is the unspoken subtext, which I pointedly ignore. He continues: 'The notes were left for me as well as you. I'm the Oracle, and that means it's my job to foretell what Anteros is planning. The old me left me information so that I could do that. And, well,' he shifts uncomfortably and meets my eyes, 'you don't actually have the right to stop me, do you? I mean, it's not like you were the boss of me. You said it yourself. We were a good team, you and me. Your exact words: "We were a good team."'

'Yes, but—'

'And anyway,' Dan goes on, 'I've seen the picture I drew after that first vision.' His face darkens. 'And if that is somehow the end result of whatever Anteros is up to, I can't just hide out in Psyche's flat reading. I have to do something!'

I look at him. I haven't got the time or the energy to fight him on this. No, actually, that's a lie. Confusions and complications aside, I do want him with me. He might not be the Dan who loves me, but he's still Dan. And I like having him around, even though it hurts. I think fleetingly of Lee Hatton; how desperate our hearts can make us. I shake the thought away.

'Fine,' I say. I glance at the green door then give Dan a warning look. 'But if you're in, you're in. So, whatever you see in there, you'd better not freak out, okay?'

'Okay.' He nods. 'Who is it?' he asks excitedly. 'Who are we going to see?'

I cast my eyes over the statue planted at the entrance, the figure of a male mortal holding a pint glass, mouth open in a belligerent jeer. The last expression that poor fool wore frozen on his countenance for ever.

'An old acquaintance of ours,' I say. 'You've read the notes. I'll give you three guesses . . .'

Chapter 15

I push the door, half expecting it to be closed – it's only late morning, after all. But no, it swings open, revealing a small, dark flight of concrete stairs heading down. Déjà vu all over again. I look at Dan to check he's ready and he nods, though his nervous expression makes me immediately question the wisdom of this venture.

Oh well. Too late now.

At the foot of the stairs we emerge into a small cave-like room, lit with a deep red glow. There's some languid music playing that runs like treacle through my head, and the air is filled with a spicy seductive scent. A long bar runs down the right side of the room and only here does this place announce its name. Ophidian. A cool enough title for a bar, the sign constructed in mosaic, tiny shards of green, brown and yellow tiles, and also a nice in-joke for those who know their etymology. I look at Dan and see that he *does* know. The penny has dropped. His face expresses a precise combination of excitement and fear.

Behind the bar a young man with a blond quiff polishes glasses. Mid-twenties, tall and broad, in a black T-shirt and black jeans, he has large brown eyes and a long face. As we walk up, the barman glances at us with a blank, incurious expression. Dan stiffens beside him in recognition: the barman looks just like one of the Anterist guards. I place a hand on Dan's arm in reassurance then smile at the man.

'Is your boss in? We need to talk to her. Tell her it's Frida and Dan.'

The barman looks at me and then Dan, his expression hardly registering the question, then he dumps the tea towel on the bar and heads through an open door.

Dan stares anxiously after the barman and then looks at me, eyes wide. 'He's one of them, isn't he? The cattle god descendants that Anteros uses as security?'

'Yeah, but he's okay. He works here now, he—' Then the door opens and Dan looks up and gawps.

Fair enough, she is rather gawp-worthy.

Medusa wears a green, long-sleeved evening dress and spike-heeled black boots. Her high hairdo is captured in a black and green scarf that glitters with tiny beaded jewels. She's every inch an elegant and dangerous femme fatale, could almost pass as human, save for the green-golden scales that cover her skin and those deadly yellow eyes, speckled with black, each pupil a narrow slit. Eyes that right now are thankfully protected by a pair of horn-rimmed spectacles.

148

Medusa's smile is lazy, amused, as she surveys us. 'Frida, Dan . . . It's been a while.'

I check Dan and see that he's doing his best to appear super-cool about the fact that I've just led him into a bar to meet a woman who can turn him to stone with a single glance.

'We ran into a few problems after we saw you,' I say casually, as though we were here just yesterday. Medusa simply smiles and shrugs and reaches under the bar for a bottle of vodka. Places it down and then grabs three glasses.

'Cocktail?' she asks Dan.

'No thanks,' he says. 'Bit early for me!' Then he looks immediately mortified at his dorkiness as Medusa pouts her disapproval.

'Frida?' She sees my face. 'Oh, come on. Please? I do so hate to drink alone.'

Oh, what the hell, I need a goddamned drink. Or, ideally, twelve. 'Sure,' I say, settling myself on a bar stool. 'Why not?'

'I thought it was dangerous to eat or drink anything offered to you by a magical creature,' Dan whispers in my ear. I raise my eyebrows and he adds, 'I read it in the notes.'

'It's fine, Dan,' I whisper back. 'Just chill.'

We watch Medusa as she moves elegantly, dispensing the vodka, squeezing a half of lemon, adding a twist of something from an ornate bottle.

'How's business?' I say, glancing around the empty bar.

Medusa looks up, frowning. 'Slow. And you know why?'

'Because you keep turning your clientele to stone?'

Medusa flashes me a wicked grin. 'Oh, him outside? He complained once too often. Now he serves as a warning to the others. Plus,' she twirls an umbrella into a glass, 'he makes a superb ashtray.'

Dan tenses up at the casual murder chat while Medusa pours some bright red juice into another glass and pushes it over to me, taking a long swig of her own. Her hair twitches with satisfaction. 'Ah,' she says, 'that's better. Now!' She turns her bright eyes on us for a proper look. When she sees Dan flinch, she gives a tormenting little smile, gently tapping the lens of her glasses. 'Don't worry, Daniel, you're quite safe.' Then her gaze lingers on him. 'Hmmm, there's something different about you,' she says, raising her cocktail glass and peering slyly at him over the rim. 'Something missing . . .?'

'Anteros caught up with us and wiped our memories,' I explain. 'I've got mine back. Dan hasn't.'

Dan blinks at my brevity. 'But I've read all the notes,' he adds. 'I know all about the . . . er . . . magical world.'

Medusa smiles as she takes in the implication of this revelation. 'But you don't remember the lovely Frida?' she asks, inclining her head to me. 'From before?'

'No, he doesn't,' I say shortly. 'As far as Dan is concerned, we only met three days ago.' My tone warns her to drop it. 'Look, Medusa, I'll get to the point. We lost the acorn you gave us. I think maybe Anteros destroyed it. We need another.'

'Oh,' she says and takes a sip of her drink.

My heart sinks. 'Is that "Oh" as in "Oh, I'll just pop out the back and get you a new magical acorn" or "Oh, there is only one magical acorn and you lost it"?'

'The latter, I'm afraid.' She taps a bejewelled fingernail

against her glass. 'There were more, but we had a break-in. Quite a while ago now. They took a lot of things, including the acorns. Which means I can no longer visit my dear friend.' She sighs. 'Poor Daphne, she does get so lonely out there in the forest by herself.'

Fuck. 'Was it Anteros?'

'I expect so.' The gorgon shrugs her glittery shoulders. 'It seems he's being very thorough. Tying up loose ends.'

I stare at Medusa, stricken. This is wholly unwelcome information. 'Okay,' I say, 'so, is there any other way of getting into the woods?'

Medusa shakes her head and the beads glitter in the low light. 'I'm afraid not, Frida. But you're wrong about the acorn. I'm sure Anteros didn't find it.'

'What do you mean?'

'If he had found it, then he would have destroyed it, and it hasn't been destroyed.' Medusa lifts her glass, sips her cocktail. 'Every magical acorn has a . . . frequency. This one is still emitting, calling to you, asking you to complete the journey you started.' She laughs at Dan's amazed expression. 'It's just how these things work. You'd have known that, once.' She reaches over the bar and boops him on the nose. 'Oh, aren't you just the cutest thing now?'

Dan takes an alarmed step backwards, presumably in case Medusa decides to chuck his cheeks as well. He clears his throat. 'Medusa, do you know what he's planning?' he asks, his tone formal. 'Why Anteros is turning the mortals against love?'

Medusa blinks her amber eyes at Dan, all innocence. '*Moi*? How should I know?'

Dan eyeballs her. I stare at him, aghast. Ten points for bravery, minus the exact same number of points for stupidity. 'Because according to our notes,' he goes on, 'you were working for him two and a half years ago. How do we know you're not still working for him now?'

I shoot Dan a look. What the hell is he doing? Does he want to get us turned into garden furniture? Dan ignores me and just stares pointedly at Medusa who, for her part, remains entirely unconcerned by his accusation.

'Oh,' she says breezily, 'I haven't seen that cad since he left us all to rot. Though why I expected anything else from a *god*,' her nose scrunches with distaste at the word, 'I really don't know.'

'So, you've no idea what's going to happen at the church on Sunday?' Dan pushes.

Luckily Medusa seems rather amused by this new version of the Oracle. She leans towards him. 'All I know, Daniel, is that it is terrible for business.' She twiddles an umbrella in her cocktail. 'We're usually full to the rafters by now, but most of my customers have left the city over the last few months.' Medusa takes another sip of her drink and her headscarf undulates again. 'What *is* he doing with all those anti-lovers?' She gives a tinkly laugh. 'It's quite the puzzle, isn't it?'

'So this is a game?' Dan asks.

I shoot him another glare, which he also ignores, so I back it up with a jabbing elbow. Medusa continues to spin her paper umbrella as she narrows her gaze on Dan, her eyes roaming over him, toying with him.

'It has always been a game to them, Daniel. Perhaps that's

152

something else you once knew and have since forgotten? Yes,' she says, 'I have a feeling that for Anteros this has all been one very long, very drawn-out game that is about to reach its conclusion.' Then she lifts an impaled olive from her glass, dangles it into her mouth and bites down with relish.

A jolt of fear goes through me at her words. 'An endgame, just like Psyche said,' I murmur. At this, Medusa's yellow eyes glow, their narrow pupils pinning me. Her snakes give a violent shimmer and she pats her scarf as they jitter and thrash. Unable to calm them, she fiddles with a knot at the base of her neck and with a flourish, removes the headscarf. Then she turns her eyes on me, as do her snakes, two dozen reptiles of varying sizes, rearing and lunging, in one fluid motion, hissing all the while, their beady black eyes a tiny mimic of their mistress.

Dan, unsurprisingly, is gawping again.

'Psyche's back?' Medusa asks and the snakes join in. *SSSykeeesss?*

I nod, discomforted under the gaze of all those snakes. 'She's helping us.'

'Really?' Medusa pouts. 'Well, isn't that just like her? Always switching sides when it suits her,' she says, cheerfully oblivious to the fact that she's doing exactly the same. We watch, enthralled, as the gorgon's snakes undulate and quiver. Medusa gives us a sultry smile.

'You must tell her to stop by. Psyche and I, we go way back, oh yes. I know her intimately . . .' Medusa winks at Dan who gulps audibly, like something out of a cartoon, and then she's on to him. With a wicked smile, she leans over the bar and

153

brings her terrible, beautiful face close to his. 'Oh, Daniel, you can imagine, surely, how nice I can be when I want to be. In fact, I bet that tonight you'll dream about it . . .' Her snakes bob towards him, their black beady eyes pinning him, their hissing soporific, their tongues licking the air, lascivious. Dan's mouth has fallen open, his eyes now also cartoony. 'I could be nice to you, too, Dan,' Medusa says, her voice low and breathy and hypnotic. 'It has been eons since I've had a mortal. I'll take these off,' she reaches up to the stem of her glasses and jiggles them alarmingly, 'and then blindfold you, adds a frisson of danger, I bet you'd like that, wouldn't you . . .?'

Dan's eyes have glazed over and he seems to be drooling a little under the impact of Medusa's snaky voodoo.

'Okay, okay, I think we are done here!' I grab Dan by the arm and steer him away from the bar. 'Dan, please go and wait outside.'

Wonder of wonders, he actually does as I ask, albeit only because he's still somewhat foggy from Medusa's charms. As he staggers away, Medusa locks eyes with me and I flinch despite myself. She tuts and wipes a finger around the rim of her glass. Her snakes lick the air. She waits until Dan is out of earshot and then she flashes me a crafty smile.

'You took the ambrosia, then?' she asks. 'That's how you got your memories back?'

I nod.

'And?'

I move the stirrer back and forth in my glass. 'And what? I don't know what you're talking about.'

Medusa scoffs. 'You've no need to lie to me, Frida.' She tips her head to one side, her eyes narrow, watchful. 'You felt it? What it can do?'

'It doesn't matter what it can do,' I say. I think about what Psyche said. How ambrosia would turn me into *something other than human*. 'I can't take any more. It's too dangerous.'

Medusa doesn't answer. I stare after Dan as he wobbles up the stairs and she follows my gaze. 'So, you've lost the old, all-knowing Dan,' she says. 'Well, perhaps that is fate.'

'What the hell is that supposed to mean?' I look at her, eyes blazing.

Medusa just smiles, and sips her drink. 'Oh, you know exactly what it means, Frida. You've thought as much your-self. Admit it.'

'I don't know what you're talking about.' But a flush climbs my cheeks.

Medusa tips her glass and drains it. Her snakes are taut, vibrating with barely contained tension as she gives me a wide smile, showing her teeth.

'Taking more ambrosia will change you, it's true. You'll become a love goddess, immortal, no longer human.' She tips her snaky head towards me. 'But do you understand what this offers you? You'll become a higher being. No more pain, no more worry, no more human frailty. You'll be everything you've ever wanted to be, only better.'

I cast another look at the departing Dan. 'And my life?' I say. 'The people I care about? What about them?'

Medusa just shakes her head. 'Oh Frida, when will you learn? You're the chosen one. Emphasis on *one*. This isn't a job share. When you come to face your destiny, you'll do so alone.' She meets my eyes. 'You've been cursed by the gods, just as I was cursed. In the end we all have to play our part. Sacrifices have to be made.'

Sacrifices? Jesus, haven't I sacrificed enough? I've only just found Dan again. And okay, so he's not exactly the Dan I knew. And okay, he doesn't love me. And yes, all the antidote is gone. But he's still *him*. He's still the man I love. (Or loved. Whatever. It's complicated.) And even though we're not how we were, I still want him in my life. But if I do what Medusa suggests, I know, in my bones, that it means the end. The end of me and Dan. The end of Frida McKenzie. The end of this human existence, which, I'd be the first to admit, isn't without its problems, but it is *mine*. I can't just give it up, can't give Dan up. Not like this. Not if there is any other way.

'You're wrong,' I tell Medusa now. 'Ambrosia is not the answer. Dan and I will find that missing acorn and Daphne will give us the prophecy and it will tell us how to stop Anteros. We'll end his games together. We've done it before and we can do it again. I know it.'

The gorgon leans towards me, then, gripping my wrist in one scaly hand, she hisses, 'Don't be so foolish, girl. You must take the ambrosia. Time is running out. What's coming is huge and dark and merciless, and unless someone stands against it, none of us will escape.' She grimaces and shivers, her yellow eyes haunted, as she says, 'Can't you *feel* it?'

And the terrible thing is, I can.

Chapter 16

I find Dan on the cobbled courtyard, bent double, as though he's going to be sick. When I close the door with a click, he looks up and hastily tries to straighten himself.

'How're you doing there, champ?'

He waves an arm at me. 'Yeah, yeah, it's just . . .' He bends over again. 'I think maybe it was something I ate,' he says in a muffled voice. 'I feel a bit queasy.'

'It's Medusa's magic,' I say and Dan gives me a beleaguered look. 'What did you expect? You challenged her. She was giving you a small taste of her power in return. It could have been a lot worse if she'd decided to take off those specs.' I stare at him. 'What was all that about in there?'

Dan takes a deep breath and tries to collect himself, straightens up and then folds again. 'I don't think we can trust her, Frida,' he says from his crumpled position. 'She was working with Anteros before. According to our notes, she tried to turn you to stone on that Valentine's Day!'

'Yes, I know that,' I say softly. 'But Dan, she's helping us. We didn't have time to update our notes, but Medusa was the last person we saw before we . . .' I let the sentence drift. 'Anyway, I didn't say that I trusted her, but she's useful. And right now, we need all the help we can get. So it would be really great in future if, before playing bad cop, you give me a bit of a heads-up. You can't just go accusing people. Especially not people whose hairy eyeball includes the ability to petrify.'

Dan nods, still with his head between his knees. 'Okay. Understood. Sorry,' he says miserably.

I stare at him. God, I hate talking to him like this. This is Dan! Admonishing him feels all kinds of wrong. 'Look,' I say. 'I don't mean to be on your back. I just don't want—'

'Me to slow you down. I know, I know, I get it.'

I stare at him. I was going to say, lose you again. I don't want to lose you again, Dan, it would break my heart beyond repair if anything happened to you.

But I don't say that. How can I?

A flash of red catches my eye, then. A group of Anterists is heading our way. I scan the area for somewhere to hide. I need to get Dan back to Psyche's but he's in no fit state to walk anywhere right now.

'Come on,' I say. 'There's a park over the road, let's sit for a while until you feel better.'

We head over and take a seat on a bench, set out of the way of passing footfall. I slip my sunglasses on and Dan does the same. On the other side of the grass, lone people are stretched out on blankets, enjoying their picnics-for-one, reading well-thumbed copies of *The Love Delusion*. Oh, how this movement was going to change life for the better; it was going to set us all free. I stare across the grass. A young girl with red hair throws a ball for her dog. It bounces into the pond and the spaniel splashes in after it and then emerges triumphant to shake itself joyfully. I smile. Simple pleasures.

I turn to see Dan looking at me. I can't read the expression behind his shades. I tip my head to one side. 'What?'

'I was just thinking how it's so weird that you actually look different to the other Frida. The one I met on the steps of the church, I mean.'

'Different how?'

'I don't know. You're ... bigger somehow.'

'That'll be the weight of the world you're seeing,' I reply. But I know what he means. It's partly the effect of the ambrosia but it is also that I *am* different. After Dan found me and told me who I was, he was right – we became heroes. The Frida I've been this last two years is more like the person I was before then. Cynical. Fearful. Oblivious.

'Do I look smaller,' Dan asks, 'than I did before, I mean?'

I stare at him and my heart aches. 'No, Dan,' I say gently. 'Not smaller. You're just ...' I reach for the same word he used, '... different.'

'Different how?'

'Is it important?' I can feel myself tensing up. This is Dan now. Is there any point in raking up how he was before? What he was to me?

159

'Yeah, it really is,' he says. 'There was this other, better version of me on that video, a Dan who was cool and brave and, from what I can gather, an expert in all of this magical mythology stuff.'

'You know stuff!' I protest. 'You knew about Psyche. I didn't.'

'I know details from games and books and films, sure, but he lived it. I need to know if I can ever become him.' He pauses. 'I want to be helpful to you. For us to be a good team, like we were. Right now, I'm just the annoying idiot while you and Psyche are the tough, kick-ass super-heroes.'

'You're not an idiot,' I say.

'Damning me with faint praise here,' he says, raising an eyebrow. 'So, go on, how am I different?'

I roll my eyes. 'Well, you used to be a man of few words, for a start.' Dan looks at me. He's not giving this up. 'Okay, you're . . .' I search for the right word. 'Lighter.'

'Lighter?'

'Yeah. Happier, I suppose. Less intense.' I look at him. 'Listen, we made a lot of assumptions before we were Lethed. I don't think we understood what it would mean. We imagined that without our memories we were still the same people just with the magical knowledge stripped out and that we could kind of reinsert that information via a document on a laptop. But it doesn't seem to work like that. We're not the same people without those memories. Losing the recollections of those experiences changes us.'

I think about who I have been for the last two years. What losing my memories of Dan turned me into.

160

'But I could become him again,' Dan says, 'in time?'

I look at him. 'I honestly don't know. Your family were the Oracle line. You grew up in the magical world, immersed in ancient myth and immortal dangers. Your whole life, you've been aware that gods and monsters exist.' I push my shades up, too, addressing him frankly. 'Without that knowledge, you're like a,' I struggle for the correct phrase, 'a parallel universe, Dan. The person you would have been, perhaps, if none of this magical stuff was real. Not better, not worse, just . . . like I said, different.'

Dan looks at me unhappily. 'Lighter, you said. Like Lite beer and Lite crisps. Not the option anyone would choose if they could have the thing they really wanted.'

'That's not what I meant at all.' I frown.

'Do you think there's a chance I'll have a vision?'

'I don't know.' I shake my head. 'I don't think so. Psyche reckons the gods who support Anteros are somehow stopping them from coming through.'

'Great,' Dan says. 'So I'm an Oracle without visions who has zero memories of anything magical. If I was a role-play character, I'd be trying to kill myself off right about now.'

I stare at him. Bad enough that we have to avert some unknown impending disaster, but do I really have to build up Dan's ego while we do it? I feel a rush of frustration and anger. We don't have time for this. It would be easier just to do it on my own. It would have been easier if I'd never gone to find Dan in the first place.

But as I think these terrible thoughts, I look at the face of the man I love and it comes back to me: what he did for me

161

when I was new to this world. I was a royal pain in the arse when he first found me, but Dan stuck with me because he knew who I really was inside. He taught me the ropes, keeping his patience (well, mostly) while I tested it repeatedly with my doubts and questions. He trusted me to do what had to be done, though I gave him scant reason to have faith in me. That's what people who love each other do.

So now I guess it's my turn.

'Dan,' I say softly. I go to put a comforting hand on his thigh, think better of it and just sort of wave it around. 'You are doing so much better than I did when I first found out.'

'You mean when I came to your office to tell you about the prophecy and you had me thrown out by the enormous security guard?' He grins. 'I read about that. You really did that to me?'

'Yeah,' I say, 'but then I got kidnapped and you made me climb through a ventilation shaft so I think that makes us even.' I meet Dan's eyes. 'Don't expect so much of yourself,' I tell him. 'You've just had a huge, life-changing shock. I think you're doing brilliantly.'

He gives me a happy lopsided grin so familiar that it hurts my heart. 'Thanks, Frida,' he says. 'You're a good friend.'

I think I manage not to wince.

$$\longrightarrow$$

We sit in the sun for a while then in comfortable, contemplative silence. A dog barks joyfully and hurtles after a ball, ears swinging. We see a group of Anterists move off further into the park.

'What made you join The Love Delusion?' Dan asks as he watches them. 'After we were Lethed, I mean?'

I stare straight ahead. Oh great, we're going there, are we? I think about all the ways I could answer that, the simplest being: I lost you, and I was heartbroken, and I didn't know why. There was a hole inside me and Anterism promised to fill it. Instead I say, 'The same thing that makes everyone join: hope.'

'Hope,' Dan repeats thoughtfully.

'What you need to understand about Anteros,' I explain, 'is that he operates like a narcissist. He has an eye for the vulnerable. He woos the mortals with his charm, tapping into our hopes and our insecurities and promising us the world, making us believe that we've found the one thing that will make us happy. He peddled obsessive, dysfunctional love to us for a long time, and now he's doing the same with the rejection of love.' I chip at a sliver of loose wood on the bench with my fingernail. 'But by the time we realise we're being used, that the thing he promises isn't real, if we ever do, we're too broken and lost to escape.' I meet Dan's eyes, smile sadly. 'And unfortunately, I've always been a sucker for damaging relationships.'

'That's horrible,' he says.

I nod. 'So, what made you protest it?'

'Well, mainly just to help out my friend.' He shrugs. 'But to be honest it always seemed obvious that the whole movement was sinister. It was hard for me to understand how anyone could fall for it. Although,' he says hastily, 'that was before I knew about evil love gods and magic and the like.'

163

It makes sense. Dan's not like me. He comes from an unbroken home, with wonderful parents who loved one another, brothers and sisters, happy childhood memories. He's that rare thing – a functioning adult male. Does he even realise how special that is?

'Lucky you,' I say. 'But think of The Love Delusion as a siren song that only certain people can hear. Only the heartbroken, the disillusioned, the mistreated, at least at first. But it's getting stronger. I think, very quickly, anyone could be vulnerable to its power.'

'And then what?'

'And then, the endgame, whatever that is.' I sigh. 'We need to hear the prophecy. We need that acorn.' I pause as I think about what Medusa said. The acorn is still out there. Anteros doesn't have it. 'You're absolutely sure there's nowhere else in the car it could be? Nowhere we've missed?'

Dan ponders this. 'I don't think so, but I'll check again when we get back.' I nod. There's a silence as I stare across the park, suddenly flattened by the impossible task ahead.

'I have another question.'

Something in Dan's tone puts me on the alert and I flip my shades down as I say, as casually as I can, 'Okay, last question, shoot.'

'Something is bugging me. Why is there no mention of the ambrosia in our file? If we knew it could bring back your memories, surely we would have factored it in? And why did that note you left say not to tell me?'

I keep my voice even. 'We got the ambrosia the day we were intercepted. There was no time to update the file. And the note I left? Well, I wanted to make sure you didn't take it by accident after our memories were lost,' I say carefully. 'I knew it would be deadly for you. I was just trying to protect you.'

'Right,' Dan says. 'Okay. Yeah, that makes sense.'

I look at him and smile. He smiles back, seemingly reassured. He trusts me. And why wouldn't he? We're a good team, he and I.

Chapter 17

It's afternoon by the time we get back to Psyche's, and Dan immediately heads down to the stuffy car park to search the car again. It's probably futile but I could do with some time alone to think, to work out what I'm going to do if we can't find that acorn.

Letting myself into the flat using Psyche's spare keys, I head for the kitchen. I locate the cafetière and make myself an extra-strength coffee. My stomach rumbles and I realise I haven't eaten lunch, so I nose around Psyche's cupboards and fridge, find some crackers and cheese, and take them and the coffee out on to the balcony. I sit there for a while, munching on the crackers, sipping the coffee, and staring over the city, watching as the sun travels behind the high-rise offices.

I take stock. It's already Monday. Anteros will be here on Sunday. I've wasted a whole day (*Oh, you've wasted more than that*, an insidious little voice whispers) and have nothing to show for it. In reality, I know it doesn't matter how long Dan searches, the acorn is gone. Maybe fallen out on to a random pavement, maybe locked in a drawer in some Love Delusion head office. Who knows? One thing is clear – without it, there's no way to reach Daphne, and without Daphne and the hidden prophecy, we have no way to stop Anteros.

That's not quite true though, is it, Frida?

After a while I hear the balcony door slide open. I turn, expecting Dan, but it's Psyche. She nods at me, walks over and leans against the balcony. Lights a cigarette. I've never met anyone who smokes as much as Psyche, but then I guess, if you can't die, what's to stop you?

'No joy?' she asks eventually.

'No. You find out anything?'

She shakes her head.

'Any trouble out there? Any Anterists spot you?'

'I don't think so,' I say. 'But Dan followed me,' I turn to her. 'I thought I asked you to look after him?'

Psyche gazes at me mildly. 'I'm not his babysitter. He insisted on going after you; what did you want me to do, knock him out? I gave him protection spells.' She takes a drag on her cigarette. 'He's more resilient than you're giving him credit for, Frida. He's been at this game a lot longer than you, even if he doesn't recall it.'

'I know,' I say. 'He did okay, actually. Well, apart from riling Medusa.'

'He riled Medusa?' Psyche raises an eyebrow. 'Well, that takes balls.'

'Balls she'd be using for paperweights right now if he'd gone any further.'

Psyche smirks and leans over the balcony again. I follow her gaze.

'I can't believe how many Anterists there are now,' I say. 'When I was last, you know, me, there were only a few hundred across the world.'

Psyche nods grimly. 'It spread fast.'

'They have a strange emotional energy.'

'How so?' Psyche looks at me.

'After I took the ambrosia, I saw something, felt something.' I describe the blackened hearts of the Anterists and Psyche listens intently, taking increasingly strong drags on her cigarette.

When I've finished, she says, 'So it's arrow magic. The lead-tipped kind that makes the mortals hate love.'

'Yeah, that's what I always thought. But he doesn't have a love arrow, does he?'

'No. There are none left. I'm absolutely certain of that.'

'Then how is he doing it? Where's the power coming from? I know he's a master manipulator, but even so, to convert this many people in such a short space of time, there's got to be some sort of magic involved.'

I think back to the conversations Dan and I had. As awful as The Love Delusion movement was, we consoled ourselves that for Anteros to convert more than a few hundred mortals would take hundreds of years. Thousands. A slow evolution. Even with Anteros's great ingenuity, we simply could not envisage how a movement so radical could embed itself into a society, in a species, that has so long believed in love.

'It shouldn't be possible,' Psyche says. 'But somehow he's done it.'

I have a heavy feeling in my guts. There's so much we don't know. Two years I wasted. And although I understand exactly why, that doesn't mean I don't hate myself for it.

'I can't believe I joined them,' I say. Not because I think Psyche is going to make me feel better, but just because I need to say it out loud to someone. 'Whatever he's doing, I helped him. I'm responsible.'

Psyche turns and meets my eyes. 'It's a waste of energy, thinking like that. You weren't yourself. You didn't know. And you'd just lost Dan, remember?'

'Dan didn't turn, though, did he? He was fighting Anteros even if he didn't know exactly what he was fighting.' I pause. 'He's a better person than me.'

'Well, yeah,' Psyche says, pulling on her cigarette. 'That's not news.'

I glare out across the city. 'I bet Anteros loved it, getting Hades to groom me. Having me worship the mighty R. A. Stone. Humiliating me like that.'

'Don't make the mistake of thinking this is personal, Frida.' Psyche shakes her head. 'Anteros does what he has to in order to serve his own ends.'

'What, like you do, you mean?'

She doesn't answer that.

We fall into silence as we look over the city. The sun is an orange disc peeking from behind the buildings. I look at the skyscraper Anteros used to occupy, the city's tallest structure.

Once it was a huge tech empire, NeoStar, whose entire purpose was to fuck up human relationships and happiness. And I brought it down. Destroyed it completely. Now it's home to a hotel, apartments and offices. I did what I was asked to do. Why is this not over? What was it all for, if Anteros is back to fuck with us so soon?

'Are we just going to fall for his tricks every single time?' I say. 'It makes me wonder if there's any use in fighting him at all.'

Psyche looks at me for a moment. Then she looks back over the balcony. 'I took Lethe once.'

I turn to her, startled by this non sequitur. 'You took Lethe water? What do you mean? Why?'

Psyche doesn't look at me as she says, 'My daughter died. Mine and Eros's little girl, Pleasure. I called her Lea. She was in her seventies by then, a very old woman in those days, but she was still my baby.' Psyche's mouth holds the ghost of a smile. 'I held her in my arms as she breathed her last and then I felt her pass on to the unknown. Somewhere I couldn't follow.' Psyche fixes her gaze on the buildings. 'I couldn't stand it. The indescribable pain. Every breath I took reminded me that I was living and she was dead. It was torture, knowing that I would keep on living, that I would suffer her loss for all eternity.'

She stubs out her cigarette and orange sparks fly. Takes out her packet and shakes another out. 'I couldn't die,' she says, 'Zeus had seen to that. But I could forget. And so I got hold of some Lethe water.' She gives a bitter smile. 'I drank it and I forgot it all. Eros, Aphrodite, the Underworld,

Olympus, everything.' She flicks her lighter and the cigarette sizzles.

When she finally turns and meets my eyes, the depth of her sadness takes my breath away. 'But I forgot her, too. I forgot I ever had a daughter.' She stares down at the burning ash on the end of her cigarette. 'I was empty inside, though I didn't know why. Tried to end my life several times, but,' she shrugs, 'that never turned out as planned. Eventually someone found me, gave me the antidote. And when it all came back, when I realised what I had done, how I had abandoned her memory ...' Pain tightens her face. 'It was the worst thing I've ever done. I swore I would never allow myself to forget her again. Even though all that sadness came back, I held on to the love and I understood: the pain was the price.'

I stare at her. I have no idea what to say.

Psyche's grey eyes are dark. 'I'm telling you this to make you understand – that's how Lethe works, and that's how The Love Delusion works, and how all dark magic works, in the end. It's seductive. It promises to take away the pain, the longing, the wretchedness of being alive. But it's a deal,' she says. 'You give up pain, you give up love, and with that goes joy, humanity and all the rest of it.'

I give a wan smile. 'And here's me thinking you didn't care much for humanity.'

She draws hard on her cigarette, eyes narrowed against the smoke, tough-Psyche again, that window of vulnerability closed. 'Turns out it's superior to the alternative.'

I'm distracted then by movement at the balcony door. Dan,

looking dusty and hot but not as depressed as anticipated. Maybe he's had some luck. As he steps out on to the balcony my heart lifts.

'Did you find it?'

'Oh . . . er, no,' he says.

I sink back into my chair, deflated. 'What've you got then?' I say glumly. 'Another Classic Rock compilation?'

'No,' he says. 'I've got what I think may be a Very Good Idea.'

He actually says it so you can hear the capitals. Psyche looks from Dan to me. 'I'll leave you guys to it,' she says. 'I'm ordering Chinese food. You want some?'

'God, yes,' I say.

When she's gone, I turn back to Dan. 'Okay,' I say. 'Very Good Idea: let's have it.'

His face is lit up and I can't help but smile. 'What if I hid the acorn somewhere really brilliant?'

'That would be fantastic,' I say. 'Did you?'

'Well, I don't know. But I've got an idea that might help us find out. Tomorrow, we should recreate the journey, up until the point where I hid the acorn. It might jog something,' he says. 'You know, like muscle memory?'

I stare at him. Recreate the exact circumstances in which the love of my life was torn away from me. What a delightful way to spend a day. Maybe I'll stick pins in my eyes and set fire to my own head afterwards to really top things off.

Dan sees my face and holds up his hands. 'Hey, if it's a stupid idea, just say.'

I close my eyes. 'No,' I say, heavily, because as hideous as it sounds, I haven't got anything better to suggest. 'It's a good idea. Worth a shot.'

Dan beams and it animates his handsome face even more. 'A Very Good Idea?'

'Don't push it,' I say, but I'm smiling.

Later, Psyche has made herself scarce and Dan and I sit on the balcony, eating takeout noodles and looking out over the city. I'm hit with a feeling of fleeting happiness. I look at Dan with his chopsticks in hand, bottle of beer open in front of him, and tell myself that nothing has changed. That we are exactly who we were – heroes who are going to stop this thing together. *Us* against the world.

And for a little while, it even works.

Chapter 18

It seems that Dan might actually have a point about muscle memory.

The following day, as I direct him through the route of our last journey together, I can feel myself physically reliving all my trauma. My body starts to stiffen, my heart pounds and my breath comes short. I try to distract myself, watching the parched yellow grass verges as we pass, but it's no good, it's all coming back to me too clearly: the hope we had of stopping Anteros. The fear.

Okay, mostly the fear. I fiddle with the hem of my black sundress, freshly laundered by Psyche, either out of kindness or more likely because she can't bear to see me humiliate any more of her clothing.

'Which lane did I drive in?' Dan asks as he indicates to join the motorway that heads out of town.

I frown as I drag my attention back to the here and now. 'What?'

'Lane. Was I a speed-in-the-fast-lane type or a bit of a slowpoke middle-lane hogger?'

'You had your memory wiped, Dan, not a personality transplant. Just drive how you'd normally drive.'

He raises an eyebrow. 'We need to get all the details right if this is going to work.'

'Okay, okay,' I say. 'Let me think. We were in a hurry. We'd just seen Medusa, she'd given us the acorn, we stopped off at mine, and then—'

'Why?'

I blink at him. 'Why what?'

'Why did we stop off at yours after Medusa's?' he asks, and when I frown he says, 'It might prompt something.' He pauses. 'We probably should have started from Medusa's, actually.'

I shake my head. 'Too many Anterists. This will be fine.' And then he waits, expectant. 'Oh, I needed to pick up my phone,' I say. 'I'd left it behind.'

'Right,' Dan says, nodding. 'So we picked up your phone and then . . . '

'And then we joined the motorway here, heading for Happy Valley Woods.'

'And where was the acorn then?'

I think about this. 'In my bag.'

'Okay,' Dan says. He indicates and overtakes the van in front. The tick-tick-ticking feels like a warning. Five minutes later I glimpse a billboard and it brings something else back.

My eyes flicker to the wing mirror, my stomach lurching in memory. 'Around here,' I say, 'I thought we were being followed.'

'You saw a car?' Dan flashes me a glance.

'Yeah, but it wasn't just that. I could feel it. Feel *him*.'

There's a pause as Dan takes in this information. 'Okay, then what?'

My eyes go to the mirror again, I see a dark-coloured car three vehicles back and my blood freezes. But it's just a navy-blue family hatchback, roof-rack full to bursting, kids packed into the back. Nothing to worry about.

'Then I looked again and the car had gone.'

'Okay.'

'Take the next exit.'

Dan nods and indicating again, swings the car off the motorway, down the slip road. Immediately the roads shrink down and that sense of suffocation returns. So, too, does the sensation, strong and undeniable, that this is a terrible mistake. But we have to do this now, just like we had to do it then. We don't have any other choice.

'You okay?' says Dan, glancing over.

'I'm fine.'

'Right, so, we headed for what?'

'The car park,' I say. 'Further down here on the left.'

I'm almost shaking now. I knew what was going to happen, there was a dread sort of certainty to everything we did that day, as though it was fated and there was nothing we could do to escape it. Why did we play our part? Why was it up to us to solve anything? We should have hidden. We could have run away together, escaped to that remote Greek island Dan was always promising he'd take me to. Anteros only Lethed us because we were a threat to him.

Just before Dan gets to the car park entrance, I speak again, my voice low. 'They headed us off here. Anterists. Brake now and twist the car to the right, we bumped that wall. Just there.'

Deftly Dan brings the car around. I look about me. The road is empty but I see them still, surrounding us.

Dan watches me. 'Then what?'

'Anterist guards got out of the car and started walking towards us.' I take a deep breath, try to quell my panic, this is not happening now, it was two years ago, it's okay. 'The car stalled. You restarted it, reversed to straighten up and then drove on.'

Wordlessly, Dan does everything I say.

As we travel down the narrow road, those same high stone walls swallow us up. 'This is where the black SUV blocked the road. It was him, Anteros. Stop here. NOW.'

Dan slams on the brakes, his face grave. He's finally getting it – what it was like, what they did to us. How they hunted us down like animals.

'And then behind us, the Anterists came. We were trapped. You said that we could run,' I say, 'but we knew it was pointless. There was no way out.' Stone walls on either side, dozens of Anterist guards. They'd soon overpower us. But shouldn't we have tried to run anyway? Should we have given up so easily?

'I thought it was more important that you hide the acorn,'

177

I say. 'So that we could try again once we'd found one another . . .' I trail off.

'What happened next?'

'I got out of the car; you stayed a few seconds more and hid it.'

'How many seconds?'

I think about it. 'Thirty, max.'

'Okay,' Dan says. 'You get out and do just what you did back then.'

I unclick my seat belt and then reach for the door handle. Then I stand exactly where I stood two years ago. Instead of staring at the black car that isn't there, I look over to the forest. We were so close. We so nearly did it. Would it have changed anything, if we had reached Daphne two years ago? Would all of this be over now?

'Then what did I do?' Dan climbs out of the car. Walks over to me. 'Are you standing just like you were then?'

I nod.

'And what did I do?'

'You came and stood beside me.'

'How?' he says. 'Where was I exactly?'

I shake my head. I don't want to remember.

'Frida, please, it's really important. If it is going to work, everything we do here has to be exactly the same.'

I stare at him and his green eyes meet mine. Slowly, leadenly, I manoeuvre Dan to where he was standing back then. I step back and survey him, sadness blooming in my chest. I bite my lip. 'A little further back, I think.'

Dan takes a step, the wall at his back. 'Like this?'

'Yeah.'

'And where were you?'

I can feel him, then, holding me, my head on his chest, the steady thump of his heart beat. My eyes prickle.

'I don't see why that matters!' I burst out.

Dan gazes at me mildly. 'Do you want to find the acorn or not?'

Suddenly, anger floods me. Fine. Why should I have to bear this burden alone anyway? Keeping the truth from him so that he doesn't feel awkward around me. I'm done with it.

'You really want to know exactly how it was?'

'Yeah, I just said.'

'Fine.'

I walk up to him, close and then closer, until our bodies are touching. Dan starts in surprise as I put my hands on him and it breaks my heart a little. Still, he asked for an exact re-creation and that's what he's going to get. I lean against him, tuck my head into the nook in his neck, and put my arms around his waist. I breathe him in. Then I lean up and I kiss him. Emotion floods through me as my lips touch his, and for a moment I am right where I am meant to be, with Dan, wishing this moment could last for ever.

But then I step away and Dan looks down and meets my eyes and where two years ago I saw the deepest love, now I just see dawning recognition and more than a little shock.

'Oh!' he says.

'Yeah. Oh.'

'Right. We were . . .?'

'Yup.'

'But you said we were just . . .'

'I lied.'

Dan considers this for a moment and I can't read the expression in his eyes.

'Frida,' he begins. 'I—'

'NO,' I shout and then at his startled expression, I soften. 'I can't talk about it, okay? Not yet.' I fold my arms. 'I only showed you because you said it would help find the acorn. So did it?'

Dan meets my gaze for a long minute, looking like there is more he wants to say, but then he turns to face the wall. Jesus, was the kiss that bad? Then he bends down and stares into a crevice. Maybe he's trying to dig a hole to escape the excruciating awkwardness? I can relate.

Then, 'Ha!' he says and swings around.

'Ha what?'

'Something has been bugging me,' he says. 'I kept asking myself, where would I have hidden the acorn in the car under those horrific circumstances? And I just couldn't come up with anything and then I realised why.'

'Why?'

'I would never have hidden it in the car. Even if they hadn't searched it, what if I had totalled the car while I was Lethed? Or sold it? Or found the acorn and just thrown it away? It's too great a risk. No,' he says, 'I would have wanted to hide it somewhere I knew was permanent.'

Then a wide smile crosses his face as he opens his hand to reveal a large greeny-gold acorn. It seems to shimmer in the light. He hands it to me and I stare at it, agog. I didn't realise how much I'd believed our chance was lost for good until I feel the relief flooding through me. It's here. It's really here.

'Dan, that's amazing!' I say. 'You found the acorn!'

'I found the acorn!' He grabs me and lifts me up and twirls me around, and our bodies fit together so well, it feels so right, but then Dan seems to realise what he's doing and he puts me down and then we just stand there looking uncertainly at one another, but then we are grinning again because he found the acorn! Oh, this is such a mess. I have feelings for him, complicated, fucked-up feelings and now he knows what we were and URGH. But still – we have the acorn. At least my humiliation was worth it.

I make a heroic effort to get things back on an even footing.

'Well done,' I say formally, like I'm giving him a work appraisal and haven't just confessed my undying love via intimate bodily contact. 'That was brilliant work.' I look over to the great expanse of forest beyond and a shiver of excitement passes through me. 'That's where we're going,' I say. 'Are you ready for this? Because once we go in, there's no coming back until we've found Daphne and that prophecy.'

Dan meets my eyes. 'I'm ready.'

'Okay then,' I say. 'Let's go.'

We climb back into the car, and Dan reverses back up the narrow road to the car-park entrance and turns in. He pulls up in the empty expanse and applies the handbrake. Ahead of us, a path leads across a field of grass, and into the lush green forest. I unclick my seat belt and feel something inside me unclench. We did it. It took two years, but we finally made it.

Then I hear something. A crunch of tyres.

I turn, heart pounding like a slow drum beat, and see a white saloon approaching. A coincidence, my mind scrambles to explain, an innocent party out for a woodland picnic! Dan is staring at me, his face tense, but I look past him, straining my eyes to look into the car. What I see gives me chills.

Every one of the five people in the car is dressed in red.

It's happening again.

'They've found us,' I say, my voice grim, my hand already on the car door, flinging it open. 'Come on!'

As we run from the car and along the path, making for the treeline, I cast a glance over my shoulder and see that the five people streaming from that white car are not the descendants of a cattle god, they're just regular Anterists with an axe to grind. Or – my gaze skitters over them and my pulse rate spikes – more accurately, a baseball bat. As I watch them, they break into a run.

'Faster!' I shout to Dan, panting. He just nods, his head down.

They must have been watching this spot. Staking it out. A message from on high, from Hades or Anteros, in case I was ever foolish enough to come back here. Or perhaps it's just bad luck, a group of Anterists on a sunny day trip who recognised my face in a passing car and decided they would be the ones to claim the head of Frida McKenzie, to win the eternal gratitude of their great leader and go down in Anterist history.

'Traitor!' an Anterist cries, and it's a howl of concentrated hatred. I try to train my attention on the forest in front of us, we can do this, we're almost there, but something makes me look back again, and I see them clearly then, these creatures who I once called my people, and their teeth are bared, their faces contorted with fury, not disciples now, but a snarling mob. And creeping inside me I can feel their desire to avenge, to punish, their longing to hear my bones crack as they show me what happens to those who betray them . . .

'Frida!' Dan grabs my shoulder and I snap back to myself, see the edge of the woodlands approaching, it's only metres away now. But the Anterists, too, are gaining.

'Judas!' comes the cry, like the baying of animals. 'Liar! Deceiver!'

Legs pumping, breath coming jaggedly, I open my hand. The acorn sits fat and warm in my palm.

'How does it work?' Dan pants, but I don't answer him, there's no time, instead I hurl the acorn on to the forest floor ahead of us.

Nothing happens.

We skid to a halt at the treeline and I stare, stricken, at the unchanging forest. Dan looks at me in alarm and then jerks his head to watch the oncoming Anterists, now almost in touching distance, they'll be on us in seconds, then—

'Look.'

Dan turns and his eyes widen. In the opening to the trees where the acorn landed, there's a silvery play of sunlight, a whispering of leaves as the air glitters and shifts, reconfiguring. Taking Dan's hand, I pull him into the woods, catching one last glimpse of the red-clothed Anterists, baseball bat held aloft, faces ruined with rage, before the forest closes up around us.

Chapter 19

We thread through the trees in silence, bathed in the pale green light that filters through the canopy of leaves over our heads. There's no sound from behind us. The Anterists could search this expanse of woods for days and never find us. We're not there any more. We are ... elsewhere.

I can hear the trickle of a stream, the calls of birds marking their territory, seeking out mates, and then other sounds, strange and evocative, not native to these woods, nor possibly even this world. The further we get into the forest, the greater the feeling of enchantment that settles upon us.

'What do we do?' Dan whispers at one point. 'How do we find her?'

I pull myself from my reverie to look at him and then give him the trusty advice I generally fall back on when faced with a situation like this: 'Just keep walking until something happens.'

I don't know how long we walk for. Time seems different here, fluid and lulling. At one point that may have been seconds into our journey but equally might have been hours, Dan says, 'Frida. About what happened back there ...'

I smile dreamily. 'The Anterists? Don't worry. They can't follow us here.'

Dan shakes his head. 'No, not the Anterists. The ... other thing. What you showed me on the road, about you and ... um ... previous me.'

I feel a prickling of discomfort as I think about what I revealed. 'Look, I really don't want to get into that now.' I stare at him. 'We've got more important things going on.'

'I know that,' he says, 'but I just want to—'

'Dan,' I say.

He looks at me. 'Frida, just let me get this out. I—'

'No, Dan!' I say again, more urgently, and point at the path ahead of us. 'Look!'

A huge stag stands there; the sheen of its tawny coat is like velvet. It locks eyes with me and I read it in one quick burst before it bows its head and trots off through the trees.

'That's Actaeon,' I whisper and Dan stares at me, mouth falling comically open. He'll have read about Actaeon in the notes, no doubt. Another of Anteros's victims. Shot with a golden arrow, the youth Actaeon lusted after the goddess Artemis, spying on her when she bathed naked. The furious goddess turned Actaeon into a stag for his impudence and he was promptly torn apart by his own hounds. Or so the myth went. Except, here he is, large as life and seemingly all in one piece.

We move quickly before Actaeon can disappear out of sight, travelling deeper and deeper into this otherworldly place, and it appears the forest has given me a new ability: to pick up on the feelings of animals. A hare stops, ears up, round-pupiled eyes fixed on us, and for a split second I feel its caution. A few paces on, what looks like a multicoloured tree bursts into butterflies as we pass, and as the insects weave between us I am filled with their giddy delight.

As our path veers to the right, we find ourselves following a stream. Shadow fish flicker deep under the clear running water and for a magical second I see their dreams. Further along, an otter is too absorbed in play with her pups to even notice us but passing her I pick up a concentrated sweet sense of joy. From the soft muddy bank a frog leaps with a throaty ribbit and I feel its enjoyment of the wet earth, the cool water and URGH! – the wiggly pleasure of a bluebottle swallowed whole.

Actaeon leads us away from the soothing trickle of the water and into an area where the trees grow dense, thick, spiky brambles sprouting up between the trunks. There are dozens of types of tree in this forest and I recognise precisely none of them. We pass one copse whose skinny pale bodies ascend far out of sight; another bunch have thick, plaited trunks, knotted with holes, like something out of a fairy tale. As we get further into the forest, the atmosphere begins to change. It's growing darker, pale green light turning grey-green as the rays of the sun struggle to penetrate the heavy coverage above.

Then I feel something.

186

I stop, holding an arm in front of Dan to silently halt him. Further down the path, the stag stops, looks back at us and bobs his head, the message clear: we need to follow. Dan meets my eyes, questioning, and I give a small shake of my head. We can't go on. There's something waiting for us in those bushes. With another toss of his magnificent antlers, Actaeon moves off again, his twitching tail vanishing behind a tree trunk. We stare after him, dismayed. Then there's a crackling of branches and I forget all about the stag as I grab Dan's hand and yank him hurriedly behind a tree.

We crouch there, Dan's body pressed close to mine to evade sight, my heart beating double time – and not just because of the unknown threat. I have a moment to appreciate the comforting, heartbreaking sensation of proximity to the man I love, and then the brambles crack as loud as gunfire, trodden by something that, by its laboured breathing and thunderous footfall, is a damn sight heftier than a hare.

We stare, transfixed, as the bushes part.

'Wha—' Dan says and then, eyes widening, '*Oh*.'

'Oh' doesn't really do it justice. I'd have gone for 'ARGGGGHHH!' myself, as a gigantic, hoary head emerges from the undergrowth. Two enormous sharp-pointed tusks curl up from a giant snout, while from the creature's mouth two further mighty sword-like tusks extend, with a couple of extra nasty-looking teeth protruding from either side for good measure.

Dan and I crouch behind the tree, frozen in horror, as the animal lumbers towards us, head down, cavernous nostrils snuffling the earth. When its whole body emerges into view, dashed are any hopes that the animal might have a dispro-portionately large bonce. This fucker is roughly the size of a small elephant.

I look at Dan and place a finger to my lips.

He widens his eyes, like: *You think?*

I return my gaze to the creature. It looks like a boar, except that it is impossibly huge, like something from the Jurassic era. I seem unable to drag my eyes away from those tusks. If this monster gets hold of us, Dan and I are going to meet our maker as a pair of jumbo kebabs.

The animal snorts and tosses its head, tiny intelligent eyes gleaming. I try to calm my mind and remember what I know about boars. I don't think they have the best eyesight or hearing. If we can just stay here, wait it out, we might get away with this.

The beast snuffles closer, bobbing its head as it swishes through the foliage, baring jagged and terrible teeth. The feeling I get is more potent than anything I've experienced so far, a kind of raw and bristling power, a deep, intense urge for destruction. The closer the animal draws, the more overwhelming the feeling, until the lust to maim and mangle is like hands around my skull, and I recoil despite myself, pushing backwards into Dan, unsteadying him. A branch snaps under his feet.

The boar swings its heavy head aloft and sweeps its gaze over the terrain. For a moment, as we crouch there, perfectly still, not even daring to breathe, I really believe that it is going to miss us, but then it sniffs the air, plants down one heavy, hairy trotter and then another. Little piggy eyes gleam and I feel its glee, black and terrible. Then, rearing its mighty tusks, it makes directly for us.

What wild pigs do have, I belatedly recall, is a superior sense of smell.

I meet Dan's terrified eyes. 'RUN!'

We run, while behind us the snorting snarling boar thunders, crashing through branches, emitting groans and grunts of excitement.

I try to use our relatively small size to our advantage, slipping through thin openings in the trees, leaping across the stream, but still the boar gallops after us, huffing joyfully, enjoying the chase. We zig and zag and zig again, but it's no use. It's tracking our scent; we have no way to evade it, no matter how many trees we run through. You really have to hand it to those mighty nostrils.

Then I realise – there is one direction this ungainly whopper can't follow us.

'We need to go up!' I shout over my shoulder and then, grasping the lower branches of the nearest tree, I climb haphazardly, hand over foot, grazing my palms and the inside of my thighs, feeling nothing but the numbness of pig-related panic. Dan is right behind me, going steadily hand over hand. I find a seat on a high, strong branch, I reach down and pull him up just as the boar rounds the corner and, realising that we have ascended out of reach, lets out a terrible bellow.

The boar paws the ground, snorting its frustration, its lust for human meat unsated. Dan peers down at the frothing animal. 'That,' he says, with winning understatement, 'is a very big pig.'

I nod my wholehearted agreement as I stare bleakly at the hairy beast. Then something comes back to me, a picture from one of Dan's books.

'Hang on,' I say. 'I think it might be the Erymanthian boar.'

'Okay. And that is?'

'Horrible mythical beast.'

Dan peers down again. 'Yeah,' he says. 'Kinda got that.'

'One of Heracles' labours was to catch it,' I add.

'Okay, great! How did he go about it?'

I squint, trying to recall the story, brightening as I remember. Then, 'Oh.' I look at Dan ruefully. 'He herded it into snow.'

'No problem,' Dan says, looking around the sunlit woods. 'We'll just make this tree our home for six months and then ... seize our chance!'

I stare down dolefully at the pig. 'But it can't climb,' I say. 'I'm *almost* sure of it.'

'I'm going to take a punt and say that, out of the two of us, I was the reader.'

I'm about to zing back a witty retort when I hear something else: a sort of sawing sound. I peer down from the tree to see the boar moving its head rhythmically from side to side. To my astonishment, I realise that it's grinding away at the trunk with its terrible tusks. I watch, awed into silence, clinging to my perch as the boar saws and saws and chunks of the tree trunk are steadily hacked away.

'Well, this is nice,' Dan says, sounding so much like his old self that I can't help but laugh. 'How long do you think it can keep that up?'

I glance down again. The boar is foaming at the chops, mean little eyes lit up with its mission. 'Honestly? I think as long as it takes to fell the tree. It didn't get a mention in the ancient myths for nothing.'

We sit there for a while, listening to the boar's insistent sawing and contemplating our fate.

'So, ahem,' Dan says, clearing his throat, 'going back to what you showed me before. About us.'

I stare at him. 'You're seriously going to have this conversation when I'm stuck up a tree hiding from a giant pig?'

'Well, yeah.' He grins. 'You can't run away, can you?'

'Is this a sneaky tactic to make me feel better about my almost certain death?' I raise an eyebrow. 'Because it's working.'

Dan laughs. 'Frida,' he says, 'I want to say something.' He pauses. 'When you woke up at Psyche's after taking the ambrosia and told me that we were just good friends, my first thought was, Oh, fuck.'

I look at him, frowning. 'Why?'

'Because I already knew that I definitely had more-than-friendly feelings towards you, feelings that must have come from when we knew each other before.'

A flush climbs my cheeks at his words and my heart pounds. 'How?'

'Well, I kept wanting to touch you and follow you around and stuff. And I felt sort of inexplicably happy around you and kind of empty when you were gone.'

'Oh,' I say, my voice small. 'Same.'

Dan smiles. 'So, when you told me about just being friends,

I figured that maybe I held a torch for you but I'd never actually told you. Or that I'd told you how I felt and you didn't feel the same.' He shrugs. 'And obviously I had no way of knowing either way.'

'Oh,' I say again. I stare at him, taking in what this means. I think back to Dan's behaviour in Medusa's, his reaction afterwards. *Do I look smaller?* All these efforts, they were just to be the Dan he was. Because . . . he still loves me.

'Hang on,' I say. 'You said I reminded you of your sister!'

'Well, I had to say something, didn't I? Didn't want to let you know that I was mooning over you just like poor old droopy-faced Maurice.' He pauses. 'Wait, you didn't put the whammy on me, too, did you?'

'I did not!' I say indignantly and then I see that he's kidding. I prod him with my foot. 'No, it turns out that thwarting the plans of an evil love god are the perfect conditions for two people to fall madly in love.' I smile sadly. 'Well, until you get to the whole "forgetting each other exists" element.'

Dan meets my eyes. 'Look, I know I'm not him. And I know that must be hard.'

I stare at him for a long moment, thoughtfully. 'Do you know that you didn't actually want to be the Oracle?'

Dan blinks at this sudden change of topic. 'Didn't I? Why not?'

'Where do I start?' I shrug. 'It was a terrible burden, the visions were horribly painful, you had to do your part in fulfilling some ancient prophecy instead of being able to live your own life. You just wanted to be normal. We both did.'

'Okay.' His brow furrows. I can see he doesn't understand what I'm getting at.

'How you are now,' I say gently, 'it's like seeing the Dan you would have been if you'd never been born into the Oracle line. You met me before I knew what I was – twice. But I never got to see the normal Dan. And although, yes,' I nod, 'it's hard that you lost your memories of us, there's an upside.' I smile. 'Dan, you've had two years of being a regular guy. A life where supernatural threats were just stories you could enjoy, where you didn't have to bear the burden of being the Oracle and saving people's lives.' I meet his eyes. 'And I'm glad for you that you had that. And I'm glad that I get to meet this version of you.' I smile at him and say softly, 'It doesn't make me think less of you. It just makes me feel like I know you more.'

Dan's eyes are shining as he listens to my words. We smile at each other, suddenly bashful.

'Does this make everything even more complicated or much, much simpler?' he asks.

'Yes,' I say.

He laughs. Then he meets my gaze, serious now. 'Okay, so . . . we take things slow. We do what we have to do, we stop Anteros and then, after all of this is over, we go for coffee,' he says. 'We start again.'

A rush of happiness fills my heart. 'Coffee sounds lovely. Of course,' I say, peering down, 'this may all be something of a moot point due to the worsening porcine situation.'

'Well, I might have had another Very Good Idea about that.' Dan looks down and then he springs into action. He moves to sit on a different branch, peers downwards and then shifts again. I watch him, wondering what he's up to as he glances across the forest and then looks back at me.

'It involves us climbing from tree to tree.'

'You do realise that if we fall, we're pig food?' I raise an eyebrow.

He looks at me, a familiar mischievous glint in his eye. 'Then don't fall.'

$$\longrightarrow$$

Dan goes first, reasoning that if the branches can hold his weight, then they ought to be able to hold mine and we clamber from branch to branch and tree to tree. But as we travel the boar just catches wind of the moving scent. Whatever Dan's plan is, I don't think it's going to work. This beast is never giving up.

Eventually, on the fourth tree along, Dan stops and rests. Panting, arms aching, I join him.

'This one might work,' Dan says.

I look around me. We're standing in the flat base of the trunk. Above us branches stretch up in a bowl shape. Dan is staring down at the sturdy tree trunk, one of the story-book types, with its twists and hollows. 'Work how, exactly?'

In answer, Dan leans down. 'Hey!' he shouts. 'Hey! We're over here!'

I look at him aghast as the boar jerks its head towards Dan's calls and then lumbers around the tree to where Dan is bellowing.

'What the hell are you doing?'

He turns. 'Do you trust me?'

I meet his eyes. 'Yes,' I say, 'I do.'

Dan nods, a smile on his lips, and then returns to boar-baiting: 'Come on then, you glorified bacon sandwich!'

Enraged by Dan's taunts, the boar emits a furious bellow. Then, to my surprise, it turns and trots away. Maybe Erymanthian boars are repelled by personal insults? Alas, no. In fact, the pig is just giving itself a run-up. As we watch in nervous silence, the boar turns, lowers its head, thrusts out its tusks, and with an exuberant snort, charges at the tree. I feel the impact, the tree actually shakes, and then . . . all goes still. There's some snuffling, a lot of heavy breathing and some rather hideous squealing.

I look down. The boar's complicated array of tusks have become hooked into the twists and holes of the trunk. The creature shakes its head, but the more it struggles, the more embedded its protuberances become.

I stare at Dan, open mouthed.

'We'd better get out of here,' he says. 'It won't stay trapped for ever.'

We climb to the next tree and the next, until we are so far from the Erymanthian boar that we can no longer hear its agonised, frustrated bellows. Then we shin down and land back on the forest floor.

I look at Dan. 'That was amazing!' I say.

Dan smiles and reaches a hand to my face and my heart flutters as he plucks a leaf from my hair. 'Got a bit of tree on you,' he says. He gazes into my eyes. I gaze back. Time stops.

Then I remember where we are and why we're here and I snap back to our mission.

'We need to find Actaeon,' I say. I turn in a circle, scanning, but there's no sign of the stag. And yet I can sense that Daphne is waiting for us. I have to trust that she'll send us a sign. We stand quietly for a moment, listening to the sounds of the forest, and then I hear something: a fluttering. Dan and I look at one another, alarmed – has the boar found us again? But no. It's a large white bird, perched in a tree ahead of us on the path. A white raven.

As soon as we see it, the corvid lifts its wings and flies to the next tree.

Dan looks at me and I nod. We know what to do.

After a while, the raven leads us to a clearing. The bird has come to rest on the upper branches of a tall tree. Actaeon is here, too. He looks up from grazing, head cocked, as though asking, *What took you?*

'Do you think this is where we find her?' Dan asks.

I look up at the raven, preening its ivory-coloured feathers, glance over at Actaeon who is nibbling a long stem of grass. Neither seems in a hurry to go anywhere.

'I think so.'

I walk around the clearing, the forest floor soft underfoot, and then I notice something. One of the trees stands slightly further forwards. It looks different to the others, too. It has pale silvery bark and delicate leaves, its branches strong and slender. As they rise, they form balletic twists, like the limbs of a dancer in flight. I walk over to the tree. Dan follows.

'This is her?'

196

'Maybe.'

'It does look like some of the sculptures of Daphne I've seen online,' Dan muses.

I contemplate the tree. Medusa gave us no instructions on how to communicate with Daphne but the gorgon came here to visit her friend, so I'd just assumed Daphne could speak, that she was a kind of person. But maybe not. Or maybe she only transforms for certain people.

I clear my throat. 'Daphne,' I say in the exaggeratedly respectful tone I usually reserve for high court judges and airport security staff. 'Nymph of the forest, we come for help. Please grant us our request, for the sake of mortal- and celestial-kind.'

We stare at the tree. Still Daphne doesn't speak. I look at Dan. 'Maybe she doesn't understand human language?'

'What are we supposed to do, rustle at her?'

I shoot him a look. I don't know what this forest is doing to him but he's sounding more like the old Dan every minute. I glance at Daphne again.

'Perhaps she's just asleep?' I say hopefully. 'Daphne,' I say in a softer voice, as I touch a branch gently and hope I'm not inadvertently fondling her anywhere indecent. 'Can you give us a sign? Can you hear us? We've come for the prophecy. We need your help.'

And then we hear a voice, as melodic as a waterfall, as cool as dewy grass on a spring morning, as Daphne says, 'Why on earth are you talking to that tree?'

Chapter 20

We turn hastily to witness a vision standing before us, though admittedly we have to crane our necks to get the full picture.

Perhaps it should come as little surprise that Daphne is tall. I mean, she was transformed into a tree, not a shrub. Still, she's a startling and magnificent sight, eight feet or so, with long, slender brown limbs and a scattering of bright green leaves across one shoulder, which flow down her torso, toga-style. She has a wide, square, handsome face, and from the top of her head sprouts a mass of skinny branches, like finely woven dreadlocks.

As she peers down at us, I see that her conker-brown eyes are ringed with coffee-coloured concentric circles. Smiling, she emits such calm centredness that it's all I can do to stop myself from grabbing her in an embrace. I never understood tree hugging before but now I totally get it.

Daphne glances over to the spindly tree we've been attempting to engage in conversation and raises a twiggy eyebrow.

'We ... er, thought that was you,' I explain.

Daphne dissolves into throaty laughter. 'Oh dear. Oh no,' she smiles, 'you won't get any sense out of that old thing.' At this, the silver tree shakes itself, lifting its leafy head with a grumble and then settles back into repose. Daphne gives us a knowing smile. 'See what I mean?'

I cast a look at Dan and find him staring up at Daphne with a familiar gooey look on his face. I jab him with my elbow.

'Daphne, I'm Frida, descendant of Eros, and this is Dan, the Oracle.' I pause. 'Dan had a vision that you were guarding a secret prophecy, one that can help us stop Anteros.'

'Yes,' Daphne says sadly. 'Anteros. His power has grown so strong.'

I stare down at the earth and scuff it with the toe of my sandal. 'We were on our way here two years ago,' I say. 'We didn't make it.'

'Time moves differently here,' Daphne says lightly with a gentle shrug. 'You're not so late, really.' Then she smiles again and I feel that smile in every part of my body. 'Now,' she says brightly, 'I do indeed have the prophecy but first, you must join me for tea. It is a while since I have had guests.' She frowns. 'My friend Medusa used to visit, but I have not seen her for ... oh, I don't know how long!' Daphne sighs. 'Ah well,' she says, her eyes faraway, and then her gaze brightens as she refocuses on us. 'But now *you* are here. How lovely. Tea?' I look around the clearing for brew-making facilities and come up short.

'Er.' I look at Dan and he nods eagerly. Seems for Daphne, he's willing to let his no-eat no-drink-with-immortals rule slide.

'Lovely,' I say. 'Tea, yes.'

'Wonderful,' Daphne says and looks skyward. 'Then up we go.'

$$\longrightarrow$$

'I was quite a different creature before Anteros shot me.'

We're sitting in Daphne's home. Imagine a tree house, except it's actually a tree palace. Above us, a domed roof of parrot feathers creates a stained-glass-window effect, reflecting the light in many colours across the wooden floor. Daphne sits before us in a throne of splayed branches. Dan and I are seated in two hammock-like contraptions made from woven grass, easily the strangest and most comfortable seating I have ever had the joy of sinking my buttocks into.

As Daphne talks, we sip a strange, wonderfully fragrant tea from cups made from large nut shells. A mouse scurries out from Daphne's chair, perches on her lap and looks at us with its tiny black eyes. I feel the attention it gives us, whiskers flicking, appraising these new arrivals, and then, in a blink, it's gone. I have a moment to wonder if this ability to know the inner life of the animals will stay with me after I leave the forest and, if so, how long I can stand the emotions of pigeons and rats and magpies before I go quietly mad. But a part of me knows that this amplification of my powers is restricted to the forest. No rat dreams for me.

Daphne turns her wise eyes on us. 'You can defeat Anteros, but first, you must understand his power.'

'Oh, I understand it, trust me.'

Daphne smiles. 'You may think so, Frida. But do not make the mistake of underestimating Anteros.' Her eyes turn grave. 'It was Apollo's failure to understand Anteros's nature that led me to this fate.'

'What do you mean?'

Daphne bows her beautiful head. 'Apollo and I were in love.' She sees my surprise. 'Oh, I know that's not what the stories tell, but you know how these things get twisted along the years.' I nod and she continues: 'Apollo used to mock Anteros, derided him as a mere child playing with toys.' Daphne threads her skinny fingers together. 'I warned Apollo to be careful, but he didn't take it seriously. To a mighty Olympian, Anteros was just a child.' She sighs, her gaze sorrowful. 'But even back then, some of us could sense Anteros's ambition.'

'Ambition for what?' Dan asks.

'Revenge,' Daphne says simply. 'On Apollo, on his brother and, especially, on Zeus, who dared to wield authority over Anteros. For a while after the Apollo slight, Anteros took no action. That is also his strength,' she says darkly, 'his incredible patience.' She hunches knotty shoulders at the memory. 'But eventually he wrought his vengeance on Apollo, as I knew he would.'

'What did he do?' I ask.

Daphne shakes her head. 'I cannot tell you what happened next, it is beyond words. But I can show you if you are

201

willing.' She stretches out a hand. Dan flashes me a worried look and I shrug. If Daphne wants to show me something that's going to help us stop Anteros, I have to see it. With a deep breath, I reach out and take one of Daphne's warm, rough palms. As I do, a pulse passes between us and –

– I'm standing in the forest watching an ancient scene play out. No, not just watching, *feeling*. Apollo has come to visit Daphne, and I see her there as she was, a delicate naiad nymph, hair coiled in a plait, smooth skin covered in a white, gossamer-thin robe, eyes alight as she spies her lover. I experience the excitement enlivening her body as she watches him, taking in Apollo's broad chest adorned by a bright red robe, strong arms opening to greet her. Her lover, her shining god of poetry, of music, of truth—

Then Daphne stops, alert. She hears something, sees a movement in the trees behind Apollo. I feel her panic; it starts as a seed and then blooms into something bleak and terrible as she sets eyes on the intruder to this private scene: Anteros, the dark-eyed god. His bow is raised and Daphne knows he's come to seek his revenge.

She tries to shout, to warn Apollo, who continues to approach, smiling, oblivious, but just as Daphne's voice pierces the silent forest, Anteros fires a golden arrow that whizzes through the trees and strikes Apollo in the back. Her lover's eyes are still on her, and the naiad has just enough time to see the adoration drain from Apollo's face, to be replaced by a hectic and violent lust. Horror trickles through her as she understands what Anteros has done, then the love god redraws his bow and fires once more and Daphne is struck by a golden arrow tipped with lead. I feel it now just as she felt it then, an agonising violation and then a shadow crawling into her chest, smothering her heart. Daphne feels herself being overtaken, her light extinguished, love seeping away, and in its place, a huge and endless hatred for Apollo, for love in all its forms.

Daphne runs, then, from her lover and from love, the shadow inside her urging her on, tormenting her about the terrible fate that awaits if Apollo catches her and now I feel choked by her panic, a wild and uncontrollable force, as Apollo pursues, consumed by his obsession, his only aim to capture Daphne, to possess her, to conquer her ...

Both know this forest well and as swiftly as Apollo chases, Daphne evades capture. Anteros looses another arrow, a dart at Daphne's feet to make her stumble and, her terror mounting, she shakily picks herself up and resumes her flight. But Apollo is gaining, her mad lover is almost upon her now, eyes crazed with the urge to consume, to destroy, and she cannot let him catch her, she will do anything, anything. In her desperation, Daphne calls out to her father, Peneus, the river god, beseeching salvation and there is only one thing her father can do to save her and it is a kind of death, but Daphne begs and she begs and heartbroken, her father relents.

Daphne feels herself begin to change.

Her legs fuse painfully to the earth and as her arms splinter and extend, reaching up to the stars, she screams a scream of pure, primal agony. And yet, within her torment, I can feel a black and bitter joy; better this, she believes, than to be *his*, to let Apollo take her, possess her; better to be untouchable, she vows, even as her skin toughens, her body thickens and her mouth is woven shut.

She's in the last throes of transformation when Apollo comes upon her and it is then that Anteros removes the magic. He wants them to know what they've done to each other. Wants Apollo to watch Daphne leave him, wants Daphne, in these last moments of herself, to see the stricken face of the lover she has lost for ever. A single tear escapes Daphne's eyes but then these too are sewn shut as Daphne completes her transformation. And while Apollo weeps in horror and shame, Anteros looks upon his work and he smiles, because he said that he would make Apollo pay and he likes the pain, you see, he thrives on the—

I jerk backwards, gasping for breath, and Dan places a hand on my shoulder. I nod at him to let him know I'm okay. Daphne is watching me, measuring me with her gaze.

'You understand?'

I nod again, unable to speak. Daphne bows her head, satisfied.

'So that is my story.' She gives a gentle sigh, like the whispering of the wind. 'I died to my old form but Zeus created a place for me here in the forest where I would always be safe. Eventually I found new life, though I am not as I was.' She pauses. 'It was a long time later that Eros came to visit me.'

I exchange a surprised look with Dan. 'Eros came to see you here? Why?'

'Because of something he feared would happen. He said he needed to leave me with a message. A prophecy. For the one who would stop his brother.'

204

My heart lifts. The prophecy! Finally, we're going to get some answers.

I stare up at Daphne. 'Can you tell us?'

In answer, the nymph stands and parts the scattering of leaves on her torso, revealing her bare brown midriff. Etched into her skin (well, technically her bark) is a symbol. It's a little like the hearts containing initials that you see carved into tree trunks, except this is not a heart. This is something else. It looks like a crude human stick figure, wearing a pointy hat and with an extra pair of arms.

'That's it?'

Daphne nods.

I frown at the symbol. It's less ancient prophecy, more random graffiti. As I stare at it, a strong feeling of recognition passes through me but it's nothing I can grasp hold of and it passes as quickly as it came.

'What does it mean?' Dan asks.

'Eros said that the chosen mortal would understand when the time was right,' Daphne says, gazing down at us with a beatific smile.

Dan flicks me an enquiring glance. I shake my head bleakly. 'I've no idea. I've never seen it before. Maybe in one of your books?' I say and then stop at his regretful expression. Because he doesn't have any books, does he? The old Dan might have recognised this as ancient Greek or Minoan or Etruscan. This Dan doesn't have any idea what it is, and neither do I. But maybe Psyche will know. We can research. We still have five days.

'Do you mind if I . . .?' Dan asks Daphne and then, taking

a pencil and paper from his back pocket, he begins to sketch the symbol.

'Did Eros tell you what he was afraid his brother would do?' I ask her. 'What this symbol is supposed to avert? Did he tell you who Anteros was working with?'

Daphne shakes her head and, as Dan finishes his drawing, she lets her leaves fall back into place and retakes her seat on the throne. 'This is all I have, Frida. I do not know what Anteros is planning, or who else his actions might serve, only that it will bring a great darkness.'

'But why hide the prophecy here?' Dan asks. 'Why not let the Oracle line pass it down, so that we'd be ready when the time came?' He rubs at his jaw. 'I mean, it would have been nice to have a few centuries to work out what it means, rather than, you know, less than a week.'

Daphne stares out over the treetops. 'The secret was too dangerous for any mortal to keep. Eros trusted me only because I understood Anteros's power. He knew that I would stay loyal.' She shakes her head sadly. 'He said it wasn't safe for any mortal to see this, not until it became absolutely necessary.'

I get a dark feeling inside at her words. 'And now it is necessary?'

Daphne nods. 'Now,' she says softly, 'we have finally reached the endgame.'

Chapter 21

Somehow in the time we've been with Daphne dusk has fallen. Dan and I stand in the clearing below the tree palace as Daphne regards us solemnly.

'There are hard times to come,' she tells me, 'but have faith, Frida.' She smiles suddenly. 'Remember, an acorn only becomes an oak when it is time.' Then she opens her arms wide to us and we finally get to hug this tree. It feels as good as I knew it would and I don't want to let go. But after a minute Daphne steps back, casting a worried look across the forest.

'Go quickly now,' she says. 'Follow Actaeon. Do not linger and do not stray off the path, no matter what you see or hear. There are dark things in the woods at night.' Dan and I exchange nervous glances – what dark things, exactly? – and then, with a last longing look at this glorious tree goddess, we follow the stag out of the clearing.

Daphne is right: something is different about the forest now. I can still hear the crickets and the birds and the gentle rushing of the stream but the atmosphere has changed, and other strange noises drift on the air sending a shiver up my spine and causing my chest to flutter with unease. I make sure to keep my eyes firmly on Actaeon as the forest grows darker around us.

'So,' Dan says, 'that symbol contains the answer.' He pauses. 'I've got to admit, I was expecting something more. A book, maybe. A scroll, at the very least.'

'I know,' I say ruefully. 'It's not much, but if Eros left it for us, it must be enough. Possibly it's a clue to a weapon.' I think about this. 'Maybe Psyche can help us to translate it?' I shrug. 'We'll get back to hers and take it from there.' I think about the image, that strange-looking figure, and once again experience a glimmer of something like recognition, but then it slips away.

Dan turns to look at me. 'Whatever it is, we'll handle it. Together.'

I meet his gaze. This journey into the woods has changed things between us. We're closer to the people we once were. What does that mean? I have no idea. But it gives me a warm feeling inside. I smile at Dan.

'Yes,' I say. 'Together.' And we carry on walking.

After a while Dan slows. 'Can you hear something?'

The four words you really don't want to hear in a dark enchanted forest. I stop. Listen. 'No, what?'

Dan frowns and stares through the copse of trees to our left. 'I think I can hear ... music.'

I listen more closely and yes, he's right. The faintest trill of pipes, a rhythmic beat of drums, voices joined in singing. Ahead of us, Actaeon stamps his hoof and I nudge Dan.

'Come on,' I say. 'We can't lose him.'

We follow Actaeon along the path but oddly the music doesn't fade, rather it seems to follow us, emitting from somewhere un-glimpsable through the trees. We continue on through the darkness, the only light from the moon and the stars. Branches crack underfoot, an owl hoots, huge eyes watchful. To our left, I glimpse the flashing black-orange of a fire and catch the scent of burning wood carried enticingly on the air. As I keep up my pace, I stare through the trees – are those figures I can see, twirling and whirling to the music, or just shadows?

As I crane my neck to get a better look, my toe hits a tree root and I lurch to the ground, landing on my already well-grazed hands and knees. Hearing my sudden yelp, Dan looks behind him and, when he sees me on all fours, he starts heading back towards me.

'No!' I shout. 'Don't stop! Don't lose Actaeon!'

Biting his lip, Dan nods and turns, his eye on the stag, and then, with one anxious glance back at me, he continues on the path but slowly, giving me time to catch up. I clamber to my feet, brush my stinging hands and hurry after him. Ahead of me the trail curves out of sight and as I follow I see first Actaeon and then Dan on the path. But when I round the same curve, surely no more than five seconds later, the route diverges into two. And both sides are empty.

I stand there, mind blank. It can't be. Where are they?

'Dan!'

I stay very still, listening. But there's nothing. Just the music, the drumming, the beguiling chorus of voices, that enticing aroma of burning wood.

'Dan!' I shout again, a note of panic creeping into my voice. 'Dan, I can't see you! Which way did you go?'

No reply. The forest has swallowed them up. I stare into the dark mass of trees, stretching gnarled limbs into a navy-blue sky teeming with stars. I can't see ahead, can't begin to fathom my way out. Left or right? Left or right? I take the left path, frightened now, praying I will catch sight of Dan and Actaeon again when the path straightens out. I picture it vividly, soothing myself, thinking how relieved I'll feel when I finally spot Dan. How we will laugh about how I nearly got lost in the woods.

As I walk, a strange thing happens. The music is getting louder, the drum beat stronger, the rhythm needling its way into my brain. Those voices joined together in bewitching harmony sound so sweet and so close. I should be leaving it behind me, but instead, I seem to be constantly moving towards it.

'Keep walking, Frida,' I mutter to myself. 'Stick to the path.'

A few metres on, I see three flat, even, stepping stones planted in the stream, invitingly. Across the water, through a gap in the trees, I glimpse that fierce orange fire-glow. I sniff the heady woodsmoke and catch other scents too, something rich and deep like ripe berries ready to burst with fecundity, the aroma of dark green leaves, the scent of damp earth just after a rain shower. Through a gap in the trees I see the dancers. In shadows cast by firelight they sway to the rhythm and there's something about this music. It's ... intoxicating, the beat matching the pulse of my blood, teaming up with my heartbeat.

Calling me.

I take one, two, three steps across the river, Dan, Actaeon and the way home now forgotten.

$$\longrightarrow$$

Using the fire as my beacon, I push my way through tangles of ivy and emerge, scratched and berry-stained, into a large circular clearing. Tall trees stand in an almost perfect circle, their slender trunks smothered in ivy and vines that sag with plump fruits. The climbing vegetation is meshed so tightly from tree to tree that it looks like a curtain, and the clearing, a stage. And in the centre, the fire.

It's even bigger than I imagined, a tepee of branches burning strong and bright, mesmerising. Around it, a dozen or so figures circle, whirling, singing and holding instruments or clasping shallow goblets, eyes flashing in the firelight. They don't appear to have noticed this interloper and so I stand there for a moment and watch.

The men I thought I saw, the ones playing double-flutes and pounding drums, are not men at all. They have partially male bodies and they dance on two legs but when they reel past me, illuminated in the firelight, I see that they have mane-like hair, bestial faces, the ears and the tails of horses and – I blink at this – enormous genitalia.

211

Satyrs.

The women are beautiful and wild, dressed in the skins of fawns, each holding a large staff from which more ivy tumbles. A green halo of vegetation circles their crowns and their long dark hair flows and whips as they dance. The word comes to me, whether a distant memory from an ancient book or simply a gift from the forest: these women are Maenads. The *Frenzied ones*. And yes, the women's eyes are glazed, ecstatic, as they sway to the music, tapping their wands to the forest floor and making something flow from the spot where it lands. I edge closer and watch as a rich, red liquid gushes forth, see a Satyr dip down in one fluid movement and refill his glass. Wine. Get one of those babies for your dinner party, and be the envy of your friends.

I look up to find someone watching. A large bearded figure in purple robes stands on the other side of the fire. This is the one they follow, he's the reason they gather, and he is the one who called me here. His name arrives, too: *Dionysus*.

I want to go, then, to turn on my heel and flee, but also, I don't want to leave. Oh no, I want to stay. To step further into the circle, to merge with this joyous, abandoned celebration. Daphne said, *Do not linger . . . there are dark things in the woods at night*. But I look at Dionysus and he smiles an easy, louche sort of smile, tips his golden goblet towards me, and the movement breaks me free from indecision and fear and I step into the circle to join the dance.

I find myself whirling and swaying to the music; it's easy, really, you just have to let it take you. I am dimly aware of Dionysus weaving through the dancers, making for me, and then, just as quickly, he's here, dark eyes burning into mine, their colour a deep reddish brown, and he doesn't just *look* at me with those eyes, he drinks me in. I'm overcome by his deep aroma of dark fruits and spices as the god loops an arm through mine and spins me until I am dizzy. 'You're just in time,' he murmurs into my ear, a ticklish, delicious sensation.

'In time for what?' I ask dreamily.

'For the song, of course,' he says, and then he releases me and I am alone.

Somehow now, in my hand, there's a goblet. I bend my nose to the cup, inhaling the scent – herby and plummy with the faint trace of honey and tar – and as I take a sip a fire is lit inside me, the *music* is inside me now, just as the music is inside the Satyrs and the Maenads and was there something I was meant to do? Someone I needed to find?

No, there is only the wine, only the music, only the fire. Only the song, now beginning.

I'm just in time.

It starts slowly, a drum beat marking the tempo, the Satyrs piping a haunting tune and the women's voices rising to meet it. I'm distracted for a moment by the sight of someone else pushing through the tangle of ivy: a mortal man, his eyes wide as he takes in the scene. He scans the dancers, sees me and something crosses his face, something like recognition. Do I know him? Then Dionysus approaches the mortal, blocking him from view. When I look again, the man has a goblet in his hand, and now he, too, is joining the dance, his eyes alight with pleasure in the fire-glow.

I gaze into the black and orange heart of the fire and I see

213

something: figures, pictures. A story is being played out in the flames. We circle the blaze, bodies swaying, as the Satyrs and the Maenads begin to sing. This is an ancient tale, telling of the powerful Titan King Kronos, who overthrew his father, Uranus, and became the ruler of the earth.

At first, Kronos was a benevolent king, presiding over the first generation of mortals in a golden age of prosperity and peace. But over time Kronos began to fear that he, too, would be usurped by his children and a dark and jealous anger grew within him. I see Kronos now in the crackling fire, and I am filled with terror, but then I take a drink and I sway and I laugh, because this is just a story, first told millennia ago, and what harm can come to us here?

The more Kronos's paranoia grew, the greater his darkness, the greater his cruelty, until his son, the Olympian Zeus, vowed to overthrow him, helped by his brothers Hades and Poseidon. And in the fire, an epic, torturous battle plays out in seconds: Zeus defeats the Titan king and ends his reign. In the orange licks and whorls, I watch as Zeus throws Kronos into Tartarus, the terrible hell prison that lies fathoms below the Underworld, interning the ousted king behind high walls of bronze. Zeus knows that, sealed in Tartarus, his father's nature will only grow more corrupted. How to seal the walls so that Kronos will never escape?

We continue to circle, turning and whirling, as the women sing and the Satyrs beat out their tune. Across the clearing I see the mortal man, dazed, his face flushed, dancing in the arms of a Maenad, her dark hair whipping across his cheek.

Now the music becomes high and hopeful as it tells of all

the ways Zeus tried to seal the walls, but I know how these things go, there will be three tries and only the third will stick. And so it is: Zeus first tried the power of worship to hold those bronze walls but worship would not hold them. At this the flutes become sombre and the dancers laugh and groan and drink and the song goes on. Then Zeus tried to fortify the walls with the power of mercy but mercy was not strong enough, and we drink and reel and laugh, because this is a story, only a story.

Then the music slows and I'm snatched up again in the arms of the purple-robed god, his fingers gripping my arms as he sways me, gazing into my eyes, and the song becomes reverent, now, almost a hymn. I'm carried along in a slow and drowsy waltz. The Satyrs and the Maenads and the mortal have dropped away. There's only a single drum, there's only me and Dionysus, gliding in circles around the fire, rising and falling to the rhythmic, ominous beat.

Dionysus leans down and whispers something in my ear, two words I don't understand but which spark something inside me nonetheless, and then the flutes start up again, the dancers retake the floor, the music lifts its tempo, and I am spun and spun, and can hardly catch my breath, and in the fire it is the third and final try, and Zeus consults Eros, who tells him the walls must be sealed with something that can never be destroyed.

At this, a trickle of awareness runs through me. There's something I need to pay attention to, something I have to do. Held tightly in Dionysus's grip, I look across the fire and I see someone, the mortal, and it's Dan! Of course it is Dan! How did I not know him? Dan's eyes meet mine, suddenly clear and shining with fear, but then a laughing Maenad snatches his hand, catching him in a jig, holding a goblet to his lips and pouring, and then Dionysus spins me again, and my eyes are drawn back to the fire. The song is about to reach its climax.

And in the orange burning heart, I watch as Zeus, on that magical third attempt, seals the bronze walls of Tartarus with love.

Everything goes quiet, then, everything slows, as I understand the truth. This is no ancient tale. They are singing our story.

And oh, Eros, what have you done?

I try to struggle from Dionysus's grasp, but the god just grips me closer, his hot body against mine, his grin loose and lascivious, eyes the colour of spilled wine. I bring a knee up to his groin with a vicious jab, and then I wrench away, spinning in panic, I need Dan, oh God, we need to get out of here, we have to stop this. But I'm trapped in a circle of dancers, the music is a hectic tattoo, the dancing wild and abandoned and there are no words any more, just music, mad and furious, blocking all thought. I'm caught up and tossed from one set of arms to another, flames flickering over naked bodies, a Satyr leers over me, crushes grape juice into my mouth, and as a sweet feeling of bliss permeates my limbs, I am tossed again and land in strong arms.

Dan.

He stares down at me, green eyes alight with recognition, and something else. I go to speak, because wasn't there something we have to do? Some terrible thing we have to avert? But as we hold each other our eyes lock with desire, the pounding, rhythmic drum beat entering our bodies and flooding into our brains.

We move, as one, to that primal rhythm and soon all thought is gone. I am lost in him, lost in us, and there is no mission, no threat, no terrible destiny, there is only the ground under our feet, the fire in our veins, the frantic throb of music in our heartbeats, and Dan, pulling me closer and closer, until his wine-stained lips meet mine.

Chapter 22

A bird trills tunefully somewhere up above. I open my eyes, wincing at the strong light drilling its way through the branches and into my eyeballs. I'm lying on the forest floor, completely naked, a warm body spooning me. Heart thumping, I turn to see Dan, asleep, his lashes dark, his lips still reddened with wine.

Oh FUCK.

I stare at him, watching his broad chest rise and fall. I absolutely must not awaken him until I've wrapped my head around this. Carefully, silently, I push myself up on my elbow and, slipping from his embrace, I stand. I quietly gather up my underwear and sundress. My arms are covered in bramble scratches. The dress is muddy and torn, stained with wine. I go to put on my sandals, notice my feet and wince. I've danced them bloody.

Rubbing a sore head, I stare around. The ashes of the burned-out fire are the only evidence that anything happened here at all last night. Did we dream it? No. The truth lies heavy in my stomach like a stone. I wish I could believe we imagined it. But the fire, the dancers, the song of Zeus and Kronos. Dionysus. It was magic, yes, but it was also real. I close my eyes as a flash of memory returns: Dionysus leaning in, his aroma of berries and dark iron-rich leaves, his breath on my cheek and the two words he spoke.

My gaze is drawn again to Dan's sleeping form, travelling over his strong brown arms, those tattoos that I know so well and those that I don't. My gaze skitters over the parts of his body that once were becoming as familiar to me as my own, and last night's memories return in flashing scenes like a 'Previously, in Frida's ridiculous life' recap sequence. You really have to hand it to me, I can take fucked-up relationships to a whole new level.

Dan looks so peaceful, so perfect, I want to leave him sleeping. But I can't. The story told in the fire last night trickles back to me, forming a pool of cold water in my guts. This is bad. Like, really bad. I bend down and gently shake Dan's shoulder. He mutters and scrubs at his face and then he meets my eyes. For a moment I stop breathing, waiting for his reaction, and then a look comes over his face, a look I know well. I've seen it many times before and it fills my heart with joy.

'Looks like we skipped the coffee, then,' he says, his mouth quirking up in a smile.

'Apparently so,' I say, feeling instantly lighter in the heart.

Dan rubs sleepily at his face. 'That was ... er ... quite a night.'

'*Quite* a night,' I agree. 'But ... you're okay?'

Dan meets my eyes. 'More than okay,' he says and then he leans over and kisses me on the lips. As his tongue pushes into my mouth, I draw closer to him, put my hands on his warm body, his hand is on my bare thigh and— I force myself to break away. Meet his eyes. I bite my lip. 'Wow,' I say. 'I ... think this forest is still having an effect on us.'

'I don't think it's the forest.' Dan's gaze roves over me.

My whole body flushes and I look at him from under my lashes, suddenly shy. 'Dan,' I say, 'while I'd love nothing more than to stay here with you like this ...'

'We need to go.'

'Yes.'

'Absolutely. Definitely we do. Yes.' Neither of us moves. Dan traces a finger along my arm and my flesh puckers into goosebumps.

'Okay,' I say hastily. 'How about we start with getting you clothed?' I clamber up and pass Dan the cargo shorts, T-shirt and boxers discarded nearby.

As soon as he's dressed, we head out of the clearing and find a trail. I can feel the difference in the air around me, in the ground under my feet. Yesterday this place was something magical, something other. Today, it's an ordinary forest again, just trees and earth and sky. I sneak a glance at Dan. Now, it's we who have changed. I take out my phone. Miraculously, I have a signal. I locate us on the map and nod down the path. 'The car park is only five minutes this way.'

We walk, going slowly on our battered feet. Dan's hand reaches for mine and I feel a rush of warmth. I don't know what this is, but I do know that it's me and Dan, and it seems that, whatever this crazy destiny throws at us, we are meant to be together. We will always come back together.

I think we belong together.

We walk in silence for a while. 'So what we saw in the fire,' Dan says after a while. 'Kronos.' His face pales at the memory. 'That's what I saw in my vision, isn't it?'

I meet his eyes. 'I think so, yes.'

'So . . .' I can see Dan trying to wrap his head around it. 'If Anteros can convert enough mortals to The Love Delusion, mortal love, as a force, will weaken, the walls will fall and Kronos will be let loose on the earth?'

I nod. 'And after he's finished with us, Kronos will head straight for Olympus to take revenge on Zeus. Anteros wants Zeus and Eros usurped, destroyed, punished. Kronos is the only being in existence capable of that.' I shake my head. Daphne wasn't lying. Anteros really is one patient motherfucker.

I see Dan's stricken face. 'But we're not going to let any of that happen!' I say. 'We have the symbol, remember? We've still got four days to work it out. And also, last night, before we . . .' I flush. 'Well, you know. Dionysus said something to me. It felt important. I think it's going to help us.'

'Great,' Dan says eagerly. 'What was it?'

I rub at my head, trying to remember. I picture Dionysus, his scent, the way he gripped me as he whispered the phrase in my ear and the words come back to me. 'Anthropos Oysters!' I frown. 'No, that can't be right.'

221

'Anthropos Oysters,' Dan repeats. 'Well, Anthro means human or humanlike ...'

'Okay, so we're going to defeat Anteros with an army of human-oyster hybrids?'

'Well, as long as they bring the mussel,' Dan says and I roll my eyes as he grins.

'You're a dork,' I say fondly.

'Yes, but I'm *your* dork,' he says and as he meets my eyes, despite it all, I'm filled with happiness.

'Okay,' I say. 'Killer oysters ...' Reluctantly I let go of Dan's hand and take out my phone again. I type the words into a search engine and try a few different spellings of the second word. Eventually, the software corrects my spelling and I get a hit.

'Right, it's actually *Anthropos Oistos*; it's ancient Greek. It means—' I stop.

Dan turns to me. 'What is it?'

'Do you have the drawing of the prophecy?' My voice is shaky.

'Yeah, here you go.' Dan fishes it out of his back pocket and hands it to me. I unfold the piece of paper. Stare at it.

The prophecy symbol. The image that Daphne has kept hidden for centuries so that we could find it. I didn't understand the image at first but now, coupled with Dionysus's words, it makes horrible sense. A black feeling of dread comes over me.

I came to these woods searching for a way to stop Anteros. Another way than the terrible solution Medusa insists is my fate.

But the prophecy has just confirmed what she told me.

The symbol. Dionysus's words. They mean the same thing. *Human arrow.*

'Frida, are you okay?' Dan asks, putting an arm around me. 'You're shivering. What is it?'

'It's me,' I say, my voice small. And then I turn and neatly vomit, red wine staining the dry forest floor like blood. Water streams from my eyes and I look up, see Dan's worried face, the concern, the care, and I think about what is being asked of me, what I will have to give up. *Sacrifices have to be made.* I shouldn't have got close to him again, should never have gone to find him, because I know now what I have to do, and the magnitude of it swells like a wave, threatening to overwhelm me until suddenly I can't breathe.

'I . . . I have to get out of here,' I pant, as Dan watches on in alarm. 'I need to get out.' And then I hare off down the forest path, limping on my bloodied feet, running, running from something that cannot be outraced. Dan chases after me, shouting my name, telling me to stop, it's not safe, the boar might be out there, and what about the Anterists? But I don't listen to him; I have to get out of this wretched forest before I go mad.

I emerge, gasping for breath, just minutes later into the open patch of land where we parked Dan's car. The Anterists have gone but they've left us a parting gift: the windscreen of the car has been smashed, the body daubed in black paint, the same word, over and over: TRAITOR. I stumble over, leaning against the bonnet, feeling wobbly and strange in the strong sunlight. Something feels weird. Something is wrong. I check my phone and, with dawning horror, I realise what it is.

We entered the woods at noon on Tuesday. It's now just after five on Friday.

We've lost three days.

223

Chapter 23

'You know what?' I say to the blank-faced barman. I hold up my glass and wave it around, sloshing Pinot Grigio. 'They can stuff it. The whole bloody lot of them, they can just . . . get someone else to do it. Yes, that's it, find some other mug.' I take a swig of the freshly poured wine, swallow, and take another. 'Because I'm not doing it. No fucking way.'

The barman continues polishing glasses without giving me so much as a glance. I place my wine down on the bar, wobbling slightly on my stool. How do you follow a Bacchanalian hangover? Well, they say the best way to get over a night on the booze is a hair of the dog that bit you. I think this is going to require the whole pelt.

'Hey!' I shout. 'My glass is empty. HEY!'

At some point between haranguing the barman into giving me another bottle of wine and almost falling off my bar stool, I hear the sound of the door opening and then catch the familiar scent of smoke and musky perfume. Psyche takes a seat at the bar beside me, the only sound for a moment the sizzle of her cigarette. Then she waves at the barman.

'Bottle of whiskey and a glass. No ice.'

The barman returns with a bottle decent enough that Psyche raises an appreciative eyebrow. She uncorks it and pours herself a generous measure.

'So,' she says eventually, 'how are you doing there, Frida?'

I let out a half-hysterical laugh. 'Oh, peachy. Really, never been better.'

She takes a sip of her whiskey. 'Dan said you just left him there outside the forest with a vandalised car. Just upped and ran away. Said he chased you but you gave him the slip.' She drags on her cigarette. 'He was out in the car looking for you for hours. Beside himself.'

Oh God. Dan. I feel fucking awful about leaving him like that. I wasn't in control of myself. It was like I was possessed. I drain the wine and refill my glass.

'I just . . .' I stare into the pale yellow liquid, shake my head. 'Did he tell you what we saw?' I ask, without turning my gaze from the glass.

A sizzle. A pull on the cigarette. A plume of smoke. 'Yeah, he told me.'

I finally face her. 'And you're not horrified?'

'This is my horrified face.'

'Well, it looks very much like your other faces.' I slump back on my stool.

'What can I say? I'm jaded.' She flicks her ash in an ashtray shaped like a coiled snake. We sit in silence for a while.

'You know what the worst part is?'

'That Anteros is releasing a Titan and he's going to annihilate the world?'

'Well, yeah, that,' I allow. 'But also, we've been so *blind*. I knew the gods underestimated Anteros, but we've done exactly the same. Just like Daphne predicted. We thought he stayed on earth to torture us.' I take a long drink. 'But it was never about us, was it? We're not even worthy of his torture. All this time, he's just been trying to bring down those walls and we were the key.'

'Seems that way.' Psyche sips her whiskey.

'What I don't get about all this is: why now?' I squint at her, trying to de-fuzz my brain. 'He's had three thousand years to create an army of loveless mortals, why do it now? Unless he couldn't do it before, in which case, what's changed?' I look at Psyche. 'Did you manage to find anything out about that?'

There's a flicker in her eyes that I can't read, and then it's gone and in my blurry wine-soaked haze I might even have imagined it. White wine always did make me paranoid.

'No,' she tells me. 'But it certainly explains why the gods are in a hurry to take sides.' Psyche picks up her tumbler and turns it in the light. 'I always told Eros his faith in mortals was unfounded. He never listened.' She places her cigarette to her mouth. 'I bet he wishes he had now.'

I take a long drink. Shake my head. 'It can't happen,' I say determinedly. 'It just can't. The walls of Tartarus falling? A Titan, here, on earth?' I get a flashback of what I saw in the flames, the sickening sight of that evil creature. 'It's just . . .' I shake my head. 'It can't happen.'

There's a mixture of toughness and pity in Psyche's eyes. 'Many terrible things have happened in this world simply because people couldn't imagine them.' She takes a drag on her cigarette. Her eyes are dark, haunting, showing all the years that she has lived. 'Your ideas about what life is, what life is meant to be, it's just a mirage, Frida. A trick of circumstance. There is no limit to the horror. No line that can't be crossed. Anything is possible.'

I stare at her. *Anything is possible*; a phrase that has long been co-opted by advertisers and the positive-thinking brigade. Did anyone ever stop to think of it the other way? That if miracles can happen, so too can their opposite? I think about the gods, foreseeing all of this and shifting their allegiances to protect their own asses. Ares and Aphrodite siding with their son. Hades aligning himself with his father, hoping it will be enough to buy his favour and forgiveness when the time comes.

And Kronos: the thing the gods are scared of.

I nod at Psyche's cigarette. 'Can I have one of those?'

She raises an eyebrow as she hands me the packet and her lighter.

'Medusa is right,' I say. I stick the cigarette in my mouth and flick the Zippo. Suck in the smoke.

'About what?'

I blow out smoke and watch it rise. 'The gods only look after themselves, Zeus and Eros included. All these prophecies, them selecting me as "the chosen one". It was never about saving the mortals from Anteros's manipulations. It was always about me saving their skins when the time came.'

Psyche frowns. 'Frida . . .'

I jab my cigarette into the air. 'It's so obvious now. Zeus and Eros fucked up. They sealed Tartarus with love, they underestimated Anteros, they exiled him to earth and he locked himself down here with us. He's been experimenting with us ever since, trying all the different combinations until he can crack us. Oh yeah,' I nod, 'they knew Anteros would unleash Kronos on them eventually. The mortals, me, Dan,' I tug on the cigarette, 'we're just collateral damage.'

'It's not as simple as that, Frida. These things never are.'

I shrug. Seems simple enough to me.

There's a silence as I smoke. It's been years since I did this. It feels bad in a good way. That makes me think of last night. This morning. A wave of shame sweeps me. After what we shared, how could I have just left Dan there like that?

'Where's Dan now?'

'He wanted to come with me but I persuaded him against it. He went to the library to do some research.'

'On his own?' I give her a sharp look.

'He's okay; he's got protection spells.' She gives me a look. 'What happened with you two?'

We fell in love again. We fell in love again and now I'm going to lose him.

In answer, I just shrug. 'It's complicated.'

Psyche nods. 'It always is,' she says. She takes a sip of her whiskey and tops up the glass. 'Dan told me about the other thing, too.'

228

'What other thing?' I say, my voice getting all high pitched.

'What Dionysus said to you: human arrow.' Psyche looks at me searchingly. 'He said that's what freaked you out. Is that why you're in here drowning your sorrows when you should be helping Dan find a way to stop this?'

'I already know how to stop it,' I say. Reaching into my pocket, I bring out the piece of paper from Dan's notepad. With the glowing tip of my cigarette, I trace the lines – the stick figure, the arrow, one laid over the other. A person. A weapon. One and the same.

'A human arrow,' I say, turning back to my drink. 'Or, to put it another way, someone who was shot in the heart with a love arrow and now possesses its powers. A human who is the subject of a prophecy that decrees she's going to stop Anteros. A human who just happens to be able to take ambrosia and survive – no, more than survive – to become a powerful love goddess, strong enough to defeat a love god.' I meet her eyes. 'Of course it's me, Psyche. It was always me. A weapon is needed to put Anteros out of the game for good.' I shrug. 'I am that weapon.'

Psyche frowns. 'By taking more ambrosia? You know that will . . .?'

'Kill me? Maybe. But not before I've stopped him.'

'I wasn't going to say that it would kill you,' Psyche says. 'There are worse things than death, Frida.' She frowns down at the symbol. 'I don't know. Taking ambrosia to increase your power? That really doesn't sound like Eros's style. Or, not the Eros I knew, anyway.'

'Even if it was the only way to save every being on earth

and Olympus?' I stare into my wine glass. 'Anteros has a dark grip over the mortals. Only another god can break that hold. Once I do, they'll believe in love again. The bronze wall won't fall.' I give a bitter smile as I remember how it felt to take the ambrosia, that this was a drop in an ocean of power that is mine to claim. 'I think, with that magic, I can make sure Anteros is never a threat to the mortals again.'

'And give up your mortal life?'

'What other option is there?' I turn to Psyche, look at her searchingly. 'Tell me. I really want to know.'

There's a silence as she thinks about this. And after a while, when she still doesn't speak, I know she knows I'm right. I pick up the glass, drink it down and refill it and then the door behind the bar opens and Medusa steps through. I get the feeling she's been waiting to make an entrance. As the gorgon saunters over, affecting nonchalance, her snakes go crazy, betraying her true feelings, and she hastily pats them into submission.

'Well, well, well,' she says, one eyebrow exquisitely arched. 'To what do I owe this honour?'

'I came to see Frida.' Psyche gazes at Medusa coolly.

'Oh.' Medusa chucks me under the chin. 'Frida's fine, aren't you, darling? She's just finally figuring out how this world works.'

'I suppose it was you who gave her the ambrosia?'

'I may have done.' Medusa flutters her lashes, coquettish. Aren't you going to thank me for bringing her memories back? We'd certainly be in a mess if I hadn't, wouldn't we?'

'I hope you don't have an agenda here, Medusa.'

'An agenda? Oh, you mean, like yours?' Medusa gives a tinkly laugh and then turns to me, confiding. 'Did Psyche ever tell you why she was so desperate to curry favour with Anteros two years ago? What it was she wanted so badly to go back to Olympus for?'

I frown, the wine mudding my memories. 'No,' I say. 'I thought . . .' I turn to Psyche, confused. 'You wanted to leave earth, didn't you? You were sick of humanity.'

'Ignore her, she's just toying with you,' Psyche replies, giving the gorgon an icy stare. 'No trips down memory lane, thanks, Medusa. We've got bigger problems right now, wouldn't you say?'

Medusa pats her snakes and do I see a tremble of anxiety? Jesus, I don't want to see fear in eyes that can turn people to stone. That seems to me like a very bad sign. Then she shakes it off and she's blithe again. 'Oh, it's fine. Frida knows what she has to do. And the sooner she does it, the sooner we can all relax, and the sooner my clientele will return.' She gazes disconsolately around the sparsely filled bar. Then she turns her gaze on me. 'Honestly, I'm not sure why we're still here talking about this. Just do it, Frida. Take the ambrosia and stop him. You know that's what you're destined to do!'

Psyche flashes her a warning look. 'Frida will make her own decision.'

Medusa laughs, delighted. 'Decision?' Then, slowly, deliberately, she strips her gloves from her arms, revealing the scales of her cursed skin. 'Did I decide to become the creature I am?' she asks. 'Did you, Psyche, *decide* to be plucked from your home because of your beauty, to be tormented by

Aphrodite, rescued by your pitiful husband and then trapped on earth, watching everyone you love die, a witness to the folly of mortals, your last scraps of humanity worn away century after century?' She shakes her head and her snakes hiss their disdain. 'No, no, I'm afraid there's no decision to be made here. You know that, and, deep down, Frida does too. No decisions, just destiny.' Medusa's yellow eyes lock with mine. 'And destiny is a cruel mistress.' She shrugs. 'Nobody has ever pretended otherwise.'

Psyche has heard enough. She finishes her drink and throws a note on the bar. 'Come on, Frida, time to go.'

I look at Medusa, her eyes are aglitter. If I stay here, listen to more of the gorgon's talk, I may become brave enough or drunk enough to do it. But once I take the ambrosia, that's it. There is no coming back from that. One way or another, it will be over for me. At least, the me that I am now. And I'm not ready to go. I never asked for this responsibility. Haven't I done enough?

'You make it sound like we're pawns in their game,' I tell Medusa. 'Well, I refuse to play.' I can hear myself, distantly, and know that I am slurring, barely making sense. 'Why should I ... should ... I turn myself into a weapon for the mistakes *they* made?'

Medusa just smiles sadly. 'Because if you don't, the mortal world will be consumed by a horror you cannot begin to imagine.' She leans towards me and her snakes train their pinprick eyes on me as she says softly, tenderly, even: 'Besides, immortality isn't so bad, Frida. Don't let Psyche tell you it is. She was fun once; we had some very good times.'

Psyche shakes her head.

'Join us, Frida,' Medusa says and her snakes are a Greek chorus. *Join usssssssss.* 'Become the powerful, immortal goddess of love you are fated to be. Join us and show Anteros, show all the old gods, that when they try to fuck with the lives of mortals, it is not without consequence.' *Conssssssequencsssss.*

My mind resists, but the latent arrow power within me shimmers a recognition. *Medusa is right,* it beguiles. *This is your destiny, Frida. Don't fight it. Embrace it. Become a great love goddess again. And this time, stop him for good. Make Anteros pay . . . make them all pay . . .*

'Frida,' Psyche says, snapping her fingers in front of my face, 'you need to eat something and you need to sleep. Come on. Come home.'

And it's that simple word that gets through to me. *Home.* I clamber from the bar stool under Medusa's slitted gaze and stumble after Psyche.

'You can't run from your destiny, Frida. Wherever you go, it will find you. Don't you know that yet?'

I shake my head, refusing Medusa's words, but the haunting sound of her laughter follows me up the stairs.

233

Chapter 24

Psyche parks me on her sofa with a pot of strong coffee, a packet of paracetamol and a bottle of sparkling water. Then she sets about making me some food.

I watch her as she moves around the kitchen and in my drunken state I seem to see a very different Psyche to the one I know. I catch a glimpse of the mother she must have been to Lea, a version of Psyche long hidden under layers of hardened self-protection, isolation and grief. She brings over a plate of cheese on toast. My eyes fill with tears at her kindness but she brushes away my thanks, curt as ever.

'Eat, drink, rest,' she says. 'When you're feeling like yourself again, then we'll talk about what comes next.'

'Myself?' I say. 'Bit of a fluid concept these days.'

Psyche looks at me, assessing, and then nods to the balcony. 'I'll be out there if you need me.'

After she's gone, I stare at the food feeling slightly bilious. I'm already beginning to sober up and it does not feel good. A ferret appears to have made a nest in my mouth and my stomach has turned to acid under the assault of wine. Picking up a triangle of cheesy bread, I force myself to eat. In between bites, I take sips of coffee and water and slowly, slowly, I come back to myself. When thoughts of Anteros and Kronos intrude – what they are trying to do, where this all ends – I force them away. When thoughts of Dan appear – his lovely face, the way he looked at me in the woods – I push those away too. It's too confusing right now. Food, caffeine, water. These are my only goals. Right now, that feels epic enough.

After an hour I start to feel better and can bring myself to pick up my phone.

The first result that comes up is a website called *Food and Drink in Ancient Myth* and as I stare at the homepage I'm reminded of how I conducted this exact search two years ago, when the idea of taking ambrosia first occurred to me. The expression on Dan's face when he saw what I was browsing.

I flick through the list and right at the top, there it is: ambrosia. I read the text quickly, skimming it, reminding myself: in some myths the characters drink ambrosia, in other they eat it, in still others they bathe in it. More fun facts: ambrosia is reported both to spring from the earth and to be delivered to Olympus by doves – that's some high-class table service – and was often consumed with nectar, another mysterious celestial substance which might have been a drink, possibly made from flowers.

I close the window and return to the search results, looking for information on what happened to those who took ambrosia. There's a story about Hera, Queen of the gods, who would bathe in ambrosia, using it to 'cleanse all defilement from her lovely flesh'. Heracles, better known as Hercules (he who herded the boar into snow), was eventually made immortal with ambrosia. And in an alternative version of the Achilles myth, his invincibility came not from being dipped in the River Styx but by being anointed with ambrosia before his mother, Thetis, passed him through a fire, making him immortal (save for the heel he was held by).

Another entry tells of Odysseus's wife, Penelope, who was anointed in ambrosia before she went before her suitors and it was said to have melted away the years from her. That explains my amazing make-up-free look. I put the phone down as I think about all of this. So ambrosia makes mortals beautiful, immortal, powerful and protected. Not too shabby. But at what cost?

I flick through the rest of the results, this time looking specifically for stories where mortals take ambrosia without the explicit permission of the gods. I can't find tales of any mortal hubristic enough to attempt this feat, but I do find the sorry tale of King Tantalus, a child of Zeus and a nymph called Plouto, who stole Ambrosia when he dined on Mount Olympus, and then dared to offer it to his guests back on earth (the ultimate in ostentatious dinner-party smuggery). It backfired, naturally, and Tantalus was sentenced to eternal punishment in – oh, look at that – *Tartarus*. Nice. Maybe he and Kronos are cell-mates.

I close all the browser windows and lie back on the couch

thinking about what I've read. I must have drifted off, because I'm awoken by a rattling as Dan lets himself into the flat, a pile of books under his arm. When he sees me, the look on his face slays me.

'Frida!' he says and rushes to my side. He kneels by the sofa and takes my hand in his. 'I didn't know what had happened to you. Where did you go? *Why* did you go?'

'I just . . . freaked out. I needed to be on my own.' I meet his eyes. 'I'm really sorry, Dan.'

He nods but I can see that he's hurt.

'Are *you* okay?' I struggle up to sitting and get a shooting headache, like someone is sliding a knitting needle behind my eyeballs. 'I shouldn't have left you there. What we saw in the fire, the whole thing, it was . . .' A memory of Dan's hot body on mine. My eyes flick up and he holds my gaze steadily.

'I'm fine,' he says firmly. 'Where did you go, anyway? Psyche said she had an idea where you might be, but she didn't divulge and she wouldn't let me come, though I did try to force the issue.' Dan ponders. 'That woman has got quite the muscles on her.'

'I went to Medusa's,' I say and a flicker crosses Dan's face so quickly I'm not sure if I imagined it. 'I just needed somewhere to think, and I knew there wouldn't be any Anterists in there.'

He nods, thoughtful. I glance over at the pile of books.

'Big library haul?'

'Research!' he says brightly. 'I'm going to discover everything I can about what that symbol and those words

237

might mean.' He sees my face. 'Frida,' he says gently, 'we can do this. We've stopped him before and we can do it again.'

A hand reaches into my chest and crushes my heart. I meet his eyes.

'I already know how we stop him, Dan. That's why I ran.' I pause. 'I'm the human arrow,' I say. 'It's me. It is literally me.' Dan is still looking at me blankly so I spell it out. 'The ambrosia boosts the arrow magic inside me.'

'Boosts the arrow magic,' Dan repeats.

'Yes. It strengthens it. On the garage forecourt, just temporarily, I could read your emotions, Psyche's, all the people in a radius around me. And,' I think about the black cloud that enveloped me, 'I could feel The Love Delusion.'

'Okay,' Dan says. 'But then you blacked out.'

'I did. But that's because I only took one drop and I wasn't used to it.' I pause. 'I think – no, I *know* – that I could take more now. That I can increase my power so that I will be strong enough to stop Anteros.'

Dan shakes his head, looking confused. 'But what will that do to you? Taking that much ambrosia?'

I give him a small smile. 'Best-case scenario is I become a powerful, immortal love goddess.'

'Temporarily, like when you glowed in the forecourt or . . .?'

'No,' I say softly. 'For ever.'

Dan stares at me. 'And worst-case scenario?'

'There's a chance it could kill me. But,' I add hastily, 'I don't think it will.'

'Frida, you can't be serious.' Dan's face is stricken.

'I am,' I say. 'This is the meaning of the hidden prophecy, Dan. It's what Eros and Zeus meant for me to do.' I rub at my aching forehead. 'To turn myself into a weapon, to save the Olympians and the mortals from the return of Kronos.'

'No,' he says, shaking his head.

'I know it's hard to accept, Dan—'

'It's not hard to accept because it's not the answer. Frida, you're wrong. You are not supposed to sacrifice yourself like this.'

'How do you know that?' I ask sadly.

'I just know!' His eyes meet mine. 'I didn't have a vision that this was how to stop Anteros, did I?'

'You didn't have any visions about how to stop him at all, Dan. That's the problem.'

'We'll find another way. I know that what we saw back there in the woods was bad, but taking ambrosia is not the answer.'

'Then what is?' I ask, suddenly weary. 'Medusa told me two years ago that this was what would be expected of me. I didn't want to believe her then.'

'But you accepted the ambrosia from her anyway, didn't you?'

I flash him a look, taken aback by the thread of accusation in his tone. 'Yes,' I say carefully, 'and if I hadn't, we'd both probably have been beaten to death by Anterists by now so, you're welcome.'

Dan nods, scrubs at his face with his hand. 'Okay, I get that, but Frida, you can't take some dangerous magical substance based on the words of a gorgon who not that long ago was prepared to turn you into a statue! And as for Dionysus, he kept us in that forest for three days, time we didn't have to waste. How can you trust what he says, what any of them say? They could *all* be aligned with Kronos for all we know!'

'I know that,' I say. 'But Dan, you saw the story in the fire. You know what Kronos is, what he's capable of. If he escapes, every single living thing in this world will be destroyed. Not in some fantasy, but here, now, for real. If I believe there's even the faintest chance I can stop that, don't I have a responsibility to try?'

'And what if taking ambrosia just makes things worse?'

I look at him. 'A Titan is being sprung from a hell prison to bring about Armageddon. How am I going to make that worse? Set it to bagpipe music?'

He just stares at me. 'How can you laugh about this?'

I smile. 'Sometimes, in this world, if you don't laugh . . .' I reach out and trace a hand across his cheekbone. 'My poor Dan,' I say. 'What a mess this is.' His gaze softens then and he takes my hand, kisses it. An electric feeling goes through me, and I just want to crawl into bed with this man, to hide from what's coming, to do what I drunkenly declared back in Medusa's bar, refuse this responsibility, make someone else save the fucking world for a change.

'Maybe I should never have taken the ambrosia,' I say wistfully. 'Maybe, in another life, I'd still be the old oblivious Frida, and you and I would have taken Psyche's money, caught a plane to some remote island and right now we'd be sitting on sunloungers, under a palm tree, listening to the crashing of the surf.'

'Drinking pina coladas . . .' Dan adds.

Tears flood my eyes.

'What?' Dan says. 'I happen to like pina coladas.'

I stare at him, heartbroken. 'Oh Dan,' I say, my voice cracking, 'what are we going to do?'

He looks at me, his eyes intense, gripping my hand so hard it hurts. 'This is not how it ends for us. I'm not losing you, Frida, not when I've only just found you. I'll find another way. I promise. Together, we—'

Just then, outside, there's a cacophony of noise, drifting in from the open door to the balcony. A huge roar and then explosions, whizzes and bangs and cheers. I struggle up from the sofa, pulling away from Dan's grasp. At first, I don't understand what I'm seeing. Out in the city, all I can see is red, red, everywhere, like a river of blood. My head sends splinters of pain into my temples as I stare out over the city streets, uncomprehending, and as the fireworks explode in a bouquet of red sparks, each one of them feels exactly as though it is exploding inside my skull.

'What is it? What's happening?'

Psyche turns to me, her grey eyes dark. 'Anteros is here.'

$$\longrightarrow$$

We watch the parade from the balcony for as long as we can stand it, then Psyche insists that I get some sleep. Dan does a few fake yawns and says that he, too, feels pretty bushed after our night in the forest, and then avoiding Psyche's amused gaze, we head to the spare room. This time, I don't go to the bathroom to change, just slip off my clothes in front of Dan's intense gaze, flushing at the desire in his eyes. Then he does the same. I step towards him, my eyes drinking him in.

'Frida,' Dan starts, but I put a finger to his lips.

'No words,' I say. 'Just us.'

Dan pulls me to him then and kisses my forehead, my cheeks, my lips. I lean against his strong body and then pull him on to the single bed. Our skin is warm against the cool sheets, our eyes meet, sparking, knowing. What's coming is too immense, to horrific to deal with, so I shrink it all down, to this room, this bed, the space between my body and his, this touch, this kiss, this moment, a world made for two, in which nothing and no one can hurt us.

And where in the forest it was frantic and mindless, now it is slow and languid, mindful and loving. A kind of reunion.

It's only as I am drifting off to sleep that I wonder if it wasn't more like a goodbye.

Chapter 25

We sleep as we did in the forest, spooned, breathing in unison, connected and complete. I hold Dan's strong arms tightly around me, waking in the middle of the night, hearing the fireworks and thinking about how the mortals down there are basically celebrating their own destruction.

The next time I open my eyes it's morning and Dan is up, dressed and fastening his trainers.

'What time is it?' I rub at my eyes. 'Where are you going?'

He looks at me. Happiness spreads across his face and oh that look he gives me, how I have missed it. 'It's half eight,' he says softly. 'I'm going back to the library.' He comes over, kneels by the bed. Puts a hand on my cheek. His eyes are excited, hopeful. 'I'll find another way, Frida. I promise you. Trust me.' Then he leans in and kisses me, with minty toothpaste lips, and he's gone.

I pull on Psyche's grey dress, moving slowly, my skin prickling with Anteros's proximity, an animal sensing a predator. I slide my hand under the pillow and pluck out the purple bag. I tip the bottle out into my hand. As soon as I do, the action seems to soothe my anxiety, quietening that fight-or-flight instinct that thrums through my body at Anteros's proximity.

Take me now, the ambrosia whispers. *What are you waiting for? I thought you were a hero. Don't you want to save them?*

But then Dan's voice: *I'll find another way, Frida.*

I slip the bottle back into the purple bag and stuff it under the pillow.

$$\longrightarrow$$

There's a pot of coffee on the table, still steaming. Psyche is at her usual station, smoking out on the balcony. I pour myself a cup and head out. It's going to be another scorching day. I stand next to Psyche and stare out across the city. Where yesterday there were dozens of Anterists on every street, today there are hundreds, as though Anteros's presence has sped up the alchemy, resulting in wave after wave of red. I can feel them, and I know even that surface façade of peace and happiness has faded. The darkness underneath is rising.

You have to stop this.

Psyche turns to me, meets my eyes, and I see that her face is pale, her impossible beauty a little tired around the edges. When even Psyche's studied nonchalance is beginning to slip, then you know you've got yourself an apocalypse. She stubs out her cigarette, takes out her packet and offers me one. I take it. Bend my head to the flame and take a lungful of smoke. Look out over the buildings, the rising heat shimmering the air. We stay there like that for a long time.

'What would it feel like?' I ask eventually.

She doesn't have to ask what I'm talking about. There's a considered silence and then she says, 'It wouldn't be the same for you as it was for me. My immortality was bestowed on me by Zeus. That's a whole different experience, far less volatile.'

'Okay,' I say, 'but just tell me what it was . . . is . . . like for you, then.'

A frown flickers across her face. She taps ash over the balcony wall. 'When you become immortal, your human relationships, your human life,' she says, 'they change. They say it's eternal life but really it's more like a death of everything you once knew.'

I think about those relationships. My mother, who is a fully-fledged member of the Anteros fan club and who completely neglected to mention that I had lost my memories. Bryony, who I have driven away with my coldness and cruelty. My work: how I dismissed my loyal PA, Penny, and aligned myself with Anterists, based only on a shared, magically created obsession with hating love. Seems like I've already done a good job of killing off my relationships.

There's Dan, though. My love for him, his feelings for me, they're real and they're strong. Doesn't that count for something?

'And time,' Psyche goes on thoughtfully. 'You don't realise how much you depend on time to give life meaning until you

245

have so much of it. There's poignancy and preciousness in our human moments because we know they're fleeting, that life is finite. There's a kind of mercy in that.' She turns her gaze on me. 'That goes,' she says darkly. 'That mercy. And without it, it's easy to find yourself following dark paths.'

I stare at her. I know what she's getting at. 'Dark paths like helping my father to his death, betraying me and kidnapping Dan, that kind of thing? Are you telling me you did all that because your life lacks purpose?' I raise an eyebrow. 'Couldn't you just have taken up salsa dancing like normal people?'

'I'm already living for ever. You'd like to see me tortured too?'

I grin and tap my cigarette on the ashtray. 'And death?' I say, after a while. 'How does it work? Do you just die over and over or . . .'

Psyche waves her cigarette, dismissive. 'No, no, nothing ghoulish like that. Death just . . . passes you by. The bullet misses. The heart carries on pumping blood. The cells never mutate. The piano, about to fall on your head, falls on someone else two feet away.' She shrugs. 'Death just becomes something that happens to other people.'

I stare at her. For the first time, I think I have an inkling of how it has been for her. I take another drag on the cigarette. 'Dan's gone back to the library,' I say. 'He doesn't think I should take the ambrosia. He thinks there's another way.'

'And what do you think?'

'I have no idea.' I realise as I say it that it is true. I don't have an instinct on this, don't know which path to take. I feel utterly lost. I turn to her suddenly. 'Do *you* think I should take it?'

246

Psyche faces me and she shakes her head, not in answer but the opposite. 'I can't tell you that, Frida. All I know is what I can sense out there.' She nods to the city. 'A darkness like nothing I have ever felt. It's happening. The walls of Tartarus are falling. As to whether this is the right call, for you to take ambrosia, to become some all-powerful love goddess?' She shrugs. 'That would have been for the Oracle to say.'

'Well, we don't exactly have one of those any more.' I fall silent. I look out over the city, seeking out the old NeoStar skyscraper. I had goddess power once. It was more than enough to stop him for good. But I let him go. And now look where we are. Is this the lesson? One more chance to put it right? To be the hero, finally, and do what I didn't have the guts to do last time?

Psyche follows my gaze to the towering building that housed Anteros's empire, once the global centre of anti-love, now just a hotel and some apartments.

'I do know one thing,' she says thoughtfully. 'When I saw you up there in Anteros's boardroom on Valentine's Day you were ... different. You had something about you, a power, a purpose. I knew you were going to beat him then, even before *you* did.'

I look at her, surprised. Psyche gives me a small smile. 'All those thousands of years I didn't believe the prophecies and then, suddenly, I did. I hated you, yes, but I was pleased too. At last, someone would be wiping the grin off that smug bastard's face.' She sees my dubious expression. 'Look, when you've lived as long as I have, you get used to holding two conflicting emotions at once.'

247

'So, what are you saying?'

'You gave me hope, that's all. Hope that this fucking purgatory that I live hasn't all been for nothing. That maybe I was stranded down here for a reason. I lost that sense of purpose a long time ago. I don't have faith in much of anything any more, but I believed you could stop him then.' She meets my gaze. 'And I still believe it now.'

I close my eyes. Time is running out, and all I feel now is panic and fear, walls closing in. Do I sacrifice myself? Become a goddess? Is that really what Eros and Zeus want from me? Dan says there's another way, but this Dan doesn't *know* that. He can't guide me the way the old Dan could. And isn't it possible he's just letting his feelings for me get in the way of what needs to be done? Aren't I, too, letting my attachment to Dan prevent me from doing what destiny says I must?

I shake my head. I'm going round in circles, and we're running out of time. I just want someone to tell me what to do.

Then it comes to me. There is someone else I can trust to tell me the truth, even if I don't want to hear it. Someone I trust with my life.

I stub out my cigarette.

'Where are you going?' Psyche asks.

I glance back and smile. 'To see an old friend.'

Chapter 26

I walk through the colonised streets, nursing a small glimmer of hope.

All my life, there has been one person I've depended on to steer me right. In the last few years, I've allowed a chasm to open up between us. It wasn't caused by The Love Delusion. It was learning who I really was. Ever since I met Dan, I've kept Bryony at arm's length, protecting her from the realities of the magical world. But now it seems ridiculous that I've worked so hard to keep it all secret. Why did I think Bryony didn't deserve to know the truth? Why did I think that I couldn't show her the real me?

Worse, in keeping all of this from my best friend, I've cut myself off from the strongest source of honesty and sanity that I have. Maybe I thought that sharing this world with Dan was enough, but I was wrong. I was only with Dan for a few months. Bryony has known me for decades. So, fuck it. The world is ending. I'm going to tell my best friend that gods and monsters exist and then ask her whether I should sacrifice myself to save the world.

That's if she believes me.

My hand is steady as I ring the doorbell. There's only silence in response. Have I missed her? It's Saturday morning, that's usually family time for Bryony, Justin and the twins, but maybe they're on holiday? Then I hear something, a shuffling, and glimpse a flash of colour behind the bevelled glass. No, thank God, she's in. I'm smiling as the door latch clicks, because despite everything, I cannot wait to see my beautiful friend, to tell her how sorry I am, how stupid I've been. To tell her how much I love her.

But when the door swings open all I can do is stare.

Bryony's eyes are red-ringed, her already pale skin is almost translucent and she looks like she's lost half a stone in the week since I saw her last. But even worse is the way she's looking at me: dead eyed, as though she doesn't recognise me.

'Bry?' I say. 'Bryony, are you okay? What happened?'

She stares at me dully for a second, then turns and walks back into the house. With a creeping feeling of dread, I follow. Jake and Joe are at the kitchen table, throwing food at each other. By the state of the place, they might have been doing that for days. Bryony just watches them blankly, listless, as I stare around me, unable to understand what has happened.

'Hey,' I say and the twins look up, grubby faced and close to tears. 'Hey, boys, it's Auntie Frida. Remember me?'

The pair stare at me, suspicious. Their cheeks are red, as

though they have had too much sleep or not enough. I look at Bryony; she's just watching the whole scene, impassive, a million miles away. I've never seen her unconcerned about her kids' welfare, never seen her anything less than attentive and loving.

I scan the kitchen and pick a box of chocolate-covered animal crackers from a shelf. 'Hey, is your drawing stuff still in the den?' They nod, silent. 'Well, how about you two draw me a picture each, okay? Your favourite animal. Go find your crayons and your paper. And then, when you've done it, you can each have a biscuit as a prize.' The boys scoot off their chairs and run into the den, leaving me and Bryony alone.

My friend stands by the table, her expression vacant. When I reach out and touch her arm, she flinches.

'Bry,' I say, 'what happened? Are you okay? Where's Justin?'

That seems to wake her up. Her eyes flicker into life and she turns on me, her expression suddenly vicious. 'Oh, you've come to gloat, is that it?'

I stare at her wide eyed. Gloat? 'No, no, of course not,' I say soothingly, though I've no idea what she's talking about. I pat her on the shoulder. 'Why don't you sit down? I'm going to make you a cup of tea.' I turn, scanning for the kettle and find it stacked behind a pile of dirty pots. I fill it and flick it on, then find two mercifully clean mugs. When the kettle has boiled I bring Bryony a cup of tea, just how she likes it. My eyes rove over her, noting each alarming detail. Her hair is greasy, her skin has broken out in stress patches. What the hell has happened? With horror, it strikes me that it can only be one thing. Something must have happened to Justin. He must be hurt, or worse ...

'Bry,' I say. 'Bryony.' I push the tea in front of her. 'Can you tell me what's wrong?' I ask gently. 'Is Justin okay?'

She seems to notice first the tea and then me. She focuses her eyes on me and they sharpen in anger. 'He said it was a friend,' she tells me haltingly. 'A friend was talking about it, he said, and he's heard me mention it because of you, so he thought he'd take a look to see what all the fuss was about. And then ...' She reaches out a shaking hand and points at me. She still wears the bracelet from her date-day, I see. Whatever happened, it must have happened soon after that.

'You did this,' she says. 'It's *your* fault.'

'What, Bry? What's my fault?'

Bryony's blue eyes hold more hatred than I would have ever believed possible. 'Justin left us,' she says. 'He's an Anterist now.'

$$\longrightarrow$$

I finally manage to get Bryony to drink the tea and tell me everything. How when she went home to Justin, ready to head out on their date, he was packing a bag. How he told her he'd been so wrong about everything his whole life but now he understood. How his eyes were lit up and he looked so happy as he told his wife that he needed to go to stay at a hotel near the church, that R. A. Stone was coming soon and he didn't want to miss it.

And as she recounts the sorry tale, I can see it all playing out. Bryony, listening to him, thinking it's all some sort of elaborate joke, and slowly, slowly, realising that he's serious.

He's decided he doesn't love her. That he never did. That his marriage, his children, this life he's been living – it's all been a colossal mistake. Bryony in her dressed-up clothes, and Justin walking past her, leaving the house without a backward glance, without a thought for the kids he loves so much. Bryony's disbelief, shock, her grief.

She's right. It's all my fault.

This same story must have been playing out in households all over the world for the past two years, and as each day has passed it will have grown worse and worse. At first, The Love Delusion siren song was only strong enough to capture the unhappily married. But if Justin has been converted, Justin who adores Bryony with all his heart, then every mortal in the world is vulnerable to it now.

I think about Anteros's sermon, to be delivered tomorrow morning. Things are moving too fast. Who's to say he'll wait until then? Who is to say he can even control it? Those bronze walls could fall at any time.

'It's a tiger!'

'It's a monkey!'

Jake and Joe barrel back into the room and as Bryony gazes off into the middle distance, I fuss over their pictures and give them two biscuits each, watching with concern as Bryony doesn't even look at her sons, just stares out of the patio doors to the garden.

'Bryony,' I say.

She turns and her eyes meet mine. She gives me a pitiful smile and then she says, 'I'm beginning to think that he was right.'

I frown. 'What do you mean?'

And for the first time since I arrived, Bryony's face takes on some life, though it's a ghastly kind of life, a manic shine to her eyes.

'What Justin said about love. It doesn't make any sense, what we've been doing. Not if love can stop like that, with no warning. As easily as turning off a tap.' She nods slowly. 'So, I think, yes, Justin is right. Love must be a delusion after all. And that's okay, you know? That's good. It's great, in fact. It doesn't hurt any more.' She offers me a smile through cracked lips. 'How stupid we've been!' Then she gets up, heads for the front door, the boys staring after her with pinched, anxious, chocolate-covered faces.

I give the boys another biscuit each and an attempt at a reassuring smile and then I follow my friend into the hall.

'Bryony,' I say softly, 'where are you going?'

'To the church,' she says. 'To be with the Anterists. I've heard R. A. Stone is here, in the city.' Her eyes take on a jealous look. 'You know him, don't you? Have you met him? Can you introduce me to him?'

With a shudder I realise that I can feel it inside her, the shadowy thing taking over her heart. I think Anteros's Love Delusion magic is floating in the ether now, spread not by a book or by rhetoric, but simply by an idea, like spores in the air, travelling across the world, invading any mortals with even the slightest chink in their faith in love.

Which must surely be almost every mortal.

I can't let her go. I place a hand on my friend's shoulder and summon up what I can of arrow power. As I touch her, a faint trace of gold fizzes, sensing the dark power, eager to act against it. 'You don't want to do that, Bryony,' I say, making my voice quiet, soothing. Some of the tension leaves her shoulder as she sags under my touch. 'You just stay here, with your kids,' I say. 'Call your mum and ask her to help you tidy up. Tell her you've been unwell. Justin has gone away but he'll be back soon. Everything's going to be okay, I promise.'

Bryony's eyes glaze and I can feel the golden power finding that fledgling wisp of dark arrow magic, circling it, enfolding it, vanishing it away. And then she looks at me, her eyes clear for the first time since I arrived.

'Frida?' she says, her pale face breaking into a sweet smile. 'Frida, I haven't seen you in such a long time! I've missed you.'

I blink back tears. 'I've missed you too, honey.' And then I wrap my arms around her. I want to tell her how much she means to me. That she has always been my guiding light. That I've let her down, done some terrible things, and that I am going to make it all better. But I don't want to scare her.

'I love you,' I say instead.

She smiles dreamily. 'I love you.'

'Goodbye, Bryony.' I squeeze her one last time, kiss her cheek, and then I walk from the house.

I came here looking for answers.

I suppose I got them.

Chapter 27

I wait outside for half an hour, watching people walk down the street and across the park. Most of them are Anterists. Anyone who is not yet an Anterist in this city will be hiding in their homes, terrified of the serious-faced mobs of red-clothed believers currently swarming over the area. When the street clears of people, I slip around the corner and let myself in through the front door. It seems weird. It's only been a week since I was last here. It feels like a lifetime.

The red paint sprayed across my front door proclaims: JUDAS! A busted lock reveals that the door has been forced and I ease it open gingerly, but I can already tell that there's no one inside. Still, my throat tightens as I walk in and pick up the resonances of the Anterists' emotions in the air – their hatred and rage, so thick it forms a sour taste in my mouth. There's yet more graffiti on my walls, spelling out in colourful terms exactly what that traitor Frida McKenzie can do to herself. My dining-room chairs have been knocked over, my lamp smashed, books tipped from the shelves. The contents of my kitchen poured all over the floor. The Anterists making clear how they feel about my betrayal.

That's nothing to what they'd do if they found you here, a sensible voice cautions, and I know. I won't be long. But I had to come. Surely I am owed at least this?

I sit on the sofa for a minute and think, for the first time, about the Frida who has been living here for the last two years, Lethed and oblivious. The Anterist Frida. I actually see her for a moment, a ghost of myself, walking around the flat, working away on her laptop, heading out to her Love Delusion meetings, so pleased with herself for having found a purpose she could truly believe in. She thought she was saving the world. Looking at her now, I both pity and envy her. Those two years were awful, but they were also so very easy. The simplest, least complicated time of my life. Isn't that sad?

A firework goes off outside and I shake myself out of my reverie. There isn't much time now. I need to get what I came for. I make my way around the flat, the hiding places coming so easily to me now that I marvel I could ever have forgotten them. There's one taped to the back of the fridge. One fastened behind the mirror in the bedroom. One folded up into a tiny, rigid square and stuffed behind a loose skirting board. For two years they have lain there, waiting for something to spark, for the faintest shred of memory to float up in a dream, for a coincidence or fate to lead us, like a trail of breadcrumbs, back to the mission we had forgotten.

I stand, staring at the photos. These pictures are a time-slip, a fragment of another life, and my heart contracts, my memory reeling backwards, to the small scrap of precious time that Dan and I had between that fateful Valentine's Day and when we knew Anteros was back. Just four months, but such deeply happy ones. Here's Dan, his arm slung around me, his face filled with love, me grinning up at him. Dan, beaming into the camera, a pint of beer in his hand, the shadows underneath his eyes fading, me cheersing with a ridiculous cocktail. We had begun to relax. We had started to believe that we were actually free.

We had no idea we were in the eye of the storm.

I look around the room. Being here also brings back less welcome memories. Like the last time I was here before I was Lethed. It was the day we went to see Medusa. She gave us the acorn and then she sneaked me that little purple bag containing a bottle of ambrosia. I hid it from Dan, asked him to stop at my flat on the way to the woods, pretending I'd forgotten my phone. I hid the bottle and my necklace under the sink, scribbling a note, then found the envelope I left taped to the sideboard and told myself where to find it.

I kept it from him, yes. Because by then he'd had that black vision. By then, I think I'd had my own premonition of how bad things were going to get. Dan thought we could complete the mission without our memories. But I'd faced Anteros once. I'd seen the look in his eyes. I knew we didn't stand a chance.

Dan's voice: *You said it yourself. We were a good team, you and me.*

But Medusa's words now echo in my ears: *You're the chosen one. This isn't a job share. When you come to face your destiny, you'll do so alone.*

'As flies to wanton boys are we to the gods,' I murmur, 'they kill us for their sport.'

And I wonder now, if mine and Dan's relationship was ever anything other than a move in the gods' game. They needed Dan to love me so that he would overstep his role as Oracle and come to find me; they needed me to love him, so that I would rescue him from NeoStar and get shot with the golden arrow. But now? Now our love is dispensable. Worse, it's an obstruction to what they need me to do. So the visions dry up. The antidote disappears. Dan is taken from me. I forget I ever knew him.

And now you have him back, a voice inside me urges. *Dan loves you.*

And yes. It's true. I believe that. But it isn't enough. Our love is selfish. It can't save the world. But it might doom it.

I think about Dan. He cares for me, yes. But the reality is he's only known me a matter of days. If I go, he will carry on. If I save the world, he gets to go on living. Just without me. And is that a true act of love?

Sacrifices have to be made.

I look at the photos, tears dripping down my cheeks. I love him. And I have to lose him. Both of those things are true. The gravity of what I have to do hollows me out inside. But into that hollow, a flickering. The spark of arrow power, recognising its chance. It's alive, this power, it wants to grow, to surge, to show me what it's capable of, what I can become.

And yes, a tiny part of me wants this too. Knows that this is where the story has always been heading.

I wipe my eyes and straighten my spine. I'm ready. The golden power inside me tells me in a soft whisper that it is ready, too. That it will complete me. That this is the bliss I've been looking for. Heroes are beyond happily ever afters.

This was never about love.

It was always about power.

$$\longrightarrow$$

Once I've accepted my destiny, all I feel is peace. I don't even notice the Anterists or the shadow that hangs over the city. I head back to Psyche's flat, let myself in. Distantly, I am aware of Dan and Psyche sitting at the kitchen table, and my heart pleads with me to say goodbye to him, to seize one last precious moment together. But I grit my teeth and walk on. I can't allow myself to do that. If I see his face, I don't know if I'll be able to go through with it.

I have to take it now, before I change my mind.

I walk into the spare room. I notice my hands are shaking when I go to the bed and take away the pillow. Stare down at the plush purple bag, crumpled, empty. The ambrosia is gone.

Chapter 28

'Where is it?'

I'm in Psyche's face, gripping her by the shoulder hard enough to leave marks on her flawless skin. She doesn't flinch, just stares at me curiously, cigarette smouldering away in her fingers. I'm flooded with an incandescent fury. 'Tell me what you've done with it!'

Psyche takes a long drag on her cigarette, blows the smoke into the air and then eyes my hand. 'You *really* don't want to do that, Frida,' she says, and although I really *do* want to do it, want to shake the truth clean out of her, I know it's the wrong move. She could kill me in seconds and, without the ambrosia, I'm no match for her. I have to be smart about this. Releasing her, I stand back, eyes narrowed.

'I should have known never to trust you. You were working for him all along, you lying, scheming—'

'Frida,' Dan says.

'Stay out of this, Dan.' I hold up a hand to him. 'You have no idea what this bitch is capable of—'

'Frida!' Dan says more loudly. I turn and meet his eyes and then I know.

'You?' I say. 'You took it?'

Psyche turns an admiring gaze on Dan. 'Well, well, well,' she says. 'Boy Scout, I didn't know you had it in you.'

It takes me a few moments to speak. 'I don't understand,' I say. 'Why?'

'Because I can't let you drink that stuff.'

'Oh Dan,' I say. I move over to him, reach out to touch his cheek, to hold him, but he ducks away, slipping from the chair and backing up against the kitchen counter, his face tense and not altogether trusting.

Psyche is watching all of this with interest.

'Listen,' I say softly, 'I know you don't want to lose me. And I can't stand to lose you again, either.' My gaze drifts to the balcony, the city beyond. I see Bryony's peevish face as she talked of going to the church. 'But things have changed out there. It's getting bad. I have to do this, Dan.'

'But that's just it. I don't think you do.' There are red spots high on Dan's cheeks. I can read him a little, his fear, and also his determination. Something about the latter scares me. 'I left myself a note, Frida,' he says. 'About the ambrosia.'

'There was nothing in the notes about ambrosia.' I frown, trying to make sense of his words. 'You said so yourself.'

'It was in code. Hidden.'

Everything seems to stop for a second. 'That's ridiculous,'

I say eventually. 'You wouldn't have kept something like that from me. No way.'

'Like you didn't keep the ambrosia from me?'

I stare at him and no words come. Psyche gets up and pours herself a whiskey. 'Look, whatever it is you think you know, Daniel, you'd better spill it. Frida's right. It's getting worse out there. Time's ticking.'

Dan swallows. 'I kept seeing a number in the notes but I didn't know what it was. Then this morning, it came to me. It was the code for a book, in the library.'

I think about Dan's excitement this morning. *I'll find another way, Frida. I promise you.*

His face is pale now, he rubs at his stubble. 'The book itself was nothing remarkable, just an old translation of *Oedipus*. But I found this hidden in the jacket.' Dan takes a piece of paper from his pocket. Unfolds it. I glance at the note. It's Dan's handwriting, I'd recognise it anywhere.

'What is this?' I ask, my voice unsteady.

'A message from my former self,' Dan says, with a tight smile. 'It says that under no circumstances should you take ambrosia. That ambrosia is dangerous enough, but mixed with the arrow magic already inside you, the effect will be far more volatile. You won't be able to control it.'

I can't speak for a moment, and when I do my voice is hoarse. 'Why would you do that? Why would you write a note like that and hide it from me?'

Dan looks at me sadly. 'I don't know. I suppose because I was absolutely sure that taking ambrosia was not the answer. And because I must have known that you'd try to.'

I absorb this. It's like a dagger to my heart. Dan didn't trust me. He hid things from me, about me.

I try to keep my focus. 'Okay,' I say. 'So what else is in that note? If you were so sure that ambrosia was not the answer, you must have had another theory, right? Another reading of the prophecy. So how do we stop Anteros?'

Dan is silent.

'You don't have another theory,' I say flatly.

'Not yet, no,' he says. 'But I have the word of the man you love saying taking ambrosia is not the way. Isn't that enough?'

'Oh Dan,' I say wearily, 'what else is there? We don't have any other way to stop this.'

'Because you haven't looked for one,' he bursts out. 'Can't you see what's happening? You hid the ambrosia from me, why? You've been keeping that bottle close ever since we got here. After the forest, you went straight to Medusa's bar, knowing she'd convince you to take the ambrosia. You haven't even tried to find an alternative reading of the prophecy because you don't want another solution. You want this one!'

I stare at him. 'How can you say that I want this?' I ask, and my voice sounds broken to my ears. 'How can you say that to me?'

'A part of you wants it,' Dan says miserably. 'Maybe you're not even aware of it.' He looks at me searchingly. 'I was worried about you, wasn't I? Before. About you using your arrow magic to influence people, about your eagerness to take ambrosia.' He shakes the letter at me. 'It's all here.'

A flashback, then, to the lock-up the first time we visited, two summers ago, when Dan and I left the video and the notes for ourselves to find. The way I touched Maurice on the arm, that tiny flicker of golden power, leaving the guard mooning after me, eager to do my bidding. Dan's eyes on me, worried and accusing. *You didn't have to do that, Freed. It wasn't necessary.* And my response, a shrug, delighted with myself. *Consider it insurance.*

I push the memory away. 'Okay,' I say, 'maybe you did have some concerns about me taking ambrosia, and I listened to you and I understood. But you loved me, Dan. You didn't want to lose me. Is it any surprise that you didn't want me to do this? What lover would?'

I hate the look I see in his eyes then. 'Yes, I loved you,' he says and I wince at the past tense. 'But I wasn't trying to stop you because I was afraid to lose you, Frida.' He meets my gaze. 'And what's more, I don't think you believe for one minute that I was.'

I look at him. My heart hurts and damn him for making me feel all these awful feelings when I was so ready to do what had to be done.

'It doesn't matter what you thought two years ago, don't you see? Back then we didn't know about Kronos.'

'But I know now,' he says. 'And I am still saying this is the wrong call.'

I stare at him. I knew this would be painful. I didn't realise just how painful. 'But you're not him,' I say softly and then turn my face away from the hurt in his eyes. I focus on Psyche. 'Listen, you know if there was another option, I'd take it. But this is the only shot we've got. And while

265

we are standing here debating it, the end is getting very fucking nigh.'

Psyche studies me for a moment and then flicks a glance at Dan. 'Give it to her.'

'Psyche, no!' Dan stares at her in horror. 'Didn't you hear what I just said? This is wrong!'

'Maybe.' She shrugs. 'Maybe not. But Frida's right: what other option do we have?'

'I believed there was another way, so why don't we look for it? We could work together. Research the symbol, come up with a plan . . .'

'The time for research is long over,' Psyche says. 'Now be a good boy and give her the ambrosia.'

Dan doesn't move.

She sighs. 'You know I'm just going to make you.'

Dan sets his jaw firm. Rolling her eyes, Psyche stubs out her fag and then she's up, pinning Dan's arms behind his back easily with one hand and reaching into his pockets with the other. She finds the bottle and hands it to me. I take it and hold it gently, reverently.

'You didn't destroy it,' I say to Dan, my eyes shining. That was my fear. 'You could have poured it away, but you didn't, because deep down you know it's the only way, don't you?'

Dan flashes me a look of disgust. 'I didn't open the bottle because I didn't trust myself around that stuff. You shouldn't either.'

But as I gaze down at the ambrosia, I know he's wrong. Ambrosia is the only thing I *can* trust. Even just holding the bottle in my hand eases my anxiety. I feel calm and settled. I know now where all of this has been leading.

'Frida, please,' Dan says. 'Please don't do this. Something very bad is going to happen . . .'

I turn to him. 'I'm so sorry, Dan, but I'm doing this for you. I hope one day you'll understand that.'

He meets my eyes and there's so much sorrow there. 'Can't we at least say a proper goodbye?'

I smile then, and tears come. 'Oh Dan,' I say. I open my arms to embrace him as Dan moves towards me and then, suddenly, he makes a grab for the bottle. Before he can reach it, Psyche has him by the arm, propelling him through the kitchen and over to the balcony. Then she pushes him on to the sun-warmed terrace, closes the door and turns the lock. So much for heartfelt goodbyes. But then, isn't that just my mortal life all over?

Dan bangs on the window. His shouts are muffled but I can feel his eyes boring into me. I don't look at him. Instead, I stare at the bottle. Its crystalline angles cast rainbow prisms across the pale walls of the kitchen, the symbol of a promise made thousands of years before I was born.

A destiny waiting to be fulfilled.

And I'm finally ready.

Chapter 29

I take the stopper from the bottle and the sweet, musky scent rises and fills my nostrils.

'Not too much,' Psyche warns. 'Just three drops. That should be enough.'

I nod and then, raising the bottle, I tip it to my lips.

I'm dimly aware of Dan banging on the window, of Psyche watching me, but then the ambrosia hits my system and I squeeze my eyes shut as the feeling rushes through me, girding and strengthening the power already inside, reuniting in a joyful harmony. It's different this time, my body isn't weak, I'm not overwhelmed by the magic, oh no, I welcome it. My being explodes into a kaleidoscope of sensations; my head is filled with the scent of spring flowers, fragrant air and something bitter, like burnt coffee. I can hear the sound of my blood pumping and see the orangey light behind my closed eyelids, as a golden tingle starts in my core then spreads, building and building, and oh this feeling – a pulsing excess of wonder, a transformation, a destiny, a homecoming.

Medusa was wrong, this isn't a curse. It's a gift.

My eyes fly open.

I see Psyche watching me, a cautious look on her face, but then just as quickly I'm not looking at her, but deeply *into* her. I see it all and I understand. The reality behind that perpetually beautiful face. Heartbroken beyond repair, eyes that have seen too much, loneliness, pain, how it has been to live all these years, as a human-but-not-human, such weariness, and no way out, unless – and something in her shimmers, then, I recognise it as hope, I reach for it, and it slips away like a fish, but I chase it and chase it and then I see: the reason she betrayed us last time. Why she wanted to get to Olympus. What Medusa knew.

Psyche wanted to return, not to be reunited with Eros – her love for him faded into insignificance long ago – no, she wanted Zeus to give her something, something she wants desperately. Now it shows itself as a gift-wrapped parcel, the single hope that has kept her from losing her mind, and I push deeper, forcing the gift to unwrap. Finally I see what she's been hiding, her greatest desire: she wants Zeus to revoke her immortality so that she can be human again.

She wants to die.

And as I stand there, experiencing every scrap of this wretched woman's sorrow, I mourn for her, for what she's had to bear, and I understand something, too. Psyche wants to die more than she wants anything else in this world. And because of this, she can't be trusted.

'Frida!'

Psyche's voice comes to me from both inside and out. I blink.

'Are you okay?'

I nod. 'Yes,' I say, my words feeling as though they are travelling through syrup. 'I'm okay.'

'How do you feel?'

I smile. Again, it feels as though I command my face to smile, and the action is carried out minutes later.

'Amazing,' I say slowly and smile again at the sensation.

'The arrow power is strong?'

'Oh yes.' I reach out a hand and a buzz of gold rushes into it. I can see a shimmer surrounding my handprint, like those drawings children do. 'Can you see that?' I ask wonderingly.

'Yeah,' she says. Pause. 'So do you have enough now? To break his hold on the mortals?'

I turn my gaze back to her. Poor Psyche. 'I do.'

'Okay, then let's go.' She makes to leave. I remain still, watching, a smile on my lips.

'No, Psyche.'

She turns and looks at me. 'What?'

'I can't risk you betraying me again.'

'I'm not going to betray you, you know that.' She frowns. 'Frida, don't be stupid. You're going to need back-up.'

'I don't need anyone,' I say serenely. 'I do this alone.'

A look crosses her face then and I feel her emotions as clearly as if they were my own. Doubt, mistrust, fear. She sees something in me and she thinks she's made an error, misjudged this, that this Frida is not—

'Shhh.' I stretch out my hand and a pulse of gold flies into Psyche's upper chest. She jerks backwards, glazing over. When she looks at me again, her eyes are wide with happiness. I stare down at my hand, entranced. So this is what it is to be a love goddess!

I think I like it.

Dan bangs on the balcony door. 'Frida, what are you doing?'

I glide over to the window and place my golden hand against it. 'Not sure,' I say thoughtfully. 'It was instinct. But I think ...' I smile more widely. 'No, I'm *sure* that I took Psyche's worries away. She's happier now. Look!' I turn to survey Psyche's guileless face. She looks centuries younger. Then, for a moment, looking at her vacant expression, I'm hit with a flash of confusion. Did I do that to her? Why? Psyche was going to help me, wasn't she? Then the golden power pulses inside me and my good feeling returns.

I stare at Dan through the glass. Shrug. 'She'll be fine. It's only temporary. She was going to stop me.'

'Frida,' Dan shouts, 'this isn't you!'

I put my face closer to the glass. There's fear on this mortal's face. What is he scared of? My brain fuzzes and then clears for a moment. I look at Psyche, standing there, blissed out and oblivious. At Dan, his stricken face at the window. I stare down at my hands.

'Dan?' I say. 'What's happening?'

He sees my fear, I feel him see it and he places a hand up to the glass. 'It's okay,' he says soothingly. 'It's going to be all right. Just unlock the door, okay? I promise we can sort this out, together. Me and you, Frida. A team. Just like before.'

'Okay,' I say faintly. 'Yes, I'd like that.' But as I reach down to flip the lock, the bottle in my hand releases a wave of scent that drifts into my nostrils and my mind grows cloudy again.

Don't open that door! He doesn't love you. He's trying to trick you! Why do you think he didn't want you to take the ambrosia? He's jealous of your power, he hates that you're the special one, he doesn't even have his visions any more, he's useless, impotent. He's going to steal that power from you, and then who will you be? Nobody. Nothing. Don't open that door!

I look out on to the balcony. Dan stares at me, so much hope in his face. Poor mortal.

'Don't worry, Dan,' I say. 'I know this world is a hard place. But I'm going to make everything better.'

He looks at me, face slack with despair. 'No,' he says, 'you're not. If you use the power like this, you're just like Anteros.'

An image comes back to me then. Valentine's Day two years ago. Me standing at the window on the 200th floor of the NeoStar building, a golden love arrow trained on the dark love god. I could have stopped him then. The goddess in me wanted to, but the human in me choked. And, well, look how that turned out.

'You're wrong,' I say. 'I'm not like him.' My eyes glow, golden. 'I'm so much more.'

Dan pounds on the door again, but the noise is growing fainter. All I can hear now is that gentle, whispering voice: *Take it all. Take it all and there will be no more heartbreak, no more confusion, no more pain. This mortal life will be nothing more than a silly dream you once had . . .*

I lift the bottle of ambrosia to my lips. And if a dim part of me suggests that I am crossing a line, that if I drain this bottle of amber liquid I will lose something precious that I can never get back, well, that's just the weak, human Frida speaking.

And we're not listening to her any more.

Chapter 30

What lies beyond the human is golden. I am transformed. I am a love goddess. Everything is easy now. Everything is right.

Well, maybe not quite everything.

I glance down at my body, at the base, undignified costume in which mortal Frida has dressed her human frame. I wrinkle my nose. Some sort of dingy sack and peasant footwear? No, no. That will never do. I feel eyes on me and, glancing up, I catch the broken Oracle watching, his face pale with horror. I nod. 'I know, right?' I say, brushing myself down. 'Hideous, isn't it? She really must have loathed herself.' I sigh. 'Ah well, that's all over with now.'

Before the mortal's unworthy eyes, I click my fingers and the ill-fitting grey dress and brown sandals disappear, replaced by a golden gown, light as air, shimmering, glistening, flowing to the floor like a waterfall, with a neckline of plunging jewels. Circles of gold wrap around my neck, on my feet, sandals of spun gold, and on my crown, my glossy dark hair cascades under a magnificent headdress of tiny, slender golden arrows, each one reaching for the sky.

'Better, yes?'

The mortal man stares, his mouth open in awe.

I smile. 'That's what I thought.'

My gaze drifts from the mortal's stupefied expression to the city spreading out below us. The buzzing emotions of the inhabitants thrum through me, the story of every human heart repeating over and over. Where there should be lemony yellows, bright oranges, vivid pinks and sky blues of joy, contentment, happiness, love, now I sense too many hearts streaked with blacks, greys and reddish browns. Anger, sorrow, pain, despair, the same infestation replicated all over the world. Because of *him*. My golden arrow power shimmers inside me. Time to end this. Time to change Anteros's heart, make him worship true love, make him worship *me*.

Something niggles at me then. What is it? Oh ... it's the human Frida. I'm not her, not any more, but she's in here somewhere, restless, nagging.

I frown. I can't be distracted from my task. What does she want?

I glance idly through Frida's pitiful life, like flicking through a photograph album; and what a sorry history this is: here she is, tucked up in bed, her father reading her a story of the gods, a happy stolen moment before her beloved dad disappears and her mother takes her daughter to have her memories wiped, fracturing her sense of self, wrenching her away from her destiny. Here's Frida studying for her exams, unaware of her lineage, using her power to set up her own practice, punishing those who scorn love, screwing over errant spouses, trying to fulfil a fate she knows nothing about.

And here are all the men in her past, hand-picked for heartbreak; here are all the ways they hurt her, shut her down, controlled her, froze her out, and here's how hard she tried to win the impossible game. And then, a miracle, or so it seemed: Dan. Such an intense love, a brief explosion of happiness and joy before he too was taken from her by the whims of those old gods. And though she should have been used to loss, hardened to it, losing Dan changed her. She gave up. Something inside her died. And that's okay. She needed to give up to make way for me.

I don't need love.

After all, you don't need what you already are.

So why is she still bugging me? An image flickers then, an irritant, the first knot in Frida's complicated emotional tangle of a life. I bare my teeth, a righteous anger building. The mortal mother tried to destroy my goddess self before I was even born, wanted to eradicate Frida's destiny. What hubris this creature is guilty of!

I turn to the watching Oracle. 'But she will be made to see the truth.' I give him a beaming smile. 'It's what poor Frida would have wanted, don't you think?' And as the mortal man watches, awestruck, my body begins to shimmer and I transform into golden light, ecstasy in motion, a human arrow with my target defined. I disappear before his eyes . . .

. . . and reappear in Frida's mother's living room.

The mother is walking from the kitchen; the TV plays a

show about antiques. She sees me and bolts backwards with a strangled cry, letting fly a small plate of custard creams.

'Hello.'

Frida's mother stares at me, mouth slack, quailing. Blinks a few times. 'Frida! What are you doing here?' She frowns. 'And what on earth are you wearing?'

I laugh. Only this woman could watch her daughter materialise out of thin air in a corona of gold and refuse to acknowledge it. She really is the queen of denial. I look into her, seeing what she did. Who she is. The complicated cat's-cradle of emotions and actions, denials and justifications this woman has been conducting since her own terrible childhood. How hard she works to hide from herself her own corrupted nature. And so it goes on. So wretched, these poor creatures. They need to be saved from themselves.

I take a step towards her. Frida's mother's eyes dart around the room as she looks for a way to escape. Doesn't she know there is no escape from the light? Why would she even want to? Only because she prefers the darkness, prefers the empty message of Anteros.

Only because she hasn't woken up yet.

'You've suffered enough,' I tell her. 'I want you to see the truth.'

Frida's mother blinks, wets her lips with a nervous tongue. 'Frida, you look strange, what's happened to you? Are you on drugs?'

'Oh, I'm not Frida,' I say, laughing, delighted. 'Well, not exactly. Not any more.'

I walk over to her and she scoots backwards until she's against the wall, her small blue eyes terrified.

277

'What do you want?' Frida's mother shakes her head, squeezes her eyes shut.

I place a hand on her head and she stills instantly, like a calmed bird of prey.

'All your daughter ever wanted from you was for you to accept her as she really is.'

'I do—'

'No,' I command and her mouth flies shut. 'How could you accept her when you despise yourself?' I shake my head sadly. 'Oh, if you could see your heart. It is black, utterly black! But I can help you with that,' I say. 'Do you want my help?'

'Yes.' She nods, 'I do. I do. Whatever you say.' Her eyes are glassy with tears.

'Good.' The Love Delusion shadow layers her heart, but it's a cobweb to the power I have now. Holding out my hand palm outwards, I send a bolt of gold into her chest. Frida's mother squeezes her eyes shut. When she opens them again, all fear has vanished. She looks at me, adoring, scrambling up from the floor and then on to her knees in worship, grovelling before me, having finally seen the light.

As it should be.

As they all will be, in time.

→

I walk through the city, wanting to see for myself the mortals I am going to be saving. As I glide through the streets in my golden gown, the humans turn, eyes filled with reverence. I look upon then pityingly. Such suffering! Even those yet unaffected by Anteros's dark magic are so torn, so uncertain, so resistant to love.

But I can help with that.

A thin man walks past and his cloud is browny black, sick, like a tarred lung, and I can see, like the rings of a tree, the daily thoughts of self-hatred that have formed this blackened aura, so dense now that he cannot fight his way out. Walking past him, a stocky woman with red hair and a drawn face, her heart harried by anxious thoughts. Fingertips itching, I twirl my fingers, and the pair stop, look at one another. Smile. There. Why suffer alone?

I pass a couple seated at a pavement café; the man's brow is furrowed, the woman's face is pained. They have been in a relationship for two years. I can see the thought forming in her mind, over and over, yet to reach her lips: *I don't think this is working*. A fizz of anger inside me at this: she wants to reject love! Foolish mortal! Before she can speak, I stretch out my arm and a tiny jag of gold shoots into her. Instantly, her colour changes to a deep, luscious pink; she turns back to the man, takes his hand, stares lovingly into his eyes.

So many broken hearts.

And I can fix them all.

This isn't you.

I pause, disconcerted. Why does the impotent Oracle's face appear in my mind like that?

You're just like Anteros.

I shoo the image away, like a fly.

I've reached my destination.

I stare up at the church. It's time. We're ready for the endgame.

Chapter 31

The steps of the church are a mass of red, packed with Anterists, camped out, waiting to be granted an entrance to tomorrow's sermon. And rising up behind them, the magnificent steeple. Somewhere in this building Anteros is waiting, a dark splinter in this world. The Anterists part as I glide through the crowd, spilling golden magic on to those closest to me, the shadow squatting on their hearts beginning to unravel and dissolve, making way for beautiful colours: pale purplish-blues, grass greens, delicate silvers. The rescued Anterists scramble up in worship, and I leave them there on their knees, my eyes trained on the church, sweeping the building for a sign of Anteros's dark magic.

We're siblings now; this golden power and its dark opposite are drawn to one another. Dark calls to light, an age-old battle. There is room enough in this world for only one of us.

But the darkness I sense doesn't originate from the church. Instead, I follow its trail around the building and find a stone structure, a row of Caryatids on either side of a red door, two bovine guards in attendance.

Anteros is in the crypt.

What is he doing down there? I frown. I know from Frida's work at this church that the crypt contains a series of catacombs and vaults that spread beneath the whole of the building. Then, with a small stab of delight, I understand: he's hiding from me!

The guards manning the red door stand to attention as I approach. I shoot twin beams of gold into them and they stop, befuddled, then kneel at my feet, devotion in their big brown eyes. I smile and pat their heads. 'Good boys.'

Then I picture Anteros's face, I dissolve into gold, and reappear in a wide-bricked corridor under an arched ceiling lit by one dim bulb. Sarcophagi and statues gurn out of the murky air. This place is dark and dank and cold; no fit place for a goddess. My golden gown is muted in the gloom, my headdress barely shimmers. I sigh. Just one more thing to despise Anteros for.

Make him pay.

Oh, and I will.

There's an opening ahead of me. He's in there. I can feel him. I move silently to the door and through it I see a large, square room.

And there he is.

He has his back to me, directing two of his red-suited guards, but he feels me, I know he does, just as I feel him: all that hatred, all that jealousy, all that rage. The depth of it, the strength of it. The power. I could almost admire it.

Then Anteros stops and turns, slowly, almost teasingly, to face me. Even in his human form, he's magnificent. His black-brown hair loose on his shoulders, those cheekbones, those penetrating, ink-dark eyes. Every inch a modern messiah. He's a worthy opponent, but I know I'm stronger than him. He doesn't have an arrow. I *am* an arrow.

As I regard him, an easy smile spreads across his beautiful face. 'Well, well, well.' Impudent eyes rove over my goddess form. 'Someone's had a makeover.' He turns to his guards. 'Grab her.'

The guards beside Anteros start forwards and with a flick of my hand, I send shards of gold into their hearts. They stop, slack-faced, and fall in supplication. I meet Anteros's eyes. 'Oh dear. Seems your devotees are mine now. The mortals you control will be mine too soon.' I tip my head to one side. 'This world? Mine. Time for you to retire, I think.'

'Is that so?'

'It is.' I twirl my finger and Anteros's hands are bound with gold. He pulls against the restraints but it's no good. He cannot fight the bonds of true love.

I walk up to him. 'You got used to feeling omnipotent, didn't you?' I stroke a finger down his cheek. 'Being the only powerful god in town, playing with the mortals, wiping memories, toying with hearts? All the while, beavering away at your little plan to free Kronos.' I see his look of surprise. 'Oh yes, I know all about it. And I'll bet you thought no one could stop you, didn't you?' I lean closer, my eyes glowing gold. 'But

I'm here now, Anteros. And I'm not a weak, pathetic mortal any more.'

'Ambrosia?' Anteros asks, a strange smile on his lips.

'Yes. Ambrosia, plus the golden arrow power inside me that only exists because you shot poor Frida in the heart. Mix them together and,' I open my gleaming hands, 'here I am. A new goddess for the modern age.'

He stares at me with those dark, fathomless eyes.

'I'm going to transform that black heart of yours,' I say. 'I'm going to free those misguided mortals from your hold.' I smile. 'No parole for Kronos, I'm afraid.' I look at his beautiful face. 'Remember when you shot Frida, you imagined you could corrupt her heart? That she would join you, help you?' I shrug my shimmering shoulders. 'You had the right idea, just the wrong way around. Once I've made you fall in love with love again, I think I'll let you help *me*. I'll be needing – what is it the mortals call it? – a gofer, to help me undo all the terrible things you've done over the last few centuries.'

I smile at him. 'It's over.'

Anteros tips his head playfully. 'Oh, I don't think so,' he says. 'You haven't seen *my* party trick yet.' Then he pulls his wrists apart. The golden ties spark and vanish into nothing and as the god steps aside, I see it.

There's a hole in the world.

Chapter 32

I can't drag my eyes away from it.

It's a void, a non-thing, the air inside it flickering madly, and from that empty space emerges a blackish despair.

'Can you feel it, Frida?' Anteros asks. 'Oh, I imagine you can. Even gods are not immune to the effects of Tartarus. And isn't that what you are now? A god?'

He's right. My golden arrow magic knows the horror of this place, a hellscape in which no magic can live, no hope.

'It was actually thought to be impossible to open a portal to Tartarus,' Anteros muses. 'And not many have even tried because,' he peers into the black hole of nothingness and then looks at me with a smirk, shrugs, 'who would want to?' He flexes his hands, now free of my golden chains. 'But in the end it was easy. The same force that holds the walls prevents a portal to Tartarus from being opened. And as the mortals turn from love,' Anteros says, 'bingo! Here it is.' He sees my face. 'Oh, I know it's only small right now, but don't worry.' He casts an affectionate glance at the black hole. 'The weaker the walls, the bigger it grows. Soon it will be plenty large enough to accommodate tomorrow morning's special guest.'

I look at him with scorn. 'All this so you can wreak your revenge on your brother, on Zeus?'

'Well, yes.' Anteros frowns. 'You say that as though revenge isn't a worthy cause, Frida, but what are you carrying out right now, if not vengeance?'

'Justice!'

'Justice?' He raises an eyebrow. 'Interesting.'

Beside him, the dark void seems to demand my attention, it swirls, transfixing me, making my focus waver. What am I doing? I have to act. *Yes! Act! Finish this*, the golden power screams in my veins. *Do it now! Shoot Anteros and close this offensive opening to hell!*

But as the thoughts form, even as my hands glow golden, Anteros is snapping his fingers and, from the gloom, four Anterist guards emerge holding two prisoners.

Dan. Psyche.

Dan is shoved roughly over to Anteros, who grabs his arm and bends it back so that Dan winces in pain. His face is pale and frightened as he bites his lip to stop from crying out. I glance at Psyche. She looks dazed, the magic I used on her starting to wear off. My mind scrambles, trying to understand how I have been outplayed. Anteros shouldn't have been able to find them. The apartment is protected.

'I sensed your power, just as you sensed mine,' Anteros

says in answer to the question written on my face. 'And for a change, Psyche didn't put up a fight.' He reaches over and strokes her cheek. She doesn't flinch. It's awful to see. 'I don't know what you did to her but I like her better like this.'

'This has nothing to do with them,' I say. 'It's between you and me. Let them go.'

Anteros stares down at Dan, and then he regards me curiously. 'You want me to let him go? You've got it.' I see what he's going to do before he does it, my eyes widen, my hand shoots out and I send golden strands to reach Dan, to catch him. Too slow. With dark eyes locked on to mine, Anteros pushes Dan into the void.

I see his face as he falls. I feel his terror.

And the Frida inside me screams.

Anteros smiles. 'I wonder how far you'll go this time, to be the hero you believe you are.' But my hands are already sparking. I'm ready to finish this.

'Tut, tut,' Anteros says. 'If you want to play the game, Frida, you have to learn the rules. If you use your power on me, then you'll break my hold over the mortals, and . . .'

I stare at him, black hatred spinning within me as understanding dawns. If I fire at Anteros, the mortals love again, and the portal closes, trapping Dan in Tartarus for ever.

'Then again,' Anteros continues, 'don't shoot me, and pretty soon those walls will fall, Kronos gets out and yada, yada, yada, the world ends.' He casts a sly look at me. 'So, Frida, what's it going to be? Are you going to sacrifice your Oracle to save the world? Can you really bring yourself to do it?'

286

His eyes are glassy with excitement. I'm very still as I contemplate my choice.

'It's a clever trick,' I say slowly. 'An impossible choice. How can a woman who loves a man so deeply bring herself to condemn him to an eternity in hell?'

'Exactly. Fun, isn't it?'

And oh, mortal Frida is speaking up again, an internal struggle is being waged between my mortal fragments and my godly power.

No. No! Don't do this!

SACRIFICES HAVE TO BE MADE.

Not like this!

I HAVE TO STOP KRONOS. THERE IS NO OTHER WAY.

But Dan is innocent! How can you do this? How will you live with yourself? I love him!

And then I understand. Anteros is correct: this is a game. A test. Again and again, mortal Frida has sacrificed her power for the men she loves. But the pattern must be broken. She has to become loyal to something higher, something greater. *This* is the sacrifice. It all makes sense. A serene golden buzz travels around my body, flowing into my hands. When I finally raise them, I see a golden bow and arrow have formed. Not of metal, but of pure magic.

I meet Anteros's gaze. 'You think Frida would risk the world to save the man she loves.' I nod. 'You're right.' As I draw back the bow the arrow crackles and fizzes and I smile, beatific. Sure. 'But, you see, I'm not her.'

And as Anteros's dark eyes widen, I let the arrow fly.

Chapter 33

As the arrow strikes the love god's cold, miserable heart, he's flooded with golden light. He bows his dark head and I stand and watch and I am pleased. Yes, I had to sacrifice the Oracle. But now it's over. Anteros is defeated and Kronos will never escape. I fulfilled the prophecy. I saved the world.

Taking a step towards Anteros, a thrill rises at the image of him kneeling before me. And as he raises his head, I'm already smiling, ready to receive the adoration of this fallen god. But the smile freezes on my lips. What I see in his eyes isn't worship. It's triumph. And the black hole behind him still gapes.

'No,' I say, and my wretched voice trembles.

'Yes,' Anteros says.

It wasn't enough power. I need to hit him with more. I don't hesitate, don't think, I raise my shimmering bow again and fire arrow after arrow into Anteros's heart. He just stands there, amused, as the darts enter his body and are absorbed, leaving him unharmed, unchanged. Time slows down. What. Is. Happening?

'Oh Frida,' Anteros says fondly, 'don't you know I never play a game I can't win?'

I stare at him. 'What is this?'

Anteros approaches me. 'I think the better question is: what's this?' he says and as he swirls a finger through the limb of my golden bow it dissolves from my hands. 'Did you think what you had inside you was the magic of pure love? A might to match that of Eros? That it could reverse what I've done?' He shakes his head. 'Oh no. If you really were a true love goddess, you wouldn't have shot me if it meant condemning a mortal to eternal hell.' He pouts. 'True Love is just no fun like that. But then, if you *did* decide to shoot me, then that proves your power isn't pure, ergo it wouldn't be able to harm me.' He shrugs. 'Either way, I win.' He looks at my rigid face with faux concern. 'Are you keeping up? I know you can be a little slow at times.'

'You're wrong,' I say, my voice hoarse. 'I am a powerful love goddess!'

'You're a goddess, yes. But what you've got inside you, that comes from grief and arrogance and rage. All wonderful things, certainly,' he adds gaily, 'but none of them have the power to stop me.'

'No,' I say, an ungodly desperation mounting in me. 'It was written. It's my destiny. I'm the human arrow . . .'

'Oh, prophecies,' Anteros says, waving his hand. 'Just more

stories you mortals tell yourselves to comfort and delude. But you're no hero, Frida. You're no saviour.' He laughs. 'Every single thing you've done has only served my cause. You made a career out of turning spouse against spouse. You peddled The Love Delusion for me – rather beautifully, I might add.'

'I stopped you,' I say, and my voice is low, bruised. 'Two years ago, I stopped you then. I can stop you again.'

'You mean Valentine's Day? Oh, did you imagine you'd hurt me, Frida?' Anteros asks. 'Wrong. What you did back then is the only reason Kronos is getting free.'

He sees the look on my face and flicks a glance at Psyche. Still gripped by two guards, she looks angry now. She's coming back to herself. 'Oh,' Anteros says, 'poor Frida doesn't know. Tsk, tsk, Psyche, have you been keeping her in the dark?'

Suddenly, I remember the look on Psyche's face when I asked her how Anteros had gathered the power to influence so many mortals. She knew something about the source of his power. Something she kept from me.

'I must admit,' the love god says softly, 'I was beginning to wonder whether it was even possible to convince you mortals to give up love. You're such a stupidly stubborn species. But then, Frida, you brought down NeoStar. Destroyed my empire. In one fell swoop, you removed all of my manipulations. Oh, I won't say I wasn't a little miffed. That was until I realised.' He leans in and whispers, 'Your actions helped create this backlash against love. You created a vacuum. All I had to do was fill it.'

I shake my head, refusing his words.

'I have to hand it to you, Frida, I'm not sure I would have

come up with it myself. Perhaps I'd become too attached to all my nasty little tricks. It is so hard to kill your darlings, isn't it?' Anteros glances into the black void. Shrugs. 'Well, for some of us, anyway.' Then he beams at me. 'But then you came along. And you made possible what I'd been trying to achieve for millennia.'

He looks to see the effect this has had on me and then, satisfied, he leans so close I can feel his breath on my cheek, inhale his spicy, evocative scent. 'So, I suppose, what I really want to say, Frida, is, "Thank you".' Then the god of love kisses me slowly on the lips.

His words, the kiss, they sink into me like poison.

I did this. I am to blame for the end of the world.

I look over and meet Psyche's eyes, see the truth reflected there. She knew it was my actions two years ago that set this chain of events rolling. She didn't tell me because she knew what it would do to me.

Anteros surveys me. 'You're ashamed,' he says now. 'Angry. Horrified. No, don't bother to deny it; I can see it in you. It's ... beautiful.'

And as he speaks, I can feel it building. The rage inside. The humiliation. The violence. It feels dark and intense, potent. Strong. And okay, it's not the pure, golden power I imagined, but what does that matter?

Power is power.

I feel the mortal Frida struggling against this, becoming hemmed in by the darkness, retreating to the last fragments of light, like a woman gasping for air in a room on fire. I don't worry about her. She'll be gone soon. And I'll be complete.

'No,' Frida screams. But her voice is so faint I can barely hear it.

Frida.

A new voice, more like a feeling, is trying to force its way into my awareness. As it does so, I feel my godly hold slip for a second and –

– I'm back. Fuck. I'm back. I stare wildly around me. Oh Jesus, I have to do something before I am subsumed for good. What can I do? How can I run from the goddess when she's inside me and she's coming and oh God . . .

Frida.

I look at Psyche. Her grey eyes lock on to mine. *Listen to me.*

Psyche, I can't hold on, the goddess, she's too strong. Oh God, I'm sorry, I'm so sorry—

My consciousness swims out again as the dark goddess begins to return. I have to hold on, I have to stay *me*, but she's coming now, and she's promising to take me to a place beyond guilt, beyond shame, beyond the terrible things I have done. Oblivion, I think, distantly. Yes, oblivion sounds good. What other choice is there?

There is one way to escape her . . .

I look up and meet Psyche's eyes. Something floats into my mind then. She's sending it to me, feeling it with every ounce of her being. An image of the portal, black, malevolent. Why?

What returns to me, then, is the dark goddess's horror upon seeing that dreadful void: *a hellscape in which no magic can live . . .*

And suddenly, I understand.

The goddess catches a glimpse of what I intend, and she rears up, shrieking in an unholy fury. *NEVER! NEVER! YOU WRETCHED MORTAL, DON'T YOU DARE BETRAY ME ...!* She battles to take back control of my body, and, resisting her with every bit of strength I have, I run past Anteros, past the red-suited guards and towards that mesmerising void.

And then I throw myself into Tartarus.

Chapter 34

Dark.

Dark and wet.

Dark and wet and squelchy.

Where am I? What the hell happened?

I muster the energy to push up on to my elbows and look around me. I'm lying on a mud-bank of sticky, black clay. It's dusk-dark and the sky is choked with a reddish smog. A cold and clammy mist surrounds me, a weariness permeates my bones, my eyes sting and my body aches, but what ails me is deeper than physical, it's like I have a virus in my soul.

And then I remember. Oh yeah. I threw myself into Tartarus.

As I lie there, it comes as equal relief and sorrow to find that the goddess and Psyche were right. No magic can survive here. All the ambrosia has been wiped from my system, the dark goddess has been vanquished and my golden gown and matching tiara have disappeared, Cinderella style, replaced once again with the grey dress and sandals. Not only that, but the spark of magic I've carried for these last two and a half years – a memento of that golden arrow to the heart – is also gone.

No powers left. I'm just normal, mortal Frida again. Wearied but also somehow relieved by this, I lie back down for a while, staring up at the dirty maroon sky as the weight of everything I have done settles on me.

Dan was right. After I was shot with that arrow, I wanted to feel its power again. The magic inside me began as something pure, yes, but the longer it was in me, the more it changed. Perhaps if I had been a different kind of person, a better person, that golden arrow magic would have blossomed into something strong enough to defeat Anteros's dark magic. But in me? – I remember my vain, selfish goddess self and wince – not so much.

And now Dan is down here and it's all my fault. Oh God, Dan! The Dan with memories would have struggled enough with this hellish turn of events, but Dan with so little experience of the magical world? Who knows what has become of him. He could be suffering terrible torments, and it's all because of me. Then I shake myself. There's no point lying here, wallowing in my guilt. I need to find Dan.

With considerable effort, I sit up.

'Dan!' I shout, my voice echoing across the emptiness. 'Dan! Are you there?' I try to stand but the mud is so slippery that no sooner do I get on to my hands and knees than I slide back down with a whoomp, right on to my face. Grimacing and spitting out mud, I push myself up again, but the same thing happens. I sink back down and dimly wonder if I'm doomed to spend eternity in Tartarus struggling and falling in increasingly comical ways, like the subject of some diabolical home video show.

Fuck that. I'm not going to let this place beat me. I have to find Dan. I grit my teeth and try again. Eventually I manage to stand, albeit precariously. From this higher vantage point, I take a look at my surroundings but the view just saps my energy further. There's nothing to see for miles but wet black mud, slimy and somehow hateful. I look up. The red gloom hangs heavy all around save for a small round patch of light above, far out of reach, suspended like a low, pale sun. I realise with a sudden, tiny heartbreak what it is. The portal. The route back to earth.

Oh God, what have I done?

None of that! No time for self-pity now. Come on!

I force myself on, seeing no sign of Dan. Where is he? How could he have got so far in such a short time? I take out my phone. Dead. Well, what did I expect? 'Guaranteed service, even in the depths of hell!' I say, laughing a little hysterically. Then I shake myself. I'm finally me again. I can't afford to lose my grip now.

'Find Dan,' I command myself, then look around. 'Dan!' I shout, to no one, and anyway my voice is swallowed up by the mud. There's nobody and nothing here, just an endless wasteland. Maybe this is how it ends, me alone in my own hell because I dared to believe I was destined to become a god.

I stiffen as I hear a noise, something like a roar, faint and far away. I squint into the distance in the direction it came from and I see the dull shine of a huge wall. I recognise it. The bronze walls of Tartarus. The only thing containing Kronos.

But for how long?

Tears come again then and I swipe at them impatiently with a muddy hand. It would be so easy to give in to despair here; I can feel it trying to seep into the gaps in my emotions, in much the same way that the mud has already crept into every available orifice. So I force myself to do what I always do when stuck in a supernatural situation that offers no easy answers: I walk.

Admittedly, that's easier in theory than in practice. As I head across the muddy plain, my sandals sink into the gunge, each step requiring huge effort, as I pull out one foot with a squelch, cursing the clay, slamming down my foot too hard so that my legs slip from under me until, yes, there I am again, face down in the mud.

That's it, the mud seems to say. *There's no point fighting. Just lie down and let me overtake you.* But then a movement catches my eye. In the gloom I can see someone. It's a man, I'm sure of it. Dan! My heart lightens and I push onwards. It's impossible to tell how much time is passing because apparently it never gets any lighter or darker here, the maroon clouds just redden to black in patches and the scenery doesn't change, it's just endless mud and black cliffs and the occasional withered tree. I keep walking, wondering how long it will take for my sandals to fall to pieces after being soaked continually in hell-mud and keeping my eyes trained on the figure.

When he eventually comes in to view my heart sinks. It's not Dan.

The man wears a tunic of rough cloth from which huge arms protrude, muscles rippling. He looks like one of those guys who drag trucks on TV. The biceps are displayed to full advantage as the hulk pushes a huge rock up a steep incline. Something comes back to me, something I read about this man, but I can't grasp it, my brain feels as if it is filling up with sludge. I walk closer.

'Hello?' I call. 'Hi, can you hear me?'

The man clearly does hear me: his face twitches with annoyance. But then he turns back to his rock and continues pushing. I watch as he hefts, sweating and straining, forcing the boulder up the hill. After a super-human effort, this he-man finally reaches the top and rests the stone on the mound's uneven surface, beaming with triumph, then he lifts his arm to wipe the sweat from his brow. It's horribly obvious what's going to happen next. Sure enough, the boulder rolls right back down the hill, the man staring after it, stricken.

'Hey!' I say. 'I'm looking for someone. A man. Have you seen him?'

The beefcake ignores me and just trudges back down the slope after his rock. It comes to me, then, who this is. I *have* read about him. This is Sisyphus, the mortal who so offended the gods with his trickery and arrogance that he was doomed to push a rock up a hill for all eternity. Not a very nice fellow, from what I can recall, but even so, it's painful to watch as he begins his long and miserable descent.

At the bottom, Sisyphus gets behind the rock and starts to

roll it again, back bent, muscles and tendons straining. I'm fixed to the spot, mesmerised as once again, through incredible effort, Sisyphus reaches the top of the hill, balances the boulder, removes his arm to wipe the sweat from his brow and – to his evident surprise – the rock speeds back down the hill again. I watch this spectacle a few more times, occasionally calling his name to see if I can attract his attention, Sisyphus studiously ignoring me, until a biting wind starts up across the plains and I decide I'd better press on and find shelter.

'Thanks for your help,' I mutter, and force myself onwards, wearied legs, dissolving sandals and all.

After some time, I see the first sign of life beyond Sisyphus and mud, and it's as out of place here as an oasis in a desert – a luscious green tree sprouting from the disgusting earth. There's fruit on the tree, a strange mixture of plums and apples and peaches, and a man stands under its branches. He wears royal-looking robes, though they're now well beyond grubby. In front of him, under the tree, spreads a pool of clear blue water.

'Hello,' I say. 'Did you see a man pass by this way? Brown hair? Tattoos . . . er, I mean, pictures on his arms?'

The man ignores me, but I know who this chap is, too. This is King Tantalus, who insulted the immortals by daring to steal ambrosia from Zeus. What was his punishment again? Well, if I really want to know, all I need do is wait.

I watch with trepidation as Tantalus licks his lips and then, seemingly for the first time, spies the ripe fruit hanging from the branches of the tree. He reaches up eagerly, his hand grasping for an apple, and I notice that he's drooling. His ribs are showing through the tears in his gown, he's clearly starving and his eyes are almost mad with delight as he reaches for the fruit. But just as his fingers make contact, the branch moves out of his grasp and his fist closes on empty air. Tantalus slumps, hanging his head.

He stares down at the ground, disconsolate, and then, again apparently for the first time, the king seems to spot the pool of water. Smiling madly, a look of intense relief on his face, Tantalus kneels down and cups his hands to scoop the water. Just as he does so, the water leeches away so the ground is suddenly bare and once again his hands come away empty. Tantalus stares at the dry ground for a moment. Then he begins to sob, horrible heartbreaking sobs of pure torment that are terrible to hear. What a place of cruelty this is.

'Hey,' I say. I walk over. 'Hello?'

Still Tantalus doesn't seem to register me. He's crouched, crying, and licking his own tears as they fall. As I get closer, he stands, still not looking at me and, straightening, he spots a peach in the tree. His eyes brighten with joy as he begins the whole terrible cycle all over again. I can't bear to watch. Maybe if I help him he'll tell me if he's seen anything.

'WAIT!'

Tantalus stops, arm outstretched, and casts a haughty look in my direction.

'Let me get that for you,' I say. I reach up and pluck the fruit, half expecting the branch to move. But no, amazingly enough, I now have a peach in my hand, warm, ripe and juicy. 'Here,' I say, and hand the fruit to the king. His eyes light up

300

as he greedily grabs the peach from me but when he lifts it to take a bite, he spits and splutters. The fruit has transformed into a perfect sphere of black mud in his hand.

Tantalus glares as me. 'What trickery is this?'

'No trickery!' I protest. 'That wasn't me!' With rather less optimism, I bend down and scoop some of the clear water in my hands and lift it to the man's grasping, muddy lips. But the second it reaches him, the water turns to black oil. Tantalus spits it out and shoots me a filthy look.

'Be gone, foul creature!'

Sighing, I lean down again to cup a handful of water, except this time I lift it to my own mouth. To my surprise it is clean and sweet. Reaching up, I pluck an apple and take a bite. Juicy and delicious. I take another drink, casting cautious glances at the beleaguered king in case he gets it into his head to attack me. But Tantalus isn't paying me any attention. Still on his knees, he's staring off into the distance, tears streaking his grubby cheeks. Then he looks up to the tree and sees the fruit. Gets up. Licks his lips. Reaches for it.

And so it goes. And so, by the looks of it, it will always go. Those poor bastards, stuck in these ridiculous, pointless loops. I walk on, chomping on the apple, my spirits revived slightly by the fruit and the water but my mind running over the problem of how I am going to find Dan. Where can he be?

It's not long before another scene comes into view, because of course this cursed place will never run out of people to torture. There is a large bath standing in the mud, and a group of women circle it. I approach cautiously and see that there are seven females, covered head to toe in mud. The bath is filled with clear water and as I watch, one woman dips a large jug into the tub, scooping up the clear water, and then brings it back, ready to pour it over herself. Except, naturally, the jug is cracked and before she can lift it to cleanse herself, all the water has leaked away.

I open my mouth to help, to explain, pointless though it might be, and then I see something else, just visible in the low light. That substance on their bodies is not mud. It has the black-red shine of something far more sinister. And I remember who these women are: the Danaids, the daughters of Danaus, the sisters who killed their husbands on their wedding night and were condemned to Tartarus to try to wash away their sins. Cautiously, I back away before they notice me, then I carry on walking.

After a while I get used to the mud, the cold, the gloom. It seems that it has always been this way. Have I ever known anything else? I walk and I walk and I walk. And then I see him. Oh, thank God!

Dan.

He's found his way to the top of a black and jagged cliff. He stands at the edge, looking out across Tartarus towards the bronze walls. But he's far too close to the drop. One more step and he'll fall.

'Dan! I'm coming!'

I start to climb. The route to Dan is arduous, and as I make my way towards him, the wind whipping up around me, I keep my eye trained on him. He's edging closer and closer to the precipice. What is he doing? Doesn't he see how dangerous it is?

'Dan!' I shout. 'No! Don't move! Stay there!'

Finally he hears me and he turns at the sound of my voice. His face lights up with happiness, but then as he moves towards me his footing falters, he stumbles and, before my eyes, Dan pitches headlong over the cliff to his certain death.

'Dan! Please, no!' I collapse to my knees, sobbing and wailing and beating my fists helplessly against the mud.

After a while, I sit up. Look around. What was I doing? Then I remember. This is no time for resting. I need to find Dan! I stand and start walking and then I see someone. A figure standing on the edge of a cliff. My heart lifts. It's Dan! He's here! But he's standing far too close to the precipice. It's not safe.

'Dan!' I shout. 'I'm coming!'

And I start to climb.

Chapter 35

Hours later, my skin is parched and caked with mud. There's a cruel wind blowing, and it whips black grit across my face, grazing my cheeks. Through the haze, I see Dan. I have to get to him. To tell him I'm sorry. The mud resists me but I redouble my efforts and force myself on. I cannot stop. The wind blows even more fiercely now and I throw an arm in front of my face as I stumble towards the clifftop.

Someone appears in my path.

I squint at them through the dust storm. The figure in front of me looks like some kind of hermit. He has a huge, bushy beard and a bird's nest of hair. His whippet-thin frame is clad in a pair of ragged trousers and a shirt whose better days might have been millennia ago. His feet are bare. As I stare at him, the man's hazel eyes shine through his dirty face and he breaks into a smile.

'Well, hello!' he says.

'Get out of my way,' I mutter. 'I have to save him.'

'Save who?' The hermit looks in the direction I'm facing. 'Who do you see there, Frida?'

For some reason it doesn't seem at all weird that this hairy individual knows my name. I spit out a mouthful of grit and jerk my head to the cliff. 'My friend is up there. He's going to fall if I don't save him.'

The man looks to where I am pointing, then shifts his gaze back to me and shakes his head, sadly but kindly. 'I'm afraid you're quite wrong. There's no one there. It's your loop, you see.'

'Can you move?' I glare at him. 'I haven't got time for this!' I look at Dan; he's too close to the edge. Can't he see it's dangerous? 'Get out of my way,' I say, swiping at the man. 'Move! I mean it!'

But the hermit doesn't move. He just peers at me with those bright eyes and smiles that odd smile. 'You don't recognise me, do you?'

I look at him and as I meet the man's soft hazel gaze I'm slammed with a jolt of memory, but before I can grasp it that mental fog descends again. I shake my head. 'Do I know you?'

'You used to,' he says. 'But it has been a long time. Years. Funny, though, I knew you straight away! "That's her," I said to myself. "That's your little Frida. My little hero."'

'What the hell are you talking about?'

'But,' the hermit continues as though I haven't spoken, 'it's not surprising that you don't know me.' He sighs sadly. 'You were so very young when I left.' He looks down at his shirt. 'And it is possible I have become a little dishevelled from spending so long down here.' Then he beams at me and that something flickers again. A memory of those kind hazel eyes. That smile. Then it comes to me. I understand who this is meant to be.

'Oh, I see!' I say. 'Ha! Very good, very clever!' I wheel around and give Tartarus a little round of applause. At some point I have begun to treat this hell pit like it is an actual being, vindictively determined to thwart me. 'You think showing me a mirage of my dead father is going to distract me from saving Dan? Pluck on my heartstrings and have me waylaid into some tearful reunion? Nice try. But I'm not an idiot. My father isn't in Tartarus. My father is dead.'

And with that, I walk resolutely around the mirage of my father. The mirage scurries after me and tugs at my sleeve. For a hallucination, he's surprisingly corporeal.

'Please stop for a moment, Frida,' the mirage says. 'It really is me. I'm really here. I was sent to help you.'

'Nope!' I say. 'Not listening!' I plug my ears and sing to myself as I plough on determinedly through the mud, my eyes on Dan, who is straying far too close to the cliff edge. The hermit-father mirage is nothing if not persistent. He plants himself in front of me so that I stumble and have to pull my fingers out of my ears to keep myself upright, letting his words in.

'Frida, listen to me for a moment. Whatever you see up there, that's not your friend.'

'Yep! That's just what a trick of Tartarus would say!'

The man smiles patiently. 'Actually, no. A trick of Tartarus would be much more likely to keep you locked in a loop of behaviour, such as trying to rescue someone you love, watching them die and then making you forget that had happened so you can try to rescue them all over again.'

I stop walking. Okay, the mirage has a point. But then I glance up at the peak and Dan is still there. He's in danger. I shake my fuzzy head, trying to clear my thoughts. 'You don't understand,' I tell the hermit-father mirage. 'It's Dan. I have to save him.'

The hermit dad's face is gentle, his eyes sad. 'No, Frida, that's exactly what you need not to do. You'll never save him, because that is not your friend. Dan is here, somewhere. Has been for days, maybe longer. I've been trying to find him myself but—'

'Days! Ha! Now I know you're lying. Dan has been here a few hours at most, he fell through just before I did.' I look at the cliff edge. 'He's up there, see!'

'Well, actually, time moves differently down here,' the hermit father says. He's awfully chatty for a mirage. 'A minute up there can mean anything from a millisecond to a millennium down here.' He looks around vaguely. 'It all depends where he landed.'

I stare at the man. I've no idea what he is talking about. All I know is he's getting in my way. 'I need to save Dan,' I say firmly.

'Agreed,' the hermit returns, 'but that's not him. And the longer you spend trying to get to him, over and over again, the greater the chance that you will lose the real Dan for good.' The hermit-father mirage looks around. 'If you really want

307

to help Dan then you need to come with me. And quickly, too; it's not safe out here.' He looks around as a vicious wind whips our clothing and grit smatters our skin. 'A terrible dust storm is coming,' he says, 'and that will bring the Harpies.'

The wind gusts at us then, blowing my filthy hair back from my face, and suddenly the hermit's face breaks into a beaming smile.

'Ah, you still have it?' he says delightedly. I look down. He's staring at the gold chain and heart pendant, now barely visible it is so encrusted with hell-dirt. As he looks at it, the hermit's hairy face turns wistful. 'I remember when I gave that to you. It was your eighth birthday. I've never seen anyone look so pleased about anything.' He tips his head to one side thoughtfully. 'Your mother hated it.'

'She said it was tacky—'

'She said it was tacky—' We speak at the same time. I stare at him. His eyes twinkle.

The Tartarus mind-fog lifts then and I see the man in front of me as though properly for the first time. Not a mirage. Flesh and blood. *My* flesh and blood.

'Dad?' I say in a quavering voice. 'Is it really you?'

The hermit smiles. 'Yes, Frida, it's really me.'

I stare at him, frozen to the spot for a moment, and then I am flinging my arms around him, nine years old again, waiting at the door for my father to return. I'm the young, wounded Frida who in some ways has spent her whole life waiting for him. Tears course down my face as I cling to my father like a drowning person clings to a life raft.

'You came back to me, you came back. You came back to

308

me. She said you weren't coming back but I knew you'd never leave me, not your Frida,' I say, 'not your little hero.' And my voice is choked, the sobs overtake me and I cry deeply, painfully, like I haven't cried in twenty-one years, and my father's wiry arms are around me as he strokes my hair and tells me it's okay, it's okay, he's here now and everything's going to be okay.

Chapter 36

I find myself in a round mud hut, a small fire crackling in the centre of the room.

After I understood that it really was my father and not just one of Tartarus's tricks, the spectre of Dan began to fade before my eyes, his outline getting hazier, until my beloved Dan was nothing but empty air. Then, as the dust storm whipped up around us, I let my hermit-father miracle lead me to shelter.

My dad now deposits me on to a bank of sofa-shaped mud, scurries off and comes back a moment later with a blanket. 'Here you are,' he says. 'You get yourself warm. Tartarus is always bitterly cold.' He pauses. 'Unless you like it cold, in which case it's always blisteringly hot.'

Obediently, I curl up, pulling the blanket over myself until only my head is visible. It seems to be made from leaves but it's soft and warm and comforting. My father perches next to me, evidently as entranced at the sight of me as I am by him. I reach out a hand and tug at his beard. Prod his thin, muscly arms.

'It's really, really you,' I say wonderingly.

'Yes, Frida,' he says softly, smiling. 'It's really, really me.'

'But how? I mean ... how?' Tears fill my eyes again and I blink them away. 'I lost you. I thought for so long that you'd left me. And then I thought you'd died in the Underworld. And now you're here.' I shake my head. 'I don't understand.'

'No,' my father nods, 'It's rather unusual. I'll explain everything. But first,' he claps his hands together, 'you need to eat.'

I put a hand against my stomach. The only thing I've had to eat in hours is the fruit from Tantalus's tree. Either the ambrosia or Tartarus has wiped all thought of food. 'I don't think I'm hungry,' I say.

'Well, you won't be,' my father says. 'Tartarus does tend to quash one's appetite – unless you're poor Tantalus, that is. But still, you have to eat. You need your strength. Let me fetch you something. Just rest, I won't be a moment.'

'Dad,' I call after him.

He turns.

I peer at him with big eyes. 'It's really you? I'm not dreaming? Because I had this dream a lot when I was little. You came back to me and I was so happy. But then I'd wake up and ... you were still gone.'

'It's really me,' he says softly, with a sad smile. 'It isn't a dream. And I'm not going anywhere. You just rest now, my love.'

311

My father – my father! – disappears through an archway and I hear faint sounds of clanking, objects being moved around. While he's gone, I look around the hut. Everything appears to be made of mud. This sofa, the bookshelves, the table are all made from the same fired black earth. My father returns with some clay bowls on a wooden tray. Fruit. Water. And a plate of – oh my Lord – snails as big as hamsters, still in their shells.

'Here you go!' he says, evidently very pleased with himself. I look down at the snails. One is still alive. It wiggles enormous tentacles at me mournfully and what little anticipatory appetite I may have had takes flight. 'Maybe later,' I say.

My father scrubs at his beard. 'Oh dear, sorry. I forgot. They are rather an acquired taste. Took me around five years to get one down, I lived on fruit and leaves before that. But I love them now!' He picks up a snail and sucks it out of its shell. It squelches as he chomps. Averting my eyes, I reach for a peach and bite into it, delicious – my father must shop at Tantalus's fruit stall, too. I take a sip of water. Then I really look at my father, examining the face behind the scraggy beard and the mud. The wide smile. His sparkling eyes. That cheerful, always-positive attitude that used to so grate on my mother. It's actually him. What madness is this? I hold out my hand and when my father places his hand in mine, it is warm and feels like safety. My dad!

Tears run unchecked down my cheeks. 'I can't believe it's you. What are you doing here?'

He squeezes my hand. 'I've been waiting for you, Frida.'

'You have?' I say. 'How? Why? Tell me everything.'

'Well,' my father says, 'I'll certainly try. But be warned, I might be a little rusty at storytelling. It's been a while since I have had a conversation with a mortal!'

'That's okay,' I say, smiling. 'Just do your best.'

'Well,' he says, 'as you mentioned, I died down in the Underworld trying to get that blasted arrow.'

'Oh,' I say, taken aback. 'So, you did die? I thought, since you were here ... you might be ... but, no? You're still ... actually dead?'

'Oh yes, completely dead,' my father says cheerfully. 'The river spirit got me – disguised as my old golfing friend Herbert.' He shakes his head ruefully. 'I should have known really, Herbert hated to swim.' He drifts off for a moment and then snaps back. 'Anyway!' he says. 'Once that happened, I died, as I say.'

He's awfully casual about it.

'Then why are you in Tartarus?' I ask, my anger rising as I think about it. 'Surely you trying to help me was a good thing? You shouldn't be punished for that!'

'Oh, I wasn't punished, I was rewarded!' my father says with evident surprise. 'I got my greatest wish, after all.'

I stare at him. 'Lifetime supply of mud?'

'Ah, you're still funny. I love that!' He laughs, rubbing his beard. 'But no, sweet-pea, my greatest wish was to help you!'

Sweet-pea. A lump forms in my throat. No one has called me sweet-pea since I was nine years old.

'It turns out that, according to the old mythical laws, I was a hero,' my father explains. 'Under usual circumstances I'd have been sent to Elysium, the paradise for heroes.' He smiles

313

wistfully. 'Imagine meeting Achilles, Jason, Hippolyta! What stories they could tell. Anyway, I was given a choice. I could go to Elysium or I could help you by coming down here.'

I can't speak. My father descended into hell, for me, twice! Then it dawns on me what this means and it's like a punch to the gut.

'You mean you've been here for twenty-one years?' I ask, aghast.

'Oh no!' he says and I breathe a sigh of relief, then he adds, 'It's been quite a bit longer than that.' I stare at him, stricken.

'As I said, time moves differently down here,' he goes on chirpily. 'In fact, it does whatever it wants,' he muses. 'Time just can't seem to impose any rules on old Tartarus.' He sucks a snail from its shell with a pop.

'How many years?' I ask quietly.

My father waggles his head from side to side. 'Oh, I'm not sure. Somewhere between a hundred and, say, a thousand?' he says. 'I lost count. But, look, I haven't aged a day!'

'But that's . . .' I shake my head. I can't stand it. It's too horrible. He's been trapped down here for all these years because of me? Am I a curse to everyone and everything in my life?

Seeing my face, my father reaches over to pat my arm. 'It's okay, love. I kept myself occupied. I spent a number of years building this hut and everything in it.'

I look about me and force a smile. 'I love what you've done with the place.'

'Well, with a bit of ingenuity there's not much that you can't make with mud and leaves.' He beams proudly. 'I even made some books, rewrote them from memory.' He gestures to a dozen bundles of leaves on the bookshelf. 'Although, I think I may have got them a little wrong. Can you confirm, did Jane Eyre give up Mr Rochester to become a pig farmer? Did Moby Dick end up beached?' He frowns. 'So many of the stories I remember seem to end with their characters stuck in mud.'

I look at my father and let out a sob. He's totally crackers and it's all my fault.

'There, there.' My dad puts a grimy arm around me. 'It's okay. I was happy to be here, Frida. It was destiny, you see!'

'What kind of a destiny is this?'

'Well, I was supposed to wait for you and then when you got here, I'd be able to help you. And here I am. And here you are.' My father's muddy face shines. 'And so I will!'

'How are you going to help me?' I wail. 'There's no way out and those walls are about to fall. And now we're both stuck down here and Dan is too!'

My father's brow furrows. 'Well, that's a rather negative way of looking at the situation, Frida.'

I blink. 'You say negative. I say rational.'

'The first thing we'll do is find your Dan,' my father says, ignoring me. 'Just as soon as the storm has passed. Yes, yes,' he mutters to himself. 'Dan is central to all of this. Sort of a . . . firelighter, as it were.'

'What?' I frown at him. 'He's going to light fires for you?'

My father looks at me, puzzled. 'Oh no, that's a lovely offer, but I can light my own fires, thank you, Frida. Wouldn't have survived very long down here if I couldn't!'

Okaaay. Mad as a box of frogs. I steer the conversation back to saner ground. 'So how do we find him?'

'Not sure yet,' he says brightly. 'Might be a bit tricky but I'm sure we'll be lucky!'

Lucky? In this place. I stare at my father's ridiculously cheerful countenance and something occurs to me. 'How have you lasted this long down here without getting caught in your own loop?'

'Oh, I didn't have a loop.'

'Why not?'

'Because I'm not being punished for anything.'

'So why was I . . .?' I see my father's face and stop. 'Oh.' There's a long silence as I take it in. 'Because I took the ambrosia?' My father nods and I give a bitter laugh. 'I'm no better than those sinners out there, am I? Unlike you, I actually deserve to be down here.'

My father ignores this. 'Dan won't have a loop either,' he muses, 'which is a blessing because once you're a full day into a loop, it's impossible to break.'

'So, Dan's not in danger?' My heart quickens.

'Oh, I didn't say that.' He picks up an apple and stares at it thoughtfully. 'You've felt what this place can do to a person. Tartarus is not simply a hell pit, it's an entity, alive itself in a way. We just have to pray that Dan has been down here for days and not years.'

'Years?' I gaze at my father, incredulous.

My father nods and bites crunchily into the apple. 'He may have gone quite mad, if so. And that's not much use to us, is it?'

I put my head in my hands. Just when I think I cannot fuck things up any more, I'm able to just squeeze a bit more fuckery out.

316

'But, not to worry,' my father says, patting my hand. 'We'll pay Arges a visit; I'm sure she'll help us find him.'

'Who's Arges?'

'The cyclops.' He sees my blank face. 'You know about Arges, surely, Frida?'

'Why would I know about Arges?' I say, bristling at his tone. It reminds me of when I was little and he found out I hadn't done my homework.

'I taught you all about Arges!' my father insists. 'Although admittedly I didn't realise before I arrived here that Arges was, in fact, a female cyclops. Her gender was written out of the ancient myths. And she's not happy about that, let me tell you!' He looks puzzled when I don't respond. 'I'm talking about Arges and Brontes and Steropes. Kronos's siblings. The three cyclops who guard Tartarus. You must remember the stories, Frida. I taught you all of this when you were little!'

I fiddle with the blanket of leaves. 'Yes, well, Mum had my memory wiped so I suppose when I finally got those stories back, they must have had a few holes in them.'

My father watches me for a moment, so much feeling in those soft eyes of his. Then he takes my hand again and gives it a squeeze. 'I'm sorry I wasn't there for you when you were growing up, Frida.'

'It's fine.' A lump has appeared in my throat.

'No, it's not.' He holds my gaze, serious now. 'I know how hard it must have been for you, especially knowing your mother's attitude towards the magical.' He looks at me sadly. 'When I descended into the Underworld, you lost me and I lost you. I would have truly loved to watch you grow up into the fine woman that you have become, but,' he shrugs his grubby shoulders, 'I think this was all fated. We are all exactly where we are meant to be.'

A silence falls then. I hold his hand and just enjoy his presence. Here I am, with my dear, departed dad in a mythical hell prison, on the cusp of the end of the world. Good times.

My father looks out of the hut. 'The storm is clearing.'

'So we can go and see Arges? She'll help us find Dan?' Untangling myself from the blanket, I leap up.

My father stands, smiling widely, nodding. 'I had a wager with her. She said you would never arrive.' He rubs his hands together. 'That one-eyed chancer owes me twenty snails!'

318

Chapter 37

We head off together across the black bog and towards the prison that has caused all this trouble.

I was somewhat fearful that Kronos would just be wandering around Tartarus, a free-range Titan. But no, it transpires there are two parts to this hell pit. The outer circle, where we are currently situated, is where once-mortal beings are detained. And then there's the high-security prison for the supernatural, with its bronze walls, built to contain the sort of monsters who can never die and must never be freed.

But just because the Titan king is currently incarcerated, that doesn't mean I can't feel him. Even without any magical love goddess abilities, the closer we get to that bronze wall, the more I sense Kronos's darkness, his emptiness, an oppressive aura of despair that increases until it feels like a thinning of the air, hands closing around my throat. Everything in my body rebels, tells me to get far, far away from here. As we approach, the walls of the prison rear up, just like they did in Dionysus's fire vision, so tall and so wide I can't see where they begin or end.

So this is it, the only way in or out of Tartarus, kept sealed all these years by the mortals' faith in love. All this time we were doing something magnificent and we didn't even know it. As we walk, I think about what my father has said. Can he really help me? Does he have a way for us to stop Anteros before – and rarely does a person get to say this and mean it literally – all hell breaks loose? But before I can ask him for the finer details, my train of thought is interrupted by the astonishing sight of a cyclops flashing me a peace sign.

'You said there were three?' I say quietly. 'Where are the other two?'

'Well,' my father says, 'you have to remember, for millennia this was the most boring and pointless job in the Universe, so a while ago, the three of them drew straws and Arges was left to hold the fort.'

'She's the only one guarding the wall?' I stare at him, alarmed.

'Oh no! We've a trio of Hundred-handed Hecatoncheires patrolling the entire perimeter. But you probably don't want to meet them.' He grimaces. 'They can get a bit touchy-feely, especially with anyone new.'

We approach Arges, who waves at us, a large grin on her considerable face. She's about twenty feet tall, with a greyish-pink skin and wears a sort of vest with epaulettes and trousers made from a combination of animal furs and skins. Her hair stands up from her head in tight corkscrews.

I can't help but stare at this tremendous creature, and Arges seems equally intrigued as she trains her single eye on me, its iris a brilliant violet.

My father beams, one arm thrown around my shoulder. 'Now, didn't I tell you she'd come? And look, isn't she just wonderful!'

The cyclops frowns and peers down at me. 'Is this your Frida?' She prods me with one enormous finger. 'Surely not! She's far too lovely to have come from a hairy bag of bones like you!'

'Hello, Arges,' I say politely and offer my hand. In response, the cyclops picks me up by the scruff of my dress, raises me to her face and sniffs me. I actually feel the wind suck at my clothing as it travels into her nostrils. I stare into her huge eye.

'I'm Frida,' I squeak. 'How are you?'

She widens her eye and then turns her gaze on my father. 'It's really her. She came!'

'Didn't I tell you? You owe me, Arg!'

The cyclops lowers me gently on to a tall platform erected next to the gate, then picks my father up and deposits him there, too. Now our faces are level, she smiles at me. 'Very nice to meet you, tiny human.'

'Nice to meet you too.'

A noise comes from behind the bronze walls, a deafening howl that chills my blood, followed by a whooshing and then the prison rattles with the impact of something very heavy and very determined. I glance at the walls nervously. They still hold, for now.

Arges frowns. 'Kronos,' she says, shaking her head. 'Never thought I'd see the day.' She grimaces, showing knobby grey teeth.

I look again at the wall and see a small shiny hole, about the size of my head.

'What is that?'

Arges looks at the hole and then at me. 'Spyhole. So I can keep an eye on my brother.'

'Can I . . .?' I swallow. 'I want to see.'

'Frida,' my father says, 'I'm not sure—'

'Oh, let her see!' Arges says. 'You're expecting her to stop him, after all. Shouldn't she know what she's up against?'

My father surveys me. 'Are you sure you want to, Frida?'

'I'm sure.'

Arges holds out a hand. 'Climb on,' she says and then she lifts me to the hole.

I peer through it. I can see something, in the distance, something dark. It takes me a moment to focus. And then . . .

I thought I had seen Kronos in the fire. Dan saw him in his vision, too, but I understand now that, as horrific as these depictions were, they were just futile attempts to capture something beyond representation. As I gaze through that spyhole, the knowledge seeps into my cells. Kronos is not a being any more. Not a monster. Not a king. Not a thing at all. All these millennia spent steeped in his own savagery has transfigured him into darkness. He is an absence, now. Wrath in shadow form. And if he is allowed to escape these prison walls, he will drain the light out of every last thing in existence.

As I stand there, mesmerised by this monstrous entity, it swirls and suddenly rises, sweeping upwards like a murmuration, darkness concentrated and heading directly for me. I want to cry out, to step away, to close my eyes, but I can't move, can't look away. He is madness and he is terror and he is desolation and *if thou gaze long into an abyss, the abyss will also gaze into thee*. Faster, faster, Kronos shoots up to the spyhole and he looks into me and he *knows* me, his sickly, shadow fingers crawling inside my brain and—

'That's quite enough of that,' Arges says and pulls me away. I reel, gasping, my heart pounding, and as Arges lowers me back on to the platform, I meet my father's gaze.

'So, now you know,' he says.

I stare at him, appalled. Now I know.

'Now, Arges,' my father says brightly, clapping his hands briskly as though I haven't just seen something truly harrowing that will haunt my nightmares for the rest of my (I'm thinking now probably very short) life. 'We're looking for Frida's friend. A mortal man called Dan. Have you seen him?'

'Another man-human!' Arges says to me. 'Boy, would I love to see another one other than this scrawny specimen!' She sighs. 'But no, I haven't seen anything.'

My shoulders collapse. Where is he?

'But,' Arges goes on, 'how about I take you for a walk around the place and we can look for him? You'll cover more ground that way.'

I look at my father and he nods, encouraging. I smile weakly up at Arges. 'That would be great. Thank you.'

And with that, the cyclops picks us up and pops us on to

what are not, actually, epaulettes but two shoulder saddles. As we strap ourselves in, Arges sets off across the plain. Travelling by cyclops. Well, why not? Makes as much sense as anything else in my life right now. As we bump over the black earth, I'm distracted from the horrifying memory of Kronos as Arges gives us a running commentary on the sights, like it's the Hollywood Tour – there's Salmoneus, younger brother of Sisyphus, standing under a rock that perpetually falls on his head; here's Ixion, tied to a fiery wheel for eternity; oh, and there's Tityos. Arges points to a giant lying on his back, seemingly asleep.

'And what's his punishment?'

'Livers fed on by vultures,' she says with evident relish. 'Oooh, look out, here they come.'

At the anguished screams of the giant, I have to cover my ears until Arges finally bores of the grisly sight and we're off again, pounding around the circumference of the prison walls. And yet still there's no sign of Dan. Since Arges seems to have run out of torture victims to regale me with, I take advantage of the silence and turn to my father.

'We cannot let *that*,' I give an involuntary shudder, 'get to earth.'

My father looks at me. 'No,' he agrees.

'Okay, so we need to start making a plan.' I pause. 'How many people have ever escaped Tartarus?'

'At last count?' he says cheerily. 'None!'

I blink at him. 'None?'

'Exactly.'

'But you have a way to help us escape, don't you?'

'Oh no. I've no idea how you do it!'

I stare at his affable face. I never thought I'd say this, but I actually am starting to see where my mother was coming from. I'm happier than I ever thought possible to be reunited with my father, but his inane chirpiness in the face of certain doom is really starting to grind my gears. I slump in the saddle as Arges continues to traipse around these blasted plains. What a mess. Even if I can find Dan, what the hell then? Everything I do just seems to make things worse.

I suddenly remember Anteros's mocking words.

'Dad, I need to ask you something.' I meet his eyes. 'Did I cause all of this? Because Anteros said that if I hadn't brought down NeoStar there would have been no backlash against love, and The Love Delusion movement would never have picked up enough momentum to collapse the walls.'

My father looks at me sadly. 'Frida . . .'

'Is it true?' I squeak.

My father looks at me for a long moment. 'Yes,' he says. 'It's true.'

I stare at him. Anteros was telling the truth. If that foul entity is let loose on earth, it will be down to me. You know how people say, 'Oh well, it's not the end of the world'? Well, now it literally is, and what's more, it's my fault. I stare at the black ground, endless miles of it, no Dan in sight. I've failed. No, actually, we need a new word for how badly I've fucked up. It's an actual fact that the world would have been far better off if I'd never been born.

'You were right about me, Dad,' I say. 'I'm no hero.'

'And when did I ever say you were not a hero?'

'You don't have to pretend.' I stare down miserably at the mud. 'You didn't believe I could fulfil the prophecy, that's why you tried to do it for me. I know how much of a disappointment I must be to you.'

His eyes widen in surprise. 'Frida,' he says softly, 'I didn't try to save you because I doubted you. I did it because I knew what you would have to become and what it would cost you.' He scratches his beard. 'Some parents want their children to be extraordinary but, in the end, the most wonderful life a person can have is an ordinary one.' He smiles. 'I just wanted to give you a chance of that. But I always believed in you, Frida. Always.'

'Well, you were wrong to, Dad. I'm not like Achilles or Jason or Odysseus. I don't have faith in the gods. I don't believe in destiny any more. I thought I understood what they wanted me to do, but it turns out that was just my rampant megalomania having its say. I don't have what it takes to save anyone or anything. I'm just a fucked-up human.'

My father doesn't speak for a moment. Then he says softly, 'Do you think you'd have fared better if you were cut from the same cloth as those heroes you just mentioned? Let me tell you something about those classical heroes, Frida. Their heroism cost them dearly.'

'What do you mean?'

'Well, Achilles may have triumphed as a great warrior, but he was killed in battle by Paris with a poisoned arrow in his vulnerable spot. Odysseus had his wiles, but he was murdered by his own son.' My father shakes his head. 'And Jason's adventures left him cursed,' he says thoughtfully. 'Eventually, he became a drifter and was killed by the falling of the rotting stern of his own beloved ship.'

I raise an eyebrow. 'Has anyone ever told you that your pep talk needs work?'

'What I'm trying to say,' he tells me, smiling, 'is I don't think the gods chose you because you were a typical hero. I think they chose you exactly because of what you just said you are: a typical mortal.'

My actual words were 'fucked-up human' but I suppose it amounts to the same thing.

'So I'm not special,' I say bleakly. 'I knew it.'

My father tugs at his beard. 'No, you're not getting it, Frida,' he says gently. 'And you might want to watch your tendency towards self-pity. It's a distraction, and a vice just as dangerous as hubris.'

I wince at this. Arges clears her throat and carries on pretending she's not listening to every word.

'Why do you think Anteros can manipulate the mortals so well?' my father asks.

I stare out at the dull panorama. 'Because he understands how mortals work and he takes advantage of that.'

'And how does he understand us so well?'

I think about this, remembering what I saw in his emotions down there in the crypt. 'Maybe because he's got all our worst bits. He's paranoid, jealous, scared, angry, arrogant . . .'

'Exactly,' my father says. 'He understands how to influence mortals because he has much in common with us. Unlike Eros.'

I frown at him. 'Unlike Eros?'

327

My father nods. 'The thing about Eros is he believes every mortal has the capacity for pure love, but he's not so hot on the other stuff – the hatred, the pain, the fear, everything the mortals have to get through to access that spark of goodness. Love is so clear to Eros, but that's not always that helpful. It's like someone who was born on top of a mountain trying to tell someone else how to climb that mountain.'

'What's your point, Dad?' I sigh.

'Impatience, too, Frida. You get that from your mother.'

I glare at him.

'My point,' he says mildly, 'is that you seem to think this whole thing would have gone better if you'd been some perfect, pious, archetypal hero. But that's not true.'

'Well, patently it is true, because look where we are!' Tears spring in my eyes and roll down my cheeks. 'I don't want this, Dad. I've tried but I can't do it. It's too hard.'

'I know, Frida,' my father says, 'but, you see, human life is hard. It's rarely fair and seldom very easy.' I look into his eyes then and for the briefest second I see what his life must have been like here. What it has cost him to exist in a hell pit for all this time. Then he smiles and it lights up his face. 'But there is goodness too, Frida. Always, there is light after the darkness.'

Not always, I think grimly. Sometimes, after the darkness, there's just more darkness. And I know then that my father's insane optimism isn't enough to sustain me.

'Listen, Dad, I hear what you're saying, but to me it's just words. You found something to hope for, even down here, because that's the kind of person you are. But I'm not like you. I'm just not that optimistic. What on earth is there even to hope for any more? Even if Kronos doesn't annihilate us, we'll probably just kill ourselves off within a hundred years anyway.'

My father frowns at me. 'No, Frida. I don't think that's true—'

'Hey, you've been gone a while.' I lift my eyes to that pale portal. 'You don't know what it's like up there. As a species we are fucked. Anteros can only do what he does because we let him, because a part of us invites it. We're weak,' I say. 'We're selfish. We are scared. We're greedy and we are hateful. Eros was wrong to gamble on us. We chose his brother's way again and again. There's nothing noble about us. We're barely more than animals.'

My dad surveys me sombrely but doesn't say anything. Maybe deep down he knows I'm right. Arges plods on, but what little light we had is fading and the wind whips black grit into our eyes. Another storm is brewing.

'We'll have to go soon,' the cyclops says, looking to the sky. 'The harpies are circling.'

'No sign of a mortal man, Arges?'

She shakes her head. 'Are you *sure* he's down here?' she asks. 'We've covered all the ground. We should have seen him by now.'

'We're sure.' My father scratches his head. 'You really want to find Dan, don't you?'

'Of course I do.'

'You were happy together? You love each other?'

'We were, we did.' I shake my head bleakly. 'I don't know

what we are any more. But he's a good man, a wonderful human being. He doesn't deserve any of what's happened to him.'

'And you were quite unfair to him, were you, before Anteros threw him down here?'

I stare at my father. Way to go, reminding me of my fuck-ups, Dad. I think back to how I treated Dan – how I refused to listen to him, led Anteros's guards right to him, abandoned him to an eternity in hell – and a dark feeling of shame suffuses me. 'I treated him horribly,' I say with difficulty. 'I don't know if he'll ever forgive me.'

I stare out at the mud, my eyes blurred by tears. Dan is lost. He's been down here for what might have been thousands of years already and it is all my fault. Now I am forced to think about it, the images come, painful and vivid. I'm disgusted with myself. Even if we found him, what could I say? Hey, Dan! Sorry I went expressly against my promise to you, lied to you, trashed all your attempts to help me, and then almost left you to rot in another dimension?

I close my eyes. Maybe it's better if we don't find him. Poor Dan is better off without me anyway. What have I ever done for him but cause him pain? What would I do if I saw him now? It would kill me to see the look in his eyes, to see his fear of me, his disappointment, his disgust at how I—

'There he is!' shouts Arges.

My eyes fly open and I watch as Arges stretches a hefty finger, pointing to a small mud cave that I am certain we have passed several times already. But sure enough, I see a figure there – torn clothes, muddy face, eyes ever so slightly wild. He staggers to his feet and waves at us.

'Do you see that too?' I ask my father, just to double check it's not another mirage.

'Oh yes,' my father says cheerily. 'That's your Dan all right.'

My heart soars. 'Arges, set me down. Dan!' I cry. 'Dan! Dan, it's us! We're here!'

Arges lowers us gently to the floor and I run over to Dan, feet hardly touching the mud, tears flooding down my cheeks as I wrap this muddy man in my arms, enfolding him in a hug so fierce that I almost squeeze the breath out of him.

'I'm so sorry, I'm so sorry, I'm so sorry, I'm so sorry.'

Dan's arms close around me; he reaches one hand up to my head, strokes my muddy hair and pulls me even closer, so that I feel his warm body against mine.

'It's okay, Freed,' he says. 'We found each other. I told you we would.' I pull back, arms still around his waist, and stare up at his face, not daring to hope.

Dan grins at me and as I look into those gorgeous eyes, I see something amazing.

He has his memories back.

Chapter 38

'God, I've missed you,' I say for about the millionth time.

Over at my father's hut, Dan and I sit on the mud sofa, arms entwined, staring at each other, wearing ridiculously soppy grins. Here we are in the depths of hell and I don't think I have ever felt so happy. Dan woke up in Tartarus with his memories returned. It seems even Lethe magic can't survive down here. I'm deeply grateful for this stinking pit for returning my love to me.

'And I've missed you,' Dan says, smiling and then wincing. He puts a hand to the gash on his cheek. 'Always wanted to see a Harpy. Kind of regretting that wish now. Evil little fuckers.'

'How did you survive on your own all these days?' I say, stroking his forehead. I'm so relieved Dan has only been stranded in Tartarus for three days and not three weeks, or, you know, three centuries. My dad was right. We were lucky.

'Mainly by eating snails. They're a bit chewy at first but I started to quite like them after a while.'

'Then you're going to go nuts for my father's menu.' I look at him searchingly. 'But seriously, what about the despair? Has it been awful?'

Dan twines his fingers in mine. 'Well, at first, what with all the mud and the torture, I did feel a tiny bit depressed,' he says. 'But then I found a shelter and a source of fresh snails and I just knew I had to hunker down and wait it out.' He meets my eyes. 'I knew you'd come for me, Frida. You always do.'

I cringe. Stare down at the muddy floor. Pick up a clay cup and study the leaf pattern my father has scribed into it. Gaze over to my father who is crouched over a box in the corner of the hut, tinkering with something. Do I tell Dan now that I left him for dead? As grim as it is, I make a vow that my days of lying to him are over.

'Okay, well, the thing is, Dan . . . I didn't come for you. At first, I mean.' I flush. 'I was all hopped up on ambrosia, and I was sort of possessed by the dark love goddess and I, well, she, really, was convinced she could defeat Anteros, so . . .'

'You tried to shoot him and close the portal?'

I stare at him.

'Oh, I know you did, Frida,' Dan says, laughing at my shamefaced confession. 'You were well gone by then.' He pulls me closer, and I tuck my head into the nook in his neck. 'But I also knew that it didn't matter, because it wouldn't close the portal.'

'How did you know?'

He reaches out and pulls one of my muddy curls. 'Because it's Frida McKenzie who is destined to stop Anteros. And that wasn't her.'

Tears rush into my eyes and I swipe them away. How does this man have so much faith in me?

'Oh, but Dan, I really fucked up, didn't I?'

Dan looks around us. 'I don't know. It could be worse. You don't have any bagpipes, do you?'

I laugh, still crying, and give him a playful shove. 'I'm serious. Shout at me, please. I need you to. I feel so terrible.'

Dan pulls me back towards him and holds my face in his hands. His gaze is intense, filled with love but with other, more complex emotions, too. Then he kisses me and I know that whatever we had, it's still there.

'You did fuck up,' he says. 'Bigtime. But so did I.'

'No—'

'I did,' Dan says. 'I should have spoken to you again about the ambrosia, instead of leaving myself notes. And afterwards, when I was Lethed and I found my message, well, I handled it badly.'

'No,' I say, 'you were right.' I bite my lip. 'Something in me wanted to take it. I wouldn't have listened to you, whatever you said.'

'It's not your fault, Frida. There was magic inside you, magic you didn't ask for.' He shrugs. 'You did your best. We both did.'

But it wasn't good enough, I think. *Not even close.*

'Dan, I saw Kronos.'

His face darkens and I know he's remembering that first,

334

dark vision. 'I don't suppose my picture was an exaggeration, was it? Or, maybe it was to scale and he's really teeny, like a small whirlwind?'

I grimace. 'Sadly, no. Kind of the exact opposite of that, in fact.'

'Right.' He sighs and then traces the line of my cheek with his finger. Kisses me again. 'So, come on then, out with it. What's the grand plan?'

Time for bad news part two. 'Well, that's just it,' I say bleakly. 'There's no way out of here. I'm beginning to think that maybe my father was sent to Tartarus so that I could be with the people I love at the end.'

My father pops up behind the sofa then, giving me a start.

'That's a lovely sentiment, Frida, but rather self-indulgent and, also, utterly wrong. I was actually sent here to give you this.' He points to the wooden box he has dragged over and then opens the lid. We stare down into the case. It contains what looks like a small, grey cannonball.

'I knew what I was supposed to do as soon as I saw it,' he says, grinning.

'What is it?' I ask.

'An Ophiotaurus bomb! Made from the entrails of the actual beast,' my father says proudly. 'Now, it won't be as powerful as it would if you had burned them yourself, natur-ally, which means you don't have the power to kill Anteros. But this will certainly be enough to render him unconscious, which should break his hold over the mortals.' He beams at us. 'Well, what do you think?'

I look down at the dusty orb. I've seen Ophiotaurus ashes

335

employed as a weapon before. Dan used them to rescue me from a kidnapping once, long ago, and they were what Psyche's bullets were made of, the ones she used to threaten Hades. But those were ancient ashes, from a beast killed millennia ago, faded in power. Not strong enough to break Anteros's mighty hold over the mortals. But this ... one bomb made from the burned entrails of an entire beast? This might just work.

Dan stares at my father admiringly. 'Did you kill this yourself, Mr McKenzie?'

'Lord no.' My father chuckles. 'Have you seen these beasts? Half bull, half serpent. Absolutely enormous!' He tips his head to one side, thoughtful. 'Although, in reality, they're actually great big softies. No.' He shakes his head. 'The Harpies got to this one. It was already dying. So I brought it in here, and nursed it until it passed. I even gave her a name. I called her Faith.' He smiles at me. 'Then I gave her a cremation. And now you have a weapon that can harm the gods!'

'This is brilliant!' Dan says.

'It is,' I say carefully, 'but – and I hate to poop the party – how are we going to use this if we can't get back to earth?'

My father scratches at his beard. 'Well, yes, that is rather a conundrum.'

'There has to be a way,' Dan says, turning to me and taking my hands. 'I get thrown into the portal and regain my memories. Your father has been waiting down here for you. And now we have a way to stop Kronos from escaping. Clearly, this is all part of your destiny. So there has to be a way back to earth.'

'Well, there is,' I say. 'The portal. It's just a shame we can't fly. Although,' I muse darkly, 'even if we could fly, we'd probably never reach it, seeing as I don't get to have what I want down here.'

At Dan's confused expression, I explain about the mirage of him falling over the cliff and me trying to save him again and again. 'I'm the same as Tantalus and Sisyphus and all the others,' I say. 'I wanted something badly and I wouldn't give up. But I couldn't have it. My wanting it made the opposite happen.' I slump. 'I bet it'll be the same with trying to escape.'

Dan is looking at me oddly. 'But you did find me,' he says. 'You beat Tartarus. So how did you do it?'

I sit up. 'Good point! Okay, so . . . hang on.' I think about it. 'You say you'd been in that cave the whole time?'

'Yeah. Why?'

'Because we definitely passed it and we didn't see you,' I say thoughtfully. 'Probably because I so badly wanted to. Tartarus was playing its tricks again.'

My father is watching me, smiling.

'Okay,' Dan says, nodding encouragingly. 'So, what changed?'

'Right before we saw you, I was feeling sorry for myself, agonising over what I'd done and thinking that actually it would kill me to see you again and have you look at me with the disgust you had every right to feel. I knew I couldn't stand that, that it would break me, and just as I had that thought—' I stare at him, eyes shining.

'You found me.' Dan finished.

I nod.

'Because you gave up trying to find me?' Dan says. He raises an eyebrow. 'None taken, by the way.'

I laugh. 'I think that was it, yeah.' I close my eyes, trying to remember how I felt. 'No, hang on, it was more than that. For a split second I wanted to *not* find you. Which I think is a bit different to not wanting to find you.'

'Are you following this?' Dan asks my father.

'I am.' My father smiles. 'Such a clever girl, my Frida.'

'And where do I get that from?' I ask wryly, recalling my father's probing, uncharacteristically insensitive questions just before I decided it would be better all round if I didn't find Dan.

'This is it,' I say slowly. 'The secret to escaping Tartarus. It won't give us what I want; it will only give us the opposite. But that could actually work in our favour this time. So, let's get this clear, what is it I really want?'

'To get up to the portal,' Dan answers.

'Yes!' I grab Dan and give him a huge, smacking kiss.

Then I turn to my father. 'I don't suppose you've got any spades?'

Chapter 39

We stand in the mud, staring up at the hole in the sky.

We'd need a gigantic structure to reach it, a ladder hundreds of thousands of metres long. And instead, what are we doing to escape this cursed place?

Digging further into it.

I stare down at the soggy earth.

'Now,' Dan says, 'if you're right, then for this to work, you need to—'

'I know, I know!' I say. As Dan keeps reminding me, I need to be thinking about digging a tunnel away from the portal and *not* about reaching it. As physically hard as this work will be, the mental gymnastics I'm attempting are far more difficult.

'Hellooooo!'

I squint through the low light and see the distant speck of

my father making his way towards us. When I told him my idea, his eyes lit up and he left the hut with the promise that he would find us some help. When he finally comes into view, he's flanked by three enormous creatures that seem to be comprised almost entirely of heads and limbs. As they approach, waving, they disappear in a blur of arms.

'Frida,' my father says, 'meet the Hundred-handed Hecatoncheires.' I stare at them. Fifty heads stare inquisitively back. 'They don't talk,' my father adds, and then, as one of them leans in and extends a hand to me, he says, hastily, 'No, no! None of that, we'll be here all year!' The creature lowers its arm with a grumble of a dozen heads, and my father turns to me, smiling proudly. 'The Hecs are going to help us dig!'

Three hundred hands. We could definitely use them. I step back and point at the rather pitiful hole that Dan and I have made a start on with the wooden tools borrowed from my father.

'We are digging here,' I say. 'Straight down.'

'You heard my daughter,' my father beams. 'Do your worst!' He leans into me and whispers, 'They're very excited about this!'

The Hecs surround the small hole and begin grabbing handfuls of the black mud in a rapid rotation of hands, flinging it behind them so that we have to duck out of the way or get splattered in the face. Within minutes, a foot-deep hole becomes a pit of several metres, the Hecatoncheires all down there in it. But eventually the Hecs, no longer able to reach the surface, are simply throwing mud around them, filling up the hole as quickly as they're digging it.

My father looks at me, apologetic. 'They're not great thinkers,' he says.

I stare down into the hole. 'Okay,' I say. 'It's fine. We just need some sort of pulley system to get the mud out.'

As my father and Dan put their heads together to see what they can come up with, the ground beneath us begins to vibrate with a gigantic stomping. We turn to see Arges making her way towards us, carrying a huge bucket. She joins us and peers down at the Hecatoncheires, who are chucking mud around with gay abandon.

'I brought your snails,' Arges tells my father, 'but then I saw your little project so I thought I'd wander over and see what you were up to.' She sniffs thoughtfully. 'Digging, are you?'

'Yes! We're trying to—'

Dan shoots me a look and I stop. 'We're trying to dig to the centre of Tartarus,' I say carefully. The cyclops shrugs, as though this is a perfectly reasonable pastime, and squints down into the pit.

I eye up her pail. 'Do you think you could help us get rid of the earth with that bucket?'

Arges beams at the opportunity to get involved. 'Yes!' she says. 'Why not?'

We get a system going. The Hecs are persuaded by my father to aim their mud-throwing into Arges's giant bucket, which is now empty (the snails, tipped out on to the slimy earth have slid away, waving their tentacles joyfully at this unexpected chance of freedom, my father watching them go, licking his lips sadly). Arges lifts my father, Dan and me down to the floor of the hole and we also resume digging, though our efforts are paltry compared to those three hundred hands. It grows colder the deeper we get into Tartarus, a clammy chill permeates my body and I dig faster in an attempt to warm myself.

We make good progress but something else is growing stronger: the black feeling of malevolence is creeping across the mud plains, the walls are rattling and shaking, the roars and howls growing ever louder, reaching us even down here in this pit within a pit. When I think about Kronos, I turn numb with fear, and so I do my best to block him out, focusing only on the movement of my body and the movement of the earth. After a while, I stop thinking about what happens if we don't make it back to the crypt or even what happens if we do. My only purpose is to dig. Spadeful by spadeful. Dig. Dig. Dig. And then dig a bit more.

But still, nothing happens. We really are just getting deeper into Tartarus. How long are we going to keep this up for? I stop for a moment, looking over at Dan and my father, watch them chatting together, swapping ancient stories as they shovel piles of earth into the giant bucket of a cyclops; I see the Hecs, still eagerly ploughing up the mud with their surfeit of hands; I see Arges lifting and returning the bucket, humming a happy tune to herself. As I look upon then, something flutters in my chest. It takes a moment to identify it – happiness. The simple joy of a team of friends working together for a common goal.

And, as the furious howls grow louder, and my body reacts with instinctive animal revulsion, I wonder if this might not actually be a good end in itself. Why not? We could dig a hole so deep that we can hide from Kronos until he has escaped

Tartarus and made for the earth. And after that? Well, we'll just stay here. It's not so bad. I'll be with my father. Dan and I could build our own mud hut. I'm sure, in time, I'd get used to the snails.

And that's when it happens.

In the blink of an eye, we're no longer in a deep dark hole. Instead, we are perched on the top of a tall, thin mud-mountain, high above the flats of Tartarus.

My father, Arges, Dan and the Hecs look around, eyes wide, as they take in what has happened. I look up. And there, above my head, just hanging in the red sky, is a large white circle. The portal back to earth. My father stares at it, and there's such a strange expression on his face: pride and happiness and wist-fulness combined. Arges looks up at it too and then gazes out from our muddy platform over to where we have a wonderful view of the bronze walls. They're shuddering.

'Well,' Arges says, 'I'll be damned!'

The Hecs beam at one another and begin a long, giddy process of high-fiving, each hand apparently having to slap each other hand at least once before they even start on one another. Then the walls shake again with an unearthly groan, sending a shockwave through the earth and causing our mud tower to wobble.

Arges nods grimly. 'I think that's my cue to leave,' she says. 'I don't think we have long and I need to be at the wall when . . .' She shoots me a glance. 'I mean, *if*, it falls.'

I walk over to her. 'Thank you,' I say. 'For being a friend to my father. For helping us.'

Arges picks me up and wraps me in a hug. 'My pleasure.'

343

Then she turns to Dan, picks him up and gives him a sniff. 'Could I keep this one?' she asks me.

I laugh and shake my head. 'I'm afraid I'm going to need him.'

Shrugging, Arges plants a smacker on Dan's face that almost consumes his entire head and then plonks him back down, where he sways dizzily.

Then she stands in front of my father. 'It has been an honour,' she says gravely, then adds, with a glint of a smile, 'you hairy bag of bones.'

'Don't go getting yourself killed. You still owe me those snails,' my father returns, and Arges guffaws and, with one fond backward glance, climbs down the mountain, the Hecs descending hand over hand over hand (etc.) after her.

I turn to my father. He holds out his arms.

'Well done, my wonderful daughter,' he says, his eyes brimming with love. 'I knew you could do it!' He gives me a hug. 'You are the best thing that ever happened to me and I love you so much.'

'I love you too,' I say, squeezing him tightly. 'You're coming with us, aren't you?'

'Oh Frida,' my father says sadly, 'I can't come with you. My time on earth was over long ago.'

Suddenly I realise that I can't feel his arms around me any more. I step back. 'Dad?' I shout. 'Dad?'

But he's fading before my eyes. The beard and mud are disappearing, the shabby clothes changing, and suddenly he's my father as he was when I was nine. Restored. My hero. And his smile now is the saddest, most beautiful thing I've ever seen.

He says softly, 'I believe in you, Frida.'

Tears rush to my eyes and I grab for my father to stop him from leaving. I can't let him go, not again, not after I have just found him, but all I grasp is empty air.

'No, wait!' I cry. 'Please, Daddy; I'm not ready. I need you!' But my father just smiles and fades, fades and smiles, and from somewhere behind him, I think I can hear waves crashing, catch the scent of brine and coconut and sun-warmed sand. Elysium. His heroes' paradise.

'Ah, there it is,' says my father, eyes alight with pleasure. He looks at me one last time, now little more than a play of light.

'Remember, Frida,' he says, 'where there is love there is hope.'

And then he's gone.

I stare into the space where my father was and my heart feels like it has stopped. I've lost him. I've lost my dad. Tears flood down my cheeks and my chest hurts and I don't think I can survive this pain. Then I feel warm arms around me as Dan gathers me close. He doesn't say anything, just holds me silently as I weep. We stay like that for a while, until my shuddering sobs become hiccups and then I still, just breathing, safe in Dan's arms.

The ground shakes again. I look up. The bronze walls are rippling. I take a deep breath and wipe my eyes. There will be time for grieving when all of this is over. Right now, I have some unfinished business.

I look to the portal. Up there is earth.

'Are you ready?' I ask Dan.

'I'm ready,' he says.

'Then let's go home.'

Grabbing the edges of the portal, I pull myself up, very much like you'd pull yourself into your loft (if your landing was a hell pit and your loft was in another dimension) and instantly my head and shoulders emerge into the crypt. I look across the room and see Psyche. She's been gagged and tethered to the column of a tomb. She watches, eyes wide, as I heave myself out of Tartarus and clamber to standing, my arms burning, Dan climbing out behind me. Then we hurry over to where Psyche is tied up, scattering hell mud as we walk.

'Hands up if you want to save the world.'

Chapter 40

Dan removes Psyche's gag and then starts tugging at her ropes. She spits and coughs and then says, 'Knife in the heel of my right boot.'

Dan locates the small silver knife and quickly dispatches Psyche's restraints. She watches him, a small smile on her lips.

'You're back now too, I see?'

'I'm back,' he says.

'Good.' Psyche stands up. She shakes her limbs, rubs wrists that are red raw from her attempts to free herself. Then she reaches into her pocket and pulls out her cigarettes. Lights one and takes a puff. Really, you have to admire her insouciance.

'Sorry about before,' she says to Dan. 'As it turns out you were right. Frida did go nutso on the ambrosia.'

'That's okay,' Dan says. 'You should have seen what she got up to when you were out of it.'

'Hey!' I say. 'I'm standing right here!'

Dan grins. Psyche raises an eyebrow. I stare around the room.

'They left you alone in here?' I ask, peering around, looking for signs of Anterist guards.

'There are four guards on the main door,' Psyche says, narrowing her eyes against the smoke. 'But they don't come down very often.' She looks at the wormhole of the portal. 'I think they're scared of that thing.' The black void is three times as large as when Dan and I went through it. It gapes and swirls, hypnotic, and a deathly compulsion grips me. I want to move towards it. Tartarus doesn't like to be tricked. It wants us back.

Quickly, I pull my gaze away. 'What time is it here?'

'Sunday morning, around seven, I think.' Psyche inclines her head. 'The Anterists are all up there. The sermon is starting soon.'

I'm distracted from Psyche's words by a blood-curdling moan coming from the portal. I think of Arges and the Hecs down there, the walls shuddering, holding but only just. That black shadow, poised, watching, waiting . . .

'We have to get as far away as possible,' Psyche says. 'Head for high ground. Hide in the caves. We let this scenario play itself out and see who's left standing at the end. You never know, the army might see him off.'

'An army doesn't stand a chance against Kronos,' I say. 'Nothing does. I saw him.' I meet Psyche's eyes. 'Once he's out, there will be no way to stop him.'

'Why do I have a sinking feeling that you've got some kind of heroic plan, Frida?' Psyche says.

'Because I have,' I say. 'We can still stop this. We've got an Ophiotaurus bomb. A proper one. It won't be enough to kill Anteros, but it's strong enough to knock him out. That should sever the connection between him and the mortals; but we have to do it before the walls fall. And that means getting past a whole load of Anterists and guards.' I meet her eyes. 'Will you help us?'

Psyche looks at me and I don't need any powers to understand what she's thinking. It's different for Psyche. Dan and I can die and then at least we'll be out of our misery. But as Psyche has said to me so many times, there are worse things than death, and if Kronos gets free, she'll experience all of them.

'Look,' I say, 'I understand if you want to go.'

'And miss all the fun?' she says drily. 'What do you need?'

'There's another door somewhere down here in the crypt that leads us to the back of the church. I'm pretty sure they won't be guarding that so closely. Once we're up there, I need you and Dan to keep Hades and the guards away from me so I can get to Anteros with the bomb.'

Psyche thinks about this. 'Okay,' she says. 'Hang on.' She pockets the knife. 'Wait here.'

We wait. A few moments later, we hear a yelp, a bang, a thump and a thwack and then Psyche is dragging an unconscious Anterist guard towards us, looking very pleased with herself.

'Disguises!' she says, when we stare at the sight. 'Well, go on. Strip him! There are another two coming.'

Exchanging a look with Dan, I strip the guard, peeling off

349

my muddy clothing and pulling on a pair of red trousers, folding them over at the waist, rolling up the hems. Then I remove the guard's shirt and tie it in a knot at my navel. Meanwhile, Dan is pulling on the clothes of the second guard that Psyche has thrown down here and Psyche undresses a third. Once we are outfitted, I survey the results. Dan's pants stop at his calves. I look like I'm playing dress-up in my parents' clothes and Psyche, well, typically, Psyche is managing to pull this look off. So unfair. Dan and I won't pass the inspection of anyone looking too closely, but I'm hoping everyone in that church will only have eyes for one person.

As we leave the Anterist guards sparked out on the floor and head deeper into the crypt, I glance back at the portal. I can feel Kronos now, just as strongly as if his eyes were still on me, and I pray to whichever gods are still on our side that the walls of Tartarus will hold for just a little longer.

Chapter 41

A flight of pale stone steps leads up to a large grey door. Psyche grips the handle and pulls gently. Unlocked. Exchanging apprehensive glances, Dan and I follow her through the opening and emerge into a small, sparse room. The vestry. There's another door directly opposite that will lead us into the church.

My heart sinks when I see that the door is manned. They're not bovine security guards, just your regular Anterists, two well-respected members who I used to know quite well: Layla, a broad-shouldered blonde, and Robbie, with his scrub of red hair and thick arms. They must have been granted the special privilege of watching R. A. Stone's sermon from backstage. Lucky them! First in the queue to be a Titan appetiser.

The pair turn as they hear us approach.

'We're here to relieve you,' Psyche says shortly. 'Requested by R. A.'

'Really?' Layla frowns. 'I didn't hear anything.' She looks at Robbie. 'You?' He shakes his head, but without concern. To the uninitiated, Psyche looks like a pretty twenty-year-old. As Layla bends her head to speak into her walkie-talkie her eyes land on me and she does a comic double take, mouth falling open, and I can practically see the thought forming in her mind: *Frida, the betrayer, here to assassinate our great leader!*

Layla starts speaking, about to raise the alarm, but Psyche moves swiftly, hitting the Anterist in the jaw. Layla's head snaps back and as she drops, her colleague turns, registers what he's seeing and surges forwards to grip Psyche. Too late we realise he has a taser. But Robbie is big and slow and Psyche is slight and quick. Dan and I can only watch as the Anterist attempts to tackle Psyche as she weaves and ducks, delivering a jab to his temple and felling Robbie to the floor, unconscious.

'Wow,' I say, appalled and admiring in equal measure.

Psyche shrugs. 'It's a calling.' She removes the taser from Robbie's belt and hands it to Dan. 'Use this on Hades. I'll deal with the guards.'

We approach the door to the church and as I stare out, I catch my breath. There are hundreds of Anterists out there, crammed into the pews, standing in the aisle, crowded at the back. Everywhere I look, there's nothing but red. Worse is their darkness, their anger, their emptiness. A sick feeling slithers through me at the sight.

Dan is staring at the pulpit and I drag my gaze away from the Anterists to see what he's fixated by: Hades, in red robes, his long grey hair flowing.

352

'You were right,' I say. 'He really does look like an evil pencil.'

Two Anterists, one on either side of the stage, are filming it all. This morning's event will be broadcast the world over. I think of what Daphne showed me. Anteros wants the mortals to see what's coming for them. He wants them to see the horror they've brought upon themselves just before they die. Torturing us might not have been Anteros's main priority, but that's not to say he doesn't enjoy it.

Psyche eyes up the sight lines. In front of us, an area that once would have been reserved for the choir is now lined with Anteros's most loyal followers. They stand between us and the pulpit, where Hades is now, where Anteros will soon deliver his sermon.

Hades taps the microphone and begins his introduction, the speech I was supposed to deliver. There's something surreal about this. Can it really be just nine days since I was standing in that exact spot, so excited about R. A.'s visit, so delighted to be chosen to introduce him? It feels like a past life. I listen as the god lays on the superlatives about the amazing R. A. Stone: revolutionary thinker, game changer, iconic leader. A lot of waffle. He's playing for time.

I look at Psyche and she nods grimly and I know she feels it too. That oncoming darkness. There's a terrible moaning from below us and I glance quickly over to the congregation of Anterists to judge their reaction, but they're so fixated on Hades' words, they don't even seem to have noticed. At Psyche's signal, we move, sliding surreptitiously along to join the Anterists in the choir. I keep my head down as the

353

Anterists dart annoyed glances at us, frowning, perhaps sensing a difference in their midst. A muttering starts up and I flick a nervous glance at Dan, but then Hades makes the announcement and the Anterists in the choir forget all about our disruption as they burst into frenzied applause. He's coming. R. A. is really coming. The moment they dreamed of has arrived! I experience a fluttering of terror, a cousin of the excitement the Anterists are feeling right now. Don't they say that fear is just excitement without the breath? Well, maybe excitement is just fear without the finer details.

Then, just as suddenly as the applause started, it stops. The room falls into absolute reverent silence.

He's here.

Anteros glides over to the pulpit, slow and commanding, his black robes a sharp contrast in this flood of red. His handsome face is animated, and as his eyes rove over the assembled Anterists, he glows with a dark purpose. His followers are awed. They have never seen such beauty. In the crowd I see a pale face. Bryony. So the dark arrow power consumed her after all. Her gaze is fixed on Anteros, as every pair of eyes in the room is, and the church is suffused with a pulsing energy so intense I think my head might explode.

'Today,' Anteros says, his voice rich and deep, 'we destroy an old world and begin a new one.' He smiles and the congregation begin to applaud again. 'Love has failed you,' Anteros booms, and they cheer and cheer, the noise building, drowning out the roars of the shadow that approaches. I look out at the crowd, clapping their own extinction, and Dan nudges me. I turn back and stare. Before the eyes of his devoted congregation, Anteros is transforming.

It's awesome in the oldest sense of the world, a sucker punch to reality. He's bigger, more vivid, hyper-real. His wings emerge, fan out, white, fading to grey and then jet black, and I have a moment to wonder how something so beautiful can be so evil. The cameras are still rolling. All over the world, Anterists will be watching in dumbstruck worship, wondering at the scale of this performance, little realising this is Anteros with his disguise finally shed. He doesn't have to pretend any more. This is the endgame.

All over the world, now, the balance is being tipped. Love is losing. The walls are about to fall.

It has to be now.

I look at Dan, give him a nod, and then I dart to the pulpit. It's only a dozen steps, but I'm spotted immediately. A shout goes up and Hades and the guards surge towards me. But Dan and Psyche are on it. As Dan holds off Hades with jabs of the taser, Psyche takes all of the guards at once, kicking and punching in a hail of falling bodies.

And I have a clear path to Anteros.

His dark eyes flicker when he sees me. 'Well, well,' he says. 'You escaped Tartarus. I've got to hand it to you, Frida—'

I launch the Ophiotaurus bomb directly at his face.

The bomb explodes in a puff of grey dust, casting a cloud of smoke that conceals him for a moment. But something's wrong. He's not frozen, not unconscious, just a little dusty. Anteros flutters his wings and grey flakes scatter through the air like snowflakes.

'Harpy ashes?' Anteros asks, amused. 'And what were you hoping to achieve with that?' I stare at the grey detritus littering the pulpit and then at the unharmed, smiling love god. *Harpy* ashes?

'Oh, Frida,' Anteros says, 'this is getting embarrassing. Don't you get bored of being a failure? Because I am thoroughly bored of you.' Then he lashes out, striking me across the face and sending me flying, crashing painfully on to the altar steps, my head cracking on the marble, my ears ringing and my vision blurring.

I lie there stunned for a few seconds and then, wincing, I push myself up on to my elbow, trying to locate Dan and Psyche, trying to tell them that we've failed, it's over. Psyche is still attacking the Anterist guards, but they just keep coming, she'll soon be overpowered. I see Dan, waving the taser at Hades and watch dismayed as Hades knocks it out of his hand and backhands Dan. Dan hits the floor.

Psyche was right. We should have run.

'Psyche,' I shout, 'the bomb didn't work. Get Dan away from Hades. Hide him in the crowd. I'll find you.'

Psyche looks up, meets my eyes. Then with a nod, she runs to Dan, hauls him up from the approaching Hades and makes for the mass of Anterists. The congregation are staring, mouths open, utterly silent. I follow their gaze to the back of the church and see why. There is no back of the church. It has vanished. In its place there's a swirling void from which something terrible slouches towards earth.

The walls have fallen.

Kronos is coming.

Chapter 42

The Anterists stand staring, unable to work out what's happening, and my heart aches for them. They brought this about but it's not their fault. How could they stand against a god, against the father of gods? They're only human. So small and so young. Why did Eros gamble so much on such fragile, breakable hearts? And oh Dad, how did we get it so wrong? Me, thinking I was the human arrow. You, believing you were sent to Tartarus to save me, with your Ophiotaurus that wasn't even an Ophiotaurus and your stupid, stupid belief in me.

Folly, all folly.

Too late now.

From the portal, a shadow emerges. It is at once a cloud, a swarm, a tornado, a nightmare. It is nothingness. It is destruction. And it is here. As I watch, spellbound, the black shadow amasses, splits, swirls, forms and unforms, until finally it gathers into a huge, malevolent face. It is the face of Kronos. A thing no mortal should have to see.

Hades sinks to his knees in worship of the father he once helped Zeus incarcerate and who he now wants to serve. Arrogant to the last, Anteros stands before Kronos, gazing upwards into that hateful being, pleased with what he has done.

The Anterists stand, mute, slack jawed, glassy eyed.

I even gave her a name, my father said. *I called her Faith.*

I frown. There's something nagging at me, what is it? I try to chase it down, something to do with my father, that mistaken beast, that impotent bomb. Then it comes to me, clear and true. What am I thinking? My father – who read every book on Greek myth in existence – could never have mistaken a Harpy for an Ophiotaurus. So why did he say what he did? Something sparks then. Could it be because he needed to give me hope? A reason to escape Tartarus? My heart starts hammering as I understand what this means. Maybe my father thought there was another way to stop Anteros. Maybe he believed that if I got here, I'd find it.

I see his face now, as clearly as if he were here with me, his smile, his eyes so cheerful: *Where there's love there's hope.*

I see Daphne's prophecy, left by Eros, that strange symbol that looked like an arrow and also like a person. To be delivered only at the endgame. Those words whispered to me by Dionysus: *Anthropos Oistos.* Human arrow. Except, that wasn't the answer, was it? It wasn't me. I've proven it, over and over again. I'm not a hero. I'm no better than any other mortal.

Kronos is growing, growing, blackness seeping from

the portal and swallowing the church, bringing a darkness without end, and—

Human arrow.

The words are spoken inside me and I drag my gaze away from the horror to focus on that thing inside me. There's something I've missed. Something I got wrong. I try to clear my muddled thoughts, try to resist the pull of the nihilistic shadow, to allow my brain to make the connection that feels so temptingly near.

I'm no better than any other mortal.

The subject of the prophecy is a human arrow.

And the Anterists, who I understand so well because, after all, I was one.

HUMAN ARROW.

The answer arrives, then, like something already known. I look at the Anterist congregation; pale, rooted with fear. I see Dan, slumped against the front pew, Psyche holding him up, and remember one last thing. *Firelighter.* And I realise that my father was right. We are all exactly where we are meant to be. And I smile. I know what I have to do.

$$\rightarrow$$

Grimacing, I stagger to my feet and make my way, limping, towards that gigantic shadow skull, my skin revolting at its proximity. Anteros turns to me, shark-eyed, wearing a smile that is wide and manic.

'Look at him!' Anteros says. 'Look at Kronos and despair. There's nothing you can do to stop him.'

'I know,' I say, and Anteros frowns because I am laughing, laughing, and it is all so simple. 'You were right,' I tell him. 'You were right all along!'

I turn to the Anterists then, all those beautiful, heart-broken souls. I believe. I believe. I believe. I hold out my hand and there it is. In the centre of my palm, a tiny spark of gold. Not arrow magic. Not ambrosia-ignited power. This is human magic. The faintest spark of pure divine love that Eros believed lives in the hearts of every single mortal.

I smile at Anteros. 'You were right. I'm not the one who saves the world,' I say. 'They are.'

And then I light them up.

Chapter 43

I aim my single, precious spark of love at Dan. Such a strong heart, his. A pure heart. I know he will keep the flame.

And yes, the tiny ember lands on him and hums quickly, effortlessly through his body and the aura around his heart ignites in gold. Psyche stares at him, wide eyed, until Dan reaches out dreamily and touches Psyche's hand, setting off the spark in her, too. Psyche's heart is a more difficult prospect, of course, but as I watch, the spark of gold inside her flickers and catches and then burns brightly. I look at these two, my love, my family, my people, and I smile. They're glowing. Then Dan and Psyche reach out and touch the Anterists beside them and I hold my breath.

This is the moment when the world ends or begins again.

The golden light enters four Anterists, makes directly for their hearts and proceeds to do battle, light against shadow, a glow, a pulsing, seeking to uncover and ignite the power that lives in all of them, a flicker of gold that can be buried, forgotten, even renounced, but never entirely extinguished. A tiny spark of pure love. Such a small thing on its own. Brought together with others, it becomes immensely powerful.

But I understand now why a love goddess could never have saved the mortals. Real love can't be forced. It has to be chosen.

I look behind me. Kronos is growing, one shadow hand emerges from the portal, a swirling mass of darkness, and plants itself in our world, and with it a terrible emptiness spreads, a hatred of all that is good, all that is hopeful.

Where there is love there is hope.

We don't have much time and yet I understand that there is nothing more I can do. It has to be them. They have to choose this. My right hand seeks out the chain around my neck, and I rub my thumb over the heart. The Anterists have already rejected love once. Will they choose it now, when it matters?

The hearts of the Anterists dim – is the fire extinguished already? Is it over? – and then – oh! – the mortals burst into colour, rainbow hues all filtered through the golden glow that surrounds them. It happens quickly now, they extend their hands, and the spark travels on, the golden fire racing like an inferno, amassing strength as it goes, so that four become sixty, sixty becomes five hundred, five hundred becomes them all, the golden fire burning the shadow from every heart.

The cameras at the back of the room are still rolling, Anterists in churches across the earth will be watching, transfixed, awaiting their doom. I need them too. And I feel them, then, the spark igniting in one heart and then many, the same conflagration repeating itself, over and over across the world.

We are all connected.

A bone-shattering roar blasts at my back and turning, I see Kronos, and his eyes are a lack, his mouth a hungry maw, his second arm snakes through the portal and plants itself on the altar. Anteros watches in delight, unaware of what's happening in the congregation behind him. All he cares is that Kronos is almost through the portal.

And once the Titan is through, it will be impossible to stop him.

I drag my gaze away from Kronos.

GET READY, I send out and I hold up my hands, palms open, and first Dan, then Psyche, and then all of the Anterists, here and in the churches across the world, do the same.

Golden threads emerge from every Anterist's hand; hundreds, thousands of tiny darts of gold intertwine and fuse into a ray of pulsing gold and I sense every Anterist watching in the world send their spark to our cause, increasing our power. The ray glows, strengthens and solidifies before our eyes, forming itself into a single, shimmering shape – a gigantic golden arrow, trained directly on Kronos.

We wait then. There is one single, blissful moment of indescribable harmonic power as we stand united. Then I send out the signal, *RELEASE*.

Then our human golden arrow shoots into the middle of Kronos's rearing chest.

The monster emits a terrible scream that fills our minds with a splintering agony, but still we stand, arms raised, the arrow a laser beam drilling into the Titan, tearing ragged strips of light in his black shadow self.

Kronos pushes back with an intense and diabolical fury, fighting us with all his dark power, and his rage fills the church with a bitter smog. He is strong. Too strong. I can feel him weakening our attack, the golden glow of the arrow dimming.

Can we really do this? He's a Titan. We're just human.

You have to believe, Frida. My father's voice. *You are not alone in this fight.*

I look out at the contorted faces of the Anterists, who have all chosen love, at this last moment, when it really matters, and I realise something. Not only can we do this. We were born to do this. *Where there is love there is hope. Where there is love there is hope. Where there is love there is hope.*

And there is always love.

Just then, Kronos thrusts out from the portal, plants two hands down in the church and, surging towards us, lets loose a bloodcurdling roar into the faces of the congregation. We can feel him in our cells now, scrabbling around, trying to invade, infecting us with his terrible absence.

But after the dark comes the light, if you can just hang on long enough. If you can just believe – *HOLD ON*, I send out. *HE'S FAILING. HOLD ON.* And then, just as Kronos's pressure increases, crawling in our heads, a repulsive, agonising pain, and it seems we cannot stand it a moment longer, the Titan is suddenly dragged violently backwards, with an unholy scream that could send a mortal mad, his face contorting, his body disintegrating, his form losing coherence,

364

the black swarm of his being swirling and whirling, as he is sucked back into the void.

The Anterists gasp, collapse, bodies aching, minds reeling, as before us the portal itself is shrinking, smaller and smaller, until it's nothing more than a pinprick.

Then I'm knocked off my feet. Anteros, in my face, teeth bared, face warped with hatred, ugly now, his truest self revealed.

'What did you do?' he screams, but he doesn't wait for an answer, just wraps his hands around my throat, and I am choking and as I gasp for breath, Dan and Psyche are pulling Anteros off me, and he's so intent on punishing me, that he doesn't see that behind him, where the black hole to Tartarus once stood, something is happening ...

Chapter 44

A star.

Or something that looks like a star.

It gets bigger and bigger and it's bright, so bright that I wonder whether Anteros did just actually kill me and now I'm in heaven. Except no, Anteros can't kill me, I'm definitely still alive and that star just keeps getting bigger, until I have to squeeze my eyes shut against the glare. Psyche and Dan fall back too, arms thrown up to shield their eyes, and the amassed crowd, no longer Anterists but also not quite themselves, have fallen into another of those hushed and reverent silences.

We wait, unseeing, and there's an immense and peaceful silence and then: 'Anteros.'

Oh, that voice. If love had a voice it would sound just like this. Anteros's hands slacken around my neck, his face sags and as though he cannot help himself, as though he would rather do anything else, he turns towards the speaker. Squinting into the shaft of light, I can just about make out a figure.

A golden man.

Eros.

If I once thought Anteros was beautiful, that was because I had never seen his brother.

Anteros roars, opening his magnificent wings, and a golden sprinkle of light drifts gently from the white hole. As Anteros tries to flee, the light swarms around him, a living butterfly net, gentle but inescapable. Anteros bats it away, screaming with rage, but the golden net wraps around him and holds him suspended, humiliatingly, in the air a few feet above the ground.

I know, somehow, that this is going to be the last time I see him. And there's something I need to say. I walk over, crouch down beside Anteros as he thrashes fruitlessly against the net.

'I just thought of something funny,' I say softly. 'All this time you thought you were using us.' I look up at the silvery portal, the immense golden being standing there. 'But I think you were being played. I think you did exactly what Eros wanted you to do.'

Channelling all of that mortal power has given me a fleeting grasp of something bigger. It may not last, but for this one moment in time, I see.

'We needed your darkness to understand our own light. To fight for it. To claim it. You helped us.' I lean in closer to the god, a smile on my lips. 'So, I suppose what I'm trying to say is "thank you".' And then I kiss his cheek.

Anteros's dark eyes burn. 'I'll make you suffer,' he says. 'I'll make you scream. I'll make you wish . . .'

I stand up and prod him with my toe. 'Bit hard to take you seriously right now, if I'm honest.'

Anteros's face bulges with fury and, as he goes to deliver one more threat, the net shimmers and tightens and he is carried across the altar. Before my eyes, he disappears through the golden portal. Gone home, though not quite in the triumphant fashion he intended.

Then there's a warm hand in mine as Dan comes to stand with me. We both gaze over at Eros and no thoughts can form as I look upon him, my heart filling with a strong and patient joy. Eros looks back at us and smiles. I think that smile could see a person through anything. Then he turns his golden gaze on Psyche and holds out a hand.

We watch as Psyche walks to Eros, tears running unchecked down her cheeks. Psyche can cry? Who knew? Then he takes her in his arms and they are a celestial tableau, two beautiful immortal beings, shrouded in light, something sacred and private and not for our eyes. Dan and I turn instead to each other, and after a while the light becomes brighter and brighter until once again we have to squeeze our eyes shut. When we open them again, Eros and the portal are gone.

There's only Psyche standing there staring at an empty space.

Dan looks at me. I look at him.

And the Anterists blink, casting a glance around them, rubbing at their eyes as though awakening from a dream.

Chapter 45

The people in the congregation are no longer Anterists. Nor are they filled with a collective divine love. They're just a bunch of people who are tired and confused and would quite like to go home. They begin to drift away as soon as the doors are unlocked. The church is soon half full, then a quarter, and then almost empty.

The Anterist guards have disappeared; they'll have to find their own purpose now. Hades is nowhere to be found. Headed back to the Underworld, no doubt. The dead might make poor sport, but they're a lot easier to predict.

I find Bryony standing bewildered in the entrance, Justin holding her hand and looking equally lost.

'Frida,' Bryony says. Her eyes widen. 'What happened? Am I asleep? Is this a dream?'

I hold out my arms to her. 'Go home,' I whisper, hugging

her tightly. 'Everything is okay.' And I think it will be. I think that Bryony and Justin and the rest of the Anterists both here and across the world will forget what they saw today. Some things, after all, are just too much for a mortal mind to keep hold of. And maybe that's for the best. Not everyone should have to live with the knowledge of what this world really contains.

All that matters is that the mortals can find the magic in themselves, when it's needed.

Dan and I stand at the altar, waiting until the last person has left the church.

'I'll just take a look around,' he says.

When he reappears I see his face and know the answer even as I ask. 'No sign?'

He shakes his head. Psyche has gone. Disappeared without a goodbye. We may never know what Eros said to her, why he didn't take her with him, and my heart hurts for her. She wants to be mortal again. Why would Eros deny her that? I wish I'd had the chance to thank her. To tell her about my father down in Tartarus, waiting for me all this time. To let her know that even her worst actions served the greater plan.

I smile to myself when I think of what she would have said to that.

When the church is finally empty, Dan and I head outside. It's a warm summer's morning and the world has not ended. I consider that a result. We stand on the steps and look back at the building.

'It's over,' I say. 'Really, truly over. Can you feel it?'

'I can.'

370

We look at one another. After everything we've been through, the things we've done, the things we've seen, there is so much to say and no adequate way to say it.

Where does it leave us? What do we do now?

'Fancy a coffee?' I say.

Chapter 46

One month later

I listen to the surf crashing, tip my head back to the sun, breath in the scent of coconut oil and sea breeze and warm white sand.

Across the beach Dan heads towards me, holding two huge bowl-shaped glasses filled with a creamy cocktail, topped with a pink umbrella, a maraschino cherry, a hunk of pineapple and a sparkler. I watch him, in his board shorts, his hair lightened by the sun, his toned body browned by our lazy days by the water, and I feel that flicker inside, like I always do. He hands me my drink and then climbs on to the sunlounger beside me. Holds out his ridiculous glass to clink.

'Cheers.'

'Cheers,' I return. 'To . . . absent friends.'

Dan smiles. 'Absent friends.'

I take a sip, lick my white frothy moustache. 'Mmmm, lovely.'

He grins.

I lie back with a satisfied sigh. We've been here for three weeks, on this beautiful and remote Greek island, and I've gone full-on feral. My skin is a nutty shade of brown, my feet are bare, my hair is 99 per cent frizz and 1 per cent sea salt. I can't remember the last time I saw my mascara.

I love it.

'How are things?' I ask.

'Good,' Dan says. He meets my eyes. 'I think it's going to be all right.'

We are mostly cut off from the world in our beach hut; no internet, no mobile-phone signal, just books and sleep and the sound of the surf. But occasionally Dan or I will head to the beach café and use the old, rickety computer to see how the world is faring.

You know, now that it didn't end.

These last few weeks I've thought a lot about that flash of understanding I had in the church. About the extreme states that Anteros drove us to. We've indulged in mad, obsessive love. We've rejected the idea of love. The pendulum has swung to both extremes. And now there are no more magical interventions or godly manipulations. It's time for us mortals to find our own way, to love, or not to love, as we choose, each according to the map of our own hearts. To try to navigate by that small spark of something divine inside us all. And to fail, painfully and often, of course, because we are only human after all.

I look at Dan's happy, handsome face. We will go home eventually, I guess. Back to the city, back to our real lives.

And then we, too, will have to learn who we are to each other without magical missions or ancient prophecies. I think we'll manage it. We were lost there, for a while, but we found each other again. I think no matter what happens, as long as we keep on looking for one another, we'll be okay.

And as I stare out at the breaking waves, something unfurls inside me, an excitement for what's to come.

There have been so many Fridas over these past few years, and now I stand on the brink of a new one. A Frida outside the prophecy, her future unwritten, a mortal with her whole life ahead of her. Not special and yet absolutely special.

I think I can live with that.

Acknowledgements

Firstly, a huge thank you and virtual squeezy hug to you, dear reader, for picking up this novel. That people take time out of their busy lives to read (and, with any luck, enjoy) my stories is an absolute privilege and a dream come true. You are why I do this.

Thank you to all the friends and family who have supported my writing. Not only did you buy the first book in the *Gods* duology, you purchased it for friends, thrust it upon colleagues, retweeted me endlessly, and generally championed me with an astonishing generosity. You rock. I am lucky to have you as my people.

Thank you to my mum and dad, from who I inherited the love of stories that compelled me to become an author, and the bloody-mindedness to make it happen. And to my wonderful sister, Amanda, and niece, Leia, who never pass a bookshop without popping in for a book-selfie.

To Kellie Barratt, Paul Connery, Adrian Hemstalk, Andy Leyland, Rhian McKay, Elaine Swords and Teresa Wilson for their friendship, wisdom and inspiration. To Susan Peak for so generously answering my questions about D&D. To Maria Roberts, Sarah Tierney and Emma Jane Unsworth, my companions on the writing road for the last fifteen years. It's been a wild ride. Here's to the next fifteen. Bring wine.

To David Lloyd, who I am now bullying in my own actual acknowledgements to write that book. You are brilliant. The world needs to hear about your ridiculous life. Get to it.

To the incredible Susan Armstrong who I am so, so, blessed to call my agent, and whose insight has made *The Love Delusion* a far better book. To my amazing editors Anna Boatman and Eleanor Russell for their commitment to making the conclusion to Frida's hero journey the best it could possibly be. To Andy Hine for championing the *Gods* duology out in the world, to Emily Courdelle and Ellen Rockell for this kick-ass cover and to everyone else who worked on *The Love Delusion* with such care and attention. You are gods and goddesses, all.

To the muse/creativity gods/whatever magical thing it is that sparks inspiration for stories – thanks for trusting me with this one. I can't wait to find out what's next.

And deepest gratitude to Nick, who keeps me sane and makes me laugh every single day. Without you, there would only be one side to this story. Thank you. I love you.